The Prince of Ambition

The Prince of Ambition

By
FRANCISCO V. MARTINS

iUniverse, Inc.
New York   Bloomington

iUniverse books may be ordered through booksellers or by contacting:

iUniverse
1663 Liberty Drive
Bloomington, IN 47403
www.iuniverse.com
1-800-Authors (1-800-288-4677)

Because of the dynamic nature of the Internet, any Web addresses or links contained in this book may have changed since publication and may no longer be valid. The views expressed in this work are solely those of the author and do not necessarily reflect the views of the publisher, and the publisher hereby disclaims any responsibility for them.

ISBN: 978-1-4401-5590-1 (sc)
ISBN: 978-1-4401-5589-5 (ebook)
ISBN: 978-1-4401-5587-1 (dj)

Printed in the United States of America

iUniverse rev. date: 6/23/2009

To João, who taught me to love history
And Maria, who taught me to love.

CHAPTER ONE
REFLECTING IN ALCÁCER
CEGUER

Just as the governor-general predicted, the Moors decamped from the perimeter of our walls this morning. The governor-general is an experienced soldier, which is to say, he understands the vagaries of youthful bravado. He knew that these boys who would be men did not represent a real threat but merely some ostentation on the part of some young, bored, querulous nobles and their retinue. Nonetheless, the sight of the sun glinting off their scimitars was disconcerting, for I do not lay claim to any military courage but rather am a devoted man of letters. I took solace from the envelope of calmness that surrounds the governor-general and was further heartened that, for the most part, the Moors prudently stayed well out of range of our German cannon.

One particular young Moor did charge briefly at our walls, riding along perpendicular to us and shouting what I am sure were heathen imprecations. He was bedecked in a dazzling white *kaffiyeh*, with a black camel-hair cord around his forehead to hold it in place, and a beautiful blue and white flowing *haik*. His mount was a powerful dappled gray stallion, and the tassels of the saddle almost touched the sand. The horse easily out-showed the rider in the spectacular hues of the cloth covering its haunches, the magnificent animal festooned with furbelows while many colored fringes fell on both sides of its magnificently flared nares. Indeed, the rider appeared drab in contrast to the bedazzled steed. The Saracen religion frowns upon adornment and any other wanton display of the human body, and the Muslims lavish their colors and raiment on their beloved horses. I must admit to agreement with this prioritization, for the beasts are simply that, beasts that are incapable of evil forethought while many of the humans of my acquaintance spin webs of deceit and malevolence. The beasts do what they do to survive, while the men I have known act out of greed, impoverishing and even killing their fellow man so they could have more. Despite having sufficient means of their own, often born into those means, these particular men want more, always more. This insatiable appetite drives them to accomplish sometimes great and sometimes evil things. The means are of no consequence, merely the ends. They are indifferent whether these goals were met through noble or base acts. But, my dear reader, I am betraying much too much of my hard-gained cynicism at too early a point in my narrative that has yet to begin.

To return to the events at hand, as this magnificent warrior rode closer to our walls, we clearly heard him yell "*Quss ummakh*," the Moor's ultimate epithet. When the governor-general noticed one of his defenders beginning to take aim with his culverin, he quickly interceded.

"Tomás don't shoot. It is not our custom to visit death upon courage."

He lied, of course, but I suspect the governor-general has witnessed too many acts of gratuitous cruelty. Like me, he is too old to do things without reason. We must conserve our energies and emotions, for it is my opinion that over-expenditure of ardor is not good for one's health, especially in this hellish climate.

In phrasing his command to the base man in noble tones, the governor-general hoped to visit some higher morality, an exercise in futility in my jaundiced opinion. Nothing appeals to these men save the urgencies of their bodies: hunger, thirst, lust, and bowel movements. In this particular case, the man appealed to continue leveling his weapon, taking careful and hateful aim.

"I have ordered you not to shoot," said the governor-general, abandoning his former nonchalance and adopting a more resolute demeanor. His right hand was now resting on the hilt of his sword, as if to punctuate his seriousness.

"That heathen called me mother a whore," replied Tomás who had not taken his eyes from his target.

In anticipation of some altercation that would pierce the dull tedium of their duty, some of the men had gathered around, hoping for entertainment. Like the rabble they are, they mostly enjoy bloodshed, any bloodshed will do, as they are not in the habit of taking moral sides. Their faces were contorted in feral smiles, exposing yellowed teeth as they looked forward to the spectacle of violence.

"And what of it?" returned the governor-general. "I am sure you have no idea who your mother was, much less your father. Besides, you may well miss the Moor and hit the horse and that would be a true sin."

The rigid ugly smiles of the men relaxed and dissolved into chuckles. The governor-general had wisely defused the mounting tension with humor. Tomás, sensing the loss of support for entertaining murder, lowered his weapon, though not without throwing an evil glance at the governor-general.

I am in awe of the old governor-general, for in truth, his authority over these men is tenuous and derives from their common hostility of the Moors waiting outside these walls and the vengeance inherent in our monthly supply ship from home. Should a man kill the governor-general, he would have nowhere to run and have to wait for the quick justice of the captain of the supply ship. Of course, I am employing rational reasoning, which these men may not have access to, as they are limited by their small, putrid minds. They represent the detritus of the earth and are not prone to weighing consequences. Many of them have committed murder, which is an act of impulse, unfettered by conscience or forethought.

None of them, save the crazies such as me, is here by choice. Alcácer Ceguer is the end of the world, a crumbling, sun-baked fort forsaken by god and beast, save for the rare visits of pride the Moors pay us. In truth, they do not want it either and would not come here but to annoy us. The weather lacks the variety of seasons and alternates from hot to infernally hot with breezes few and black, querulous flies many. As I have said, the garrison of men represents the dregs from our land, mostly comprised of murderers, pederasts, and, at the top of the hierarchy, thieves who were not given a choice as to the service of their sentences. As a small, underpopulated kingdom, we make use of all our citizens, even the criminals among us. In reality, these men are in prison, the Saracens outside acting as the bars while the authority of the supply ship represents the fetters. There is no escape other than trying to survive the mandatory five years of blinding monotony, guarding a fort no one particularly wants to take.

Most men do not survive in their entirety, as they are low beings and are constantly quarreling among themselves over trifles. The issues are always small but the consequences heavy. For the most part, they are cowards, preferring to take their revenge on their perceived enemies at night while they slumber. I have often been jolted out of my sleep by an inhuman shriek. At first, I thought it was the sound the devil makes with his genitals pierced, but then I learned that it was the utter surprise of a man who awakes with his throat cut or worse. The men of the garrison are geniuses when it comes to deviltry. Kill a man, and you simply take away all he has and will ever have. You have taken away the use of his senses and whatever pathetically small enjoyments he may have, but with death, he will lose his misery. Now if you maim a man, you can prolong and deepen that misery. Whatever form of vengeance, it is an awful sound, not produced anywhere else in nature, as animals do not go around killing and crippling each other in such a base and cowardly way. It is uncanny the sound a cut larynx can still make. No one ventures into the night to go see what we all know has happened, save the rats that greedily cluster to drink the victim's warm blood. In the morning, the body lies stiffened in its cot, an astonished look on its face, a mixture of surprise and terror, with the pervasive, acrid smell of excrement.

Their appetites are unrestrained and given full vent. With no women about, they perform unspeakable acts with each other. Warped allegiances combine with the bad alchemy of petty jealousies that would be comical if the outcome was not so deadly. A furtive look at another man's lover can lead to a cut throat. Whether they are appeasing their lust or hate, brutality is always present. It is their medium as the sea is to fish.

When the men returned to their posts, the governor-general rested his left leg on a notch of the sun-baked crenulated wall. Loose grit fell from his boots, reverting to the sand it once was. He methodically rubbed his arthritic knee in the manner of a man trying to dispel the infirmities of his age.

"Besides, it's not profitable to shoot him," he added. Now he was telling the truth.

In his younger days, the governor-general, who was not a governor-general at the time but a mere yet artful thief, had captured a number of Muslim princes and exacted handsome ransoms for their return. I am certain that the sums I have heard rumored that he received are inflated with the natural exaggeration of time, but even if it was a tenth of what was mentioned, the governor-general can look forward to a comfortable retirement next year without having to risk his grizzled neck outside these walls in attempting to capture this reckless youth. Besides, the governor-general no longer has his *"alfaqueque"* to act as the go-between to arrange for the exchange. The partner he was reputed to have used, Frey José, has long since returned home, waiting for death in comfort in a monastery in the more temperate south of our nation. Besides speaking Arabic, Frey José was a Franciscan, the only Christian clerics the Moors seem to tolerate because of their vow of poverty. That morning, I saw the governor-general shrug with just a hint of remorse over this missed opportunity and stamp his foot hard on the stone floor to get the circulation moving in his damaged leg, or perhaps he was frustrated at his limb's loss of vigor as old men are who can still remember their youth.

With the hardness of the unyielding stone, he recovered from his revelry as his old blood trickled back into his gnarled leg. The governor-general explained to me that those young heathens were just out to prove how brave they were by confronting their infidels and had no real interest in spilling their blood to retake such an unimportant outpost as Alcácer Ceguer. The governor-general is not vainglorious; he is merely stating fact. Ceuta is expensively garrisoned with twenty-five hundred men, befitting its importance, while Alcácer Ceguer can only boast of two hundred fifty miserable defenders, existing in man-fashioned hell and exacting revenge from each other since they are unable to visit their wrath on higher powers. In Arabic, the Alcácer Ceguer means "little castle," which is only half correct, for it is indeed small. It is a sun-baked speck on the coast of Morocco, nestled between the succor of Ceuta and the menace of Tangier, each a hard day's ride away. I often stand here on the crenulated walls, my eyes straining across the sea, knowing that home is less than a fortnight's journey away. At times, I imagine the onshore breezes bringing whiffs of pine forests, redolent with resin, or I think I smell translucent onions bubbling in hot olive oil or the heavy robustness of my father's magenta wine. The weight of the years has crushed many of the cravings I once had, but surprisingly, some appetites have been honed, such as the pleasure I take in food and drink. I am like one of those few priests who actually take their vow of celibacy seriously but then overindulge in other appetites of the flesh such as gluttony. Despite my best efforts and the expenditure of large quantities of silver, the gourmand in me remains starved, as gourmet treats are rare.

Our food must be brought from across the sea, as the Moors will not trade with us. Befitting our low station, the victuals brought are foul: half-rotted potatoes, green with mold; thin strips of salt-encrusted cod, more bone than flesh; and rancid meat. In addition to the bimonthly caravel from Lagos, there are some irregular visits from the Genovese who used to trade here before we took the town, but they charge enormous sums for poor-quality luxuries. But what am I to do but pay? Like most old men, I have grown fond of my small luxuries. I have learned that sin is a zero-sum game; the sins we disabuse ourselves of as we age, such as carnal lust, are replaced by others, such as gluttony. Sometimes I look up at the blinding white sky and envy the jubilation of the swallows that can fly back and forth with such ease, oblivious to the allegiances men must make to their princes and gods.

Alcácer Ceguer, such as it is, was the last conquest of my prince. It is here that I have come to write another chronicle lauding a minor lord who does not pay well but does so in advance, allowing me to subsist and gloat over the few Genoese delicacies I can purchase. It is the year of our

Lord 1473, and my prince has been dead for over thirteen years. During this time, his fame has grown throughout all the Spains, which I attribute, with no false modesty, to my chronicles of his participation in the conquest of Ceuta and role as patron in the conquest and discovery of the coast of Guinea. I have heard that my chronicles have been read as far and wide as the Italies and even England, where my prince stands in good repute, owing to his Plantangenant blood.

But where are my manners? Even the heathen Saracens will not begin a conversation without first introducing themselves, reciting their cursed lineages with a litany of ibns. My name is Gomes Eannes de Zurara, a chronicler of history and esteemed member, or so I thought, of my prince's posthumous household. I was also the head curator of the Royal Library, the guarda-mor of the Tombo Tower, and commander of the Order of Christ in former, more heady lifetimes. This last title still causes me much dismay, but it is not the time nor the place to air my grievances. My chief fame derives from my aforementioned chronicles, and I am widely known as the chief panegyrist of my prince, Dom Afonso Henriques, *infante* of Portugal and the Algarve, knight of the Garter, governor of Madeira and all of Guinea, and grand master of the Order of Christ. The English, who tend to be drunkards, have referred to him erroneously as Henry the Navigator. Actually, Henry despised sea voyages since he was prone to extreme seasickness. He assiduously avoided any sea voyage but made spectacular use of those he was forced to undertake. Less generous souls have referred to me as my prince's chief sycophant and general ass kisser.

In my chronicles of his conquest of Ceuta and Guinea, I described Henry as the perfect prince, a chaste and temperate man who remained celibate throughout his life and eschewed wine and other easy pleasures starting from adolescence. His sole obsession, according to me, was the defense and spread of our true faith and the exploration of the unknown world for the greater glory of God. In my depiction of him, he was a serious and solemn man; even as a youth, he was not known to be amused by trivialities, and as a prince, he was more apt to command respect than elicit love. I lionized him as a man of unbending moral character and austere, even monastic, personal habits. This is the prince I introduced to the world. In part, much of what I write is the truth, but as you, kind and tolerant reader, must have already suspected, not all is strictly fact. All myths must contain kernels of truth if they are to endure. Moreover, some of the greatest lies are not explicit, but perpetuated by the omission of exactness.

I was part of and lived in his extended household for over forty years, yet I cannot claim to have truly known what constituted the gist of my prince. If you were to listen to the account of a man's closest friend and admirer and somehow mesh it with the opinion of his most adamant enemy, you may very well get a reasonable proximity of the truth. Since there are no written vehement detractions of my chronicles regarding my prince, I have taken it upon myself to play my own devil's advocate. No, I have not come far enough to become my prince's enemy. I am merely trying to humanize the deity I created, perhaps also to amend the paid-for exaggerations and thereby gain a better seat in the pantheon of history.

These pages are not to be construed as a confession or penance for any wrong done on my part. I am not ashamed of my work; I was merely carrying out the duties of my chosen trade as a paid propagandist. I am not apologizing for my chronicles, much as a cooper would not apologize for a barrel he manufactured or a draper blamed for exaggerating the quality of his cloth. Like any tradesman, I used my given and acquired talents to earn my bread. In my particular case, I was able to earn enough to buy jam to spread on my bread. But who among you, my dear readers, can lay blame on a man for seeking a bit of comfort in this uncomfortable world?

My prince was a shrewd man; he recognized the value of a positive public image. The image I manufactured for him served to predispose popes to approve his petitions and gather adherents and adventurers to his endeavors. By wearing the mantle I wove him, my prince was able to persuade those less intelligent minions that his endeavors were for the greater glory of God and bereft of any personal gain. He was precociously aware that the printed word is imbued with a truthfulness that completely overrides anything that is merely uttered, the sound soon lost upon the wind. The printed word endures, serving as a testament to posterity. Who would dare to put a lie on paper under the ubiquitous eye of historical judgment? It would indeed take an audacious man who was supremely self-assured to make use of such a power, precisely the kind of man my prince was.

So my motives are not inspired by any sense of penance, but rather manifold. First, my pen is motivated by a dying wish to show you, my public, that I am not the hack you take me for. There is no use in denying it. I have heard the loud whispers and the suppressed titters as I pass by. Though old, I still retain excellent hearing. Second, there is the matter of professionalism. I was not paid in full for my labors, and as such, I feel I am at liberty to edit liberally what I have previously written. Last, there is an inexplicable compunction to keep on writing. It fills my soul, as I believe everyone has his purpose. Mine is to scribble away, while my prince felt compelled to send his intrepid sailors to the ends of the world for purposes that still remain shrouded to my ken. Yes, I believe that Henry was mostly motivated by an insatiable need to accumulate more land, more wealth, more power. But there was a less obvious hunger that drove him. Yes, my prince was avaricious, but he was also possessed with an unquenchable curiosity, which I find to be a partially redeeming quality. Each truly sentient man possesses compulsions. My prince was compelled to amass wealth and discover the physical truth of our world. As for me, I am compelled to write like other men feel themselves driven to fornicate and as moths are enticed by the flame. It is a need much akin to a bowel movement, and many of my critics will agree that the end product of my literary forays is the same as that of a bowel movement.

So every evening after I have bid the governor-general a cordial adieu from our conjoined company, as I am the only other man here who is not a complete brute, I retire to my cell. Before submitting to my routine of writing before I go to bed, I usually look up at the turgid sky, the spiral of stars so thick upon the firmament that I feel they are about to smother me. The stars are so dense in places that you cannot distinguish any individual star, but rather, they form a pervasive glow, an aura where God may live should He choose to have a physical abode. On this cloudless night, my jaws agape and the crook of my neck begins to ache. I stand witness to a cacophony of light. I am constantly amazed at the sight of the teeming heavens, heaving with the weight of a creation that I cannot fathom. When I gaze upon this munificence of God, the only emotion I am constantly aware of is my own insignificance.

I notice an ovate yellow moon, which, upon closer inspection, is compressed by two thin lines of clouds. Our senses are poor instruments of reality and frequently confound the intellect with false signals. My so-called godfather, the Benedictine priest I was told to address as Uncle Bernardo by my poor, suffering mother, may God rest her soul, often pointed to the beauty in the heavens as proof of God's existence and benevolence. At the time, I took his word for it, but with reflection and the advantage of prolonged hindsight, I do not necessarily see the link, as this evidence is filtered by our all-too-easily-deceived senses. I again tread on perilous ground, but I am removed from the sharpened, yellowed talons of the inquisitors our foolish current sovereign has allowed into the kingdom from Castile. It is the distinct advantage to live at the edge of the world, far from the perils of civilization.

I now withdraw to my cell and devote one-tenth of a candle's length to my current insipid patron and the remainder of the precious Genovese wax to the reconstruction of my prince. I will leave it up to you, kind reader, to judge the veracity of my recollections. I am cognizant that time can distort memories, but I am also aware that, as a man approaches his death, as am I, he is subject to fewer and fewer vested interests. I feel entitled to perfect my fiction by the admixture of some truth. It was, after all, my lies that created Henry's myth, but isn't all art a lie? No, readers, do not get upset with me; I do not call my chronicles art, as I can already hear the laughter gurgling up your collective throats. My work was pure propaganda used to justify my prince's various agendas. I am no Herodotus, but even he was not altogether impartial, as he clearly glorified the Greeks over their Persian enemies. I was paid to create a persona and am not ashamed to admit it, but now I feel inspired by a higher authority: the truth. So let us begin.

Chapter Two
Further Introductions

*W*e cannot help but form opinions of the people we encounter, yet like all the other misconceptions we commit, owing to our faulty senses and lack of complete information, these opinions are usually based on laminas of appearances and false shadows of evidence. It is as if we were judging a book strictly on the quality of the vellum cover or the lack of such a cover. A man we meet in our daily meandering might be labeled a brute, a woman a wanton, without any thought of the interceding events that brought them to our presence. Was the man mistreated by those he was supposed to trust as a child? Was the woman repeatedly raped by her trusted uncles? People are molded by the physical and mental trauma they endure. It is my belief, matured with time, that our righteous God cannot commit any soul to eternal damnation since, by definition, God is ubiquitous and therefore aware of all extenuating circumstances. This, dear reader, or so I shall refer to you hereon since a bond between us must perforce be formed by your very act of reading these pages, is my own personalized version of God, not God as presented to us by the Church. I am free to say these calumniates, as I am near death but far from the ungentle inquisitors in Lisbon.

My God, the God I have conjured, could not damn anyone to perdition, as He is all seeing. Take Tomás for example; you remember him as the would-be assassin of the Moor on that dandified horse, tempting his death. The governor-general was correct in supposing that Tomás did not know who his father was. For that matter, I do not believe his mother knew either. No, my well-fed reader, she was not a wanton slut, but perhaps merely hungry. Who are we, the well nourished, to judge the morality of human need? I am not speaking of mere predilections but of real need, the need for air, food, water. Until I gained the vision of old age, I could not conceive what a person would do to alleviate the imperial imperative of hunger.

I mean hunger, real hunger, not the kind the privileged occasionally encounter, that sauce that will enhance the food we are assured of getting. That is a welcomed visitor, a harbinger of impending satisfaction. There is another kind of hunger, a hunger not so easily dismissed, as there are no simple remedies for it, such as a waiting meal. It is not merely a temporary discomfort, but rather the finger of death eviscerating your intestines, an agony before the release of death. My poor reader, I may be shocking you, sheltered as you must be from these importunities, but death does not come easy to the hungry, but in slow increments. Christ was lucky to have been crucified, as starvation is slower and much more cruel.

Hunger is a persistent tormentor. It disallows peaceful sleep; there is no possible comfortable position you can find. Hunger imposes in inopportune rudeness, making humans go mad to alleviate it. Tomás jokes about the hunger he endured; he must or else go mad. We at the fort all know that hunger ranks above all God's commandments, and certainly no just god would have unleashed such a demon upon his creations.

From these and previous, perhaps careless, words, dear reader, you may have already formed, however inchoate, an opinion of me, namely, one of a sickly and cynical old man, godless and friendless, awaiting death far from hearth and kith. You are, of course, partially correct, but I beseech you stay your final judgment, to the degree that there can be any finality in the course of human relations, until I can acquaint you with some of the catalysts that helped form my character, such as it is.

I was born in a village called Mangualde, located in our intemperate north, where summers are hot and prolonged and winters sleeted, accompanied by a cold, damp chill in the mornings that gels the very marrow of your bones. In this kind of clime, you try to keep under the bedcovers until your bladder mandates otherwise. As with too many of the places in our poor kingdom, Mangualde possessed nothing much to distinguish itself other than poor, niggardly soil that did not gratuitously yield crops, but rather, the crops had to be wrestled out of the earth by rough-hewn men, fighting for sustenance as soldiers fight for survival in desperate battle. Their reward was just that, survival, they got no other laurels. It is understandable that these men would become brutes, for that is what they were forced to be in order to chisel away at the granite and transform it into obdurate soil.

I often refer to my village as a land of the blind, for what is illiteracy but a loss of one's eyes? Despite their immense physical strength, the men of my village were all emasculated by their inability to read and write. Though it was no fault of their own, in my constant, jaundiced view, it was a result of a secret conspiracy. Safe in their low-rafted taverns, they would ridicule each other's infirmities but never touch upon their ignorance, more ashamed of it than the venereal diseases that often visited them. Their eyeless servility catered to the vested. The landlords were assured of cheap labor, the merchant vessels had access to a plentiful supply of disposable seamen, and the priests were free to interpret the Gospel as they saw fit, making sure these strong, physical brutes remained mentally docile.

My mother, may God rest her lithe soul, was the village beauty. I know what you are thinking, dear reader: all our mothers look beautiful to us, and surely, mine did to me. But I do not refer to subjective perceptions. I speak to the memory of the furtive and none-too-disguised hungry stares my mother would elicit wherever she would go. I grew to hate those looks, the tightened, suddenly moist lips, the smarmy smiles, the lubricious double entendres that pursued her wherever she went, the ingratiating manners, and the overt leers. This raw lust formed a low opinion of the male animal in these early formative years of my youth. It is an opinion I am powerless to change in any significant way, and I am sorry to say it has been confirmed with my life's experience. Lust in a man is akin to hunger, only junior in priority. It is much easier to satisfy in a brief shudder of release.

Women must perforce be constantly on vigil against the male's constant onslaught, for theirs is but a brief moment of pleasure, while the female is saddled with shame and the impediment of an unwanted child. She has to be virtuous, unless, that is, she also happens to be hungry and must respond to the necessity of survival and worry about her virtue at a later time. This is how Tomás and all his ilk come into this world.

My mother was human flesh: a gaping mouth, a gnawing stomach, and, alas, a fruitful womb. If God were indeed a good engineer, He would have designed women better so that they could not procreate when their bodies were deprived of nutrients. But God is an indulgent engineer who favors life over sense.

And so my mother succumbed to the exigencies of her

human stomach and exchanged her virtue for a reliable supply of kale soup with an occasional joint of meat. My father was the village priest, Dom Bernardo, who never publicly acknowledged my reality. In one sense, I was very lucky, for often priests father many children, as the supply of vulnerable women is plentiful. Dom Bernardo had taken his vow of celibacy in all seriousness and was ashamed of his weak flesh, so he remained loyal to my mother as atonement.

I have said that my mother was a beauty, and my father was well aware of his blessings. I remember him well: a stout man with large teeth and an indulgent smile. He was a true scholar in that he loved Ovid, despite the Roman's Godlessness. I believe it was through him that I was able to see the beauty in the classics, though he admonished me more than one time not to tell anyone of the single book he kept hidden behind the clay cock on the mantel shelf.

I was privileged indeed, Dom Bernardo's only child, but also a highly visible target for abuse, as was my mother. Narrow minds prey on small issues. Slit-eyed leers would follow my mother about the town as she saw to her errands. From the women, there were the superior arching of eyebrows and the occasional throaty whisper, "whore." I heard the word; without even knowing its meaning, I understood its tone. Sometimes I would escape my mother's tight and imploring grip and kick a shin, much to the indignation of the woman and to the amusement of the men. My mother would inevitably retrieve me, grab my hand and quickstep away. There were the rough-hewn men who would follow us, even roughly lifting me by my armpits while I helplessly thrashed the air with my stunted four-year-old legs.

"Quite the little man, your son, Dona Emilia," or so they referred to her, despite the glaring fact that she was not married. I can only speculate what they called her in the safety of their dark, vinegary, bawdy taverns. For all their leers and lewd jests, there was not one of them who was not secretly in love with my mother.

I am not relating this to you to claim sympathy, dear reader, as there were many bastards in our small village. I was more privileged than most since I knew the identity of my father, as I was only a bastard by the dictionary's rigid definition while there are many legitimately born who earn that title with their behavior.

As I have stated, my mother was a rare, aquiline beauty. Her skin was fair, untainted by any Moorish vestige, unlike so many other females, with their thick-skinned complexions and sprouting mustaches past the age of twenty. My mother's face was perfectly symmetrical, her left side in proportion to her right. Her nose was small and straight, forming a bridge that divided two gleaming eyes whose color changed with her gentle moods. Her hair was thick, abundant, and gypsy black, parted straight down the middle of her scalp so that it flowed down upon her angular shoulders like a rich woman's shawl. Endowed with a gentle disposition, which, combined with her natural beauty, made her charms irresistible. For all their bravado, I am sure that the men were in awe of her, even when ensconced in their taverns, where men are given the freedom to boast of talents and courage they do not possess.

Despite the overt forwardness of the men and the contempt of the well-fed women, everyone was constrained by the invisible leash my father held. She walked with freedom from attack past the sticky aura of lust since she was the village priest's housekeeper and known concubine. My father, "Uncle Bernardo," was himself a "nephew" of the bishop of Viseu. Thanks to my privileged illegitimate birth, I received an education, not only learning to read and write but exposed to the Greek and Roman classics, though warned by my grandfather, the bishop, of the innate evils of Godlessness these authors possessed, their beautifully written passages notwithstanding. I never received these admonitions in seriousness, perhaps because my teachers, to a man and priest, secretly admired the classics, despite the authors' pagan beliefs.

Besides Ovid, my father liked other ancients, though not with the same fervor, if I may use that adjective for a priest. Sometimes on Sundays, we would make the day-long journey to Viseu and visit the library in the cathedral where there was a great collection of books, perhaps as many as one hundred. What seemed astonishing to me was that each book could find something novel to say.

Here I encountered the Godless authors Homer and Virgil, espousing their version of truths before Christ had trod the earth. In their works, passion ran rampant, while Plato's words were measured and devoid of heat. When I asked my father where our God could be found in their reason, he could not answer. In the ensuing years, I have come to realize that we needed to create God to justify our insignificance in relation to the ancients. You see, I can say these things because I am far away from the inquisitors' talons.

My father and other teachers gave me my life; they gave me my eyes, and I was lucky enough to be able to prioritize my mind over my stomach. Indeed, both were well nourished.

I was well taken care of within the confines of home, but outside the protective walls, I was prey to the fists of stronger boys with little to dissuade them as to retribution. Despite the pinches I received from jealous boys, I did count myself fortunate, as I was given eyes to see the light. My hands were allowed to remain childlike soft, albeit constantly ink-stained, and I never was visited with that hopeless hunger, the ever-present companion of many of the boys my age. And so you may wonder, dear reader, why such a privileged youth as I was turned into an old ingrate. Granted, the circumstances of my birth may not have been optimal, but to this day, I would not exchange legitimacy for an empty stomach nor, worse, an empty mind.

I first questioned my faith in God upon my mother's premature, meaningless death. Yes, I am well acquainted with His mysterious ways, but when mystery becomes injustice, a thinking man must sit back, stroke his chin, and decide what unseeing hand lies behind the haphazard events that come to pass, where thieves are rewarded with stolen wealth, the gluttonous are satiated, and the righteous are thrown into early graves. It was the early summer of 1415 when a plague swept through the whole of Iberia. To add to the perversity of her death, she succumbed to the great black abyss on the very same day as and to the very same flux that killed the queen, Dona Phillipa, Henry's mother. Apparently, the distemper was unable to distinguish between her nobility and my mother's low birth.

To his credit, my father was openly inconsolable. There were lesser beauties that quickly gathered around him, shedding false tears, but who were more than willing to exchange their virtues for the comfort he could offer. In his grief, or perhaps because he had arrived at an age where carnal lust fades, my father returned to his vow of celibacy. I cared not for the reason but was pleased that it benefited my future.

After my generous education was concluded, I had the great fortune, thanks to my bishop "great uncle," to attain a position as a scribe in the Royal Library when the then thirty-seven-year-old Henry summoned me in the late autumn in the year of our Lord 1431. Despite the intervening years since the great victory at Ceuta, he seemed still flush with hubris, as if he had just returned from the battle. He was only twenty-one in 1415 when his great triumph took place, but since that time, his fame had grown to legendary proportions, and I was a bit frightened to be in the presence of his august personage. Although just a scribe, I had achieved a certain modest reputation as a scholar and had proved myself a friend of the royal family, the House of Aviz. It was with great pride and humble ambition, though admittedly also with hope of patronage, that I wrote some paeans in honor of our illustrious king and Henry's father, Dom João I, master of the House of Aviz and defender of the realm, after his great victory over the avaricious Castilians at the battle of Aljubarrota in 1385. This was many years before I was born, but I felt a sense of obligation to the king for having vouchsafed the liberty and wellbeing in our small but stubbornly independent realm. It was God's will to preserve us despite being outnumbered by the invading enemy.

In my account of the battle of Aljubarrota, there is the perfunctory heavenly omen, in this particular case a flaming sword. It is a misplaced omen since both sides were Christians and both claimed the allegiance of God to their cause, but every important battle must have its omen. Since I did not witness the battle nor interview anyone who partook in it, I will not bother to repeat my fictional account, save that our forces prevailed. Whether the victory was due to God's intervention, the force of two hundred English longbowmen on our side, our superior defensive position, or the possibility that a glob of pigeon shit fell into the Castilian commander's eye at a crucial moment, I cannot say.

With the victory, Dom João I assured himself a place in history and, perhaps more importantly, ensconced himself on the throne. Dom João I, like myself, was illegitimate, the bastard of the king, Dom Pedro I. His half-brother, Dom Fernando, had a much more legal claim to the throne, but what of it? Legitimacy often depends on who has the greater force of will and whose army is bigger. Unfortunately for Dom Fernando, neither his character nor his army matched his legitimacy. He would have been better served to lead the life of a merchant or an ecclesiastic, given his methodical plodding character. Lamentably lacking in ambition, regrettably bereft of political acumen in marrying Leanor, a hated Castilian, he made himself easily disposable. The couple remains vilified to this day, especially Leanor, though I have no inkling of her true nature, never having met her. Being an accomplished liar myself, I know all too well the power of the propagandists to take history seriously. History and its progenitor, myth, are invariably written by the victors. I am of the opinion that the genres are interchangeable.

Dom João I married more judiciously. His wife, Dona Phillipa of Lancaster, was both English and a Plantangenent and therefore palatable to the vested interests comprising the court. Her father, John of Guant, had supplied the aforementioned archers that may or may not have been instrumental in the victory at Aljubarrota, the flaming sword notwithstanding. It is common knowledge that enemies of the English are known to cut off their middle fingers whenever they encounter a yeoman so that they could not wield that murderous yew. Prior to any battle, the English will often display their middle fingers to their enemies. But I digress.

Henry was one of six surviving children of that happy, but more importantly, politically expedient, union of the Houses of Aviz and Plantangenent. Even Englishwomen can be fertile when properly seeded. With two older brothers, Henry had no serious hope to inherit the throne, despite the steely ambition I noted in him from our first meeting. It was not for lack of aspiration that he did not pursue the throne through the usual machinations of nobility: poison and other subterfuge. Henry possessed a greater vision. Why be king of a small strip of land bordering the cold Atlantic when there is a continent to conquer and rule, a continent far richer than anything that could be imagined on our poor soil? He would be king of a new world, a realm wrested from the pervasive ignorance of our times, where men feared encountering beasts whose mouths were in their stomachs so the better to consume them or had eyes in the palms of their hands so they could watch their victims agony as they strangled them.

Henry first received me in his private quarters in the St.

George castle, overlooking our beautiful city of Lisbon, and I was much appreciative with this gesture of intimacy. He was unusually tall for an Iberian, but then again, he was half English, a people known for inordinate proportions and large appetites. Against the prevailing custom, he was clean shaven and wore his dark hair short, against the vanity of the times for flowing tresses. His general countenance could be said to be pleasing to the eye, but an austere expression detracted from those good looks, giving him the weight of a man twice his age. There was an aura of heaviness about him that suggested that he was not overly fond of the frivolities normal to one of his youthful years. Despite the cordial reception to his Spartan quarters, the quasi demigod who was my prince made me feel ill at ease beneath his brooding expression. I had heard the reports of the battle to take Ceuta. The prince had reputedly been merciless with the captured Saracens and was said to have personally beheaded more than a few. Henry was only twenty-one at the time, and the lack of charity in one so young bespoke of an iron character, whereas most of us still harbor compassion and are still molten metal at twenty-one, awaiting time to shape us into what we will become. Even at well past sixty, I still wait to find my unique mold. It is a misfortune of mine that is rarely shared by others.

At sixty, I am a rarity. At forty, the governor-general's body is more infirm than mine, but he has used his body while I have spared mine save for my eyes. I have witnessed death upon young boys with no more than an impacted tooth turned infected. I have seen stalwart muscular men turned to fetid mush overnight and pink-cheeked youths fade like blossoms in an arid clime over some triviality, a cough, a minor scrape turned gangrenous. In our parlous world, the slightest infirmity can bring death. I have survived a long, mundane life and am not sorry one iota, for I would be a live dog any day over a dead lion. Again, the infirmities of my age lead me to digress; let me return to the interview.

The austere room held a great fireplace large enough for a man to walk into, but despite the cold and dampness, no ashes littered the hearth. A plain wooden crucifix hung above a simple bed pressed against the sweating white-washed walls. A hair shirt prominently displayed across the bed reeked of penitence, the combined smell of animal musk and the ferrous odor of blood. Three bulbous knotted ends of a whip hung on the wall and appeared to have smeared blood on the wall, as if a sin had maculated a soul, and dripping pools of the same had darkened the wood floor beneath it. I quickly averted my eyes from such an intimacy.

He was unsmiling in my presence, but I took that to be quite normal for someone who had lost his beloved mother to the pestilence on the same day that I lost my own. My own lovely mother had also died swiftly, like a dove smothered in some giant's beefy hand. He was a noble and I but a lowly bastard, yet my mother was a beauty while Dona Phillipa, despite her lineage, had the face of a pig with a spike rammed up its ass. I have been told that she was never seen to smile, her face rigid, as if a victim of extreme constipation. This was the woman whose death was sublime as I limned it, dying serenely with a halo about to form over her square skull. She didn't so much die as deliquesce.

Her propagandized death was so unlike that of my mother whose lips turned black and brittle with disease, whose bowels loosened, despoiling the already piss-stained sheets. Now, dear reader, while not present, I will venture that Dona Phillipa also expelled noisome offal before she gave up her soul. I will also venture that there were no swords proffered to the princes but a geyser of pale yellow vomit from which all present shrunk in disgust and horror of the possibility of infection, that the only boxes present were not japanned with slivers of crucifixes but a single pine box already laced with a layer of lime.

But I was paid to uplift the human flesh of the nobility

above our own. We must die in obscurity, our throes only vaguely remembered but best forgotten while the nobles must pass on to the heavens, smelling of lilacs with rose water dripping from their cocks and perfume emanating from their arses. I was paid to paint such pictures, for that is what a conglomerate of words does; do not judge me too harshly, dear reader. I was but that rare, one-eyed man in the kingdom of the blind who wrote odes to the well born, and it was that talent that attracted the attention of my prince. And so I was summoned, and with plebian alacrity, I hastened.

After a brief and awkward obeisance on my part, I offered my condolences on the death of the revered Phillipa of Lancaster, whom God took to His bosom shortly before our fleet sailed to take Ceuta. I even took it upon myself to relate to him the coincidence of our mothers dying on the same day to the same pestilence. I had prepared a small speech of consolation beforehand and was just about to begin my second sentence when Henry held up his hand with annoyance clearly indicated on his face.

"I am familiar with your literature and believe you possess the talent for an undertaking that I am proposing to you."

An exaggerated bow and an ensuing silence signaled my willingness to listen and obey.

"Our Christian kingdom has attained a great victory over the infidel. The conquest of Ceuta must be proclaimed for all Christendom so that Europe may behold and give thanks to God and the force of our arms be made strong at His bequest. You must write it in Latin to give it weight and universality."

"Sire, my Latin suffers a dire inadequacy."

He looked right through me, and I felt as if I had been stabbed by a merciless sword that seemed to project from his brooding, deep-set eyes. Then, as if he had merely encountered a minor obstacle, another avenue occurred to him, and he brightened from brooding darkness to saturnine.

"No matter. Write it in our native language, and we can always have a monk translate it."

His tone was sententious, and I felt as though I was in the audience, watching some accomplished actor perform one of those incomprehensible pagan Greek tragedies of which some of my tutors were so fond. I waited to ensure that he had completed his thought and, at his curt nod, responded with servility punctuating my language.

"My Lord, I would be most honored to write this epic, for surely it is of Homeric proportions."

"I have heard of these pagan writers. You must refrain from any kind of obvious emulation of their heathen art. We must make this ours. In another hundred years, these pagans will be dust and forgotten, whereas I want to leave a Christian legacy behind that will be read until our Lord Jesus returns to judge us all when the temporal world ends."

I repeated my delight at the privilege or some other such babble and backed out of the room, bowing and averting my eyes from the bloody intimacy of the bed chamber together with its instruments of carnal self-reproach.

The high and mighties seldom care whether you glimpse their soiled undergarments. He was a prince and I but a seeing-eye lackey. As far as Henry was concerned, I was no more than a pony with an unique trick. With another curt nod that bespoke of his innate sense of entitlement, I was sent away.

As I was dismissed, Henry told me to return on the morrow after his morning regimen when we could begin work. All the way home, I cursed myself that I had had not the courage to speak about any compensation. My nepotistic position at the Royal Library held much prestige but unfortunately little in the way of monetary compensation, and as my dear worldly reader must be aware, prestige cannot purchase bread.

Now, dear reader, bread is not nectar or ambrosia, but I was most humanly in need of it. There was also a need for

German thauler, or silver as they call it here, as there was this certain Ofelia whose true love could only be obtained by it. I was young and quid pro quo seemed understandable; it still does. At the time, I was a prisoner of the youthful exigencies of my loins, and Ofelia, if that was her real name, appeared beautiful to me. If that opaqueness of lust had been lifted from my eyes, I would have, of course, seen that she was anything but beautiful; rather she was encumbered with a manly chin and the sloping forehead akin to the representations of mastodons I had seen in the library at Viseu. As I was blindly bound to her, so was I now bound to my prince as only silver can bind a man in need.

The next day, I returned at what I had imagined to be the proper hour, only to find my prince pacing to and fro, impatient by my tardiness.

"I have received assurances from the most esteemed bishop of Viseu that you are a serious young man, and here you show up well past the ninth hour. The sun is practically wasted for this day."

"I am most heartily sorry, sire," I responded, my stomach knotting while I tightened my sphincter muscles to avoid an accident. "I am not acquainted with Your Royal Highness's regimen, and I dared to err on the side of indulgence of sleep."

"Do not mistake a royal birth for lassitude of character. On the contrary, I believe royalty must outdo. My sacred Christian duty demands I serve as a paradigm for my fellow man. The immortal soul takes precedence over the transitory body, as most assuredly you must believe."

Too frightened to believe in anything save for the preservation of my skin at the time, I think I may have simply nodded with my whole torso in dumb agreement. To this day, I am ashamed of the ludicrously cowardly figure I must have cut, but Henry's title and bearing were too intimidating for a mere mortal such as me.

"I abjectly apologize and will henceforth arrive at ... at—"

"Six, even with the cock."

"Six, to commence our work."

"No, I attend Mass at that hour and wish you to serve as the acolyte, as I have been led to understand that you know the Latin liturgy of the holy Mass."

"Indeed, I do."

"We will begin now."

It was fortunate that I had brought my own quills, ink, and parchment, for there were none to be seen in his sparse quarters.

Before I could speak of any forthcoming pay I could expect to receive, he began to instruct me on the proper tone of the narrative.

"You must refrain from using superlatives; they are not appropriately Christian and lack humility. Also, refrain from using any turn of the phrase that is known to be already in print and try to mint new meanings, employing adjectives to innovative uses. Always be sure to portray our crusades as driven by only Christian zeal, unlike the Saracen's who use theirs as an excuse to exploit venal commercial ends. Always portray their gods in direct conflict with our own true one. Imagery is not to be over used; however, it may be appropriate to convey a slain Christian knight to heaven on a golden chariot. Do not use the same image for slain men-at-arms, something more humble perhaps. An escort of a cohort of angles comes to mind. It has occurred to me that the image of huge black hands reaching out from the underworld to take away dead Saracens is especially efficacious. Also, please ensure that every Christian decapitates at least twenty Moors before he himself is killed. Most importantly, the Moor must always pale and run before our charging army as we shout for Portugal and St. James. It is a theme I wish you to return to repeatedly, though with slight alterations, so as not to make the prose tedious or contrived."

He further lectured me on sentence structure and permissible laudatory terms to be used with respect to members of the royal house. I tried to listen to his advice with humility while also trying to keep my growing irritation from noticeably swelling in apposition as was my wont in my youth or showing any outward manifestation of disagreement. In an effort to divert him away from his lection, I asked if he would deign me with some details of his youth before the present great deed.

His features darkened, and he knit his brow, signaling that he was troubled, but then he seemed to relent. Henry was clearly not used to being led, but he was also a man who gave thought before raging at perceived insolence. I watched as he gave weight in his mind to my words and saw the resignation on his face as he realized that he must shake hands with my particular devil.

"I was born on Ash Wednesday, itself an omen, in the year of our Lord 1394. Not only my saintly mother but others who were in the birth room can attest that I emerged from her womb clutching a simulacrum of the holy cross. This vision so impressed the queen, my mother, that she sent for her personal astrologer, a Jew that called himself Juda Negro. I suspect that you are wondering why my mother would consult a Jew?"

"No, my Lord," I quickly answered. "They were the original path to God, which we, to our everlasting salvation, did not ignore, while they, to their damnation, have abandoned, refuting Christ as our savior."

"Quite so. Juda Negro was a learned, and I dare say, holy man in his own way, or my mother would not have placed such trust in him.

"After a careful and rather prolix study of the alignment of the stars, Juda Negro foretold that I was destined to accomplish great things. When I was later informed of this prediction, I took it very seriously and began the preparation of my mind and body. I believed that my participation in the conquest of Ceuta and my subsequent knighthood at the hands of my father proved that the prophecy was indeed correct."

His speech remaining lofty as Henry informed me that, upon his knighthood, in the aftermath of the battle, he had adopted the Anglo-Norman motto, *talant de bien faire*, hunger to perform worthy deeds.

"Indeed, this Juda Negro was assuredly a gifted scholar."

"Does he still belong to your household?" I ventured to inquire and immediately regretted my curiosity. I have learned not to elicit any un-volunteered information from superiors, lest it be embarrassing. Let princes limn their victories and bury their defeats. With Henry's glower, I knew that I had crossed over an uninvited threshold.

"Following my sainted mother's demise, Juda Negro disappeared. I am uncertain of his ultimate fate, but I was away fighting in Morocco. I do know that my sister, Isabel, harbored some unexplained animosity toward the harmless Jew and may have held Juda partly responsible for our mother's death. She is a willful creature and further hindered by the passions of her sex. Without the sobering guidance of her male family members, I fear she may have done some harm to the helpless old man. Perhaps Juda should have predicted an equally roseate future for Isabel as he failingly did for my poor mother.

"I have heard of seers from past ages who candidly foretold their patrons' doom as well as good fortune. There was the oracle of Delphi and the sybil in Rome. If these seers did indeed tell their powerful clientele the absolute and horrible truth instead of what served their vanity, then I suspect they had the advantage of immortality. Vulnerable men like Juda Negro are much more likely to tell great kings and especially their sisters what they want to hear and thereby live longer and retain their patronage. In not doing the same for a spiteful child, he may have doomed himself once the protection of Dona Phillipa was lifted by her death."

At times, Henry could be honest regarding interactions between the great and lesser estates.

ي

What followed was a maelstrom of activity as I methodically awoke and became an automaton rushing up the steep street to St. Georges, perennially squeezing my buttocks lest I arrive late or somehow displease him in some unpredictable manner. Yet despite all his earlier admonitions, it was Henry who was invariably late, offering no excuses. The privileged have, as their right, our attendance upon them. The time of the rich and powerful has more value than that of the common man, and the latter must never forget it. The longer the wait, the more important the person, yet our God is supposed to heed us immediately. It has been my unfortunate experience to be kept waiting for days for an audience with some self-important nabob for the only purpose of aggrandizing his ego. To be fair, my prince never specifically kept me in attendance for that low purpose; my wait was simply a matter of his convenience and not an intentional sleight. I was too insignificant a person for Henry to go out of his way to offend.

Despite the humiliations, these were heady days for me. There I was, a mere speck on God's cosmic ass, in private audience with one of the most powerful people in our kingdom. In the ensuing days, I watched him pace to and fro from the corner of my eye as he dictated with an inner fervor that made him impervious to the damp frigidity of his fireless chambers. I believe that, at times, captured in his delirium, he forgot that I was even present. So he spoke, and I copied his words verbatim with the intent of adding some art to them at a later time when I was away from his brooding eyes and there was some warmer blood pouring through my fingers. What I produced was the version that must be familiar to you, dear reader, for I wrote it as dictated by my prince, of course with the necessary aforementioned literary embellishments. You have read and marveled at the example of Christian chivalry and daring displayed by my prince in the short siege of the great city of Ceuta. In the reality of history, Ceuta was only a minor fortress, but I have heard vicious rumors that Troy itself was also only a small village. Conquerors must exaggerate their feeble achievements. My pages limned that, when Henry and his two older brothers, Duarte and Pedro, came of age, their father, the king, had wanted to arrange a spectacular tournament in their honor with jousting contests so that the young princes could earn their knightly spurs. The wars with Castile were thankfully over, so the king had to devise other means for his sons to win glory. According to Henry, it was he who dissuaded his father from such ostentatious and useless display and instead heeded the wise advice of the venerable royal treasurer, Afonso de Alenquer, to attack and take Ceuta, across the straits from Gibraltar on the Moroccan coast. With the conquest of Ceuta, Afonso Alenquer argued, Portugal would control the entrance to the Mediterranean, possess the terminus for the caravans bringing riches and gold from the African interior and gain a base for the further conquest of Morocco for the greater glory of God.

"There were good and strong reasons for the taking of the fortress," he dictated to me on one particularly cold, clammy morning. Despite the accumulated dampness that had settled in his chambers, Henry did not deem it necessary to order a fire lit. As my cold fingers clamped around the stiff quill, I strove to keep pace with his muscular tongue. I shivered in my robes, perhaps with more exaggeration than was warranted, hoping to draw attention to my discomfort. Henry took no notice and continued pacing to and fro as he spoke.

Henry related that it was Alenquer's contention that we were perfectly within our rights to retake the city, as this present-day Morocco was but an artifice, that, in reality, had been the previous Visigoth province of Mauritania Tingitana. Therefore, as we were the natural heirs of these Western Goths, we possessed a proper claim that precedes the Moor.

With all the gravity of a bishop, my prince detailed how he transformed himself into the main impetus behind the holy expedition, overcoming the objections of his reluctant father.

"I toured the green north of our kingdom, recruiting heart and sinew for God. Our people rallied to the cause; some cynics say it was because of the lavishness of the food and drink of the feasts I offered, but I preferred to think this was not so. I could discern their earnest desire to serve God and their king glowing behind their eyes as if they were possessed with the crusading spirit of the Holy Ghost."

As I dutifully committed his words to paper and posterity, I believed in the honesty of the people's fervor. I was still young, and it never occurred to me at the time that religious fervor and hunger radiate much the same light behind one's eyes. Never having suffered the beast myself, I was naïve to the lengths men will go to procure a meal and temporarily drive off the painful throes of an empty stomach. With the dubious advantage of honest and remorseful hindsight, I now realize that hungry men have little choice in matters. Future plans are circumscribed by the limitations of procuring the next meal, never beyond that short, miserable time horizon. Only the rich care about next year or even next month. The poor must contend with the next hour. Hungry men answer to any cause. It need not be godly as long as a meal awaits as their reward.

"In his arguments against the expedition, the king, my father, had wisely pointed out that the cost in men and materials would be too large for a poor country such as ours, exhausted as it was from the continuous wars of first expelling the Moors and then having to repel the avaricious Castilians. My father also pointed out that there would be the expenditure of maintaining a suitable garrison once the city was taken. There could be no hope of obtaining victuals from the hostile countryside outside the conquered walls. Lastly, the king warned of the opportunistic Castilians, capable of taking advantage to invade our kingdom if the army was away doing God's work.

"I was able to counter these arguments suitably and was consequently able to win the king's blessing. My main point was that making war on the infidel was the will of God, a posture no one could refute. There were also Afonso Alenquer's reasons as to the control of the straits and riches to be had. I dismissed the threat from Castile by saying they would be cowed by our feat of arms and dare not invade, as dire retribution would be taken upon our army's return.

"With the king's concurrence, I aided in forming a great armada, enlisting an army. The men themselves proved to be strangely incurious as to where they were going and as to the purpose to which they would be employed in battle. They were happy to serve God, and I was pleased to feed and quarter them as befits men who are doing His work. My father, my brothers, and I rendezvoused in Lisbon's deep harbor at the beginning of the summer of 1415. I can still remember the headiness of our reunion, especially my brothers and me who had yet to taste the glories of war. Our father, as can be expected by majesty, was more subdued, having already partaken the nectar of victory. He released sufficient energy to meet the requirements of the moment, and no more. Amid this giddy happiness came the plague, perhaps God's way of reminding us who is ultimately in charge of our affairs.

The Holy Mother Church has taught us that God's reasons are inscrutable, and we can never hope to understand them, only to tolerate what must be inevitable. I cannot examine too closely His purpose in afflicting my sainted mother with the flux. Admixing misery and mercy, my mother died three days after her first symptoms. I can still vividly remember our teary gathering at the foot of her bed. Despite her own weakness, she admonished us not to delay departure. As we choked back sobs, she presented Pedro, Duarte, and me with beautifully jeweled swords to be used in the upcoming battle for the greater glory of God by slaying the infidel. She then presented each of us with japanned boxes containing pieces of the holy cross. With a last gasped blessing, she sent us on our holy mission."

Henry related these events in a sententious tone, making me wish at the time that my own mother who had died on the very same day of the very same flux had behaved with such calm dignity. Instead, as I can recall with eidetic clarity, I see my poor, shrunken mother thrashing about on her narrow, thin cot, alternatively vomiting thick, black bile and expelling noisome excrement while viscous blood oozed from her eyes and ears. There was no relief from these base symptoms until merciful death released her from torment. At the time I was listening to Henry's version of his mother's death, I was convinced that nobility endured the flux with sublime serenity and without the horrid sights and smells visited upon the poor rank and file of our kingdom.

With the benefit of my mind's vision, even as my actual eyes fade and my orbs grow cloudy with age, I can more readily imagine how the queen died, not as Henry falsely described, but rather as a fellow human, subject to the same dehumanizing symptoms, as the plague does not distinguish between stations. The excrement of queen and housekeeper is equally noisome, perhaps more so for the former, owing to the richer diet. The excrement of the poor does not smell as foul as that of the rich, just as the droppings of a rabbit appear harmless compared to the rancidness of a pig's.

As to the awarding of the swords, I leave it up to the

discretion of you, dear reader. Neither of us was there to witness the event. The basic truth of the matter is that I do not particularly care. I do have an opinion regarding the slivers of the true cross, since, if all these relics that circulate in our Christian Europe were to be brought together, there would be enough lumber to build a man-o-war. I am aware that I am again guilty of sacrilege, but by the time you, dear reader, peruse these pages, I will have been long dead. Besides, the good father inquisitors are not likely to leave the comfort of their well-heated great halls to come to this pest-ridden hell of a place to interview such an unimportant fly fleck such as myself. There is a distinct advantage to being a nobody living at the edge of the world.

It was nearing the end of our interview when my last quill dulled and I entreated the prince to pause his commentary so I could sharpen it, but he either did not hear me or ignored my plea, as he continued on sonorously, as if he were in a trance.

"We gathered again at our southern city of Lagos, and there I invoked the king to grant me two requests: that I may be the first to disembark and that when the king's royal ladder was set upon the walls of the city, I be allowed to be the first to ascend it."

I half committed his words to memory as I feverishly honed my quill.

As you will later learn, it was totally beside the point whether Dom João I granted these petitions, as the historical chronicle, as reported by eyes with no vested interests, proved otherwise.

Dear reader, I was enthralled by my prince's narrative of the battle, as I am sure you were upon reading my chronicle. I could not but admire his pure courage as he led his men into the fray, slaughtering infidels as a farmer reaps ripe wheat.

"It was a warm day, even accounting for the season and latitude. From experience, I can tell you that nothing unmans a soldier more than thirst. It is a horrid urgency, driving away all complacency and ardor for the cause. Nevertheless, on that day, I endeavored to ignore my thirst as well as the other exigencies of my body and strode forth ahead of the seventeen men that comprised my personal guard. It was then that I encountered some five hundred or so of our men, their tongues paled and swollen with thirst and fear, fleeing from the counterattacking Moor. Seeing this reprehensible spectacle, I raised my sword, the late queen's present, and, shouting for Portugal and St. James, ran forward. The men, recognizing me and most likely ashamed of their cowardice, took heart and rallied, driving the Moors before them like frightened sheep. The day was won with the fortress falling to our arms in a single short but desperate battle."

All this and more, the prince related to me in the course of three days as I dutifully noted. At the time, I was much younger than Henry and felt to be a child in the presence of a demigod. Again, I tread on sacrilege, but in an orthodox way, as my prince's stature and reputation have grown geometrically since his death. Again, I must take modest pride in being partly responsible for this quasi deification. I have even heard rumors of canonization, given his widely reputed celibate and holy life. I must admit that I was put under the spell of his self-assuredness, and I believed that God must indeed be whispering his holy afflatus into his ear, as no man that I had known until him could have acted with such certainty of purpose.

I was collecting the parchments and my writing materials deliberately, trying to get up the courage to inquire as to monetary compensation for the upcoming labors. He must have sensed my unease and asked me what matter was.

"Well, my prince," for such I now considered him, "I was wondering if my stipend from my duties at the Royal Library might be increased to reflect the added responsibilities."

His brooding mouth opened in wonder as if he had not

understood a word I had said. I quickly explained the worldly matters to my perplexed prince.

"You see, my prince, I will need to buy parchments and writing materials, most of which are imported from the Germanies and Holland and are therefore expensive. The ones I used are all I had and must be replaced. There will also be the printer's fee and the expense of dissemination of the finished texts."

"Make a list of the expenses and give it to my secretary, and I will see that you are reimbursed."

He began to walk out of his small, austere room when he stopped at the door and said without turning to me, "Zurara, I know you are not a rich man, but you are a deserving one. Be loyal to me and my Godly causes, and I will make you part of my household and possibly sharer of great fortune on earth and even a greater one in God's kingdom."

I was young then and believed every word he said.

س

I have taken the first tentative steps toward immortality. Fame is the only way to overcome death, for you must be truly dead when the living cease speaking of you, as the ancients believed. There is solace in paper and ink, immutability equal to that of God; it is the only true way of challenging Him. Despite their celebration of Godlessness, Homer and Virgil endure and may continue to do so when even God is dust. Dominicus must whip me twenty times for the thought. I want to be a hero, wrathful and undeterred from my sacred and personal cause. My, but he is an angel, those fleshy ruby lips and the girlish shiver of those slight shoulders. I allowed him to see me, to witness my suffering on his behalf, the dried blood on the wall and whip, what I must endure to eschew his love, that fire that consumes me and, at the same time, leaves me whole, only to burn again. Oh, dear God, why have You taxed me so? Is it I? Is it a test of character? Must I earn my station? If I were certain, I would rejoice, stripping my proud flesh of raiment, all its vanity, discarding the false temporal idols, capricious whims, seeking a higher plane among bodiless Titans who have evanesced into the sublime. Why do I love the pagan so? It is against all my pretenses of modesty, for deep down in the gist of my core is this undying ambition, and still, I know myself to be immodest. I am compelled to erect Babel so that I can spit in God's eye. Be calm, my indomitable animal; the greater the rage, the more dire it is to subdue the beast, adding vivid colors to each other: the blood reds, the yellows that take your breath away, and the purples that cannot be ignored by man and nature until the mundane emerges. Brown, that totally forgettable hue, claims kin to the color of excrement and of Franciscan robes. I will punish my vanity with it. He is a beauty, this boy, and I will tell him a story of gods and demons that will make him love me, just as I despise myself for what I truly am. No one need ever know, not even me, for I will convince myself otherwise by constant mantra. I will do God's work to strangle the beast. It is the beast I most fear, he that makes the walls sweat and that swells my hateful member. I must drive the red beast from myself, lacerate flesh, to do without comfort of food or drink, think of Christ's crucifixion. Yet it is precisely that image that resurrects the animal that is barely caged within me. What is it about that holy image that causes such disgraceful sacrilege? I would stab the moon seven times to be rid of it. The horrible visions I have, I cannot relate them in confession, for surely I would be excommunicated. Dominicus is the only one I can trust; he does not judge but merely absolves and does so repeatedly when I say I am truly sorry, and at the time of the utterance, I am. I cannot be above God, though I feel myself above mortal, insignificant men. They are so small in their base appetites of today's meal and the vulgar disgusting lust for female pudenda. I am above such perdition but yet entranced by my own insanity. My inner world is a vivid hell, so I will go outside it and find a route to India around Africa—I am sure it exists—and take all opportunities to slay the Saracen in the name of and to the glory of God. This I swear.

CHAPTER THREE
JOÃO AFONSO DE ALENQUER

Time is an inscrutable machine; it can only be measured after it has occurred, but the precise moment elapsing can never be captured. The accumulation of the present makes a coherent past. The event that is occurring may not take on great importance, but once analyzed, recorded, and filtered through a man's intelligence, that same event may become significant, perhaps even a milestone in history. I have read the great Herodotus who was said to have invented history, but even his rendition of the events was hearsay and subjected to a mortal man's prejudices. Our memory and records of the past are protean, subject to lapses, imagination, and outright lies. Great chunks of our past disappear, much like those fleeting memories of dreams that evaporate within our minds as dewdrops do upon a single blade of grass under an intense August sun. It is as if a man went to market with a hundred *dobras* in his purse, and at the end of the day, he tallied his purchases but could not account for thirty of his coins. In my youth, months would vanish from my memory; I could not account for how I had spent, or more likely wasted, those precious days. Time is squandered on youth, unfeeling to the preciousness of it. Old men know how to husband their remaining resources.

With the subtraction of the sum of my days, I now regret the great swathe of my life that was dissipated on trivialities. This particular of mine, of course, pertains only to thinking, effete men such as myself, for the mindless peasant wastes none of his time in his single-minded, often Herculean task of keeping himself and his family from starving. The peasant labors, the peasants eats, and then he digests, no more. His wakeful hours are dedicated to mindless labors, with no sinful luxuries squandered on speculating intangibles.

We so-called educated men, free from the demands of the soil and assured of our next meal, are the ones who are guilty of disrespecting the calendar since the seasons do not bind us to the requisite rites of planting, weeding, and harvesting. Free of necessity, we privileged have the options to devote this freedom to accomplish deeds, great and small, pray to a senseless and insensitive God, or, as is more likely, indulge in ephemeral hedonism. I fear the great majority of this minority devote much too much time in praying and fornicating and too little toward pursuits that elevate the mind and cleanse the soul. I, of course, number myself among these dissipaters of time.

Alas, my youth was wasted on being young, praying for underserved boons, sighing rather than inhaling, and humming when I could have learned how to play a musical instrument. As I have deteriorated into old age, whole years have been extinguished into nothingness. Perhaps that is how death maneuvers, blotting out time and memories until all life is absorbed. These ruminations are assuredly sacrilegious, but I am unable to stop my mind from randomly wandering away from dogma. It is a weakness in which I let myself indulge.

I do remember with an eerie clarity one raw day in early April; it was not long after my chronicles on the conquest of Ceuta had been published. At the time, I was enjoying the privileges and limitations of being part of my prince's household. I had amassed nearly twenty years of service, and the privileges were indeed many but were outweighed by the circumspect conduct I had to maintain by being associated with the perfect prince I had invented.

I was tacitly forbidden proximity to anyone save my prince, as aloofness inspired royal awe while intimacy was apt to reveal human frailties. Needless to add, pleasures of the flesh were strictly taboo. There could be no more Ofelias in my circumscribed life. Even marriage was frowned upon by Henry, as he believed the union with a wife would blunt resolve. Henry's household was composed of zealots to the cause of Christianity and its spread and perpetuation to the heathen lands of Guinea while at the same time fighting and killing the Moor whose beliefs were anathema to the true faith.

Though my own weak flesh desired a woman's heat and my lax conscious at times yearned for release from severe sobriety, I was willing to make these sacrifices in order to associate myself with what I thought was living history, the moment that I was capturing, a moment to be revered by posterity. I thought I could confound the inscrutable machine and stop time and etch the moment. I took immense pride from the modicum of renown that I had brought Henry through the dissemination of my writings throughout Christendom. I was now working on another opus that also celebrated his ongoing accomplishments, namely, the conquest and discovery of Guinea. Some business had taken me to the royal city of Tomar, and one of my privileges was an appointment as a lay member of the Order of Christ by my prince who served as governor of the holy order. As a member, I would be lodging at the Order's massive monastery in Tomar. The Order of Christ was the successor to the Knights Templar and had inherited a part of the vast wealth that the Templars had amassed. Indeed, my prince had hinted many times of the rewards that could await me in return for loyal service to his household and, in particular, his person. It was widely rumored that some of this physical wealth was entombed somewhere in the bowels of the very monastery where I was staying.

I will admit that it was with some immoderate pride that I passed through the massive gates of the monastery. Just above the gates was the carved escutcheon of my prince; chiseled into the quickly aging green limestone was his eight-pointed cross of discovery surrounded by five artichokes, the miraculous fruit that keeps our sailors from coming down with scurvy while on prolonged voyages of discovery.

A young, nervous acolyte came to my cell and presented me with a note written on parchment, a sign that the sender was no poor man. I was accustomed to missives bearing invitations from local gentry, as my name had gained some fame, and I was, after all, associated with and had access to the ear of my powerful prince. I blessed the shivering, rain-sodden acolyte, as I had no copper coins on my person, and he gloomily withdrew. The message contained an invitation from Afonso de Alenquer, the former treasurer of the realm who had figured prominently in my chronicles as the germinator for the invasion and conquest of Ceuta. In my humble estimation, I regarded his invitation as more of a summons, and after a quick ablation, I reported to his house, which was quite near the monastery, a gift from my prince for services properly rendered.

I must admit to some surprise on finding the house modest, but perhaps I was still under the influence of the granite majesty of the neighboring monastery. At the time, I remember feeling that Dom Afonso had merited a grander abode, but then again, perhaps Dom Afonso was much like my prince who used ostentation as a political instrument while, at the core, he was more comfortable with austerity, better to be nearer our savior.

An ebony black slave, or so I assumed he was, let me into the sunlit atrium. I was curious, as I had never been so close to an Ethiopian, and I stared with undisguised fascination. He most likely was quite used such curiosity and ignored my impoliteness. He was taller by at least a head than most Europeans, with broad, squared shoulders. He stood with an erectness of posture that projected an arrogance of nature or a natural nobility, I know not which, that belied his humble status of servitude. I was most gratified to notice a crucifix dangling from his thick, well-shaped neck. He looked well-fed, and there were no whip marks visible. This former heathen was assuredly better off as a pampered creature of this household, and by converting him to Christianity, we had saved his immortal soul from eternal damnation. We had done him an immeasurable service by saving him from man's darker humors, the pun was not intended. This was the state of my thoughts at the time.

As I was led through the house, I was impressed by the interior's sumptuousness when compared to the simplicity of the unassuming exterior. There were luxurious Asian carpets that lined the walking area that seemed to reach up and caress my feet as I gingerly stepped on what perhaps could be years of someone's toil. The walls were decorated by painted wooden masks with beastly elongated heads. At first glance, I was appalled by these heathen representations, but then the colors and the artistry began to convert me to their innate beauty, despite the infidel hands that had fashioned them on the hard African wood. It occurred to me that Dom Afonso's house was much like the ugly mud-daubed abodes of the Jews who slyly hide their wealth from jealous eyes while lavishly furnishing their interiors. The Jews have learned how to hide in comfort.

An evil suspicion took root in my breast at that moment when gazing at all that un-Christian beauty. Could Dom Afonso be one of those crypto-Jews? Henry has often said that there were many of these devils incarnate hidden among the innocent in our kingdom. They were sons and sometimes even grandsons of Jews who had converted to our true religion rather than endure the purging fire of the *auto da fé*. But their conversion was a false one, and what was worse, the heresy they harbored was passed on to their children.

Living in constant deception brought out a thirst for vengeance in the Jew. As we all know, the Jew never dares face a Christian man-to-man, for he is an innate coward, preferring to amass wealth through deviousness. The Jew prefers to snipe from a hiding place. My prince told me of instances of poisoned wells or circumstances when Christian children went missing, most likely victims of the Jew's unholy ceremonies. It was through Henry's own insistence that the *auto de fé* still remained in our kingdom, despite his brothers' tepidness, especially Dom Duarte who openly criticized the practice and fervently believed that the accusations of Jewry were a result of envy or private grudges.

Henry remained steadfast and insisted that an iterant group of Benedictine monks investigate accusations at his direction. More often than not, no overt event such as the disappearance of a child need have occurred; all it took was a whisper that took root in small hearts and weak minds.

It is true that most of the accused were wealthy men whose acumen for business might have aroused envy. It was also true that accusations were often thrown at political foes. Once accused, adamant denial was a sign of guilt. Offer passive acceptance, and you are also guilty. There was always a solution, with the accused acquiescing to whatever my prince sought in return for a devout baptism in return for the dropping of all charges of crypto-Judaism. At the time of my gazing upon Dom Afonso's hidden wealth, it struck me that someone's cowardly accusation might prompt an accusation of Jewry.

Like a man suddenly doused with frigid water, I dismissed

my suspicions, for Dom Afonso de Alenquer was a nobleman who had served both God and my prince well. Moreover, Dom Duarte, then king, had mandated that the accuser must come forward if the *auto de fé* were to proceed. It was one thing to stab a man in the back but quite another to do so when you have to face him. And so following Dom Duarte's requirement, the number of accusations dropped precipitously. It would indeed take someone blessed with Herculean testicles to openly accuse a man like Dom Afonso, well connected as he was, with a false accusation of Jewry, for Dom Duarte had mandated that false testimonies would have to face the fire, and I have been told that any form of death is preferable to that, for the voices I have heard were witnesses to the fact that the victim does not immediately die but suffers hell on earth for quite some time until he is released to eternal damnation. Dom Afonso was safe from frivolous accusations, I concluded.

The Ethiopian led me to an Eden-like garden in the rear of the house and then departed with a slight but courteous bow. The humble exterior's mask of the house's hidden treasures seemed limitless. The garden was fashioned in the Arab style, with an abundance of flowing water. At one end of the garden was an impish statue of a child holding a pitcher from whence an endless stream of water flowed. The other fountain featured a deceptively mundane semicircle of stone, from which a gentle geyser emerged, alternating spurts as if to punctuate pleasure. The sound of the streams had a soothing effect upon my overexposed nerves, and I unconsciously found myself admiring the Moor's design. It the desert, water is an art form.

In between the fountains, there was a small wooden table and three chairs shaded by a trellis with overhanging vines. Since it was but April, there were still no grapes, but I could well imagine the splendor of the place when September arrived and the dark purple bunches swelled above your head.

I imagined myself sitting there, a tantalus reprieved from torment.

Sitting at the table, I espied an old man wearing a wide-brimmed hat against the mist of the day, with his gnarled hands clasped behind his back as he oversaw a young man pruning his vines. The curvature of his spine indicated the weight of years that pressed upon him. He seemed to sense my presence, for he immediately turned with a dexterity I had not credited him with and faced me as I approached. His eyebrows had grown unruly and a bit satanic, as is the nature with old men. His beard was long but looked trimmed and well cared for and clean, and I mentally credited the Ethiopian slave for his general well-kempt appearance. Most men of his apparent age tend to be slovenly, and one can often find remnants of last night's dinner among the knotted tresses of their beards. Despite his stooped frame, this old man bore himself with nobility, and I could not help but notice the active intelligence that pierced defiantly through his rheumy eyes. In the perspective that my old age has given me, I have learned that it takes more than sharp, young eyes to see things as they truly are. It is now evident to me that Dom Afonso's inner vision, even at his advanced age, was superior to my own relatively fresh eyes.

He bade me sit in the shade of a trellis flowing with vines that dangled pleasantly overhead, laden with tiny, hard, little, acrid balls that would become the grapes I had previously painted upon the canvas of my mind.

"Ever since I read your chronicle on the conquest of Ceuta, I've wanted to meet you. You are, of course, much too young to have assisted in the battle, so I am curious to learn how you acquired your facts."

I told him of my long and frequent interviews with our prince.

"I thought as much," he said pensively.

"Darfum? Darfum, you black heathen, bring us a jug of wine and two glasses."

The Ethiopian arrived bearing an earthen jug and two goblets accompanied by a half loaf of mealy bread and a saucer of olives swimming in sister olive oil. With grave majesty, he departed without saying a word.

"His name is Darfum?" I inquired.

"That was his name when we stole his freedom; I see no reason to steal his name as well. But getting back to Ceuta, your description of the events leading up to the conquest is all wrong."

I must have been visibly shocked by this declaration since Dom Afonso was basically stating that my prince had lied. He began to laugh at my apparent distress, but his old man's cackle segued into a fitful hacking cough that is often a harbinger of impending death.

"Sorry to have frightened you so much. No, it was all wrong. Of course, there were many truths interwoven among the lies. You have to clothe lies in partial truths to be believed. Pour yourself some of my wine; it is from two seasons ago and my best from this vineyard."

I did as he requested, but some self-preserving egotism in me told to escape while I could. Yet my feet were unable to move, overridden by curiosity and the insatiable yen for the truth. Pure truth is enthralling; it purifies the soul and releases all malaria. I desperately wanted to abscond with my complacent lies but did not dare. If some prankster leads you to a pit and cautions you to cover your eyes, for what you may see is the ugly truth, how many among us could refrain from sneaking a peek?

"The biggest lie is your credit to me for conceiving the conquest. I did no such thing. I was and am a simple civil servant, not a regal strategist as was our great king, Dom João I, may God preserve his soul. The king himself began preparations for the invasion in 1409 when your prince was only fifteen and had just barely learned how to get out of his breeches before he shit in them. Our king was one of those rare men who did not wait for his destiny to define him, but took it by the throat and shaped it to his own iron will. He wrested the throne from that idiot, Fernando, his half-brother and legitimate heir, and defended it against all odds. When those avaricious Castilians attacked in 1385, our weak and putrid nobles sided with the invader. They were landed, and the Castilian brute promised them the retentions of their estates in return for betraying their country. Noble nature being what it is, they acquiesced, citing the fact that Dom João I was not a legitimate heir as the bastard son of Dom Pedro. It was the smart alliance to make; Dom João I was outnumbered at least two to one, but he was not without support among the people and, more importantly, among the merchants who rightly feared that the Castilians would reassign their privileges to their own men of commerce. It was lucky for our king that our merchants were prosperous. They provided the funds to arm the army, and there was even enough to hire one hundred English longbowmen from John of Gaunt who was to become our king's father-in-law and permanent ally against the common Castilian foe.

"After Dom João I succeeded in driving the Castilians away in the great battle of Aljubarrota, he quickly moved to defrock the traitorous aristocrats, awarding lands and titles to some of his most ardent supporters. The trouble was that there were not enough lands and riches in our poor kingdom to make everyone content. There was also the problem of the numerous landless knights who had rallied to his cause. Ambitious himself, Dom João I knew how that sin—or is it a virtue? I know not which it is—can lead men to question authority and intrude upon hard-won privilege. These knights were witnesses to the monetary fruits that can be reaped through force of arms. It was with these dilemmas in mind that our king conceived of invading Ceuta and unleashing the dogs of war upon the hapless Moor. The provisioning of the armada at the expense of the common taxpayer would continue to fill the coffers of the merchants while the war on the infidel would serve as an outlet for the malicious energies that accrue in the restless souls landless knights.

"It was also true as you recount that the preparations for the invasion were carried out through mazes of secrecy and deceit. As our king and his sons amassed the army and armada, the Christian kings grew fearful. The king of Aragon worried openly that his island of Ibiza was the target. Even the all-powerful Castilians themselves fretted that we sought to wrest the Nasrid kingdom of Grenada away from their prior claim to it. Our king said nothing to Juan of Castile other than if you claim it, take it. All of Christian Europe speculated and trembled.

"When Dutch privateers harassed some of our merchant vessels, our king made a great show of the relatively small incidents and did not deny the rampant rumors that emerged that Holland was the target. He even sent a trusted emissary to Count William of Holland to proclaim in his public court our king's grievances, and the emissary went on to make military threats. Our emissary was also instructed to seek a second private audience with the count and explain the ruse. The count was both pleased and relieved and continued to support the feint with false preparations and alarms.

"It is also true that our king sent the prior of the Order of the Knights Hospitaler to Sicily, ostensibly to ask for the hand of the horribly rich but horrible ugly princess for Pedro, the eldest son. You should have seen that petulant child jump up and down in the throne room, vowing that he would never marry a woman who had more facial hair than his brother Henry, noted already as unusually hirsute at twenty. How both the king and your prince chuckled at Pedro's outrage.

"On the way to Sicily, the prior's small, unarmed caravel harmlessly anchored under the protection of the port of

Ceuta. This was the prior's real mission. He took soundings of the harbor and reconnoitered the defenses of the city. Upon the prior's return, he built a model of the fortress from two sacks of sand, a roll of ribbon and half a bushel of beans. The man had missed his true calling, a strategist wasted in serving Mass.

"Your account of the armada did not do it proper justice. I saw it sail from Lisbon and will never forget the sight of the red-crossed sails of one hundred ships bearing fifty-four hundred men-at-arms, nineteen hundred mounted bowmen and their steeds, and twelve thousand unmounted bowmen and footmen. The crested sails, the spirited cries of the men, the terrified neighs of the horses stomping about nervously in the nether holds of the ship; it was a sight to behold. Even as they left, only a few aboard the ships knew of the armada's true destination.

"So you see, I had nothing to do with the germ of the idea, much less your prince who claims in the chronicle to be the main impetus behind all the machinations. The other untruth is your description of the battle itself, but in this, I cannot enlighten you since, in Christian honesty, I was not present. But I have been audience to many who were, and I suggest you go speak with them. I will refer you to someone who lives here in Tomar who was not only there, but served notably."

"This is all very interesting, and I assuredly will speak with this veteran, but I also understand that you have been a member of the royal household for many years and witnessed the princes as they grew into men. As you have wisely pointed out, my own chronicle of Henry is one-sided and lacks dimension. My prince has never revealed anything more to me than he wishes. What was he like as a boy?"

"Now, chronicler, you have hit the bone and revealed the marrow. You should have come to me before writing that rubbish. But before I continue, I will need added refreshment."

So saying, he shouted to Darfum to bring another jug of wine and a basket of figs, as his bowels needed encouragement. With old age; vanity diminishes.

س

"The first three boys were just over a year apart in age. Despite Dom João I's frequent travels, intrigues, and mistresses, he managed to keep Dona Phillipa pregnant almost constantly for the first five years of their marriage. Of course, Dom João I was one of those loveable villains, able to eviscerate an enemy and eat his liver in the morning and endear himself with gracious jocularity to a potential benefactor in the evening of the same day. It takes a cad to become a great king.

"And a great king he was. He never betrayed what went on in his mind, save in retrospect. He smiled both to enemy and friend. Whatever he thought remained in his head. He kept both friend and potential rival close, often sending them on fruitless errands that both distracted and engaged ambitious minds. He was magnanimous in tolerating fools but woe to the cunning man. There were frequent 'accidents,' with these cunning men constantly falling off their horses, though it was a stretch of the imagination how such an accident could result in decapitation. The Benedictine monks were judiciously circumspect upon issues. Church and state are constantly at odds in the accumulation of wealth and power. One claims the privileges for God and the other claims it for man in the name of God. But if a king is to be successful in thwarting the Church, the priests will inevitably petition the pope for succor, and it is a sagacious temporal who does not push the clergy too far. Dom João I was wise enough to limit his despotism, not agglomerating too much power upon his sole person.

"Dona Phillipa ruled the boundaries of the household with an iron will and fist, just like the English bitch she was. She was politic in ignoring her husband's dalliances, provided they remained discrete, and the wench was acutely aware of her place, somewhere above a knot in a tree and below a ewe in heat. I distinctly remember one young wench, a daughter of some minor nobility, who forgot her place in the hierarchy and thought she could possibly replace the queen in the king's affections and on the throne. The wench quite literally disappeared; as if she never existed, as the queen was subtle. Any public offender of Dom João I would have been flayed and then hung by his ankles until his flesh was consumed by vermin. The body of Dona Phillipa's putative rival was never found, while her family was prudent enough to lodge no protest.

"The queen was like a mother crocodile in the protection of her offspring in that she would defend them at all costs but was not above eating one or two of her own issue should she deem it necessary. She oversaw her children's education, ensuring that they were taught the accumulation of lay science, irrespective whether the precepts conflicted with Christianity. Independence of thought was fostered; however, the children had to attend Mass every morning. As the proud Plantangenant she was, she made sure all her children spoke the English language with equal fluency to our own.

"Dona Phillipa brokered no rivals to the succession to the throne. She assiduously married off all the king's bastards to suitable spouses, meaning of lineage so low that they could never lay claim to the throne. As I have suggested previously, great kings and queens are made of sterner stuff than mere mortals, rendered omnipotent by doubts of conscience and guilt. The meek only inherit the thin layer of earth that covers their shallow graves, that is, until their bones turn to dust or dogs unearth and eat their bodies. The audacious, like

Dom João I and Dona Phillipa, do not wait passively for their inheritance; they seize it.

"Coming back to the children, Duarte was the eldest and pale and sickly from birth. After surviving three successive unlucky wet nurses, he was entrusted to the care of a Franciscan nun, Sister Lucia, who had spent some time in Grenada with our enemies, the Moors. There she had learned the apothecary science and was said to know how to cure many diseases and to restore strength to the weak.

"I can only guess what admonitions our stern queen must have threatened the hapless nun with, for she behaved like an exposed nerve. Every time Duarte so much as stumbled, she would run frantically to him, shouting holy explicatives. Surrounded by such a protective shroud, in addition to the boy's natural physical infirmities, Duarte grew up with the assurance that the world was a parlous place, rendering him fearful of body and loath to make decisions without extraneous counsel, no matter how trivial.

"His brother, Pedro, was next in age, a physical replica of his short, stocky father but lacking in his sire's wiliness. His was an open sou. Subterfuge was alien to him, making his emotions easily readable on his visage. As the hale younger brother, he was the instigator of torment to fish, fowl, and siblings, especially his older brother, Duarte, who frequently joined in the persecutions if only to avoid being subjected to them himself.

"It was my joy to see the mirth on Pedro's face as he scaled a cherry tree while the timorous Duarte watched fearfully from below. Sister Lucia was present to ensure Duarte did not attempt the climb, though she need not have worried, as the boy showed no disposition to try. Her shrieks were often heard, admonishing Pedro and constantly reminding him that he served as a poor model for his brothers.

"Henry was the third oldest and an enigma from birth. Unlike Pedro, his face betrayed nothing save for a sustained brooding that could not be interpreted with any precision. From the start, he lacked the spontaneity of a child, conducting himself from infancy with the weight of a morose adult. He suffered no intrusions on his privacy and woe be to the hapless servant who did not take care to knock before entering his chambers. While his siblings naturally fidgeted and pinched each other playfully in chapel, Henry knelt in apparent rapture, in comatose prayer as if he were in direct communion with God, begging forgiveness for sins I cannot conceive a ten year old could be guilty of. His saturnine appearance added years to his actual age, so he became used to deference from adults early on. At twelve, a coarse mustache appeared on his upper lip, and he was now taller than his two older brothers. This precocious virility manifested itself in a natural athleticism. Henry was a fearless tilter and excelled at the sword. Even at this age, he could pull the drawstring of an English longbow as far back as his ear. His prowess in the arts of war endeared him to his father and swelled the pride of the queen who saw the blood of Richard the Lionhearted flow through her son's veins.

"Yet despite all the precedents of virile youths, Henry's nature did not manifest itself in the expected ways of the times. His brothers indulged in the entitlements of their birth station, drinking and retching, but Henry remained apart from such nonsense. Yet it is not natural for such a young man to refrain what must be in his nature.

"Most male children receive religion as if they were being dosed with a bitter but necessary medicine. They dutifully but only reluctantly open their mouths and swallow the nasty stuff and then grimace with the aftertaste. Not Henry. He splendored in that pasture. He would crucify himself for hours on his knees in the cold, damp chapel, rapt in prayer as if he were in private audience with God.

"Now Dom João I's reverence was perfunctory; he tolerated the chapel but always made sure the officiating priests knew they may have God to pray to but he had a sword to resolve any argument. Consequently, the priests knew to speed up their litany, and the Latin words ran into each other as if they were one long syllable. My king was a true man of this world; religion was but a political necessity. He could jovially drink to the health of a man and have that same man murdered in the same night. Henry's subterfuge ran deeper.

"While Henry's body gelled into sinew and muscle, his spirit withdrew into some impenetrable inner sanctum. Although he was not only equal but superior in strength to his elder brother, Pedro, Henry climbed no trees nor did he scale vine-covered walls to peek into maids' quarters, as was his brother's wont. Rather than seek out other lads his own age for company, he elected a severe young Capuchin monk by the name of Frey Dominicus as his confessor and constant companion. This monk was given all responsibilities for his person, even emptying out the prince's chamber pots, a task forbidden to the servants. It would seem that Henry did not want any gossipy witnesses to his own human frailty. I remain a reverent man, but this Frey Dominicus represented to me all that was wrong with the priesthood. A sour disposition, devoid of any humor, and intolerant of human weakness, I thought him a poor companion for the prince. In the monk's ever-frowning face, I saw an obdurate misery that wished itself on his fellow man. The severe priest was a human who despised humanity. I am sure that he despised his own weak body and would have rather been born directly as an immortal soul. He openly hated mirth and would angrily leave a room at the sound of laughter. Priests may be priests, but they are also men; Frey Dominicus was neither.

"A short hiatus followed, then came the births of Bianca and the youngest, Fernando. As soon as Bianca was weaned, she was sent away to a convent school in preparation for a proper marriage. The queen had little use for her own sex. I hardly can remember that child, though I have heard she grew up to marry one of the kings of the Spains; I forget which since there are so many and all immodest.

"Of all the children, the adorable Fernando was the most beautiful; that infantile smile could even melt the heart of the queen. His hair tended toward curliness, something unseen in his siblings, and formed one large cone atop his head that fell upon an angelic forehead. He was prone to a wide-cheeked smile as his older brother, Henry, was to sullenness; however, they attracted each other like opposite ends of lodestones. Fernando grafted himself on the willing trunk of his brother, following him with still unsure steps wherever the older boy went. Henry appointed himself his youngest brother's protector, and woe to Pedro should he try to visit his humor on the helpless Fernando. Henry was quick to punish his older brother, thrusting a fist into a muscled but yielding abdomen, or, if the offense was particularly galling, an elbow straight to the jaw, causing Pedro to lose four teeth before he turned eighteen, until he grew wise enough not to challenge Henry in anything physical. Neither parent intervened in these battles since the stronger must perforce vanquish the weaker, and lessons learned young are lessons learned best. Pedro's bruised flesh went without comment.

"It was refreshing to witness the adulation in the wide eyes of the child, Fernando, as he waddled after his protector brother. Even through the heavy mist of hypocrisy of the court, the sincerity of their mutual love still brings tears to my cynical eyes. It is a memory I can no longer bear, knowing what subsequently happened to that poor hapless child. I would not have recounted this now if not for your persistent solicitude and the lubricant of the wine. Now go away. You have made me sad on this day, and I don't have that many days left to enjoy. Remember to seek out the veteran of Ceuta; Darfum will give you his name and where he can be found."

With this rather one-sided interview, I was gently dismissed and shown the door by the muscular Darfum. As

I left, I thought I detected a smirk on his ebony face but could not tell for sure, as these people have different expressions. One thing I was indeed sure of was that the pedestal I has installed my prince upon was somewhat lower than it had been that morning when I awoke.

س

There are witnesses other than God to my conduct. I am even fearful that those witnesses inhabit our earth. When the unholy peel the shrouds of my humanity, what must they judge but weak, trembling flesh such as their own? There are so many of these on this earth, those who cast aspersions upon the means without taking the ends into account. I feel myself so alone and unique. What is God's purpose? I know Him to be inscrutable, throwing His most daunting gauntlets to the most deserving. I am a prince, and yet at times, I wish I were the ignoble plebian, able to satiate the basest of appetites without censure. I have killed all those who intuited my true nature; they were easy, simply priests. But what of the others? The aroused suspicion? Even a prince's arms are too short to do battle with God and His multitudes. The old witnesses of my youth will soon die, and then I will rewrite my history.

CHAPTER FOUR
A HUMBLE MAN'S ACCOUNT OF
THE TAKING OF CEUTA

*M*y interview with Dom Afonso festered under the skin of my soul like an ulceration in dire need of lancing and exposure to the cleansing light of truth. Once doubt sets into a mind, it takes hold, spreading like a virulent weed; its grip cannot be loosened by will alone. It occurred to me that I had been much too ready to accept Henry's version of the events as the literal truth. It also occurred to me that it had suited my interests to believe him in every detail. I began to feel ill at ease with my weakness of character, or so I interpreted my gullibility. Those tight smiles from some of the nobility I now reinterpreted as sneers. Yes, dear reader, I had already heard the whispers that referred to me as Henry's toady, a literary hack for hire. Previously, I had been able to dismiss these calamities as envious susurrations, but I now reevaluated. These hitherto dismissed detractors could be telling a truth I had refused to hear.

Again, I tried to bury my doubts. After all, Dom Afonso could be wrong; he was an old man, perhaps even senile.

Yet as much as I tried, I could not convince myself of any willful malevolence on the part of that honorable gentleman. I then tried a different tack to assuage the ever-encroaching doubt. It is a rare man indeed that can be utterly objective about himself. Prince Henry was no different; he merely admixed some of his own perceptions with the reality he had experienced. No man sees the world as it actually is, but rather filters it through his own prism of prejudices.

For the next three days, I tried to go about my business but could only devote part of my active attention to the endeavor; the greater part of my mind was obsessing on the possible lack of veracity of the details of the battle my prince had related to me. Finally, I could not resist, and I summoned the nervous acolyte and showed him the name of the tavern where Dom Afonso had said I could find the witness to the battle.

"My Lord," he shyly stammered, "I know not of any taverns, but I am told that some of them are rough places. I would suggest that you go speak to the hostler of the monastery. He is a profane man and is likely to know how to direct you. I would also suggest that you hire him to accompany you; as I said, these places can be rough indeed, and your clothes and manner will give you away instantly to ruffians who may not wish you well. The hostler is a tree of a man, with wrists as thick as my leg, and he can be trusted, for he would lose his position here should any harm come to you while under his care. I would also suggest that you arm yourself with *dobras* should you need them. You will be safe with the hostler; no one would dare rob you while you are under his protection."

I thanked the seminarian for his solicitude and went to the stables to seek out this hostler whose name I was told was Nuno. He was easy to recognize from the acolyte's description, as he was indeed a stout man, at least a head and a half taller than me and twice my heft. He sported a blunt forehead and a square jaw that projected brute strength, but no particular astuteness.

I showed him the tavern's name, The Hole in the Wall, and he put his massive arms akimbo and whistled in astonishment that one such as I would wish to visit such a place.

"It is indeed a rough place, frequented by men with no love for nobility such as Your Lordship. The good seminarian was wise to counsel that I accompany you. I would also suggest that we take along my cousin here, Fernando, for added protection, for many of these fiends carry daggers and such, and he owns a sword."

When I inquired as to their fee, the hostler stroked his chin in mock thought and then impudently quoted a whole *dobra*, taking me aback at the steepness of the price for their escort.

"But, Your Excellency, what is this pittance to a man of your rank, a member of the Order of Christ and rightful heir to their fortune? Surely, Your Lordship's wellbeing is worth more than a mere *dobra*?"

His audacity almost made me want to go complain to the prior to have him dismissed. He must have caught that danger in my face, and he began to wheedle how he was a poor man with six mouths to feed, including his widowed mother. His groveling tone mollified my pride, and I agreed to the price, though I dare say I received the worst of the bargain. This granite-jawed man was perhaps not as dull as he appeared.

With the hostler leading the way and his cousin following behind me, I was led through a maze of narrow alleys I never knew existed in Tomar, though I have visited the city many times before. The hostler's wide shoulders barely fit between the green-veneered, moss-covered walls of the gray stone houses that seemed so a kilter that I feared they may collapse upon us at any moment. As we passed, old, toothless crones curiously stuck their yellowed heads out from above and cackled some obscenity to the hostler who did not dignify their taunts with an answer, my presence apparently lending him augustness. After countless twists and turns, we came upon a slanted doorway, and the hostler ducked his head and stepped into the miasmic darkness while his cousin dramatically held my arm with one hand while his other hand was placed on the hilt of his sword. Apparently, my *dobra* also included a bit of theater.

From inside, I heard loud greetings and hail-well-mets, announcing the appearance of Nuno. A moment later, he emerged, grinned sheepishly, and motioned for me to enter.

The interior of the tavern resembled more of a primeval cave than any structure fashioned by Christian hands. As I blinked the sun from my eyes, I discerned the low rafters crisscrossing at precarious angles and strewn with accumulated sheets of spider webs, dust, and grime. The air was heavy and dank, infused by the collective poisonous exhalations of diseased lungs and other humors excreted by unwashed bodies. Added to these malodorous fumes was an acerb tang of cheap wine, and suddenly, an acute vertigo came upon me at this onslaught of smell and scene. All around, hollowed eyes stared at me like wolves eyeing their quarry with undisguised gluttony.

The combination of the alcoholic mist that permeated the low tavern and the sudden and irrepressible fear that overcame me must have unsteadied my sense of balance. An arm was thrust under my elbow to steady me, I know not by whom, but I suspect it was Nuno earning his *dobra*, which I no longer begrudged. The shadows around me sat still and quiet, more like stalking beasts than men. As I looked about, I wondered what daily existence must be like for them to seek out such a horrid place as a haven. My thoughts were interrupted by the hostler who led a man to me.

"This is the proprietor of the tavern and the man you seek," he said with the satisfaction of a magician who has just pulled a rabbit out of a hat. With that, the hostler joined his cousin who already stood at a crude, wine-darkened wooden bar, engaged in hearty conversation with the other regulars who were peppering him with questions about me as their heads bobbed in and out from behind Nuno's fleshy mass.

The man, or more exactly, the remains of the man, who stood before me was prematurely stooped and grizzled, as I knew he was not yet past thirty-eight. A long, angry scar ran aslant of his face and crossed a closed eye socket that had been sewn shut to prevent infection. His stoop was accentuated by the fact that his left leg appeared shorter than the right. All of a sudden, he grimaced hideously, exposing blackened teeth, and I was about to appeal to my protectors when he pointed to a table, and I realized that the horrible expression was actually a smile.

We sat, and two cracked, age-yellowed bowels of wine were served to us by a boy I took to be his son. I introduced myself with immodest grandiloquence, as I have said my name had gained some fame within our small kingdom and even beyond, but he just one-eyed stared at me in confused blankness. I then told him that Dom Afonso Alenquer had referred me to him, and he grimace-smiled in recognition.

"Ah, then you're the fellow who wrote about the battle of Ceuta? I've heard of these writings."

"You haven't read my chronicles?" I asked in surprise.

"No, my lord, witless soul that I am, I can't read, though my boy knows his letters and can tell you whether it's an A or B; can't you Felipe? I hope someday I can send him to school to learn how to put them together and be able to read in a proper fashion like a priest, but right now, I need his arms here. What can I do for Your Excellency, as there isn't anything I wouldn't do for Dom Afonso, kind man that he be."

I explained that I sought an account of the battle of Ceuta, as I was led to believe by Dom Afonso that he was present. He smile-grimaced and called out to his son to bring us a jar of wine.

"This'll take more time than a bowl of wine. What do you want to know?"

"Everything."

His lone eye slid from side to side as that of a animal suspecting a trap.

"Your Excellency, Prince Henry has already told you what happened at Ceuta. I'm sure he told you everything as it happened."

"But you say you have heard of my writings? Is what you heard what happened?"

Again, the telltale eye wandered suspiciously from side to side.

"It was as Prince Henry says it was," he said with a finality that indicated a dismissal. I was about to arise when I noticed the grinning faces of the men at the bar, apparently delighting in my failure. These men with so little were taking pleasure from my setback. For some inexplicable reason, their smugness gave me added resolve, and I again put my full weight on the chair from a mid-standing position.

"I will swear you an oath on my honor as a member of the Order of Christ that I will tell no one of our meeting nor of anything you tell me. You may be perfectly truthful with me. I can assure you that the prince will not hear. Besides, I would not want to let it be known that my version of the conquest of Ceuta was in error."

"You wouldn't want to write another history?" he asked, his single eye focused on me.

"No. The information I seek from you is for my own curiosity."

He maneuvered his deformed head aslant, a signal that he did not understand.

"I just want to know for myself what happened that day."

"But Prince Henry ..."

"Prince Henry was not everywhere. He could not have

noticed everything. I just want to hear from you what you saw."

"Your Excellency, you're an educated man whilst I can't even sign my name. You're of the Order of Christ and surely closer to heaven than me. What you promise I must surely believe since if you, as Godly as you are, lied, then heaven itself would fall upon us all and crush us into dust."

He grimaced a smile as I tried to ascertain whether he had just threatened me. Before I dared confront him with my suspicion, his eye looked up at me with a gypsy astuteness.

"I'm a poor man."

I had been unconsciously waiting for the price of truth, since it did come with some risk, and internally thanked the acolyte for his wise suggestion. I looked around me, and the skeletal grins intensified as they sensed that one of their own was about to have the better of one of their betters. I reached into my purse, counted the *dobras* and prudently drew out ten, half the enormous amount I had brought. His one eye darted to the golden pile, more money than he had probably ever seen in his life, and reverted back to me in silent negotiation. I sensed the building greed of the riff-raff around me intensify. I drew out another five golden coins, but this time, his eye remained motionless, still stabbing me with uncompleted negotiation. I began to suspect that he knew how much money to the coin I had with me and was determined to strip me of it all.

Now, dear reader, pride is sometimes detrimental to accomplishing one's ends. Here I was, a member of the Royal Court, an important and educated personage, haggling with an illiterate vestige of a serf. Again, I was indignantly about to rise.

"Yes, Excellency, I was there as you can well tell from what is left of my body. I was in the thick of it all and assigned as part of the prince's bodyguard. That was the most important day of my miserable life, and I can remember every detail better than what I did this morning."

With all abandon to exasperation, I reached into my purse and slammed the remaining five coins on the wine-soaked table, indicating my own version of finality. The grins about me relaxed in victory, and every ear attuned itself to hearing a good story. A hush descended upon the tavern like a velvety fog. The men took small, furtive sips of wine and set the crockery down gently, lest any noise interfere with what they all greedily wanted to hear, for oral lore is the literature of the illiterate.

س

"I'm called Vasco Martins, born like all you see around you here: poor and desperate. Me and my brother were taking our small flock of sheep to market in Braga, where there was this great feast going on. We were fed good meat and given good wine at no cost to us. As we gnawed on the gristle, a great lord got up from a platform. He said he was a prince of the Portugals and surely he must have been by the look of him. He was grand and handsome with a full head of black hair and a manly mustache, though he couldn't have been much past twenty. He was clothed in fine garments that glimmered against the sun and was surrounded by other nobles. He said he was going on what he called a crusade against the heathen Moors, whoever they were, and he needed strong men with stout Christian hearts. We all kept chewing on the remaining, more stubborn gristle as he spoke, but then he said that there were untold riches to be won, and we stopped our gnawing and listened with interest. That was all the convincing I needed. I enlisted on the spot and was told to be in Oporto on such and such a date and given a whole *real branco* for expenses for the journey. My brother also tried to enlist, but the lords there didn't take him, as he was a puny lad from birth. These lords must have been plenty smart, for the poor lad died that very year, shriveled as a raisin and coughing up rose-colored blood. Such is the lot of the people. My parents had eleven children, and only me and another younger sister survive to this day. The rest were taken to God's secret embrace and are now in heaven, where there is no hunger and no suffering, may the Lord be praised for His generosity.

"Well, I got to Oporto and was put on a cart along with five other sorry-looking lads. As we passed the shops, we stared, as none of us had ever seen so much meat in one place: slaughtered whole pigs, rabbits, skinned and pink, and something like a large chicken that someone in the cart said was a goose. Our mouths were agape with wonder as we rattled by the stands piled high with kale and mustard greens. Who would eat all this food, I wondered, but then I saw the immensity of the city. There were buildings taller than I'd ever seen, some five stories high. The houses were crowded together so that none even had gardens for growing greens or a sty under the house for keeping a pig. The rich men who lived in these houses of ease were assuredly the ones who ate the food I saw in the market. Save for our village priest, there was no one back home who didn't till the land in order to eat, and here was a city full of people rich enough to not have to scratch the dirt.

"We were garrisoned nearby and trained in arms. The broadsword came naturally to me; it was easier than swinging a hoe or an axe from dawn till dusk. I got so good that I could cleave a giant October gourd in two with just one mighty chop. The instructors included old soldiers that had served with the king at Aljubarrota. One was called Ruy Gonçalves, and he wasn't given to compliments, but I could tell he was impressed with me, so I tried all the more to please him. Nothing adds more resolve to muscle than living through poverty. Unlike my brother, my body firmed hard from the farm work while my stomach was like that of a goat's, drawing any and all nourishment from the moldiest and hardest crust of bread or soft, almost porous turnips. At that age, my arms were muscle, sinew, and bone, and I had a natural talent for the sword. Such was my skill and Ruy's influence that I was assigned to the prince's personal retinue., in reality, his bodyguard. There were seventeen of us, all the best men with the heavy broadsword.

The prince's *barca* sailed from Oporto in early August to join the rest of the fleet that awaited us in Lagos. In the harbor of Lagos were the royal banners of the king as well as the prince's bother, Pedro, flying with majesty in the warm winds of the Algarve. My lord, when I saw the forest of masts clustered in the harbor, I nearly wept with pride, and my chest swelled with patriotism. So many ships. So many men. Surely, no other kingdom could boast of such power.

"At Lagos, the priests came on board, scattering among the vessels, and began to proselytize to our raw, crude souls. They sprinkled holy water on the ships and on us and told us that to kill the Moor was righteous and was the will of God. A priest came to bless the prince's bodyguard and said we were among the anointed, whatever that meant. I was too frightened and ashamed of my ignorance to ask him what 'anointed' meant. After the priest left, I asked one of my mates who shrugged his shoulders. None of us knew, but I've come to believe that it means we were chosen for battle. At the time, I remember wishing that 'anointed' meant something about better rations.

"We then departed with the southerly winds billowing the sails tightly while the priest that remained aboard our *barca*, a certain Franciscan named Frey Bernardo, said Mass with us gathered along the sides of the ship. I was standing close to the prince, a solemn young man whom we imitated throughout the ceremony, kneeling when he knelt, standing when he stood, and crossing ourselves when he did. After the Mass, Frey Bernardo told us that we were going to do

God's work by fighting the infidel. Rude fellows that we were, our blank faces turned to each other in silent inquiry as to whether the man to our right or left knew what an infidel was. Frey Bernardo saw our bafflement and shouted that the infidel was Godless, as he had rejected our true Christ. One of our braver fellows asked aloud if this infidel was like the Jews who lived in our midst, tolerated yet kept apart. Frey Bernardo's voice grew harsh, and as he spoke, spittle flew out of his mouth. He shouted that the infidel, the Moor, was worse than the Jew, as they were intent on destroying our Christian faith and taking our lands. Landless as we all were, save the prince and his nobles, we nonetheless bristled at these words. Raising his arms over his head, Frey Bernardo warned that, left unchecked, the Moor would return to our country, possess our land, burn our churches, and rape our women. Virgins that most of us still were, we again bristled. If anyone was going to rape our women, it would be us, begging Your Lordship's pardon for my coarseness.

"With that, the prince rose to speak. I noticed that he was not the same stout lad that had boarded the *barca* in Oporto. He seemed to have shrunken in stature while his complexion had paled. He looked a bit wobbly as he fought the pitch and roll of our vessel rather than accepting that the ocean held sway over its own kingdom. As a boy, I had acquired my sea stomach from accompanying my uncle who owned a longboat and lived from the sea. It was a rough life and dangerous too, but I recognized the green pale of his face from my own first encounter with the sea when I was just ten and could barely haul in a line with a struggling cod at the end of it with my small hands, chapped and bleeding from the cold and the friction of the rope. There was no doubt in my mind, our noble prince was seasick, and I smiled inwardly at this very human display of weakness from my better. But he put on a brave face as he fought back the vomit that must have swelled in his throat so that he could speak to us. He repeated that we were on a holy mission that was God's will and many other things the priest had already said to us, and we nodded in tame, obedient agreement like the trained animals we were. I again beg Your Worship's pardon if he takes any offense at my coarse, unschooled language. He then said that there would be riches in the great castle we were about to conquer and that we would be free to loot, but he admonished that the riches must be collected in a communal pile from which we all would have a share. With that, our ears perked up, and we were all in favor of pursuing this particular will of God. He further warned that any man caught hoarding treasure would have his hands cut off, and there was a general hum of agreement on the punishment that fit the crime. We were all risking our lives equally, and so it was just that we should share in the plunder equally as well.

"It was on the tenth of August that the fleet entered the Straits of Gibraltar and was met with one of those sudden summer storms that scattered our formation. Our *barca* heaved to and fro like some child's toy, and we felt helpless in the swelling arms of the sea. If we were on God's mission, why was He apparently thwarting us, I remember thinking. His ways were mysterious indeed. The prince's greenish hue intensified, and his retinue, me included, was made to stand along the deck to shield him from the vulgar eyes of the other men on board. With my back turned to him, my eyes were rendered useless, but not my ears, as I heard him wretch out of mouth and squirt from his arse, again begging Your Lordship's pardon, for I remain a roughly hewn man without the genteel words to employ. With nothing left to heave or squirt, the prince ordered our captain to turn north, away from the onslaught of the cruel, thoughtless storm, but into the unfriendly nearby Castilian coast.

"I could plainly see that the captain wanted to protest, but in the face of the authority of the prince, he obeyed. Our *barca* was followed by all the vessels in our sight, some ten in all, including three flat-bottomed, clumsy *naus* containing the mounted bowmen and their horses and sundry caravels. The storm was now at our stern and quickly pushed us onto the Castilian shore at Punta Carnero, causing much consternation among all of us, as we were fearful that the Castilians might mistake our landing for an attack. The captain fervently suggested to the prince that we put back to sea, but he said we should wait until the storm passed, confessing he could not swim. The captain, trying to keep his tone neutral, countered that he could not swim either nor most of us on board, which was sure to make us better sailors.

"Luckily, like many summer storms, the skies cleared and the wind died quickly, and we resumed, setting a straight course for Ceuta. There, we found the majority of the fleet at anchor, apparently waiting for us. Our *barca* located the king's banner, and we pulled alongside.

"The prince walked across a plank, shakily gathering courage from his intestines and redirecting it to his heart. The king was at first relieved to see that no harm had come to his son, but then his face turned to stone as he barked at the boy, complaining that his maneuver had cost us the dearly won element of surprise. I imagine we all tried to close our ears to the tirade, as anyone would in the midst of a family quarrel. We were also embarrassed to witness the prince abased, and somehow we felt as though we ourselves were being punished.

"The city of Ceuta stood before our anchored fleet, and I forgot about the majesty of the armada as my jaw fell agape in wonder and fear, for it looked so unconquerable. Without realizing what I was doing, I sidled closer to Ruy Gonçalves. His face was calm, and I took some comfort from it.

"'The king knows what he's doing,' he said evenly, and those few words kept many of us from vomiting and shitting in our breeches with fear; I know this for myself.

"The city was sited along a low-lying tongue of land,

running eastward into the sea, and I judged the peninsula to be about a full league in length. We could not see the city itself, for it lay behind seemingly impenetrable walls. The foot of the peninsula ended in a round massif that Ruy said was called Mount Almina and was equal to the height of perhaps one hundred thirty men standing head to head. There was a moat dug across from sea to sea, where the peninsula joined the mainland, and behind the moat, the walls of a castle.

"With the fleet fully assembled, we lost no further time. Our *barca* rushed forward, pushed by the wind, and beached herself while the caravels began firing on the castle to keep their cannon at bay. Our caravels could fire at will since the Moors had no navy save some corsairs who had fled at the first sight of our fleet.

"Ruy Gonçalves was the first man to jump ashore, and we all closely followed him, believing there was safety to be gained from staying in his shadow. We set up a defensive perimeter, which allowed the prince to come ashore without fear of ambush. At the prince's nod, we advanced to the massif and found the king already there and directing his large retinue to scale it and set up pulleys at the peak to bring up our light cannon. The king ordered us to the walls of the castle and to begin the attack as soon as his cannon opened fire from the peak of Mount Almina down into the city.

"To a man, we rushed forth, our strength bolstered by the reinforcements coming ashore. We had brought planks and easily crossed the moat while the enemy was forced to keep their heads down from the fusillades from our caravels. As we approached the walls of the castle, a number of defenders ran forward to meet us, while, from the crenulations, their comrades were frantically waving their arms, shouting in heathen, apparently urging them to return behind the protection of the castle walls. Henry, the prince, rushed ahead, shouting for Portugal and Saint James, and Ruy followed him while we followed Ruy. The defenders were soon outnumbered and overwhelmed. I saw the prince cleave a man's arm off and, may God forgive me, I brought down my sword on a defender's head as he turned to flee. When we examined their smallish bodies, we discovered that they were mostly boys, no older than fifteen or sixteen, the age of true courage and absolute rashness. I was already breathing hard from this small encounter and feeling a bit guilty at the murder of this boy, but before I could question myself, our cannons began to shoot from the top of Mount Almina down into the city. The walls were now useless to them. The angle of our cannon allowed us to rain fire on them with impunity. At first, the rate of fire was slow, owing to the need to send up the balls and powder by just one pulley. As more ropes were added, the rate of fire increased, and the fiery balls were hurled over the wall, tearing flesh into unrecognizable remains so that you couldn't tell whether the scraps had once been a man or an ox. It was not long before the defenders came roaring out. Ruy hoisted his broadsword over his head, and we followed in the wake left by his courage.

"A man's head is not like a gourd; it bobs and weaves while below that head are arms that are attempting to cleave your own precious head in two. With little to lose but my misery, I struck forward and encountered not a boy, but a man my own size wielding an arced sword. We engaged, and after a powerful thrust missed me, I struck back with all the might I possessed, and the sharpened edge of my sword found flesh and bone. It is a sickly sound, very unlike the slaughter of a pig which is done with precision and care so as not to spill any of its precious blood. The sound of a blade slicing into a man is an unnatural one, as it severs flesh you will not eat and cracks bones. Then comes the blood, a flood of metallic-smelling, viscous liquid. I never imagined a single man could have so much blood! It clings to your hair and sticks your hand to the hilt of the sword. While your bowels are coping with the sight of so much blood, the stench of shit is unleashed, and the vapor wraps itself around you. I was unsure whether it was my shit or that of the man I had just slain. I had cut this man nearly in two, with his blood and my own sweat flowing into my eyes and stinging horribly. My knees buckled in agony from the effort, and my eyes burned, but I dare not lay down my sword. A broadsword weighs twenty-five English pounds, and it was a dog day of August. Even young and strong as I was and accustomed to hardship, I was gasping for air amid the acrid smell of death infused into the heaviness of an August climate.

"Then Henry burst forward, and we, his bodyguard, dutifully followed. There was a brief skirmish as we all tried to protect the prince, and before I knew it, I had entered the city, the first of us to do so. I was about to appeal to Ruy to set up another perimeter around the prince when he ran brashly forward past me, waving that damned little fancy sword his dying mother had recently gave him, again shouting Portugal and Saint James. In horror, we saw him disappear into the city's maze of warrens, and we desperately followed. Dumb oxen that we were, we still guessed our likely grisly fate if anything happened to the prince while he was under our care.

"We found him surrounded by determined adult defenders who looked well fed and confident. The prince waved his sword in defiance, and this act gave us heart, and the seventeen men of his retinue dove into the fray to rescue the prince. I cannot describe to Your Excellency what happened; there were blows and screams from all sides. Then a blade fell heavily across my face and gave me this scar that Your Excellency has politely not looked away from like most, who find it hideous. My chest and face were covered in blood, and I could only see from what was my remaining eye. I expected to be beheaded at any moment as I knelt, senseless to my surroundings and praying that whoever was to kill me was skilled enough to do it mercifully, with one mighty stroke. Instead of the sharp edge of a scimitar, the strong hand of a friend fell upon my nape and pulled me to my feet. It was Ruy, also bloodied and August rancid. Blinking through the blood, I noticed that our seventeen was reduced to just the two of us, but the prince was safe.

"Later, I learned that the whole battle had lasted no more than thirteen hours. To me, it had felt like an eternity. I was too weak from my wound to join in the looting, but Ruy assured me that he would look out for me and that I would have my share. I was too dazed to tell Your Excellency what happened, as I fell in and out of consciousness, all the time getting closer to home aboard ship.

"Well, as Your Excellency must know, we found little or nothing in the way of loot in the city: no gold, no silver, just a few jars of spices. I turned out to be one of the lucky ones; because I was the first to enter the city and had saved the prince's life. I was awarded fifty *real broncos*, which allowed me to purchase this tavern that gives me and my family a living. I am proud of most of what I did that day. It was a great victory."

Vasco then looked off with his one eye in sweet revelry, as nostalgia is a suave liar. I asked him whether he saw the prince rally his fleeing army, and he bristled, saying that the army never fled but single-mindedly advanced. This perturbed me since my prince had plainly stated that he had rallied five hundred fleeing men, but then again, even Vasco admitted that he could not be sure of what happened after he was wounded. He described the chaos of battle and that no one man, least of all an ant within an army of ants, was likely to be aware of the whole panorama.

"Your Excellency, as I have said, I was a mere ant, but if you want a man's point of view, you must go see Dom Pedro de Meneses who was appointed governor of Ceuta after the battle. He was an officer and saw everything."

I asked about Ruy Gonçalves, where he lived and might I go speak to him as well, and Vasco's scar grew crimson.

"The truly noble Ruy died not long after the taking of Ceuta. He never recovered from his wounds. He died in poverty but swathed in glory, which I am sure will gain him entry to paradise. But like me, he was also an ant. Go see Dom Pedro de Meneses who was a man among us ants."

I was unsure whether I wanted to speak to the former governor, as I might hear things better left unheard. As I left, I pressed a remaining copper coin into the palm of the young Felipe and stepped out into the street and, for the first time in my life, actually smelled the fresh air I had so long taken for granted. It was not until I got to the gates of the monastery that I realized that Nuno, the hostler, and his cousin had remained at the tavern. They did indeed get the better part of me, flat-headed brutality notwithstanding.

س

I awoke last night again covered in thick, beaded sweat, gasping for air. Which of my frequent nightmares did I endure? Was it the one with that ruby-lipped fiend who teasingly smiles at me, his mouth slightly open in lascivious invitations? No, not that one tonight, thankfully, as I always must flagellate myself for soiling the bed with my seed.

In the confusion of the pitch darkness, my mind raced to another tormentor. The slit-eyed devil with the skin of a reptile who sometimes beckons to me to lie with him. He smiles at me brutally as glutinous saliva oozes from the corner of his hideous mouth. At my apparent disgust of the invitation, the monster begins laughing while holding his engorged member with both hands while performing the unspeakable before my cowering eyes. As I atone somewhat because I am repelled, I flagellate myself less for that dream.

But this night, my dream was neither. I was back on the beach at Ceuta. I try to move forward to join in the battle, but I sink knee-deep into the sand. I struggle to extricate myself only to hear the laughter of the men. Our men are then joined by the Moors who place their arms on each other's shoulders and join in the laughter. Their combined mirth reaches a crescendo, and I faint, but only to awake naked, surrounded by Duarte and my father and mother who are intently studying my body.

"Is this really my son?" my father asks.

"Of course not," answers my mother. "I copulated with the lusty ram on a moon-filled night. I can still feel him thrust this monstrosity into my womb and smell his hot breath upon release of his seed."

"Then he is not my brother?" asks Duarte.

"No, but he will be your master, a lord of the netherworld. He will have savage powers and appetites. He has ruined my womb; from now on, I can only give birth to females and eunuchs. Beast that he is, he will devour the earth, his hunger insatiate."

"Tell no one this," says my father. "I will pretend that he is of my loins."

For this dream, I do not flagellate myself. Experiencing it is punishment enough.

Chapter Five
Intervening Circumstances and an Interview with a
Fidalgo

The supply ship is nearly three weeks overdue. The normally querulous men have turned into rabid dogs. At mess, envious eyes are cast upon a neighbor's trencher. Should a slice of moldy cheese or green-encrusted bread be deemed too large, suspicions of favoritism are unleashed and brawls break out. The governor-general wisely waits, hoping that a wound settles the matter, but lately, as the men grow more desperate and become hungrier on the reduced rations, they are not satisfied with drawing first blood but want to kill. The governor-general is forced to intervene, and with his trusted three-man squad, shouting oaths and swearing threats, he tries to separate the combatants before they kill each other and then go on to kill us. So far, he has been successful. But with each successive melee, another ear is loped off and another bone broken, and his hold on order grows more tenuous. He has warned me on more than one occasion to remain in my quarters and not go gadding around the compound, a warning I have taken seriously and to heart.

It is the most prone to violence who become the natural leaders. Tomás the would-be slayer of the dazzling Moor, comes to the fore as a cork in water.

"They're leaving us to die in this shit hole. Who are we to the nobles in Lisbon but some soulless scum to use and kill as it serves their purposes? We are but fleas on the arses of their dogs. Do they even know that Alcácer Ceguer exists? We'll be dead of hunger in a fortnight, and they won't even stir in their sleep. I say we go to Ceuta, taking what we need as we go along. I'd rather die mercifully from the sharp scimitar than suffer the slow death from hunger."

Though I am appalled, there is much logic and truth in what he has said. The sheep who pretend to be men also see the argument and grumble in agreement. Tomás bunches his hands into willful fists and glares at the arms cache in silent command. The governor-general must intervene, and true to his sense of urgency, he does.

"Are you men crazy enough to listen to him? You would all be dead before you could travel three leagues from these walls. And what if you made it to Ceuta? How would traitors and deserters be received by my friend the governor-general there, Dom Pedro de Meneses? Do you think he will slaughter five lambs and open a keg of new wine in your honor? I know him very well. He is an older soldier than me. He will hang all of you from the city's gates and let the vultures pick at what is left. That is, after he scourges all of you.

"I tell you that Lisbon has not forgotten us. We remain an important outpost for kingdom and God; this I swear to you all, but God help anyone who disobeys me."

The men make a trembling retreat. They are but feathers subject to the prevailing breeze, with no true will of their own but to survive. It is that instinct that now takes hold of them as empty stomachs growl, giving them rudders and a resolve that they do not normally possess. But the governor-general knows how to decapitate.

"You, Tomás, will be the first to die if my command is disobeyed."

With that, his three-man squad levels their culverins within an unmissable distance. Tomás is neutralized for the very short time being. A mere battle of countenances ensues, with the governor-general silently daring Tomás to utter another word as the culverins remain leveled, though some start to wobble from the weight of the weapon. The conclusion of the encounter is now foregone, as Tomás rejoins the multitude of his brethren so as to make a less conspicuous target. The men disband begrudgingly, the threat of mutiny still manifest in their defiant lingering.

That evening, as is my wont, I dined with the governor-general in his stark quarters. Perhaps "dine" is not the proper term; I go gnaw on some thick-crusted bread that is my contribution to the dinner table while the governor-general attacks some dried beef with the consistency of leather from a cow who died of old age, with his eight remaining teeth. In the comfortable silence of old men, we sit in the meager light of a single candle as I choke on the edge of a sharp piece of bread that my weakened saliva cannot soften. The governor-general produces a goblet of wine for me in collegial compassion.

"My sir, I cannot. Water will do."

"Water might do but not while there is still wine."

"It must be your last."

"What if it is? Most likely, by tomorrow, we will all be dead, or wishing that we were. Let us gnaw and sip and not worry."

I do not want to ask the question for fear the governor-general will tell me the truth, but I cannot resist.

"Did you believe what you said about us being an

important outpost?'"

"Not a word. In fact, I think that rascal Tomás exaggerated our importance by comparing Alcácer Ceguer to a flea on a nobleman's dog. Drink up, my friend. Tomorrow we die."

After a moment of reflection, I rejoin, "I have always been afraid of death, for I fear it is an eternal abyss with nothing beyond it."

"That cannot be true. There is a God and a heaven. I know that I have not always merited God's grace, but I have spent some years in atonement of my sins, such as they were, as I am not sure whether it is sinful to do what one must to eat. Dom Zurara, you must hold onto your faith and not be like that rabble out there who would crucify Christ himself again for a leg of mutton if that would ensure their miserable survival for another miserable day."

I had learned not to argue the point with the religious man; it is not an argument you can win nor is it a pleasant one since faith and logic cannot prevail over one another. Furthermore, I am much too tired and assuredly too hungry to counter and do not want to offend my host. Besides, if I had deduced myself into perdition, why would I want to drag anyone else with me, especially someone I respected?

There is nothing left to say for the evening, so the governor-general brings out the game board and the rest of the wine. We had both become enamored with a game the Moors called *shesh-besh* or six-seven, as that is the most fortuitous first roll of the dice. Calmed by the game's mixture of strategy and luck, as well as the caress of the wine, the evening continues in sweet, dull peace until the candle begins to sputter.

س

My current distress has distracted me from recounting my tale to you, dear reader. I do not apologize; it is merely a statement of fact. Not to worry. My insatiable curiosity still remains; however, it is currently trumped by more primordial needs, let us say more insatiable appetites.

I spend the next three days in an ever-amassing panic. To me, the governor-general represents order and law. Should anything happen to his person or authority, I am afraid the worst that humankind could unleash will occur. The last of the most treasured dogs had disappeared, much to the dismay of their masters. I could even swear that, all of a sudden, the insects themselves have been consumed, for there are none to be seen. I even consider venturing away from the walls, as it would be more humane to be killed by our enemies than be eaten by my brethren. I am sure the governor-general will not be able to preserve order for much longer. I see it in his eyes, pupils dilated in acceptance of death, his face an ashen pallor in expectation of paradise. The men again ominously begin to congregate in the parade ground before the gate; circling, Tomás awaits his war cry.

In history, I believe there are hundreds of similar circumstances with the expected occurring. Mutiny runs rampant, superiors are killed, and anarchy prevails with the mutineers themselves ultimately dying from infighting and starvation. However, as far fetched as it may seem, just when the situation seems at its most dire, the look-out atop the walls yells.

"A sail, a sail."

An eternal moment ensues as we all look deeply into each other's faces, as in prayer to our mortal brethren. The younger men scamper up to the walls and stare out into the sea in silent agony. With all the composure of his age and position, the governor-general bids one of his cohorts fetch him his glass and then leisurely climbs the flimsy ladder to the balustrade, his moral superiority on plain display.

"The sail has a red cross," he says evenly, not shouting. It is the men, including myself, that do all the shouting.

ﺱ

It takes another two days for the caravel to approach and anchor. The captain is one Flávio de Souza who is surprised to learn that a notable such as myself would choose to live in such an extremity of the empire, or so he refers to our meager grapple hold on parts of the world. He claims to have read and enjoyed my chronicles of our great Henry the Navigator, or so his English cousins had dubbed him. At an earlier age, I would have believed him, gratified by his praise, but jaundiced as I am, I take it as no more than supercilious flattery. He is full of news.

"Good King Dom João II now sits on the throne. You will be happy to hear, Dom Zurara, that he is following faithfully in Prince Henry's footsteps, or shall I say wake, and has continued the exploration of the Guinea coast. This last year, the great explorer, Bartalameu Dias, returned with the news that he had rounded the cape of the Guinea continent. India and its riches must be close, for the king named it the Cape of Good Hope and has commissioned Dias to return, round it, and reach India."

The amiable Flávio surely goes on to mention other notable occurrences, but the Dias accomplishment is the only one I remember from the evening, for I, indeed everyone in the garrison, am busy compensating for the weeks of scarcity. After we eat, en masse, we retire to our cots for collective sleep in order to give our bodies the needed concentration to digest the victuals.

Over the next few weeks, the contents of the caravel are off-loaded while the ship's carpenter makes repairs. Even a relatively short and uneventful voyage takes its toll on our fragile wooden vessels. I could not imagine one enduring the months at sea it would take to round the so-called Cape of Good Hope. Before setting out, Flávio informs the governor-general that he has brought along three "volunteers" to replace men who, by their comportment, have merited release from garrison duty. The governor-general wisely chooses the trouble-rouser Tomás to be among the returnees. We all climb up the balustrade and watch the sail slowly disappear until there is nothing left but a longing for the sight of it. The umbilical cord to our homeland is cut, and every man feels abandoned and homesick, especially the three new "volunteers" who whimper all night until one of the hard veterans curses and kicks them into silence.

س

Now, dear reader, I know I have been remiss in the relation of my tale to you, or should I say the mental rewriting of my chronicles. You must understand that the exigencies of puny flesh override any other pursuit, no matter how noble.

In the history that is my life, I never really thought much about higher pursuits, I must admit. Survival is so precarious that altruism is a luxury vouchsafed for the rich and powerful. We smaller men must make do pursuing mundane exigencies. Yes, I know what you are thinking, dear reader: I was indeed among the privileged, but you see my sense of security was evanescent. With a quick word and a nod, Henry could have sent me back to obscurity and day-to-day existence. Even after death, Henry remains the reason why I am in this Godless place.

All that being said, my curiosity about Henry became a motivating force. I wanted to speak to this ex-governor-general of Ceuta, as the maimed soldier, Vasco Martins, had suggested. Suddenly, what had not been merely of importance before, namely, the truth, became an obsession. I sent a courier to our northern city of Viana, asking the old retired soldier, Pedro de Meneses, for an audience. My haste for the interview was fed by my aforementioned obsession and the fear that the old soldier, now Count of Viana, was a very old man. Truth is mortal like the men who carry it within their bosoms. The courier returned within a week with a message that Dom Pedro would see me. I petitioned the Order of Christ for funds and was granted a few silver coins from the stingy hands of the prior. Bidding farewell to my helpful acolyte as well as the strong but useless hostler, I set off.

Dom Pedro's grand house, more like a castle, was the exact opposite of Dom Afonso de Alenquer's. Where the latter's house was humble on the outside and lavish within, Dom Pedro's abode dominated the height overlooking the city, and its facade was composed of crenulated walls, lending it a military aspect. The interior was stark, large, cavernous rooms with no artwork on the massive walls and almost no furniture. In this mausoleum, there was no gentle and accommodating Darfum, but austere men in livery who bore themselves erect and square shouldered. In his retired life, the count chose to remain under the rigor of military sternness.

Dom Pedro received me in a great room with a large fireplace, big enough to roast a horse. It was blazing though the weather was not cold, but I understand the old prefer to be warm to the marrow of their bones. His face bore several scars and was grizzled as a bear's. His eyebrows were huge, gray crescents with wiry hairs that fell down into his orbs, much like that of a sheepdog's. His clothes were disorderly while he exuded a smell, much like that of a rain-sodden, rotting log. I introduced myself as he waved a hand at me dismissively, in the manner of someone well acquainted with my history. He nodded thoughtfully and remained deep in reflection, or perhaps, I feared, dozing, but then he began to speak.

"Dom Afonso is a good, God-fearing man, and anything he told you was the truth. As to that tavern keeper, I seem to recall him; he was a brave soldier and saved the prince's life. Brave soldiers seldom lie. Well, I have read your history of the conquest of Ceuta, and it's rubbish. I should think you must already know this, or you wouldn't be here."

Dom Pedro then heaved his prodigious body onto a great wooden chair with a unicorn fabric pattern. Despite the heft of the chair, the wood groaned under his gravitational assault. Reaching for a peach, he broke it in half with his claw-like hands and began to chew mechanically. Taken aback by this lack of civility, I took it upon myself to sit in the plain wooden chair opposite him, feeling discomfort from the fire.

"True enough, the pup was courageous in battle, but he was also rash, causing the death and mutilation of his entourage, that Vasco barkeep included. It was the king's beautiful plan that won the day; once we took Mount Almina, the city was helpless against our cannon. But I am sure that Vasco already filled you in on the details of the battle. You said in your note that you wanted my point of view.

"There were many personalities there, some at cross purposes. You already know what the king had in mind, perhaps foolish in the long term but accurate in serving the purpose of the moment. The king's second oldest son, Pedro, was just a naïve boy; he merely wanted to earn his spurs, a naked child without any guile. His younger brother, Henry, on the other hand, inherited enough guile for ten Castilian lifetimes. At twenty or so, he was already scheming to become the viceroy of Morocco; Ceuta was merely a stepping stone, not a small goal for such a young pup.

"There was also the count of Barcelos, the king's bastard son and half brother of Pedro and Henry. Much older and much craftier, he already had a lifetime to amass a man's hate. He was dismissive of his brothers' military prowess, but he reserved a special contempt toward the innocent Pedro. I can't tell you why, as sometimes animosity springs from unjust causes. It is just the same when you put a dirty rag and a rotten apple in a jar and surely the materials will transform themselves into a rat, unexplainable dark alchemy. Then there was the fact that Pedro was second in line to the throne. Perhaps Barcelos thought he could control the simple heir, Duarte, but not the virtuous Pedro. Henry, in my opinion, was the sliest of the king's five sons but had no intent on this particular throne; his aim was to create a parallel kingdom, and so he was no threat to Barcelos.

After the city fell, we found a number of Genoese merchants and even a small Franciscan monastery. The Genoese had tried to take the city back in 1395 and had failed. In return for promising never to try again, the Moors had granted them trading rights. So your history is not true in declaring Ceuta a *terra clausum* to Christianity. When we finished ransacking the city and found no wealth to speak of, save some measly urns of spices, Henry's ire rose to a froth, and he put a dagger to all the Genoese's throats and forced them to sign over their bank accounts to the Order of Christ, of which he was governor. I know not whether the Order, or more precisely Henry, ever collected, as I am certain that the Italians rushed home to close their accounts.

"The captured governor of Ceuta was called Salah ben Salah; a thirtyish man with a shaved head and a nose like that of a hawk's. He was spurting fury at himself for having rescinded the order for reinforcements from Fez. When our fleet first appeared, he had sent a courier to Fez, but when the storm dispersed the armada, he had supposed, wrongly, that we had left and recalled the courier. His was the agony of a leader who had made a bad decision. Nonetheless, Henry strode up to him and thrust a dagger to his throat, demanding to know where the treasure was. 'What treasure?' Salah screamed. 'You ignorant Portuguese infidel, there is no treasure here.' I then saw Henry's eyes grow cold as a shark's, and it was only the interception of his brother Pedro that saved Salah from being skewered like a spring lamb. 'Lords do not kill other lords,' I heard Pedro admonish.

"Henry was livid at being remonstrated by his older brother

in front of the men. He marched up to one of the Moorish captives and demanded to know where the treasure was. Even before the cowering soul could answer, Henry plunged his dagger into his throat, and the poor soul fell, gagging and drowning in his own blood. He gasped for a minute before God mercifully released him; infidel that he was, he did deserve to die so. There was no treasure in Ceuta.

"Before we could recover from this scene, Henry pulled another captive away while Pedro screamed at him for mercy. Upon pulling his *kaffiyeh* off, a young boy's face emerged. His visage was so beautiful that he could have passed for a girl, those piercing black eyes with a soft fuzz that covered his cherub olive cheeks. Henry stared at this apparition for what seemed to me like an eternity, and then he abruptly released him as we all gave a collective silent sigh of relief. I remember thinking that perhaps there was some honor and humanity in this wolf pup.

"The arrival of the king, who had been delayed at the gate with a slight leg wound, put a stop to these ghoulish theatrics. He called for a meeting of his advisors, one of which I was proud to be.

"It was decided that we leave a twenty-five-hundred-man garrison to hold the city; for what purpose, I still do not know. Upon hearing this, none of the *fidalgos* wanted to stay; it took all the king's persuasiveness to extract volunteers. Your history says they were all avid to remain, a pure falsehood. Ceuta was a pit in the estimate of these spoiled children, and they wanted nothing to do with it, especially since they were not enriched by the conquest.

"The king then appointed his old lieutenant, Martim Afonso de Melo, as governor of Ceuta. He was an old colleague of mine and had commanded the important left flank at Aljabarrota, where we sent the Castilians limping back to their home and boasted to everyone who wanted to hear that the simplest way to Castile from Portugal was to follow their bones. Dom Martim visibly blanched at the announcement and begged the king to reconsider. He rightly claimed to have served the throne honorably for over twenty-five years and had already lost his left arm and two sons at Aljabarrota. He now wished for nothing more than to return home and watch his grapes and grandchildren fatten under the warm, paternal, Lusitanian sun.

"The king looked around our small circle, and his questioning but demanding eyes settled on me. I too was a veteran of Aljabarrota, though younger than Dom Martim, and had lost no sons nor limbs from the battle. I did not feel I possessed Dom Martim's moral height to refuse, and so I accepted with false thanks.

"Before taking leave, Henry lectured me in front of the assembled garrison on the best methods of repulsing the counterattack that he was sure would come. You cannot imagine my mortification at having to listen to this young pup tell me about my business. It was only my sense of duty to the throne, his father, that kept my tongue in my mouth and my sword sheathed. Henry then magnanimously presented me with the keys to the city and departed along with the fleet. I was allowed to keep ten of the best armed caravels for defense.

"All these events took place in August of 1415; in the following year in February, the king decreed that Henry would bear the sole responsibility for Ceuta, failing to define, in true royal fashion, where our respective authorities stopped. This ambiguity was resolved with my eating some breast of crow, arriving at a *modus Vivendi*, whereby I cooperated with Henry's grand design of ultimately ruling Morocco. You see, my young pup's lackey scribe, Ceuta proved to be a disaster. The Moorish caravans stopped coming, and we were cut off from the hinterland. We were therefore totally dependent on our homeland for necessary supplies. Given this situation, Henry established the *Casa de Ceuta*, a royal company that requisitioned grain at below market rates. This practice naturally infuriated the farmers, but it also rewarded the merchants who had remained loyal to Dom João I during the Castilian investiture.

"I myself devised ways of raising revenue through the capture of Moorish princes and ransoming them back to their rich families. They often came to our walls like moths drawn to a flame. It was dangerous work capturing them, for their entourages were formidable, but it had handsome returns. I also employed the caravels as corsairs, raiding Moorish shipping as well as Christian vessels suspected of trading with the infidels. I shared a full 60 percent of the spoils with my reticent men, bribing them to remain, and another 20 percent went to the Order of Christ, namely, Henry. The remaining 20 percent enriched me, and I felt no qualms. Unlike Henry who received his share with no risk, I was putting my life in hazard for the spoils. With this arrangement, everyone was kept more or less content, to which I attribute my longevity as governor of Ceuta.

"For the next ten years of my tenure, we operated in like fashion. The Genoese, Catalan, and Sicilian vessels we attacked could not appeal to the Holy See, for they would have to admit trading with the infidel. And of course, my own *alfaqueque*, a Franciscan I had captured when we took the city, arranged some clandestine trade with the Moors. We traded grain, horses, and textiles for exotics from the interior of Africa, such as oryx skins, ostrich eggs, civet musk, and gum arabic.

"Men are quarrelsome—I know I am—and so the status quo could not remain. The city had been taken too easily, and Moorish pride was hurt. In the summer of 1419, the allied armies and navies of Morocco and Moorish Grenada attacked, and I immediately sent word on our fleetest caravel to Henry, requesting reinforcements. We had taken the precaution of mounting cannon and culverins on the summit of Mount Almina; we would not commit the same mistake as the Moors.

"The sea battle was brief and decisive. Their clumsy dhows were no match for our maneuverable caravels. Their ships had flat bottoms and rode deep in the sea. Turning these monsters was a tortuous affair, requiring much too much time. Our smaller caravels, on the other hand, were yaw, with long rudders and mobile lateen sails that allowed us to change directions on a wine cask. Moreover, our cannons were situated lower on the decks, making it easy for us to blow holes in their sides below the water line.

"It is strange that the Arab is a great astronomer and thereby gave us the celestial map that guided us upon the open sea. Yet despite this contribution, the Arab remains a poor sailor, hugging the coast in rightful reverence of the sea's omnipotence.

"After three of their vessels were sunk with no reciprocal losses on our part, the Moorish fleet fled. The Moors did not fare any better on land, as our shot fell upon them from Mount Almina. After less than a week of easy slaughter, the Moors retreated, shouting imprecations with many a fist shaken at our implacable walls.

"In the proceeding days, as we buried and blessed our dead, Henry arrived in a dither along with three thousand men. He was plainly relieved to see his city still in our hands. I must credit him with commending me just as publicly as he had previously lectured.

"During my tenure, I watched Henry protect this useless enclave at all costs, including the life of his younger brother, Fernando. I have never understood his attachment to Ceuta, as it only brought us grief with little gain, at least in the kingdom of man. The city gave us nothing but exacted so much from our poor realm. Since then, I have followed Henry's endeavors with growing admiration as he pushed our captains down the coast of Guinea. Perhaps it would be wise for you to speak to these returned men from our ships of exploration before you finalize your history on the discovery of Guinea so as to avoid making the mistakes you made on the conquest of Ceuta. Ah me, we all struggle and scheme, but in the end, it all comes to naught. The powerful schemer dies much like the mindless serf. But I do grow weary. Would you like a peach?"

This evening, I bade my confessor, Frey Dominicus, bring me some wine, as the demons needed to be drowned. Frey Dominicus is obedient, though I can feel his silent rebukes and agonize in his disapproval when I allow him to flagellate me for my sins. I can hide these sins from men but not from God. My transgressions must be countered with great deeds and sacrifice. For the sin of overindulgence on wine, I will not partake of meat for a month. I impose my own penance, for if I left it to that heartless skeleton of a man, Frey Dominicus would flagellate. The demons that visit me in my dreams need further expiation, for I know that I welcome them. For this inherent evil, there must be a great penance. I will give a continent to God in atonement. Surely, God understands that I must employ human means to achieve this; even charity must have an earthly provenance. A god that is as God is will condone and recognize that which I do is in His name. How else can a continent be conquered without availing myself of the necessary riches to pay the wages of the mercenary? Not all men are motivated by their love of God.

The wine is nearly gone, and I dare not tell Dominicus to bring me more, as he will surely take gusto in the next time I allow him to flagellate me. I have removed the hair shirt, as it sticks to my still-fresh welts, may Dominicus be damned to the deep recesses of hell. The cot entices me, yet I am afraid of the voluptuous demons that visit me in disturbed sleep. Weakling that I am, I want to welcome them. Has God sent them as a test? He only tests those He expects great things of. If so, I am among the anointed, like David in the Bible. In my soul of souls, I know that I was indeed born apart from other men, strange and different. If this is not so, why am I so driven to accomplish? Why am I so tormented? God's grace is not a light burden, but I will be vindicated. I will have more wine this evening, and I promise not to eat meat for two weeks in penance, Dominicus's glares be damned!

CHAPTER SIX
THE ATLANTIC ISLANDS

A man's life is never linear. It may sometimes appear so when you read the work of bad biographers who limn their subjects as going from victory to victory, such as my own chronicles of my prince. In my work, Henry had but a few purposes in life: to serve God and explore His world for His greater glory. Men are invariably more complicated. The meanest man can one day perform the most unselfish act, and a normally brave man may cower in fear. On any given day, we are as mutable as the stars. The real Henry was often distracted by minor details, and like any other mortal, he knew failure. We all have heard of Alexander the Great who was said to have wept before he was thirty because there were no more worlds to conquer. But even Alexander must have tasted some secret defeats, although perhaps not in battle. Alexander's legend and his distance from us in history may have beclouded his human frailties, much like the sun makes the moon seem to disappear. Henry is closer to me in history, and I know some of his setbacks.

Before describing to you these setbacks, there is one achievement I did admire: his concept of a school of navigation. He aptly chose Sagres as the site for his school, situated as it was on a promontory overlooking the angry Atlantic whose waves crashed menacingly against the stone massif in constant, menacing attack. At Sagres, there could be no possible delusion of man's mastery over the sea; the incessant attack of the waves was a constant reminder of man's powerlessness in the face of the vastness of the sea. Sagres was both a humble monument to the Atlantic as well as a challenge to the ocean's omnipotence.

Dear reader, I know not how, but word spread throughout the world of Sagres's existence and its purpose. In a world of darkness, the faintest light is discernable from afar. Astronomers, cartographers, and physicists toiling away in dingy laboratories in the universities heard the silent call, and they came. They came from the Spains, Genoa, Venice, Grenada, and England. They were Christians, Jews, and even Moors, all working in harmony, arguing their conceptions of our world amicably, though sometimes with heat. To want to know necessitates pragmatism, and pragmatism engenders tolerance. I was privileged to be among the first nonscientists to be invited to stay, as Henry thought he may want to record his founding of the first school of navigation for posterity. I was instructed not to publicize his endeavors in any way without his permission, least it attract the suspicion of necromancy from the Vatican.

The physical school was actually a refurbished old fort, its stones bleached almost white from the sun and salt from the pounding waves. There was a round courtyard in the center, where painted white stones of almost the same size were arranged in the shape of an astrolabe, a tacit tribute to the Arab. A large rotunda overlooked all with glassless windows facing the ever-boiling sea so that the spray was free to permeate every nook and apse. Henry reasoned that all our materials, including the parchments we used for the maps, must be exposed to the same elements that the mariners will encounter. The older, more vulnerable maps and rudders were carefully stored in a cedar chest, and Henry kept the only key constantly on his person.

Because Henry bore the expense, the accommodations were far from regal. The prince would bear the expense of outfitting a dozen caravels but would quibble at the spending of a few *dobras* on such luxuries as candles or firewood. The sleeping cells were small and damp. The food was plain but nourishing. Sagres was not a place one would go to enjoy the better advantages the world had to offer.

Owing to the early popularity of Sagres, I had to share a cell with another man. Luckily for me, he turned out to be a fellow countryman. As we were both roughly of the same youthful age, we made friends easily, as we are pliable in those tender years. His name was Tristão Vaz, and his pleasant visage and generous smile endeared him to me from the beginning of our acquaintance. His excitement was easily contagious, and soon he had me believing that we were indeed fortunate to be at the hub of the world. Some days after we met, we spent a long night sharing bread and wine as well as each other's history. I will, of course, dispense with mine, as you, dear reader, are already familiar with it. To this day, I still remember his words. It is strange how I can recall his narration in vivid detail over so many decades when, in all honesty, I could not tell you, dear reader, what I had for breakfast yesterday nor even if I had breakfast at all. He spoke without assumption, and his tale still resonates in my mind's ear.

"My mother could read and write, and she named me Tristão after some star-crossed lover in a legend. I took her name, Vaz, as I did not rightly know who my father was, and my mother refused to tell me in fear I may do something foolish with the information. She did say, under God's oath, that my father was dead, but since I was born during the Castilian war, I can only hope that at least he was Portuguese, though my mother never confirmed it one way or another.

Death, mayhem, and birth are all related occurrences in the world as God has devised it.

"My mother, being educated herself, knew the value of literacy, so she made every sacrifice to place me in a Jesuit college. I was fortunate to encounter one particular teacher, Frey Luís, whose mind was universal and not limited by the strict pedagogy of our Catholic religion. I trust you will be discreet with what I am saying to you. As a much more learned man than my humble self, I imagine you too believe that the catechism we learn by rote does not possess all the answers to our roaming questions. Frey Luís's particular fascination was geography and navigation, and his passion was so ardent that it proved contagious.

"After the regular lections, we pored over the old maps that Frey Luís had been able to amass in the library at Coimbra. There was the Catalan, Jaome Crespes's, Insula Palola chart that depicted various islands off the coast of Guinea, believed to be luxuriant with ample water and abundant timber. Frey Luís subscribed to the common belief that there was a Christian kingdom beyond the land of the Negroes ruled by an isolated Catholic prince called Prester John. If we could only make contact with him, Islam would find itself surrounded and constricted by Christian armies.

"The library at the University of Coimbra was a treasure trove of old charts, and we studied various theories of both theoretical and empirical geography of the world, such as the 1401 chart by the Frenchman, Gadifer de la Salle, who showed the Guinea coast continuing beyond Cape Bojador in a normal fashion with no perils. The Florentine map of Laurentian Portolano amalgamated the ideas of his predecessors and showed various islands off the coast of Guinea and extrapolated that the coast must continue past Cape Bojador, contrary to the superstitious chart by the Venetian cartographer, Giovanni Pizzigani, whose map depicted the continent of Africa ending at Cape Bojador and that, beyond it, the sea turned poison green and was a boil and fraught with giant sea serpents. Frey Luís dismissed the Venetian's concept as ridiculous, as he believed these visions of poison seas and monsters did not fit into God's logical design of the world.

"Frey Luís also introduced me to the use of the compass as well as the concepts of latitude and longitude. He taught me the use of the astrolabe in determining latitude and dead reckoning in the attempt to assess the more difficult if not impossible longitude. He freely borrowed from all cultures, even commenting that the lateen sails we used on our caravels and the astrolabe were Arab inventions, so too our knowledge of the stars. When I expressed surprise at his blatant admiration of our hated enemy, he responded by saying that, when the whole of Iberia was under Moorish rule, they were generally tolerant of our religion and brought irrigation and oranges to our hopelessly arid land. He then mused a while and lamented that the Moor had suddenly stopped contributing to the universal weal and seemed bent on retrogressing. He then shrugged in resignation of God's will.

"Frey Luís suggested that I send my credentials to Prince Henry who was congregating men with interest in exploration of the yet-unknown world at Sagres, at the southern tip of our kingdom. My mentor said the prince was in need of intrepid and curious men such as me. He recommended the prince to me as a venerated man who neither touched alcohol nor women in order to concentrate his energies in serving God through the exploration of our globe and conversion of the heathen to our true faith while at the same time fighting the Arabs by denying them these new lands and their innocent natives.

"The prince is lucky to have access to a whole kingdom of intrepid men, as there is no better spur for audacity than poverty. Our kingdom is full of landless men who are never sure of their next meal. Desperation is an incessant goad that makes brave men out of the timid since death holds no particular threat to a man who has only his hunger to lose.

"To my surprise, I received an immediate answer from the prince within a month, requesting my presence at Sagres where I could join his companions. I borrowed some adulterated silver coins from Frey Luís, copied his maps, and set off; enthusiasm saturating me like young September wine.

"When I arrived here at Sagres, it was like an epiphany, and I understood why the prince had sited his school of navigation here. It was truly an altar to the sea, with solid granite cliffs descending vertically into the angry waves; as if the sea was assaulting the land. Sagres indeed looks like the place where the land ends and the sea begins. The roiling waters look merciless, as if daring us to take up the challenge and sail our flimsy vessels upon an ocean, a force confident of its ultimate victory over us puny men."

It is strange how I can remember his narrative over so many decades when I tend to forget what occurred only yesterday. His tone was totally unassuming and still resonates in my mind's ear.

س

Tristão's passion was sufficiently enervating, but he was able to sleep peaceably through the night, and in the morning, he was gone. Our destinies took us to different places, and I did not run into Tristão for months, though I did hear that he remained at Sagres while I attended to small tasks hither and thither at the bequest of that dreaded Frey Dominicus, as Henry no longer gave his orders directly to me. There was a singularly frightening aspect to this priest, and I wondered why my prince had chosen this austere man as his confessor. To my mind, Frey Dominicus was the opposite of the *infante*, small-minded and limited by blinding dogma. But perhaps that was the reason for his selection, that is, to keep Henry's wandering mind from straying too far from strict catechism. I was seeing much less of my prince, as he remained cloistered at his chapel to the sea that was Sagres, but in the fall of the following year, my travels took me there. I was hoping to share the same cell with Tristão, as I was very curious how he had fared at Sagres in the intervening months. I must also admit to enjoying his amiable company and that irrepressible smile that erupted on his pleasant countenance. To my dismay, I was quartered with a foreign-looking, swarthy man who smelled of piss and could barely speak our language. His demeanor was saturnine as he grunted affirmatives that were barely discernable from his negatives. After a few such one-sided conversations, I assiduously avoided being in the cell, save for going directly to my cot and embracing Morpheus as soon as I could to escape the unpleasant company.

The next day, my disappointment was somewhat abated when I caught sight of Tristão in the courtyard, deep in conversation with a gaggle of men twice his age. I waved and engaged him. In the short, intervening months, he seemed to have changed. He appeared more self-assured, and I somehow liked him less for it. Perhaps it was jealousy on my part that he had progressed while I had remained the same, a tree trunk to his wandering vine. One thing I was sure of from his barely contained exuberance was that he had much more to communicate than I had.

"I am quartered off the rotunda now in a damp cell where the cold mist of the Atlantic invades every nook, and I swear to you, Zurara, that I wake with half the Atlantic swirling in my lungs. Some three weeks ago, I was summoned and ushered into the august presence of the prince. I was initially surprised not to be able to discern him out of the congregation. He was indistinguishable from the men who surrounded him. He wore a plain black robe and was hatless with short dark hair and a frown seemingly pasted permanently on his countenance, which I attributed to the hair shirt that prominently protruded from the neckline of his robe. Frey Luís did not exaggerate as to the holiness of this man. Despite this overt act of humility, I remained skeptical of his ultimate motives, for as Frey Luís had taught me, without skepticism, we are powerless to superstition that fills in the vacuum to the inexplicable.

"When the prince began to talk, he projected a majesty that belied his humble attire. His rank was augmented by the fact that he was a full head taller than anyone present, which most people would attribute to nobility, but being the skeptic that I am, I credited this to a better diet than most of us are afforded in our early years.

"When I arrived at the circular chamber with open views of the cold, boiling sea, the prince was deep in conference. They seemed mostly a motley collection of foreigners; two of them were obvious Jews, with their telltale skull caps, and the others appeared to be various Italians. It was one of the Jews, a cartographer called Alcides, who beckoned me forward, saying that he knew of and admired my mentor, Frey Luís. My surprises accumulated at this Jew's admiration of a Christian priest, but in retrospect, I believe that he did not esteem the cleric as much as the scholar.

"I presented my credentials to the solemn prince, and he simply nodded and returned to poring over the charts that he and the group were studying. Not knowing what to do, I looked over their shoulders and observed.

"The prince was an avid participant in the debate but allowed for challenge and interchange of contrary opinions. He listened to these contrary views with an equanimity that surprised me, for most men of noble birth are not tolerant of any opinion but their own.

"Then Alcides invited me to espouse my opinions, and I brought out the copied charts I had brought with me and began to postulate on the coast of Guinea as well as the outlying islands I was sure existed. My words fell on kindred ears and served as a catalyst for high-pitched but amicable debate. It was in the midst of this lively discussion that it occurred to me that this collection of men had stopped being Christians, Jews, or Arabs, Portuguese, Catalan, or Genoese, and become rather a brotherhood of curious scholars. It is so strange to contemplate that I have been afraid of Jews and Saracens my whole life, but devoid of weapons and armed with ideas, we become allied in the same cause.

"That evening, I shared a simple dinner of broiled cod, greens, and potatoes. Perhaps in deference to the prince, everyone partook of the wine in modest amounts. There were no women present, which I felt to be normal, as the sciences are of no interest to their sex. The prince presided but remained fixated in his project, which was to go down the entire coast of Guinea until the continent ended, round it, and find a new route to India since our old land route was blocked by the Moors when Constantinople fell. Seated next to me was a man about my own age who introduced himself to me as João Gonçalves Zarco, and we became immediate friends, as the like-minded young are apt to do. Zarco had no inkling of cartography; his experience was firsthand with the sea. He had started out as a *pagem* on a vessel at the age of eight. In his short lifetime, he had grown to love and respect the sea, but he especially admired the caravel, the little ship that dared to challenge the unquestioned might of the world's oceans. He began his encomium thusly:

'It is a marvelous craft, maneuverable yet with a shallow draft so that you can move close to the coast. The secret is in its lateen sails that are directly attached to the yardarm by the *parrel*. The sails are thus freer to move and catch the wind so that we can sail fifty-five degrees into the wind as opposed to sixty-seven degrees for a square-rigged vessel; that means less tacking and quicker voyages.'

"I nervously looked out on the boiling sea and tremulously asked how big the caravel usually was.

"'Not big, just forty to fifty tons. There is little comfort since there is no forecastle to allow for the free movement of the sails. The navigator gets the best quarters, in the sterncastle, which offers the greatest protection for the maps and instruments. It takes a crew of twenty to properly man her, and she can make a speed of ten knots with the wind behind her, though six is more the norm.'

"As Zarco continued to explain the merits of the caravel, his eyes gleamed with enthusiasm like a man in love with a beautiful woman. Without consciously knowing it, I began to share in his opinion of the caravel, although I had never set foot on one. I noticed that the prince, who was sitting solemnly at the head of the table, had fixed his eyes on us and our animated conversation. He neither smiled nor frowned, so I was at a loss as to whether or not he was pleased by our conviviality.

"After dinner, the prince pulled Zarco and me aside and asked if we would be willing to captain a caravel manned and waiting at Lagos. We almost tripped over ourselves, agreeing in unison. 'Good,' he said, 'I prefer sending men out who can get along with each other and have complementary skills.'

"That evening, as I made my way down to my damp quarters, I looked out into the swelling sea. Despite the comfort I had temporarily borrowed from my new friend, Zarco, I cringed at the ocean's immensity and power, set against the flimsiness of a fifty-ton wooden ship, and I silently commended my soul to heaven.

"So I am to sail with Zarco in the early summer. I am beside myself with excitement and cannot trust that I am not dreaming."

We parted that night, and I must admit that I harbored an inexplicable but insidious jealousy over Tristão's newfound but ardent friendship with this Zarco and wished that I shared in the same interests that would have brought us closer. I retreated to my friendless cell, loathing the night and the snoring of my inhospitable roommate while Tristão would go on to riches and glory.

ي

Through the years, I followed Tristão's trajectory with both envy and pride, never really knowing which emotion was primordial. I had just returned back to Lisbon from Viana from my audience with the former governor-general of Ceuta, Dom Meneses, which I have already related to you, dear reader. As we are intimate friends and inhabit alternate dimensions, I will confess to you, my reader, that I was in a foul mood and now thoroughly disgusted with my small role in misleading Christendom regarding Henry's true contribution to the commonwealth of our realm. I was replete with self-pity and self-recrimination at the ease to which I was employed as a cat's paw.

Upon my return to Lisbon, I found an invitation to dine at the monastery of Jeronimos. In my peevishness, I was about to refuse when I realized that my housekeeper was away and the monastery's kitchen was famed.

There were many of the same faces there whom I greeted with my usual perfunctory charm. I espied a number of people congregated around a stout man with the loud voice of someone accustomed to being attended, or perhaps he was just drunk. Although the body was unfamiliar, I had heard and seen that voice and face before, yet I could not place the circumstances. As I stared at the vaguely recognizable visage, I felt I was looking at someone I knew through a thick glass prism covered in mist. The stentorian speaker went on with his discourse, unaware of my constant gaze. At one point, he inclined his head to make a point, and with that gesture, I recognized my old friend Tristão Vaz.

We never notice ourselves age, save for when we encounter someone we knew when we were both young. Tristão had grown quite corpulent as the self-made man is apt to do, especially one who had tasted hunger as a child and wishes to make up for past deprivation. I stood there as if seeing myself objectively and realized that I had also grown old. We hugged, we laughed, and we wept as old friends will do, since the bonds we make in our youth are not easily severable.

"The last time I saw you at Sagres, you were commending your soul to heaven," I said gaily, trying to disguise the immense sadness I felt for finding myself so aged.

"Come to my home. It is not far from here, and I have a carriage outside. We must talk of the old times," he said.

"I wish to hear about Madeira."

س

We sat upon sumptuous French chairs, hand embroidered with visions of unicorns and mythical beasts with shooting forked tongues. A servant lit a fire without request and then, also without bidding, brought out sweet meats, dried fruits, and an earthen jug of thick wine, all of which Tristão partook of prodigiously, arming himself, as it were, for the task of narration.

"I will begin some five months after I last saw you at Sagres. You may remember that the prince had just assigned me as navigator with Zarco as captain. As it was the beginning of June and the most propitious time to sail, we left the very first week of the month. The ship was everything good, as Zarco had extolled, and, at the same time, everything I had dreaded. Indeed, it was highly maneuverable with its lateen sails and pleasing lines, but it was also miserably small. It took no more than forty paces for a large man to go from prow to stern. Privacy was completely nonexistent, and every man had to perform the basest bodily function in full view of the crew.

Yet despite the suffocating heat and proximity, morale was high, for the crew was composed of good lads, most not even yet men, with silky faces and accustomed to sharing small spaces and extracting every bit of conviviality they could find. So despite the cramped quarters, we were a congenial crew, with laughter erupting easily. The shared hardships made us brothers who cleaved to one another when sharing poor, simple pleasure: a dry blanket or a good biscuit broken in half and offered. Pleasure and friendship are heightened in the face of dearth.

"We set off in early June of 1420, with the southern winds billowing our sails so that the red cross of the Order of Christ showed prominently. True to tradition, someone in the crew had painted an eye on the prow so that we could find our way. Our mission was to explore at least sixty leagues of African coast beyond the limits of the kingdom of Morocco, where the great desert started. The prince wanted to know exactly how vast this desert was, that which the Berbers called the Sahara, and where the land of the Negroes began, for there was said to be huge quantities of gold and ivory as well as yet unknown riches.

"Our ship was laden with biscuit, dried beef, pork, salted cod, wine, olive oil, assorted barrels of fruits, and, of course, artichokes to ward off scurvy. There were also as many barrels of freshwater as we could carry. The weather being balmy. We slept on deck on mats stuffed with dog hair and covered with goatskin blankets. We stank but dared not use precious freshwater to bathe and could not rid ourselves of the lice that somehow accompanied us on board. Washing our clothes with seawater would have ruined them, as the clothes would have shrunk. Moreover, the salt from the sea clung to the cloth, making our shirts and pantaloons unbearably stiff and scratchy. So our clothes reeked, but we soon became used to the smell enough to not notice it, overly.

"With the prevailing southerly winds at our stern, Zarco

ordered the jib sail rigged, and we flew along at ten knots. Our speed gladdened the inexperienced hearts of the crew, but a few of the older hands frowned with worry, as they knew the return trip would be against the wind just as our supplies would be dwindling. Zarco noticed my anxiety and tried to insert steel through my withering spine by reminding me of the close hauling capabilities of the caravel, and besides, we were sure to find freshwater somewhere along the coast. I smiled weakly and again commended my soul to heaven.

"As I said, we left in early summer when the ferocious Atlantic is in its meekest mood, but as is often the case; the petty plans of men collide with the inexplicable will of God. The southerly zephyr breeze that had propelled us away from home suddenly turned into an angry westerly storm that whipped our insignificant little bark away from the coast of Guinea and into the vastness of the sea. There was no use fighting omnipotent nature. Our only hope remained in riding out the storm and resuming our course once it had subsided. Despite the season, it was a particularly fierce tempest, and even though we had stripped the mast almost bare, save for the minimum sail we needed to maneuver, we soared along at speeds of over fifteen knots, carried along in part by the prevailing current. In retrospect, my mind tells me that the storm lasted four days, but at the time, it had seemed like an eternity, and many times, I had given myself up for lost when, just as suddenly as the storm began, the winds died down and the ocean became tranquil, as though there had never been a storm at all.

"The crew proved to be just as protean as the weather; one moment, they were all hovering below deck, crying and expiating their sins in preparation for death, and the next, they were busily engaged in repairing the damage the storm had wrought on our sturdy little ship. I went to the stern castle to find most of my charts ruined by the seawater, but luckily my instruments remained intact.

"Zarco was about to order the helmsman to put about back toward the coast of Guinea when the lookout shouted land ho to port. To a man, we all rushed to port, causing the ship to heel precariously, and Zarco shouted to the helmsman to compensate while at the same time cursing us. Chagrined, I moved to starboard, ordering along half the crew to come with me. I squinted into the horizon and discerned a only a vague haze sitting in the distance in torment. I knew the lookout had a better angle, yet I myself could not see anything but a slight discoloration of the horizon. After a day's sailing, the haze took form, and as we neared it, the island began to take shape and become greener so that we could soon identify individual trees and brushes. I noted its latitude and approximate Hail Mary longitude on one of my few remaining dry charts and took it upon myself to call it Porto Santo, in honor of our salvation from the tempest. Miraculously, we found anchorage and sent the skiff ashore with five men, led by me. We armed ourselves with cutlasses and muskets, and we each said a heartfelt Act of Contrition before setting out for the island. There was no way of telling what heathens may be lying in ambush; I just prayed they were not cannibals. Death is death, and our physical bodies should be indifferent as to the means and cause. Yet somehow I felt my skin tighten with dread and even nausea at the prospect my dead flesh would be burned and consumed.

"Upon landing on the coarse-sanded beach, I ordered the men to light the flints on their muskets but to keep them uncocked, lest we begin to shoot at shadows and at ourselves at the sound of a falling coconut. I cannot speak for my men, but as myself, I had to squeeze my buttocks tight so I wouldn't shit in my pants.

"The island was indeed lush with vegetation, which meant that there must be abundant freshwater somewhere. Within an hour, we had successfully reconnoitered the entire island, as it was small, and we were reasonably satisfied that it was uninhabited, finding no structures, not so much as a footprint. I climbed to the highest prominence, and to the west, I saw another, much larger island on the near horizon. On the way back to the skiff, we tried but failed to find any surface water. The thick vegetation must have been supported by rain or underground wells. In either case, the water was out of our reach.

"Reporting my finding to Zarco, we set off the fifteen leagues or so to the large island I had seen from the prominence of Porto Santo. It was even more densely forested than Porto Santo and, indeed, many times larger. I appointed it in my chart with latitude and longitude and named it Madeira, after the abundance of trees evident.

"Unlike Porto Santo, there were no beaches where we could land but rather steep cliffs that fell vertically down into the sea. The ship's carpenter fashioned a ladder, and the same intrepid five of us set off. We found the approach difficult, as the sea swelled, and we were afraid of smashing the flimsy longboats into the wall of the cliffs. After several fretful approaches, we found a cove of a sort where the sea was becalmed enough to allow us to approach the massif.

"The climb was fraught with danger, but we managed. The foliage in the interior was so dense that we had to employ our cutlasses to carve a path through. It did not take long for me to ascertain that it would take weeks to properly reconnoiter this much larger island. Nonetheless, it seemed apparently uninhabited, even though, save for the lack of beaches, the island seemed a veritable paradise: fertile soil, abundant freshwater, and moderate climate. God had presented us with a partial version of Eden.

"Satisfied with our discoveries, we returned home on just four tacks, Zarco again proving himself correct on the maneuverability of the caravel. Prince Henry was pleased with the news, and he almost smiled. After a brief respite, we were ordered back to sea; this time, we were a small fleet of four caravels. One of them was captained by a Genoese by the name of Bartalomeo Pallastrelli who had brought along a clutch of rabbits to release on Porto Santo. This had been the prince's idea, and again trusting in your discretion, it proved to be a singularly bad one. I do not want to disparage the memory of my patron prince, but the introduction of the rabbits, which we both know only eat and fuck, proved to be an utter disaster. Without the counterbalance of our native wolves, foxes, and hawks, the rabbits multiplied and turned the island into a wasteland within months after their release. Prince Henry, I suppose in a sardonic mood, rewarded the hapless Pallastrelli by appointing him governor of the now-barren Porto Santo. Wisely, Pallastrelli did not remain at his post for very long but returned to Lisbon where he met a fellow Italian who was haunting our courts in the hope of receiving command of a fleet by which he hoped to reach India by sailing west. It was a ludicrous idea, as Frey Luís was sure that God had not made the earth so small, and the better route to India had to be east and around the horn of Africa. This Italian, one Christopher Columbus, married Pallastrelli's daughter and eventually took his inane petition to the more gullible, now-allied courts of Castile and Aragon.

"Madeira proved to be an economic success from the start. In order to assure his thalassocracy over the Atlantic, Prince Henry told Pope Eugenius IV that he had freed Madeira from the Saracen yoke, a blatant falsehood, but the prince got his sovereignty over Madeira and the rediscovered islands to the north, which we called the Azores, after the hawks that were found circling them. We Portuguese suffer from a singular lack of poetry when naming *terra incognita*, as we are often too literal. One of our explorers, whom I shall not name, came upon a small atoll he named Bird Shit Island. The name, thankfully, did not take hold, and it is renamed for some obscure saint who I cannot remember. There were many other islands from the charts we had collected in Sagres.

The Azores in particular appeared in different places on the accumulated maps, yet the exact longitude had remained a mystery.

"In Madeira, we were soon producing dragon tree resin, but with the soil being so fertile, it enticed us to bring in sugarcane from Sicily and our own vineyards. Unlike Ceuta, there was a steady stream of willing settlers, and before long, the island was a commercial success. Zarco and I were rewarded by the prince; he made us donataries, and we each received 5 percent of the island's export of dye, sugar, and wine. Prince Henry reserved for himself the monopoly on the sale of salt, saw mills, ovens, and soap, all of which the islanders needed to import from the mainland. He petitioned his father, Dom João I, to appoint him governor of Madeira and later convinced his brother, Dom Duarte, who inherited the throne in 1433 after the great king's death, to confirm his appointment. Again, between you and me, the indecisive Dom Duarte would have appointed Prince Henry pharaoh had his younger but much stronger-willed brother had asked."

"What about these Azores?" I inquired.

"As I have said, the Azores had frequently appeared on the old maps that Frey Luís had shown me. The Azores were not as lush as Madeira, but by 1439, Prince Henry gained permission from the crown to start planting settlers there. The son of the true king, Dom Duarte, granted his brother, Pedro, the largest island, São Miguel, as his personal property. This irked Prince Henry to no end, and I fear the prince never forgave his older brother for usurping what he believed to be rightfully his property, although you must forgive another indiscretion: the prince was avid in jealously, guarding the islands of Santa Maria, Flores, and Corvo for himself, exacting the same monopolies from the settlers he had acquired in Madeira.

"It was then that Henry's half brother, the count of Barcelos, petitioned the poor, vacillating Dom Duarte to be made governor of Corvo. The bad blood the count stored within himself stemmed from the fact that he was the oldest son of the king, Dom João I, but because he was a bastard by birth and, you keep this to yourself, also bastard by nature, he had no claim to the throne. Pathetic as he was, Dom Duarte could not refuse any entreaty made in his presence, as he was afraid of confrontation, something true kings relish. Prince Henry was unable to exert his considerable influence, as he was now mostly cloistered away in Sagres. The count of Barcelos played his cards, namely, his unfortunate birth and what the House of Avis owed him for that, his moral ascendancy to the throne as the eldest son of their father and the knowledge that this vacillating half brother, who had to call in his advisors to select which attire he would wear on any given day, would not refuse him anything just to be rid of an intrusive presence and the overriding guilt the count skillfully heaped upon his naïve personage. Thus the count was granted the governorship of Corvo in perpetuity, and the prince added another fraternal enemy to his list. The Azores did not prove to be the immediate economic success enjoyed by Madeira, yet the prince held onto his resentments as if they were precious gold coins. I petitioned the court for the governorship, or at least a portion of the profits, from one of the islands but was ignored. There were other predators to feed, but I cannot complain from the rewards I received from the discovery of Madeira.

"As in our adventure with the discovery of Madeira, a Castilian ship was blown off course and came upon on what proved to be a chain of islands they, also unimaginatively, called the Canaries, after the wild dogs that roamed there, after the Latin *canus*, meaning dog."

"What happened with the Canaries?" I asked.

"Oh, that is a sadder story," replied my friend, Tristão.

"Not satisfied with the governorship of Madeira and most of the Azores, the Canaries became a pernicious obsession for the prince. In my correspondence with my wise mentor, Frey Luís, it was his opinion that, since the prince had no vices, he must perforce expend his energy in other endeavors lest he burst like a pig's bladder during a heated football game.

"The Canaries had been plotted on many charts, as Frey Luís had showed me, and their initial discovery lay in the fog of history. The larger islands, Tenerife, Gomera, and La Palma, were inhabited by particularly fierce aborigines who had driven off several European incursions, despite pitting steel against stone. Yet some parts of the islands had been settled by Castilian, French, and Catalan colonizers. As was his wont, Prince Henry paid no heed to their antedated presence; he was determined to own some, if not all, these islands for himself, as they were situated not far north of Cape Bojador and, with plenty of freshwater, would provide an excellent jumping off base for the exploration and conquest of the continent of Guinea.

"With this mania deeply implanted in his brain, in the year of our Lord 1424, Prince Henry sent a two-thousand-man expedition to take Grand Canary in the face of the Castilian claim to the island. I was administrating to Madeira at the time and fortunate not to have been inducted into this disastrous and rash attack. Prince Henry had his eye fixated on the large island and its aboriginal inhabitants. This time, there was no reason to lie to the Pope; he meant to convert them to the true Christian faith. In among those dozen *barcas*, there were Benedictine and Franciscan friars who were present to exploit and save souls of the natives. We also brought shackles to subdue their heathen natures. After all, had not the Holy See declared that it was far better to live as a converted slave and ensure the kingdom of heaven after death than to live as a free savage and be damned?

"It is without some generous dollop of self-flattery that I say that one of Prince Henry's particular talents was in choosing the right man for the task at hand. He was an astute judge of human capability. He was also a good appraiser of empty stomachs. Unfortunately, he was also in debt to a number of merchants, a particular one who wanted his nephew to command the expedition to take Grand Canary. That man, or more precisely boy, whose name I cannot remember since it is not worth the effort, was a complete incompetent. It is a great boon to us self-made men that talent, unlike wealth, cannot be inherited.

"Again, I implore you, my friend Zurara, to be discreet, for despite my wealth, I am not immune to assassins. Rather than moving inland en masse, this particular genius of the mixture of nobility of the rich merchant class, most probably a product of too many intermarriages of first cousins, decided to split his pathetically small force into fifteen columns since he was unsure where the hidden enemy lay. The natives, having lived on the island since Adam spliced his rib to create woman, knew exactly where they were. The idiot brought along one hundred twenty horses but kept them in reserve. Horsemen are meant to be used, Zurara. One thing I have learned is that, when attacking someone's home ground, use a mallet on the nail, eschewing the mere hammer. If the foe has ten men to defend, you must have thirty to attack. If the enemy is covered in tin, you must shield yourself in steel.

"Our men dutifully marched single file into easy ambush. A javelin was thrust into a man's exposed hindquarters, disabling him and making him a liability to his comrades, for two men had to be released to bring their wounded comrade back to the ship. A stone slung from a sling crushed a nose and four front teeth, and a hail of arrows fell upon visors and breastplates, but occasionally found exposed flesh. They all took their toll on thirsty, weary men, still seasick from the to and fro of the ships from which they had recently disembarked.

"The men charged, yelling Portugal and Saint James, but the enemy melted into the foliage. They simply refused to fight on our terms. When we turned our backs, they reappeared, spewing all sorts of projectiles on unprotected napes, arms, and thighs. In the end, we were defeated by primitive tribesmen with stone axes and wooden javelins, but then again, they were defending their homeland, and men are apt to be braver in doing so, as righteousness equals strength. They appeared in a split second, too short a time to take aim, too distant to thrust a sword into. Our men cursed these agile pagans and even cursed their own God in childhood petulance, but it did no good. Badly led and without moral height, they were not the same men as their fathers who had repelled the Castilian invader. Defense of one's home brings out the hero, while avarice can only take you so far, well, before you are willing to die.

"The failed expedition was totally financed out of Prince Henry's pocket, which is to say the Order of Christ, so when the Castilian king, Juan II, remonstrated, Dom João I could honestly claim innocence on the part of the Portuguese throne, though I am sure he practically burst with pride at his son's audacity. Juan nonetheless threatened war, which would have been disastrous, given the impoverished state of the realm, but Prince Henry, true to his nature, had calculated that consequence well. The Castilians were besieged by the French from the east and the Moors from the south and could ill afford to open another front to the west. This he related to his father who approved of the gamble.

"Upon hearing of the fierceness of the natives of Gomera on the Canaries chain, Prince Henry, ever the opportunist, bade his corsairs to befriend them. The Gomerans were barrel-chested heathens with primitive gods who believed their salvation lay in dying in battle, perfect for the prince's plans. Our corsairs made friends through appeasement with gifts of salt, wine, and olive oil. The chieftain, who we baptized as Benedict, was especially fond of our wine and, as a culmination of our trust and esteem, was presented with a horse, which died within a month, owing to lack of care. Prince Henry did not trust them with modern weaponry, nor did the pagans seek it, believing that redemption lay in living or dying using their own primitive weapons. They were the perfect cat's paws. Thus allied, our corsairs enlisted the Gomerans, and they were taken to neighboring islands on slave-hunting *razzias*. Throughout his endeavors on the Canaries, Juan II of Castile threatened havoc while Dom João I protected his throne and son by adamantly stating that he had nothing to do with these exploits and would his distant cousin forgive the antics of his overly ambitious child and uncontrollable freebooters. Juan of Castile was hard-pressed from a number of sides but still managed to send his distant cousin a succinct answer: 'Bullshit!'

"All was going to plan for the prince when one of his overzealous captains, whom I will not name, because I do not like him, seized twenty Gomerans and brought them back as slaves. Perhaps he was overenthusiastic, but in my opinion, he was just lazy. It was much easier to capture trusting Gomerans than venture into the dangerous bush after more elusive prizes. Fool that he was, he displayed them before the prince in Sagres. Henry flew into a rage over the betrayal of allies. With the twenty former Gomeran captives bearing witness, he ordered the captain bound and hoisted over the walls of Sagres, where he was repeatedly dunked into the cold ocean until he was within a hair's width of death. The Gomerans' wounds were then covered with balm, and they were clothed in soft robes. The penitent captain, after having been fished from his ordeal, was forced to kneel in front of his former captives and beg forgiveness. The Gomerans gave no clue as to their disposition. Once safe back on their island, they related to Benedict their ordeal and how these Portuguese could not be trusted. Benedict kept his religion but promptly changed his allegiance to the Castilians.

"The prince's mania was frustrated for the time being, but

not his indomitable spirit. In 1436, the prince again attacked the Canaries with his private fleet of corsairs. This time, the target was Tenerife. Five rotund and unseaworthy *barcas* with a complement of five hundred men-at-arms surprised a small community of Castilian settlers and proceeded to 'convert' four hundred natives. Unable to establish a permanent foothold, and running out of supplies, the fleet retreated with their now-captured, but spiritually saved, slaves.

"With these expensive setbacks seeping his funds, the prince took a lesson from his caravels and tried another tack. Apparently in a fit of abject debauchery, the Castilian king, Juan II, had granted a partial lease for the Canary island of Lanzarote to a handsome Frenchman by the name of Maciot de Bethencourt in 1448. Bethencourt was twenty-five, and the Castilian was fifty-two, practically at death's door, but he still fancied round French buttocks. The prince's spies in the Castilian court apprised him of his cousin's infatuation, so Henry again dipped into the Order of Christ funds and purchased the lease from the reprobate Bethencourt whose female sensibilities were only too happy to exchange gold for some fanciful claim on a remote island. The prince then proceeded to establish a small number of squires and tenants on the island, but it did not take long for the Castilians and what remained of the natives to drive the hopelessly outnumbered Portuguese off the island.

"Thus it all ended. Through all Henry's machinations, the Canaries remained in Castilian talons. For all Henry's stratagems, the Canaries proved a dissipation of money and manpower while at the same time putting the kingdom at risk in a renewed war with Castile. By all accounts that I am aware of, the prince never showed any particular remorse in putting his realm in jeopardy, nor did he ever display any overt pique over the failure to take the Canaries. He remained a man who would never learn from failure but could only profit from success."

س

My dear God, why do you frustrate my designs? Am I not your chosen? If I were not, surely, You would not descend these tribulations upon myself. Those careful designs lay in a heap like a cathedral destroyed by Your hand in a massive earthquake, an occurrence that we poor mortals are still trying to decipher. Why do You let mere mortals hinder my efforts? Why do You also let my enemies claim You, my dear Lord, as their ally? I would burst my lungs, burn my larynx in savage complaint to Your apparent deaf ears. You have made me different with a purpose. Tell me, dear God, I know it is I. I would not suffer so if it were not. I do not presume.

Please, dear Lord, just let me be instrument of Your will. Let me slough my humanity and come close to You since You have seen fit to task me. If I could, I would take my sword and smite my enemies, if they were not both in me. I would put a dagger to my thin-skinned neck and dare those demons to approach.

Dear Lord, I damn Your mysterious machinations. You made me born a prince. Are You trying to teach humility? Do I not abase myself to Your glory and majesty sufficiently? Dear God, make my flesh strong and lead it away from temptations. I will bestow a world to You as long as it is your purview to give me temporal jurisdiction. I have sensed Your touch impel me forward, but I plead not to be led into further failure. I am Your instrument. I will receive this failure as a lesson in humility. But, dear Lord, let me proceed unmolested.

CHAPTER SEVEN
ENTR'ACTE

*I*t snowed overnight, a rare event for these climes. The men of the garrison woke up as they usually do, in glum acceptance of another day only to find their grim, gray fort covered in a coat of pristine downy snow. The beautiful white mantel hid the ugliness of the place and even made it look festive. Most of the men stationed here have never seen snow so, they whooped and hollered, romping about, throwing the fluff all over themselves and their companions in the innocence of revisited childhood. The gates were opened, and they continued their celebrations. Some ingenious fellow compacted the snow into a ball and threw it at a friend. Soon, they were all imitating this delightful exercise. It occurred to me then how I had forgotten that many of these so-called men were really still boys, not yet twenty.

They continued to throw these cold orbs at each other with such wild abandon that they did not notice the Moors come. We shouted from the ramparts but could not pierce the din they were making. It was not until the Moors were well near that they finally noticed them. It was too far to see who threw the first snowball, for this is what it was, and soon they were all screaming like children engaged in play. The governor-general saw this spectacle and shook his head but, wisely, did not try to stop it. The merriment and frolicking went on for an hour before the men started returning to the fort, their hands too frozen to continue the game. Without a word, they returned to their grim duties, a vestige of a smile remaining on their cold, red-colored countenances. No one spoke of what had happened as if it had not occurred at all. I found it refreshing and pleasant to see them as children once again. Why are the pinnacles of joy so short-lived while the valleys of gloom so prolonged? But I must return to my narrative.

س

Over the last two goblets of wine, dear reader, I have merely recorded the testimony of witnesses to my prince's conduct in his various enterprises. I would now like to retake the stand, so to speak, and relate to you some of my own perceptions of those earlier years, following the conquest of Ceuta. At that time of his life, my prince was perceived in different manners by different people, much like the blind men touching various parts of an elephant. Even to me, who had accompanied him over the years, he remained a piebald horse whose color depended on the angle of view. To Dom Alenquer, my prince served as a mere pawn in the grander plan of his father, Dom João I. In the eyes of the navigator, Tristão Vaz, my prince was a valiant but reckless soldier in the army of Christ, intent on vanquishing the infidel. If you were to believe the old governor-general and soldier, Dom Pedro Meneses, Henry was a mere whelp, full of vainglory and impetuosity. Which of them was Henry? He was all of them, naturally, with one common element binding these personalities: audacity; it was the mortar that bound the edifice of his character.

Now audacity is one of those neutral traits in that it can be employed for either good or evil. I was still young and dazzled by his luminance, so I believed Henry utilized his courage for good purposes. In retrospect, his audacity led to reckless decisions, caused undue and horrific suffering, widened our knowledge of the earth, and disgorged tremendous wealth. Unfortunately, none of the latter ever came my way, though Henry did make a fortune for Tristão and many like him. I do not envy their well-deserved rewards but do lament my ill-deserved fate, but then again, deserving has nothing to do with life. We are all but dead leaves released from tree limbs and moving to and fro at the whim of the prevailing breezes until we alight on the ground and are interred.

One other apparent aspect of his character was that Henry wished to leave a legacy behind since that is the reason he hired me as his panegyrist. He was cognizant of the image he wished to bequeath to posterity and thereby attain some kind of immortality on this earth, for as the Romans used to say, you are not truly dead as long as someone remembers your name. But this public persona he wished to project was not his true self, as I slowly began to learn in those early years of out tenuous relationship. Like all astute politicians, Henry cultivated a public image that was grander than the underlying individual. The public image he wished to project was godlike in nature. I am not blaspheming but trying to convey to you the image of a man who was above others in his lack for low passions. He did not imbibe wine nor consort with women, while constantly referring to himself as God's instrument, even when pursuing personal interests. He never complained of human discomforts such as hunger, thirst, or fatigue; in this, he was above other men whose flesh is composed of weaker material. He tried to live his public life as altruism personified.

I was once acquainted with a dissolute but ultimately insightful young man at school who claimed that all men were motivated by basic needs. This acquaintance of mind was well-read and could even decipher the ancient Greek, which must have caused his head to turn toward pagan tendencies. In his purview, since most of the people on God's earth were poor, every act was performed to assure the procreation of their next meal. Once hunger, thirst, and shelter from the elements were secured, he believed the devil then takes men by the hand. In my acquaintance's profane opinion, once man's basic necessities are seen to, carnal lust is the next in line to demand satisfaction. He was, of course, speaking solely of the male, as, thankfully, women are free of this dark desire. In my most humble opinion, dear reader, the female is both more ethereal and more pragmatic. Once a woman's basic necessities are satisfied, she, by instinct, seeks to nidify and, as such, is drawn to what she believes will be the best provider, indifferent to the physical appearance of her partner. In short, for a woman, wealth trumps beauty.

Having expostulated on the nobler nature of the female, to my shame, I believe that there is more than just a grain of truth in my profligate acquaintance's opinion on the male constitution. May God take pity on my weak flesh, but I myself was born in this visceral world and can still vividly remember the incessant call of the blackest of lust as a boy of thirteen, even as I kneeled in church to pray for forgiveness. But for the gross talk of some of my schoolmates, I would have thought of myself an abomination. I was also blessed to have a confessor who told me that these urges, horrible as they may be, were normal and sent to us by God as a test of our character. God allows the devil's afflatus into our ear so that we might battle successfully with evil, and that is why Christian canon existed, to help us curb these nefarious appetites, unlike the heathen who fornicates indiscriminately and is consequently condemned to the ravages of eternal hell.

I am an old man now, and confession of youthful transgressions comes easily to me, so I can tell you, dear reader, that I myself was only partially successful in curbing my carnal lust. Besides my brief but unforgettable relationship with Ofelia, I will not enter into my own confessions of nocturnal visits to fleshpots. The evil irony is that knowing I was committing a vicious sin made it all the more exciting and fed my lust. I remember thinking that God was indeed a cruel engineer of the human psyche. It is now useless for me to seek absolution. There is much too much hypocrisy in this world for any guilt to pierce my armor of disillusionment. Apart from the circumstances of my own birth, I still know of so many of our own Catholic priests, even bishops, who keep none-too-secret mistresses and even wives and families. Again, the opinion of my dissolute acquaintance comes to my mind, as does my own history.

But what motivated my young prince? As a man born of woman, he must have been susceptible to the call of the insatiable flesh. Despite his noble birth and fictional public persona, he too was made of friable bone and quivering flesh. The hair shirts he frequently wore attest that he too was tempted. Yes, he was prone to the same low urges as we male mortals, but he was able to punish his proud flesh into submission.

At Sagres, where he spent most of his time, my prince lived in a world of men, save for some ancient female cooks and drudges. His last real female contact was with his departed mother, Dona Phillipa de Lancaster, and he had not sought their company since her death. He thrived in the male culture. He loved to hunt and was a frequent host to masculine tourneys, where bones were frequently broken and sinew ripped into permanent disrepair. He freely, and even comfortably, displayed his virility on the battlefield and in the tilting contests. My prince also liked to host lavish and costly displays of pageantry, both at court and abroad, replete with good food and fine wine. Some in the court, most particularly his own half brother, the count of Barcelos, openly suggested that there were political motives behind all this feasting, though Henry never laid claim to the throne and defended the ascension of his brother, Dom Duarte. Nonetheless, the count claimed these pageants were aimed at gaining political favor with the lesser nobility and to impress the merchant classes who were easily impressed my mere ostentation. He was most likely correct in this opinion.

I was frequently in attendance at these feasts and paid close attention to my prince's conduct. Despite the abundance of food and drink, Henry partook abstemiously of nourishment and almost never imbibed any wine. He was a model of virtue, publicly living the image he wished to leave posterity. It was at these pageants that he came in closest contact with the young, marriageable daughters of the nobility and richer merchants who tried their best to attract his attention. They were brazen to the point of sinfulness, yet it was understandable; he was a prince of Portugal and wealthy beyond private speculation. They batted their eyelashes until those tiny muscles must have ached from exhaustion and intruded upon his invisible male *cordon sanitaire* by asking silly questions and dropping clumsy hints as to their affection for him, all to no avail. My prince merely smiled politely, not lending himself to any particular suitor but paying them all in the same small coin of barely tolerable civility.

These young women were mostly composed of the same breed, flighty and given to excessive giggling and crimson blushing when they dropped boulder-sized innuendo that the prince either chose not to understand or simply ignored. I myself thought them frivolous, but I did admire their tenacity, for the more aloof the prince was, the more they redoubled their efforts in worming their way into his attention.

I must also admit that most of these young women were indeed pretty, as youth has a forgiving aspect, while a few were exceptionally beautiful. They all knew their basic catechism by rote and were skilled in needlework and at least one musical instrument. They possessed just enough education as is proper for a woman, for too much knowledge, much of which can be brutal, cannot be of benefit to their more delicate disposition and may well interfere with the happiness of the household. It creates a more harmonious environment when the wife recognizes and accepts the mental superiority of her husband and does not challenge him on any subject, save perhaps for the care and education of female offspring. Moreover, with an overemphasis on literacy, these young women may start to read these pernicious romances that abound, which can often excite emotions unsuitable to females.

My prince's decorum was indeed admired by the men of the court but frustrated the daughters of the gentry and merchants no end. I myself was in awe of his control, as Henry was so unlike his own lusty father, Dom João I, who was never one to pass up an opportunity to sate his enormous sexual appetite, fathering scores of bastards by grand ladies and wenches alike. The queen, I was told, tolerated her husband's trysts, as most wise women are apt to do, as long as he was discreet about it. If the king were to dote for too long on any particular paramour or the temporary object of the king's loins proved to be too ambitious, Dona Phillipa was quick and merciless to act, and the woman in question would find herself expelled from the court, if she were lucky. In tacit compromise, the king never remonstrated with the queen when his paramour of the month disappeared. It was as if she had never existed.

Henry was unlike his father. Since these women seemed all wrought from the same mold, it was my opinion at the time that Henry was searching for someone like his own mother: a strong, intelligent, worldly woman who, at the same time, was virtuous beyond reproach. There was not a one of these noisy furbelows that had any semblance to the dead queen, save for one.

Her name was Dona Eulalia de Albuquerque, and she was from one of the noblest and wealthiest families in all the

Iberian Peninsula. Her mother had refused marriage until the man she eventually married agreed that her lands would remain under her name and not automatically transfer to the husband, as is the custom. At her untimely death, Dona Ximene, for that was her name, bequeathed the title of her estates to her only daughter so that Dona Eulalia owned estates in Aragon, Castile, and Portugal. In the direct possession of this wealth, she was unlike any of the women who flocked to Henry's pageants who depended on their male relatives for their wellbeing. I suppose strong-willed women tend to engender strong-willed daughters, as it is such an uncommon and unbecoming trait in a woman.

There were other dissimilarities to the lacy furbelows that were her supposed rivals. One overt difference was that she was unusually tall, just half a head below the height of the prince himself. She had deep-set, predatory eyes that did not look daintily away when confronted, causing some men to demur in her concrete presence. Her cheekbones were prominent and darkened from the sun, for she was an avid equestrian, eschewing the more proper dray or carriage.

Her education also set her apart from the other young women of her age. She was said to be as learned as any Benedictine scholar, and she could debate subjects ranging from religion to the natural sciences with ease and confidence. I often saw men, who I deemed erudite, visibly ill at ease in her august presence, lest she prove herself better or more learned than they, as she was apt to do. Should a point of pedagogy prove an issue of disagreement, Dona Eulalia was ready to quote the provenance for her opinion, leaving the male sages hemming and hawing while they themselves tried to recall the particular work she was citing with the ease of the scholar that she was.

She was unafraid to argue a point with any man and would not concede it without being proved wrong, which was rare. There were few men who had the courage to enter into discourse with her, as they had everything to lose and nothing to gain. She had to rely on male overseers to manage her multitudinous properties but put short reins on them. God have mercy on the fool who tried to deceive her in business dealings, for Dona Eulalia would have none and persecuted those who had wronged her to the full extent of the law, which was considerable given her exalted position over the lowly transgressor. Many such fools found themselves on garrison duty in places worse than Alcácer Ceguer, if it can be believed that there are even worse places.

She disdained those frivolous romance readings, admiring the works of the ancient masters as well as St. Thomas Aquinas's *Summa Theologica*. She could read Latin and was fluent in a number of our modern languages, including French, Castilian, Catalan, and English. She did not giggle, although she was prone to mirth. She enjoyed a good laugh with the robustness of a man. In short, she was everything that would make her ineligible to the proud men of the time. We all professed to want docile, timid creatures, yet despite these assertions, when a woman refused to submit to the mold, we flocked to her like love-starved eunuchs, our heads full of the same prattle we despised in our women. I will confess, dear reader, that I was a bit in love with Dona Eulalia myself. Perhaps it was because of this infatuation and the absolute unlikelihood of any reciprocation.

ي

I happened to be in Coimbra on some small business on one of our notoriously hot days. The sun beat down on the smooth, foot-worn cobblestones with such fury that only the well-shod dared walk on them during the high hours surrounding midday. The barefoot poor did not dare venture out, for the cobblestones were heated enough to fry an egg in less than a minute. The normally gregarious sparrows did not deign to leave their leafy, shady perches.

I was taking refreshment under an awning, hiding from the pernicious sun, when I was approached by a liveried servant bearing a message. It was an invitation to dine with Dona Eulalia and some of her family who happened to be present in the city at her residence in Coimbra. I immediately returned to my rooms and began grooming myself for the occasion. If I could have licked my own eyebrows, I would have.

Dona Eulalia's so-called residence turned out to be a careful reconstruction of an ancient Roman latifundium, recreated with care and attention to the detail of the majesty that had once been. The ample courtyard was replete with lattices from which thick grape vines hung, shading it from the sun. A long table had been set under a particularly thick awning of vines. It was sumptuously prepared with the best of glazed clay plates and well-shined silver cutlery. The sun dappled through the wide leaves of the vines and, with the gentle breeze, set points of sunlight dancing about the rich mauve tablecloth. Everything spoke of understatement and elegance. Although the table was large and long, there were only four place settings; my audience with the noted noblewoman was to be intimate, and I felt my pulse race in expectation and nervousness. A young couple in rich brocade approached me and introduced themselves as Dona Eulalia's cousins; their actual names were an afterthought, and quite frankly, I do not remember them to this day. I was aware that their presence was merely for the sake of propriety, as a young, unattached woman could not have a private audience with a man.

Dona Eulalia quickstepped over to me, beaming her welcoming smile. She did wait for her male cousin to introduce us as custom dictated. At her station in our class structure, the usual protocols were elastic rules and bended with wealth and power.

"Dom Zurara, at last we meet. I have read, no, I have *devoured* your wonderful chronicle, and now I hear you are working on yet another, detailing the exploration of Guinea. How marvelous, and how erudite you must be. Your chronicle makes me wish I were a man in order to experience such adventures and serve God in such a direct manner."

I would not call her attractive in a physical aspect. She was indeed tall, but her face bore the remnants of the pox and was thickly covered in paste to disguise the scars. Her forehead was a bit too large to be feminine, and her eyebrows thick and unplucked, as was the custom. She carried herself with a masculine purpose. Yet despite all these less-than-feminine attributes, she possessed a singular attraction I could not explain.

She bade me sit at the head of the table, insisting I do so despite several demurrals. She was unlike any other woman I had ever met, engaging and engaged, unafraid to display her intelligence and even more unafraid to admit ignorance on a subject and asked questions unabashed, yet I noticed that the questions were intelligent ones. She also knew the arts of a woman and frequently asked questions which were merely meant to inflate my ego, though some were indeed out of curiosity. When she laughed, as she was apt to do, she did so heartily and with genuine mirth, not like the shallow teeters of the young, flighty women of her age, with nothing in their heads other than gossip and what headdress the queen was wearing in Madrid or the doge's costume in Venice. In the short time between the salad and the fish course, she had thoroughly endeared herself to me and made me her slave. That was indeed her purpose. She continued to spin her web, and I was only too happy to luxuriate in her captivity. Her onslaught of charm was maintained through the meat course, but when the fruit was served, she got to the point of her business with me.

"Dom Zurara, I will assume that you have to be one of the closest people to Prince Henry."

"My lady, the prince is not an easy man to approximate. He is majesty and purpose while I am but a humble man and his willing instrument."

"Well said, but as one of his closest associates, you must have been privy to his being more than any man on earth?"

I was downcast as the real reason of our meeting occurred to me. Dona Eulalia had no interest in me other than as a source of information. Prince Henry continued to loom large, and I was an insignificant in his shadow. Armed with this knowledge, I ruminated and answered.

"My lady, I am told that there are certain awe-inspiring statues in Egypt, half lion, half human. To look upon their cryptic faces, it is said that you expect them to communicate something profound at any second. These statues, sphinxes the natives call them, can entrance you with anticipation so that you can stare upon their visages for hours in anticipation of some ultimate truth that never arrives. They just maintain that secret smile, intimating that they know something you never will. My prince is a bit like these sphinxes."

"My dear Dom Zurara, even without realizing it, you have already told me much. Yes, Henry is an unique man; I can see and feel it. I admire the scholar, unlike most of the beasts we have that pass themselves as nobility but could not parse a single Latin verb. But Henry is a warrior as well, and without the overt braggadocio and brutality that most men claim as prerequisites for courage. Am I correct, Dom Zurara?"

"To the letter, Dona Eulalia."

"His interest in navigation, tell me about that."

"My lady, it is a complicated scientific subject, and I myself have a poor grasp of it, while you—"

Dona Eulalia's air of hospitality suddenly popped like a

soap bubble upon a thorn. She could not dissemble a glare of disapproval, for she, as intelligent as she was, went on to finish the sentence I had foolishly started.

"You mean to say that I, as a woman, could not comprehend such science?"

I stammered an apology and began perspiring profusely. Noticing my ill ease, she quickly sought to soothe my wounded pride.

"Please, Dom Zurara, do continue with what you do know about his navigational pursuits. I did not take any offense. Please, I pray, continue."

Continue I did. I told about Sagres, the maps, the theories, and Henry's obsession with the exploration of the Guinea coast for profit and God. I confessed that I was unsure of the order of priorities. She absorbed this information like that hole in the sand one digs on the beach as a child. You bring pail after pail of seawater to fill it, but the water only disappears; the hole never filled. She did not interrupt my narrative but let me ramble on until I came to a conversational cul-de-sac, but she always had a catalytic question prepared to make me continue.

Dona Eulalia had a special gift of drawing a person out beyond that person's predetermined boundaries. I spoke at length about things I was both sure of and unsure of with the same authority. I was giddy upon parting, having forgotten Dona Eulalia's true purpose. The wine and her undivided attention were equally intoxicating. I did not mind being used.

س

I did not see Dona Eulalia again for uncounted weeks until I returned to Coimbra, where I accompanied Henry who was hosting one of his pageants. Colorful tents had been set up in the city's square before the imposing moss-covered granite walls of the university. All the city's notables were seated in a U-shaped table, with Henry presiding at its center while I sat at the left elbow of the table, uncomfortably ensconced between an old gentleman who kept referring to me as Dom Vicente, despite several corrections, and his corpulent wife who farted a great deal more than she spoke, which I believe the better of the existential trade-off. Between avoiding the noisome gases emanating from the mouth to my left and the arse from my right, I espied Dona Eulalia approaching Henry on the arm of the ashen-faced cousin I had met at her palatial residence. The young man whose name still escapes me was visibly ill at ease, and it was obvious to me that he had been enlisted for the sake of decorum. As protocol required, Henry rose from his seat to greet the notables before him. Expecting a short exchange of platitudes, Henry blanched when Dona Eulalia began to converse with him.

My prince was not used to intercourse with women, the pun is intended, but she was from an extremely important family, and there was nothing for him to do but cordially invite her to sit at his table in order to further pursue her thoughts.

With her cousin pale and mute beside her, Dona Eulalia set course upon an avid conversation with Henry, and it was soon evident that she was almost as familiar with the subject of exploration as he was. Obviously, Dona Eulalia had taken it upon herself to learn as much as she could about the science of navigation since our interview. Henry spoke tentatively to her at first but soon warmed to the topic, given Dona Eulalia's grasp of his own passion. The exchange became so intense and lasted for such a long time that rumors were soon rampant that my prince and Dona Eulalia were very likely to wed. These rumors suited Dona Eulalia's own expectations, and she hunkered down in her estate near Coimbra to wait for Henry to make the next effort, as the decorum of our times dictated. Then weeks elapsed and accumulated into months and no such overture was received. Dona Eulalia was not a passive sort, so she borrowed an audacious rib from my prince, whom she obviously hoped to make her husband.

There was nothing of the coquette in Dona Eulalia's fiber. She believed in firm action rather than passive attendance upon the male's fickle whim. She sent a letter to Henry that he showed me. It read as follows:

15ᵗʰ of September, Year of Our Lord 1425
Coimbra
Your Excellency:

It has been some months now since you graced our humble but erudite city with your noble presence, and I pray that this missive finds you in good health and in God's protection. To be perfectly honest, our conversation on that day has weighed upon my mind, and I have devoted some time and resources to some of the problems we discussed, and I hope that my sex will not prevent you from considering any wisdom my words might impart. I will confess that the counsel I am about to proffer is not entirely of my own creation, as I have consulted some well-placed members of my family as well as made liberal use of the well-stocked library that we are privileged to have at the University here at Coimbra.

First, regarding Your Excellency's interest in the Canaries, my sources in the Castilian court fervently believe that Juan will never cede any of these islands, no matter the cost. If necessary, the court of Castile will redeploy forces from their southern border with the Moorish kingdom of Grenada in order to defend the Canaries from the "private" investment by Your Excellency's corsairs. I would therefore dissuade Your Excellency from expending any more precious time and resources in trying to wrest any of these islands from Castilian control. Also be warned, do not approach my cousin Philip, since the throne of Aragon is allied with Castile on this issue. Moreover, it is Philip's intent to eventually unite the kingdoms of Aragon and Castile with the marriage of his infant daughter, Isabela, to Castilian infante, Ferdinand.

I have studied all the Moorish maps we have here, guided by the cartographer, Abraham de Ribeiro. As his name implies, he is a Jew, but I am told that Your Excellency frequently relies on the counsel of members of their tribe. They are a devious people, but it is wise to be tolerant when there is profit to be made from their advice and acumen. I share Abraham's opinion that the coast of Guinea continues well beyond Cape Bojador, and there are several islands further south that most likely will have freshwater and can serve as a haven for our men to invest inland. Abraham is of the opinion that the great Nile turns west into the Niger, the Nile of the Negroes, and flows into the sea. There, he believes, as do I, that Your Excellency will find the terminus to the River of Gold, in a land the Arabs call Senegal. All these superstitions of poison seas and monsters are all fabrications by the demonic Moor to keep us from penetrating the land of the Negroes, where they now trade horses for slaves and gold. Find these islands and bypass the Canaries.

Regarding Morocco, I believe that Your Excellency should expand the foothold you so valiantly established at Ceuta. The Visogoths were our great grandfathers, so rightly Morocco belongs to us. The caliph of Fez is reported to be a weak and indecisive man, more concerned with deflowering young boys than military strategy. He is unlikely to commit his full forces to any counterattack once the fortress is taken. I am told by my family members that Fez is too powerful a stronghold but that Tangier is vulnerable. I propose that Your Excellency send a scout to reconnoiter the fort, much like your father did with Ceuta, but do not use the prior again, as that would arouse Arab suspicion. There is a willing Genoese in my service who would gladly go and is unlikely to raise any eyebrows, for he frequently goes there to trade.

I hope Your Excellency accepts my womanly counsel in the same vein as the advice wisely doled you by your sainted mother, Dona Phillipa. I am an unbeliever of pagan oracles, but I do have a sense that Your Excellency was meant to accomplish great deeds as per your adopted motto. I write to endorse and add my feeble female support toward Your Excellency's lofty aims of discovering new worlds and converting the Negro heathen to our true religion so as to save countless souls from perdition. I hope to ally myself and my house to your holy endeavors and remain.

Your humble and obedient servant,
Eulalia de Albuquerque

I was at Sagres when my prince received Dona Eulalia's missive and was called to his presence. He was sitting alone in the windowed round rotunda overlooking the ever-turbulent Atlantic. This solitude took me by surprise, as he was usually huddled over maps, surrounded by advisors, cartographers, and captains. He was visibly ashen when he showed me the letter.

"This is a new sort of creature to me. Zurara, you are a friend of the household, what does this woman want from me?"

I felt the innocent weight of the question as if someone had placed an anvil on my chest. This man, this prince, who was so sagacious in politics, a deceiver in warfare, was a complete naïf about women.

"Perhaps, my lord, you should take it at face value, that she merely admires you and wants to offer her help and counsel in your various endeavors," I said a bit lamely and very much wanting to be someplace else. He then looked at me incredulously, as if I were a fool.

"Don't you think she is angling for something, perhaps one of the Azores? I just do not understand why the Albuquerques would not send a male negotiator."

"My lord, Dona Eulalia is quite wealthy in her own right. I do not believe she hungers over more estates."

"There is no such thing as owning enough lands," he spat out with more venom than I had ever witnessed.

"But, my lord, not all are motivated by your pristine fervor to convert the heathen and defeat the Moor. Some people, especially women, seek much more mundane goals."

"Such as?"

I could not evade the question as I could not ignore the point of a sword pressed against my heart. I hawed a bit, cleared my throat several times, and sweated profusely on this extraordinarily warm day in late September. As his eyes bore into me like an awl, demanding the truth he thought I knew, I finally blurted out the obvious, obvious to all but Henry.

"I believe, my lord, that Dona Eulalia wishes to wed you."

My words echoed off the granite walls of the cavernous room and hung in the still air, slowly coalescing into comprehension like raindrops gaining the necessary mass within a cloud before they fall to earth. His eyes transformed from narrow slits of suspicion to round orbs of surprise and amazement. He began to pace quickly to and fro and speak in staccato bursts of breath.

"But this cannot be. I have given this woman not an iota of

encouragement. I have sworn myself to the service of Christ and chastity. What can I do to dissuade her?"

"My lord, Dona Eulalia belongs to one of the most influential and richest families on our peninsula. Would you not even consider an alliance with such a family, as it would further your aims?"

He suddenly stopped pacing and leveled a look of such malevolence that I feared it would pierce me like a sharp blade.

"I will not prostitute myself for a single *real branco*. I am a prince of Portugal, and the Algarve, governor of Madeira and the Azores, and I lay head of the Order of Christ and have the resources to accomplish my goals without the need to soil my body."

"But, my lord, marriage is a sacrament."

"Only if it is accepted as such."

"But, my lord, the aid she and her relative can provide—"

"Ah, well and good, but I have no need to marry a pig to enjoy the ham."

It was now my turn to become irate. You see, dear reader, I was still young and not fully in control of my emotions.

"My lord, I am acquainted with Dona Eulalia, and she is a comely woman of considerable virtue."

My prince waved his hand in a sign of having meant no literal disrespect.

"Well, indeed, she has provided me with some wise counsel and information. You are correct, Zurara; she may prove to be a useful ally. It is she who has begun our dialogue on such a platonic level and so it shall remain. Given her wealth and position, I dare not insult her, so I will answer her letter, supplicating for more advice."

As I took leave of my prince, he recommended pacing, three steps to and fro in a fit of uncharacteristic agitation. I spent that night in the empty altar to the ocean, that is, Sagres.

On the way to my chamber, I encountered Frey Dominicus, the prince's old, dour confessor. He was one of the righteous priests and is fastidiously celibate, yet I did not like him; I preferred the licentious hypocrisy of our more human clergy to the inhuman pedagogy of this pasty-faced demigod. Frey Dominicus looked at me with his customary ill will, for he disapproved of all literature that did not strictly praise God alone. I bowed my courtesy and silently wished his feeble stick of a body to hell.

In the still quiet of the night, only the sound of the ocean dominated. Between the crashing of the waves against the massif, I thought I discerned a rhythmic sound, as though a door was being slammed open and closed by the wind. But it was a calm night. With curiosity overcoming my natural reticence, I opened the door to my chamber and crept toward the source of the noise, which turned out to be my prince's rooms.

Feeling like a thief, I put my ear to the oak door and listened to the slaps of leather on flesh. Yes, dear reader, I have been to many public punishments and know well the sound of the cat-o'-nine-tails. After each blow was delivered, with a vengeance, I might add, I heard the distinct cry of pain. It was the sound of the humbling of proud flesh. I dared not venture farther into the intimacy of a prince and his God.

In the following weeks and months, Henry continued to correspond with Dona Eulalia. The tone of the interchange remained platonic, as Henry never let it abase into the personal. Dona Eulalia was bound by her own code of a high-born noblewoman and could not breach the topic that was foremost on her mind without besmirching herself before God and her proud family.

As time wore on, Dona Eulalia's letters became more infrequent until they stopped altogether. Despite her resoluteness, she was defeated by my prince's stony indifference. I will confess to you, dear reader, my estimation of my prince was diminished. Whereas I had once admired his chastity, I thought him a fool to eschew the hearth that was offered him in all good faith. Also, I felt uncomfortable with Henry's rigid chastity, as I felt uneasy with Frey Dominicus's strict inhuman virtue. I somehow believed that human beings were meant to be like yews that sway in the winds of temptation, not like oaks that refuse to bend, and thereby may break.

Having committed her energies to the one man in the world she admired, Dona Eulalia never deigned to pay attention to the courtiers that still pursued her. She suspected that most, even the richest, were after her money and position, and she would not agree to marry beneath the status that she had adopted for herself in her soul. Yet she endured, ostensibly a female within a powerful clan, but *de facto*, the family's guiding intelligence and ultimate arbitrary of all family disputes. I had finally discovered what motivated my prince. My dissolute acquaintance was wrong. It is not always carnal lust that spurs men into action; it can also be a lust for fleshless power and glory.

س

The sin of Eve continues to manifest itself. The female is ever the temptress. She insinuates her vile flesh and fetid pudenda in a never-ending crusade to strip a man of his chastity. They are an abomination to our race. The Arab is correct to drive the female from his presence, to clothe her from head to toe to render her powerless to persuade. Dear Lord, lay waste to their subterfuge. I wish I had the power to scourge every female in my kingdom. Humble them, wretch their smug arrogance away from their prideful faces, disembowel their wiles, and make them all quake in my presence. I resent the decorum that binds me. I despise these rules that limit my will, but these are the tethers that God, in infinite wisdom, has seen fit to bind me. I will obey, but not without tugging at the restraints the way a good horse tries to defy the reins. I would banish these poisonous creatures, save for the necessities they serve. Let them procreate in excruciating pain amid the middle-aged administrations of old hags. They are all witches, and I will have nothing to do with them. May they all burn in everlasting hell. I will find new worlds where I will rule only second to God. My own concept of civilization will be imposed, and I will at last be free of these man-invented tethers that do not envision my genius.

Chapter Eight
Wooden Ships; Iron Men

*H*enry kept me close by during the explorations of the coast of Guinea. Once a week. I was called to his august presence in his austere chambers off the rotunda at Sagres so that he could dictate his linear successes. I remained his dutiful slave and recorded the events as he spoke them with no interpolations.

Sagres became an increasingly crowded place, full of the learned and the adventure seekers, and I was forced to share my quarters with a motley crew of men, though none of them ever came into my heart the way Tristão did. I suppose I was past that fancy age when friendships are made in heaven. Now closeness had to be earned rather than given beforehand. As we age, we become less flexible both physically and emotionally. Most of my roommates were rude adventurers drawn by the rewards of pillage. Avarice comes easily to poor men. Apart from the very narrow subject of navigation, there was little in common between us, despite the proximity of the space we shared and our age. They were largely of the opinion that I was the prince's agent, if not his complete toady, and so avoided me in all respects while remaining aloofly civil to a fault. They were all of the opinion that whatever was said in my presence would be immediately communicated to the *infante*.

One morning, a page came to me with a missive from someone in a high position in the Order of Christ requiring my presence at a place I have long since forgotten. As a potential donatary, all such requests were mandatory, and I prepared to travel to Braga as ordered, hoping that the weather would cooperate, as it was still only April when the climate can be protean. Of course, I communicated my duty to the prince as well as all concerned, including my current cell mate, a certain Fonseca, a captain in waiting for a ship. He was a coarse man with whom I was forced to share a bed, though he stank of week-old piss and thirty-day-old sweat.

Sometime before vespers, another messenger arrived with an urgent note that my trip had been cancelled, owing to inclement weather. I was very much relieved, as I am not a good traveler, even in the best of circumstances, and tend toward motion sickness in a swaying dray, not to mention the jolting my bones endure when stiff wooden wheels are forced over rain-created ruts on the road. It is a discomfort I would rather eschew, and I well understand why the majority of our common-born population lives and dies within three leagues of where they were born. I remain of the opinion that travel pares years off a man's life.

I had not had the occasion to advise anyone of my aborted trip and so repaired to my quarters, much relieved from that particular onus. As I have said, my quarters were off the rotunda and among the most spacious. It was with great surprise that I found my cell full of men waiting in line before the two cots. The cots were both occupied by grunting men, one I recognized as Fonseca, atop strumpets, with glazed expressions and emitting feigned sounds of passion. My own descents into velvet lasciviousness told me so, but as telluric men, we do not pay much attention to the play acting as long as the female's pudenda is wet and warm and the thighs thick with distaff flesh.

Upon my intrusion, the men waiting in line disbursed with hands over their faces to prevent me from recognizing them. Fonseca and the other pinned under the strumpets were powerless to act as quickly, so I had a full view of their sheepish faces. They extricated themselves with difficulty and remorse from their respective harlots and stood there naked with their hands covering their organs, still erect from carnal lust. The harlots in the meantime laughed at their cowardice and brazenly showed their nakedness, exposing buxom buttocks and round, drooping breasts, as harlots tend to be well fed. I was fascinated with the view of their exposed flesh. My eyes became lungs as I inhaled their essence. Inexplicably to me, it was their imperfections that aroused my lust the most: the thick thighs and the hanging, pendulous breasts. It was also the bold insouciance at the leisure and sheer pleasure they took in clothing themselves before my apparent hungry eyes. It was clear that these harlots knew the absolute power their peripheral bodies held over low men like myself. As they strutted out, the older one lifted her skirts and passed her hand over her pudenda and offered her palm to me to smell, and I inhaled the luscious sin to my everlasting shame. In this my old age, I can still remember that acrid, corrupt odor of sin and salvation. The harlot caught the ecstasy on my face and laughed in taunt, a deep-throated chortle of someone who has exposed hypocrisy. She knew that I would have been only too happy to get on line.

The next day, I experienced a tomb of silence from what normally was a cackle of gregariousness. Eyes avoided me, as everyone expected me to tell my prince of the occurrences of the night. I can still remember wondering how those ingenious men ever got those harlots past the male sanctity of Sagres, and I secretly commended them for their improvising spirit. Yes, they all expected me to tell my prince of the base nature of their flesh. When days and then weeks went by and there were no inquiries, I began to encounter smiles and an occasional nod of approval that I had proven myself a fellow man with all his warts. From that time, I was trusted by the men at Sagres as a man of discretion and, more importantly, as a man. Word of my discretion spread quickly, so returning seafarers came to me to unburden themselves after they had reported the half-truths to my prince.

And so, dear reader, I will remain on the witness stand for a while longer, as I wish to relate the events that took place at Sagres in my presence and away from the purview of my prince. When you read my nearly completed *Chronicles of the Discovery of Guinea*, you may get the impression that Henry's interest in exploring the coast of Guinea never wavered and that he was relentless in pushing his captains farther and farther south toward the land of the Negroes and, ultimately, the land of gold. This impression was meant to be conveyed, and it was my prince's intention to portray himself as such, but like so many of the linear biographies of the saints we read, it was not so. So it was my prince who did proceed along the coast of Guinea in fits of energy and sudden stops, as his attention was continually diverted to other enterprises, such as the Canaries or Morocco. He reminded me of those jugglers we frequently see in our fairs who take hold of additional flaming torches in their act until one finally falls to the ground, if they're lucky enough not to burn their hands.

Apart from my prince's multiple tasking mania, the financing of the building, provisioning, arming, and manning a caravel created quite an expense. Whenever possible, Henry preferred to have the financing borne by a third party, with which he would agree to share 20 percent of any riches found and brought back. If Henry bore the entire expense himself, he required half of any booty taken. In such a poor kingdom as our own, there were few merchants, and even fewer nobles, who were willing to bear the cost, so the voyages mostly fell upon Henry's purse, which everyone thought to be bottomless, given his position as lay governor of the Order of Christ.

My prince commenced his explorations modestly in 1420, even before receiving Dona Eulalia's wise letters of counsel, which he chose to conceal from his advisers. I did not need any instructions from him that I was not to speak of the letters he received from Dona Eulalia. It was a tacit order. He chose a poor squire from his household by the name of Gonçalves Baldeira. This squire's poverty and the extreme indigence of the crew made them willing participants, as wealthy men are unlikely to risk their more precious lives on the treacherous Atlantic.

Baldeira set off on his lone caravel from Lagos and was gone for just three months. Upon his return to deep anchorage at Lagos, he and the voyage's scribe went at once to Sagres to report to my prince. Henry put a scribe aboard the vessel to act as his representative and record all treasure found and laded. Henry was a realist, though he professed to trust his captains implicitly.

Baldeira reported, and the scribe concurred, that he had explored nearly one hundred leagues of the coast of Guinea and had landed ashore several times to reconnoiter. He complained that these incursions inland were hampered by the lack of horses and recommended that future voyages take along two or three horses. My prince thought it a wise counsel and made a note of it, bidding Baldeira to proceed.

There was little that Baldeira could report; his men did not encounter a living soul upon landing but found merely uninhabitable desert as far as their eyes could see. Having established that there was no freshwater for one hundred leagues, Baldeira suggested that future voyages lade more barrels of water, and Henry also made a note of this suggestion as well.

Baldeira reported that the winds were predominantly southerly and that the coast he explored was free of sandbars.

He also said that the ocean teemed with fish, so there was no need to carry as much dried meat, allowing for room in the small hold of a caravel for the additional barrels of water. Again, Henry made a note and appeared to be satisfied with the results.

All in all, I thought it was rather an unremarkable voyage and an inauspicious beginning. I personally did not see any merit to continuing the exploration of Guinea. Nonetheless, my prince rewarded Baldeira by appointing him *almoxarife* for the city of Oporto. As collector of taxes, Baldeira's living was assured, and he thanked my prince profusely. He would have kissed Henry's feet had my prince not ordered him to refrain from such abasement and not act like a groveling infidel.

Now, dear reader, you may be of the opinion, as I was then, that the reward bestowed by my prince was overly generous and not in proportion to the feat accomplished. After all, Baldeira did not bring back any gold or even any rumor where it could be found. He did not bring back as much as a single coconut. But our vision is small, dear reader, while my prince had a grander plan. Word of Baldeira's fortune spread like the pestilence in July, and soon, seafaring men all over the Christian, and even the Arab, world flocked to Sagres to serve Henry who had the luxury of choosing among the best of them.

In spurts and stops, other voyages followed, each one going further south but resulting with no profits and no word where the gold could be found. We knew that the Arab caravans brought nearly all the gold that was in circulation in Christian Europe from the interior of Guinea, but where was the source of it? The continent remained enigmatic. Henry determined that our ships simply had to sail farther south, around the caravans, until the source of the gold could be discovered. Only it was not so simple.

ي

The subsequent voyages began in the year of our Lord 1422. They were tentative and cautious explorations with ships full of wild-eyed men who still believed that monsters awaited them with toothsome mouths agape to rip their flesh and swallow them piecemeal. There were also nervous captains who quietly shared the crew's doubts. In my *Chronicle of Guinea* that is soon to be released, dear reader, you will find a list of these captains who dared but failed to round the dreaded Cape Bojador. Lessons had been learned, and Baldeira's advice was heeded so that these subsequent voyages brought along horses so as to explore the interior where suitable landing places were found. The captains were further instructed by my prince to erect crosses upon the shores where they landed, inscribed with the date and claiming the land for the *infante*. Also, Henry asked that natives be captured and brought back to Sagres for questioning, only there were no natives to be found.

With the horses, patrols of two or three mounted men invested into the interior but found nothing in the first six years. All they could see was desolate sand dunes with no signs of any civilization. It was as if even God had abandoned this land. But as the voyages inched farther south, our patrols began to encounter small camps of nomads who lived in tents and herded sheep, goats, and camels. With their horses and superior arms, our men were able to capture several individuals who were brought back to Sagres for interrogation.

These shepherds and goatherds were ignorant men, so the interrogations proved fruitless, as none of them had ever even seen a gold coin. Yet Henry was patient and treated the captives well; in fact, I suspect that these evil-smelling infidels lived better lives at Sagres than they ever had in their desolate land. They ate prodigiously, though they would not drink wine nor partake of pork, much like the Jews that live in our realm. One great benefit of this interchange was that a number of squires in Henry's household learned their foul, guttural language, most notably one man called João Fernandes who became so adept that the Moors were said to say that he spoke as well as they did. Fernandes was one of those rare individuals who have a facility with strange tongues.

With time and careful, patient interrogation of the captives brought back, we learned that the great desert extended many leagues beyond Cape Bojador. Moreover, as the education of some of our captives improved, we further learned that the desert was not as desolate as we had imagined but that there places where freshwater was available that the infidels called *wadis*. The more learned captives told us that, beyond the desert, at a river they called the Senegal, the land of the Negroes began and that it was lush and deadly. It was there that the gold came from.

Our voyages continued, albeit with those infamous nonlinear starts and sudden stops. The captains, straining for rewards, brought back what they could: more captives who confirmed the information we already possessed and exotic things such as huge eggs from a flightless bird that our Roman ancestors had called *astruce* that became our word "ostrich." Henry was eager to taste the egg, but the cook was unable to crack its extremely hard shell. A sword had to be brought into play, and just one egg produced a prodigious omelet that left Henry quite sated. He ordered that none of these beasts be killed, unlike the dodo bird that quickly succumbed to our sailors' hunger for fresh meat. He did not want any more extinctions on his conscience.

The captives were returned home with the proviso that they tell their kinsmen of their good treatment by the Portuguese. There were a few that begged to remain, and so they were granted permission but nothing else in the way of favors. As our voyages continued, other exotic foods and animals were bought back. There were caramelized dates, the fruit of the palm, that were delicious to eat, as well as the soft center of the palm itself that we called heart of palm. Our captains also brought back small animals. There were wide-eyed monkeys that the ladies of the court soon fastened a fascination upon, so captains were handsomely remunerated for bringing these creatures from Guinea. Some intrepid soul managed to capture an ostrich that, it was found, could disembowel a man with a swift kick. My prince, in his majesty, tried to approach the animal after it had slain his servant with the surety of harquebusiers aimed at the creature. When it reared to kick, a volley was fired. The meat proved stringy and not at all tasty. In anger, Henry revoked his order regarding the ostriches. The ostrich was saved from extinction in that it was lucky enough not to be tasty as the dodos and, to my knowledge, survives to this day. There was this very nervous small dog that lived on carrion that was called by the natives a jackal and an ugly, evil-smelling, brute of a dog called a hyena that also was a disgusting carrion eater and could crack bones apart with their massive jaws to eat the marrow as no other creature on God's earth can, as far as I know It was a hideous creature with devilish eyes, but the prince was fascinated with its strength, if not with its elegance. He conjectured that, despite our captives telling us that the hyena was strictly a carrion eater, he believed such a powerful and motivated animal could also hunt. Most of us despised the animal and were not too sad when the cold dampness of Sagres did away with the ugly brute, as it began hacking in its cage and was found dead one misty morning.

Despite their constant failure to find gold, the returning captains were received with kind indulgence by my prince and often rewarded out of proportion to their accomplishments. Henry's largesse ensured a steady stream of volunteers and even attracted a trickle of financing from wealthy merchants eager to gain the prince's favor, thus partially relieving

Henry of bearing the full burden of funding all the voyages of discovery. Also, some of the goods brought back from the explorations were gaining in favor. The previously mentioned impish-looking monkeys were highly sought after by some of the less attractive noblemen since the contrast was thought to make them look comelier. In my opinion, it was the monkeys that outshone the ladies both in manners and appearance. Also popular were multicolored birds. This exotica fetched handsome prices and motivated investments in ships.

ي

In the year of our Lord 1433, our great king, Dom João I, was ill, and it was generally feared that he was dying, owing to his advanced age and profligate life. The churches of our small, poor kingdom filled with people who prayed for him, since he was the only king that any of them had ever known. The great Dom João I had repelled the Castilians and kept us free and, while he had not brought overwhelming prosperity to our lands, at least he maintained the peace that enabled us to at least pursue it.

At Sagres, we lived in another world, far removed from the anxiety that wracked the court in Lisbon. Yet enough unease filtered through to inspire one of our more intrepid squires, Gil Eanes, to vow to round Cape Bojador in honor of our dying king. Contributing some of the funding from his own pocket to expedite the voyage, Eanes set off in the benign month of May with an unseasoned crew of seventeen men and one page. Also aboard was the prince's ever-vigilant scribe, a member of the crew that had grown increasingly unpopular with the men, as he had no duties aboard, save for spying on them. Many of the scribes met with untimely accidents and were prone to falling overboard. Henry was forced to warn captains and crew that he would not tolerate any more of these accidents, making the men responsible for the safety of his scribe. Henry also had to increase the scribes' pay in order to induce these timid souls to go on the voyages. Within four months, Gil Eanes returned, crestfallen, but with his ship and crew intact. Eanes reported that he had indeed spotted the dreaded Cape Bojador. He described it as composed of red cliffs, and as the ship approached it, powerful currents swept his vessel out to sea.

As much as he tried tacking to approach the shore, the wind and current worked against him. What the current and wind had accomplished in a mere half a day took them a week to repair, necessitating much tacking. Nonetheless, he remained steadfast in his determination to catch sight of the coast and Cape Bojador again. The coast proved elusive and was still out of sight, though it was thought to be near, as the lookout could see birds circling in the far distance. It was then that the ship lurched to a standstill and all the men tumbled about the deck. Luckily, no one had fallen overboard, not even the scribe, but unluckily, the ship's keel was stuck fast in a sandbar. They had been close hauling at an approximate speed of eight knots, so the keel was firmly embedded, and everyone aboard dreaded the inevitable slow death once the water ran out, for it was too far to swim to shore, and the small rowboat and could only hold four men. Putting on a fifth passenger to ferry to shore would overload it. Moreover, the men would have to fight the current all the way. None on board volunteered to venture in the small boat. They sensed the cannibals salivating at their predicament.

As Gil Eanes related these events to my prince and his entourage of advisers, tears of frustration started to flow liberally down his weathered cheeks, yet I do not believe that anyone present thought of it as unmanly. His most optimistic hope at the time was that the tide would lift the ship off the sandbar, but this optimism proved futile, for they had indeed rammed the sandbar at high tide, so as dawn approached, the ship settled deeper into the grasping muck and the ship tilted to port. There was nothing left to do that day but wait for the next high tide and try to pole the ship astern and off the sandbar.

That evening, the men took turns at the poles, exhausting themselves but putting all their efforts into the endeavor until their hands all bled raw, but the ship would not budge. By sunup, the men's mouths were agape and their eyes sunken in despair as they lay haplessly about the deck. Eanes believed that the men were beginning to partially accept their own death; he could see it in their hallowed eyes and panting chests. Yet desperation can be a formidable force.

Eanes ordered the small rowboat overboard and attached hawsers from it to the stern of the ship. He manned the rowboat with the strongest rowers and ordered them to row out until the hawser line was taut and then standby.

Only four of the remaining men on board could swim, so Eanes volunteered them. Sheets were tied around their waists, and taking turns of two at the time, they dove under the ship to hack at the sand with spades and cutlasses while severely admonished to keep clear of the hull. Even the strongest of them could only remain below for just a minute, given all the energy and air they expended in trying to free the keel. After repeated tries, the men began to vomit the swallowed seawater upon the decks and had to wait longer and longer intervals to recover. When the divers reported that they believed they had made substantial progress in clearing away the sand, Eanes ordered all four of them again overboard and simultaneously ordered the men in the rowboat to pull on the oars for all they were worth, while the remaining crewmen were set at poling. The men in the water came up for air but courageously dove down again. The movement was imperceptible at first, but then everyone left on board could feel the ship budging off the sandbar until, with one great lunge, it floated free. An exhausted cheer wafted from the men while Eanes ordered the pole men to keep the up their pressure lest the ship slide back into the sandbar with the current.

With the ship free of the sandbar, Eanes proposed to continue southward, but his proposal was met with sullen faces. This was a secret part of communication that Eanes did not relate to Henry. I was, after all, a trusted man. The men obviously did not want to tempt providence, saying almost in unison that their running aground was a sign sent by God not to continue, for the legends of poison seas and huge serpents were true. At this point, Eanes asked the assembled men if they indeed wanted to return as poor as they had left, to which they all unanimously answered yes. Fearing outright rebellion and pity for the ordeal his men had underwent, Eanes turned northward and came home to report to the prince. Eanes related the rest to me; as far as the prince was concerned, the voyage was a huge success, for the vast sandbar had been carefully noted on Eanes's rudder.

The assembly of advisers grew quiet, allowing the prince to ponder the words of the squire. After all, it was Eanes's own funds that had financed the voyage, so it was his loss not to have rounded the Cape. The prince then said the Eanes had proposed to round Cape Bojador as a prayer for his beloved father, Dom João I, king of Portugal and the Al Gharb, or all the west. The king, he reported to Eanes, was dead. Long live the king, his brother, Dom Duarte. The prince proposed to re-provision the still-serviceable caravel and for Eanes to set out again. He said he was to use the same crew, and he was assigning him the same scribe who had miraculously not fallen overboard. This voyage was to be in honor of his father, whom God hosts in heaven. Eanes was to round Cape Bojador in praise of his departed father's soul and to honor God. It was an offer that Eanes could not dare refuse.

Eanes set sail on the same caravel with the same crew in the early spring of 1434 and returned six months later, having successfully rounded Cape Bojador. Beyond the Cape lay normalcy, more ocean with no monsters, no poisonous seas, nothing but the world as we knew it, though unexplored and unexploited. The news spread through Europe, and Henry's prestige was exalted. My prince appealed to the Pope for a bull, granting indulgences to anyone who crusaded in Africa, as Guinea was known to the Italians. Pope Eugenius IV granted the bull and further granted Henry a monopoly on any trade south of the Cape.

Meanwhile, Eanes had reported to the prince that he had used his previous experience as a guide. He had steered a course seven leagues out to sea as they approached Cape Bojador. Even with this precaution, Eanes ordered a continued sounding of depth. When a cove was seen, Eanes cautiously approached the shore. The coast was barren, save a few succulents, which Eanes brought back to the prince. He told him that he had named them St. Mary's roses. He said he sent two scouts on horseback into the interior, but they returned with nothing to report. Running short of freshwater, they returned with his meager cache but with the important information that there were no monsters beyond the Cape. The prince was pleased, as his name was now known throughout Christian Europe, and the Holy See had granted him a monopoly on trade. Eanes and his crew were rewarded, but not overly.

Henry had succeeded in dispelling myths of monsters. He had always despised superstitions and fervently believed that these myths were created to limit man's curiosity. He could now dole out rewards since Cape Bojador had been rounded, but he wanted tangible results. He wanted gold, ivory, and civet musk. He had proven that there were no monsters, and the forthcoming crews would have to earn their keep, as crippling superstition had been slain.

Gil Eanes, proving himself tenacious, returned to Guinea the very next year. This time, there were two caravels, one commanded by himself and the other captained by Afonso Gonçalves Baldaya, my prince's official cup bearer. Giving

Cape Bojador a wide berth, the small fleet proceeded forty leagues southward, finding a safe haven in a bay they named Bahia dos Ruivos, after a fish there in plentiful numbers. When a mounted scouting party went ashore, they found the rounded footprints of camels and ashes from campfires.

Going farther south, ever careful to take depth soundings, they again found another haven in the tranquil waters of a bay they named Porto de Galé. Here, when they went ashore, they found recently abandoned villages and decaying fish nets. It seemed the farther south they sailed, the less inhospitable the land. Eanes again sent out mounted scouts, and they soon returned with three bedraggled Moors in tow. The prisoners were treated well, as per my prince's instructions. Two of them were morose, for the Moor understands the concept of slavery, and sat upon their haunches in silent misery. The third proved talkative, and Eanes knew just enough Arabic to able to communicate with him on a rudimentary basis. This Moor told him that his name was Adahu and that he was a prince in command of a hundred men and owner of a dozen horses. While Baldaya was elated at the capture of possible ransom material, Eanes remained skeptical, as the ragged Adahu did not look like the prince he claimed to be. Moreover, his eating habits were as uncouth as his less royal companions.

Nonetheless, Adahu told Eanes and Baldaya that he was worth sixteen Negroes in ransom, while the other two could fetch as much as ten slaves. He proposed to go to his people and negotiate for the Portuguese, but Eanes was wary of this arrangement, fearing that Adahu was really a scamp and would disappear. A compromise was reached in which the two lower-ranking Moors were released to bear the offer of ransom. Within one day, Moorish tribesmen appeared with ten Negro slaves in tow, and both Eanes and Baldaya were delighted with the exchange.

Adahu now proposed that he go negotiate for his own

release, giving his word that he would bring back sixteen Negroes as payment. Although Eanes was still skeptical, he was more open to believing the affable Adahu and released him, even providing him with a valuable horse to expedite his errand. When the days accumulated into three, it became evident that Adahu had lied and had moreover stolen one of their horses. To worsen matters, Eanes believed that, rather than bringing the promised Negro slaves, Adahu may very well bring his tribesmen to attack them. With water running low and not knowing exactly where the nearest *wadi* was, they left.

The Negro slaves were treated well on the return voyage, so all ten survived and could be given as a present to the prince. Despite attempts at communicating with them, their language was incomprehensible. Upon meeting with my prince, he showed them gold, but they just stared at it as if they had never seen it before. Henry was a bit disappointed but hardly defeated. He donated the ten Negroes to the Church of São Vicente in Lagos, where they were to be converted to Christianity and served God.

س

I knew it. I knew it. Cape Bojador was a myth, a mere superstition created by mindless men. The world is as we see it, no monsters, save the one we wish to create to intimidate ourselves. We set our own limitations. Man himself is limitless in the visage of God, for He made us in His likeness. If Cape Bojador is a lie, what other lies did the ancients convey? We need irrefutable experience so that the truth comes to the fore. My dear God, I know that You have set me upon the earth for a purpose. There are worlds to be discovered, riches, beyond mild measure, and humans to be saved for God's holy bondage. You have chosen me as Your ally, may I be worthy. I know that You have imparted Your license to me, and I will render unto You a new world in Your glory and perhaps, in recompense, a small profit to me. Are we not allies? I have heard Your voice. I understand the torments You have sent to me as tests of my allegiance to You, dear God. I promise to spread Your word, Your will to this brave new world. You are my God, but let me decree myself the king of this ocean in Your honor. I will even convert the fish to Your worship.

Chapter Nine
The Mahgreb

Sagres turned out to be a place of extremes. During the uncomfortable warm months and the miserable damp, cold ones of the year, my body was never at ease, either goose-pimply frigid or unnecessarily hot and sweaty. I was spending more time there as Henry's scribe, as my presence was required to record the occurrences that Henry would later interpret for me for the *Chronicle on the Discovery and Conquest of Guinea*, which I had been assigned to write. By tacit agreement, only successes were to be recorded for posterity, and the chronicle was to be strictly linear.

Despite the discomfort of the quarters, I was actually happy to be there. Sagres was abuzz with activity, as more scholars and adventurers amassed there after the rounding of Cape Bojador, which proved to be only an imaginary barrier. The circumnavigation of the Cape confirmed many privately held theories and reinforced man's rationality over unobserved superstition and gave feeble man hope that he had at least a tenuous control over nature.

I had deservedly earned a reputation for discretion since the incident in my cell that went unreported to chaste Prince

Henry. As a consequence, many of the more gregarious visitors to Sagres sought me out to confide in me, and many of the confidences were of a nature that I would not have volunteered to be privy to, but so be it. I did enjoy the knowledge in others that I was not a complete toady to Henry. They knew what they told me would not reach the ears of the prince, and somehow that consoled me, to be considered someone who could be trusted.

Take any amalgam of humanity at random, and you are bound to find braggarts, sybarites, ascetics, cheats, heroes, truth, and falsehood. The sample of flesh and souls that gathered at Sagres was no different, save for lack of a single coward among them. Of course, I liked some, loathed others, and did not even notice a few of the nonentities. One particular man stood out for his wit and intelligence. I believe I have already mentioned the linguist, João Fernandes.

Until him, the only ones who had previously shown an interest in learning Arabic were priests who foolishly thought that they could convert the Arab to Christianity. After a number of them were murdered in most hideous ways, the priests stopped their proselytizing and put their linguistic talents toward more pragmatic use as *alfaqueques.*

João Fernandes's interest in Arabic was much more secular than those of the priests and conveniently coincided with Henry's interests. The Arab caravans brought gold and other riches from the interior of Guinea to the ports on the coast. Being the eternal pragmatist, Henry would much rather trade with the Moor than fight him, as the former practice was much easier to accomplish in attaining his multiple goals of amassing gold and using what it can buy to find a route to India and its riches. With gold, he could outfit the ships and impel the explorers to round Guinea and find passage to India.

João Fernandes cultivated every Arab that arrived at Sagres, making them feel welcome and comfortable. He did not allow any Christian to so much as cast a gloomy eye toward them and stood by his guests in every quarrel. In so doing, he gained their confidence and gratitude, but he wanted something much more precious: knowledge of their language and culture. Surprisingly, the Arabs did not have to be coaxed or cajoled but were only too glad to teach their language. They were flattered that an infidel wanted to learn the language of the Koran. João Fernandes spent hours each day, at first haltingly and then progressively smoother, in conversation with his varied teachers. It was a mystery to us all how he could reproduce those strange, guttural sounds. As he became more proficient, his mind began to incubate a plan.

Dear reader, up until we rounded Cape Bojador, we had been mere gnats swarming around an elephant but afraid to bite. Our scouts had thus far only penetrated a day's distance of a horse trot into the interior, too afraid to wander too far from the relative safety of our ships. My linguist friend first broached his inchoate plan to me to see what I thought of it.

"I propose to disguise myself as a Moor and go into the interior to explore and gather information. I have leaned much about their customs as well as their language. The Moors have an implacable code of hospitality, and any Muslim cannot be denied food, water, and shelter upon requesting them."

"But you're not a Moor."

"They won't know that. My Arabic is good, and besides, I come from the south and have dark features. With the right clothes and a little more sun on my face, I could pass for an Arab."

"You're crazy. They'll find you out, open your jaw, and pour molten lead down your throat like they did to the priests who wandered there to preach, that is, if you don't die of thirst first in that boundless desert."

"I'm going to propose my plan to Prince Henry," he said

with a conviction that left me speechless. João Fernandes did not give himself time for any inner debate but went directly to Henry the next day to propose that he be allowed to go into the belly of the beastly continent to collect information from the Moors, especially those who participated in the caravans that brought the gold to Tangier. He outlined a plan that was not a plan at all, but a mere hope of one. There was no certainty that he would encounter anyone in the interior nor any water, as our scouts had told of a vast desert beyond Cape Bojador; their description was of a forbidding land not fit even for snakes and lizards.

I was hoping that my prince would not allow my friend to throw his life away. I was counting on Henry's humanity to counter his curiosity of the interior of Guinea and his avarice for gold. In these expectations, I was thoroughly disappointed, for Henry readily agreed and even congratulated João Fernandes on his plan. As for myself, I could not discern any method, only a blind foray into hell on earth with nothing but the surety of a lingering death.

João Fernandes set out on the next available ship. He was put ashore some one-hundred-fifty-leagues south of Cape Bojador, where our scouts had seen the most evidence of habitation, and given a date of seven months hence when he would be picked up at the same place. No one aboard that ship ever expected to see him alive again, but to everyone's surprise, he was waiting there at the appointed time and place. At first, our sailors did not recognize him, as his skin was as dark as a Moor's and he wore a filthy stripped *haik* and fetid *kaffiyeh* on his head. After much celebration aboard ship, he was brought directly to Sagres to report his findings to my prince who greeted him with great ceremony. His report was lengthy. I was assigned as scribe. I still have the original with me here; I will read it to you.

ي

First, my prince, there were conversations I had with the Moors that might offend you. Should you wish me to abridge my report, please say so, otherwise I will endeavor to recreate every word I heard.

I thank Your Majesty for your wise tolerance.

I was put ashore some one-hundred-fifty-leagues south of Cape Bojador, where we already knew the ship could approach the coast without risk of running aground on a sandbar or being torn apart by submerged rocks or reefs. As I embraced my companions in farewell, I could feel their anguished grip of their arms around my ribs, as much as saying goodbye forever rather than merely farewell.

In our previous landings on this particular coast, we had found signs of life: footprints, fishing nets, and the ashes of campfires. There appeared to be an apparent path into the interior, beaten hard by feet and hooves, so trusting my soul to God, I set off along it. The landscape about me was harsh, but not desolate. There were small copses of gnarled acacia trees as well as flowering bushes, including St. Mary's roses. Birds were plentiful, including familiar ones like sparrows and doves as well as others that I had never seen before. One bird particularly fascinated me, as it walked about the plain on stilted legs and had a feather sticking out of its head, just as our scribes do when they put their quills behind their ears. It looked about like a heron and was obviously hunting, and then I saw it pick up a snake with its beak. The snake bit furiously and repeatedly at the bird's leathery legs, but to no avail. The bird then shook its prey violently and beat it against some rocks until it was dead then swallowed it down in one obscene gulp, head first. The presence of the sparrows and doves was comforting since it meant that there must be water nearby. There was a hawk ominously circling the azure sky, which accounted for the doves remaining within the protection of the thorny acacias.

While the birds were a good omen, swarms of hideous

black flies plagued me and tried to land on every part of my exposed body. I now realized why the Moors wear the *kaffiyeh*, as it covers most of the face, keeping the flies and sand from your mouth and ears. Nonetheless, the flies swarmed around me, landing furiously on my naked eyeballs. I cursed them, but it was useless, so I plodded on down the worn path, feeling it with my feet as my eyes were slit to the bare minimum in order to avoid the pernicious flies and flying grits of sand that could injure my eyes, given the velocity the wind carried them.

That night, I camped in a dry riverbed, digging deep to find muddy water as my Moorish tutors had taught me. Despite straining the water repeatedly through my *haik*, it still tasted more like mud than anything else, but I was glad to have it. The night was starlit such as I have never seen before; nonetheless, I built a large fire as I had been advised. The night was as cold as the day was hot. All around the perimeter of the light from the fire, I discerned the yellow, glassy reflections of the malevolent eyes of hyenas and the smaller slits of jackals. That first night, I slept fitfully and frequently started awake, afraid lest the fire die and the hyenas come to tear me apart with their huge jaws while gluttonously howling their hellish laugh. I will admit to you, my prince, I was particularly afraid of these ugly beasts, and I think I would rather die quickly in the jaws of a noble lion than be torn apart by frenzied, cowardly hyenas.

For the next three days, I followed the visible path, but I was increasingly preoccupied, feeling I had made a mistake at the choice of a landing place and was merely on the road to perdition. At night, surrounded by all those yellow, glass-eyed reflections, weaving and bobbing menacingly, I will confess to Your Majesty that I had begun to despair of my venture and started cursing my bravado for undertaking such an obviously suicidal mission. If the hyenas got to me, not even my bones would survive to serve as remnants that I had ever existed.

But that night, the ugly brutes did not enter my dreams, thankfully. In my continued fitful sleep, I dreamt that some day an infidel would come upon my bones, picked clean by scavengers and bleached white by the unblinking, merciless sun. In such a state, my mind regressed to near dementia, as I began to have conversations with my mother and father, long since dead, and to argue with my brother on the reasons for volunteering to go into the interior of Guinea. In these dreams, my brother was winning the argument. In this arid, monotone place, the regression turned geometric, and I feared that I would lose my mind. But my dogged tenacity and sense of pride prodded me on deeper into the hinterland. If I were to die, I refused to accept it passively.

As I trudged on, my toes began to scrape the coarser sand and the landscape became less bleak. To a European eye, it may have been still, featureless desert, but having experienced true bareness, the landscape actually started to look lush by comparison. The acacia groves were thicker, and the tough grasses grew in large clumps, though the black swarms of flies continued to be a horrid nuisance. Toward the apogee of the sun on the fourth day, I discerned a patch of thick greenery off in the distance. Hoping I had not descended into total dementia, I began to trot toward what I hoped was a *wadi*, like a disillusioned hermit who wants to be around life again.

Since I was downwind from the *wadi*, I smelled the smoke before I could actually see the fire. It was evidence that there were people there. I slowed to a cautious stalk, fearful that they would most likely treat me as enemy. The Moors I had encountered up to this moment were our prisoners or guests and therefore at our mercy, but these were free men, free to do me harm. My trump cards consisted of speaking Arabic and an understanding of their customs, the primordial of which was hospitality, which was a basic, given the inhospitality of their habitat.

I first came upon two women bearing large clay jars of water upon their heads and covered in the black *chador* with their faces hidden behind their *yashmaks*. As soon as they saw me, their eyes bulged white like a peeled, hard-boiled egg, and they ran crying out, "*ferengie*," foreigner. I was quickly encircled by five men wielding scimitars with the assuredness of practice, each of them looking at me through hostile slits of their eyes.

I raised my right hand and uttered the mantra I had been taught: "*As-salaam aleikum*," peace be with you."

They immediately sheathed their swords, their once tense shoulders visibly relaxing. With the protocol established, they all repeated the mandatory reply in unison: and unto you, peace. The iron rules of hospitality were automatically enforced. My heart continued to pound hard against my chest despite the sheathed swords, and it took me a while before I recovered from the shock of a close encounter with a violent death. I looked about the lushness of this particular *wadi*, resplendent with a thick groove of palm trees and tall grasses and said, "*Allah karim*," God is generous. Again, they visibly relaxed, and four of the men touched their foreheads and withdrew, leaving me with what I assumed to be their leader who intoned, "*Allah ma'ama*," God is indeed with us. I was invited to sit on the single rug they owned in front of the leader's tent and offered some *chay*, or tea, a word close to our own *chá*.

The leader of this motley clan called himself Ismail ibn Abrahim and revealed his advanced age as he stiffly lowered himself down on the rug spread just outside his tent. I could sense that he was curious about what a lone man was doing in the middle of the Mahgreb, for that is how he referred to the desert around us, but courtesy kept him from asking what was on his mind. First, we had to drink the sugary tea and praise God in sundry and poetic ways, and only then could he get down to the business of conversation. I introduced myself as

Ibrahim Abdel, a name of one of our captives who had helped me learn Arabic. I said I was on a *hadj*, a pilgrimage. Ismail's eyes narrowed in suspicion, and it was evident that he did not believe me, but it would have been rude to insult his guest by calling him a liar. I could see him stare at my garb, wanting to know which tribe I belonged to, for my Arabic was a medley of pronunciations, depending on the teacher I had at the time. To compound his suspicion, my clothes were a mixture of tribes. The restraint of the iron rule of courtesy was only thing that kept him from asking questions that were sure to reveal my true identity. To alleviate his suspicion, I told him a story I had prepared for such an occasion. I explained that I had been set upon by thieves who stole my camel and left me almost naked. Some kind shepherds came to my rescue and clothed me in a diverse array, for which I was thankful, as God is great. I concluded by praising God's mercy while hoping that my host would not ask me to which tribe I belonged, for I was unsure of the answer I would give. Luckily, Ismail appeared satisfied with my proffered explanation and did not probe further, saying only that God is merciful.

With a sweeping wave of his arm, Ismail said that his clan was *Tuareg* of the *Imazighen* and that he personally owned over fifty sheep, numerous lambs, eight goats, and four camels. I complimented him by saying that God is generous, to which he quickly agreed. After more formalized conversation, he become frustrated with my evasiveness but nonetheless offered me a tent where I could spend the night. It was time for the *salat il'asr*, the prayer before sunset, and I joined them as instructed by my various tutors.

The next morning, I again went through the lengthy, formalized greetings. After the greeting came the tea and then time for conversation. I asked my host if he knew where the caravans passed from the land of the Negroes. He asked me why I wanted to know, and I answered that I was seeking protection by joining one since a man alone is vulnerable. He said he did not but that his cousin over on the next *wadi* to the east was likely to since he occasionally traded with the caravans. He said he could not take me there since he was currently feuding with his cousin and feared that he might be killed on sight by him.

I then asked if I could purchase a camel, whereupon all the men of the clan were summoned to share in the negotiating. I had brought some adulterated silver coins and as much salt as I was able to carry, for my tutors had told me that salt was more highly valued than silver. The negotiations were prolonged, and there was much shouting back and forth, and my patience was taxed several times, but I persevered until, finally, one of the men agreed to sell me one of his aged animals and a two-horned wooden saddle for two sacks of salt, which was half of what I had. I suspect that if they knew exactly how much salt I had, the price would have been higher. The coins were disparaged, as they did not prize silver, but only valued gold.

During my stay at Ceuta, I had learned to ride these filthy beasts. You must hook your right leg around the front horn and tuck it under your left leg. It is painful but preferable to walking in the desert. Like all camels I have encountered, this one was contumacious and tried several times to bite me with its ugly, yellow, bowed teeth. Whenever it could not bite me, and I was foolish enough to be in range, it would eject a horrid spittle from its fetid, old mouth that oozed off me like mucous. Despite these beasts' foul temperament and evil odor, I have come to respect their usefulness as modes of transportation in the desert. Camels possess wide-splayed, double-toed hooves that distribute its weight evenly on the soft sand, unlike the nobler-looking horse whose hooves sink into the sand up to its fetlocks, requiring extra effort for the animal to move. Also, the camel can store enormous quantities of water in its cavernous stomach and sweats much less than a horse. For all their ungainliness, these beasts are indispensable to the Arabs in the Mahgreb.

Following an obvious trail, I rode to the east, where I indeed found a *wadi* just where Ismail told me it was. Riding a camel, I looked less suspicious and hailed the encampment from afar so as not to cause the same panic. I introduced myself to Ismail's cousin, Assam, and we went through the same litany of praising Allah and tea. Assam then asked if I had purchased the camel from his cousin, to which I responded in the affirmative. At this, he was interested in knowing how much I had paid for it, and out of courtesy, I felt compelled to answer. "He cheated you," he said derisively. "My cousin, that eater of dogs, expects profit from every sale, even to his own kin." I said nothing to this and let him vent his bile. I liked Assam from the beginning; he was a more open individual and much less suspicious than his cousin, so I stayed with his clan for two weeks, paying for my food and lodging with some of the salt and helping with the herding of the sheep and goats. Assam showed me his large herd of sheep with pride, saying that he was much wealthier than his dog-eating cousin. God is generous, I said to his satisfaction.

In addition to his openness, Assam was lax about his religious rites and prayed only in the morning and evening but dispensed with the mandatory five prayers per day. He claimed that God would understand the necessities of poor shepherds and to live in piety is enough to please Him. I hope Your Majesty does not take offense when I say that I am usually more comfortable with people who take their religion in moderation. In this, the Arab is much like us. A man who is not a slave to dogma is easier to deal with. Again, I beg Your Majesty's indulgence, but I am referring specifically to the Arabs I met.

One evening, I asked Assam where their king was, and he looked at me strangely.

"King? We have no king but God. The *Imazighen* are free

men, and each one is a king within his own tent. What is a king but a grand thief? Take ten generations of successful thieves, and you have a dynasty. Then they begin to make up rules of property so that other thieves will not take away what they have stolen. This is very common in the lands of the infidels, where their church helps and abets with its rituals and crownings. But it is a farce. Their kings are just organized thieves who pay others to defend their pelf.

"We of the Mahgreb are independent, self-sustained men. It is me against my brother, me and my brother against my cousin, and me, my brother, and my cousin against the world. We need no king, only the grace of God."

I found this defiance and individualism admirable in a way, begging Your Majesty's pardon, but hardly practical where alliances of men under a common cause and banner is necessary for civilization. I fear the *Imazighen* will never accomplish great deeds but will remain shepherds and goatherds. I again apologize, but I am only relating his words so that Your Majesty can further appreciate how the Moor thinks. It is important to know your enemies.

Assam told me where the caravan routes were: farther to the east, perhaps fifty leagues with a respite at Fez before traveling on to Tangier and then the coast. I asked what goods the caravans brought from the land of the Negroes, and for the first time, I saw his face cloud with suspicion, uncommon to him, and he claimed not to know. I did not want to press the issue and so thanked him and praised Allah in profusion and went on my way. We bid each other an emotional farewell, and Assam claimed that I was a good man but from a strange-thinking tribe. I said nothing to counter his opinion, and we parted on good terms.

After these weeks spent with them, I began to piece together a general concept of these people. The Arabs to the east called them *El Barbar*, while the pagan Greeks knew them as Libyans and our Roman ancestors named them

Moors, where we get our term for them. There are many tribes besides the *Tuareg*, including the *Riffis*, *Chenwas*, *Mozabites*, and *Chleuhs*. They are at continuous but restrained war with each other, and personal feuds can last generations, even past the memory of the initial insult. Tribes tend to fight over grazing land, with *wadis* a central point of contention. Water is highly prized and jealously guarded. Many blood feuds have originated over a dispute over a well. If a member of another tribe is caught drinking from the well, it means instant death. There is no court to appeal to, and there is no mercy neither asked for nor offered. Life is harsh in the Mahgreb, and it takes harsh men to survive in it.

The women are unapproachable, and any communication with them has to be made through the auspices of a close male relative. Their marriages are arranged without their consent, much like our own nobility; however, unlike our female nobles, these women lead such harsh lives that I could not tell the difference between the calloused hands of a chieftain's wife and her maid, while their faces remained hidden behind their *yashmaks*. It was dangerous to stare at them, as a male relative would take offense, and it would be his duty to slay you to preserve the honor of his family.

In the fifth month of my peregrinations, I wandered into the magnificent camp of Beni ibn Hamid who I had been told by Assam had served as a *sheikh al kara*, a leader of caravans, in his earlier years. Assam had said that Beni ibn Hamid was his uncle, with overt pride, and I began to suspect that everyone in the Mahgreb was somehow related to each other. Hamid was one of those handsome old men with a snow white beard and a beguiling smile, with an evident appetite for the pleasures of this mortal life and blessed with resources to be able to pursue them. The sugary tea he had consumed all his life had corroded his teeth to yellowed stubs, which seemed to be his only woe. He possessed crystalline eyes that projected an erudition accumulated over the years and an avid curiosity that was matched by his appetite; he was especially fond of lamb with lentils. His curiosity and knowledge reminded me of Your Majesty, if I may be so bold. He owned fifteen beautiful books bound in lambskin that were his prize possessions and that he esteemed over his three young but illiterate wives. He too, like Assam, took his Islamic belief in moderation, praying just twice a day, yet he was a paradigm of hospitality, as his religion and culture required.

Hamid was no simple shepherd, but a scholar, and he immediately saw through my guise. As Your Majesty knows, I am from the southern part of our kingdom, where our hair and eyes tend to be darker than the north. The months I had spent in the Mahgreb had further darkened my complexion to a tawny hue, but Hamid was an astute man and, because of his education, a tolerant one, luckily for me.

He leveled an intelligent gaze at me and smiled as he offered me a second cup of tea.

When I hesitated out of fear, he whispered, "*tfaddal*," please, with a conspiratorial tone. I thanked him and accepted the proffered cup; to reject would be against the rules of a proper guest.

"You speak the language of the Koran well for a *kafir*; please do not take the word 'infidel' as an insult, but that is what we call all unbelievers. I take it you are a Christian," he stated without menace but sure of his words.

To deny his truth would be an insult to his obvious intelligence, so I trusted his benevolence. My lungs deflated in resignation, and I felt that I was plunging down into the sea but managed to whisper, "*Mashallah*," what God has willed. Hamid smiled kindly and asked if I was from the Spains. I answered truthfully that I was Portuguese and that we had gained our independence from the Castilians in a great battle and were, like the *Imazighen*, free men.

"You are not like us at all but slaves to your king and

princes. You think these so-called royals are greater men than you, but they are not. They eat, fart, shit, sleep, and die just like you and me. I have heard that your great king, Dom João I, has died, and I honor him. He had the courage to take Ceuta from the sultan of Fez. Your new king, his eldest son, Dom Duarte, is weak. Unlike our majestic Arab horses, it seems humans are unable to pass on nobility from generation to generation. That is why it is better to have no kings at all."

Begging Your Majesty's pardon, I am only recounting his words. I could tell where his nephew, Assam, had gotten his opinion of kings.

I then asked him whether he planned to reveal who I really was, to which he laughed heartily.

"I have few intelligent men with whom to converse. I want you, my smart *ferengie*, to tell me the absolute truth: why are you here?"

Faced with astuteness, the best thing is to tell the truth, or at least a partial version of the truth. I told him that I served my prince who wished to explore the interior of Guinea as well as go southward into the land of the Negroes. I told that it was curiosity that impelled us, the zeal for discovering new worlds.

Again, he smiled that tolerant smile of his.

"Yes, I have heard of your prince, an admirable scholar in his own right. Some of our Arab cartographers are his guests, I am told. But truly, you only seek knowledge, not the gold that comes up from the land of the Negroes in our caravans?"

I said that our kingdom was impoverished after the war with Castile, and if we were to maintain our independence, it would take money to provision an army and buy cannons from Saxony that had the iron and the coal to make them while we did not.

"You do not lie, yet you do not tell the entire truth. I believe that your prince is truly a curious man and partly driven by a hunger to know. I also suspect that he is an ambitious man, and I have heard that he covets the viceroyalty of Morocco. Perhaps that would not be a bad thing since the sultan of Fez is an idiot and a pederast, but there are other motives for wanting gold other than to defend your homeland. There is pure avarice, something I do not understand. You see, I am a wealthy man by our humble standards. Why would I want more? You can only live in one palace, eat one meal, and be with one wife at a time."

I answered that his insights were profound but that I myself was driven mainly by curiosity.

"This I believe, João Fernandes. Do you know your own history? It may be a sign of what your destiny will be. In the year 711 of your Christian calendar, we *Al Babars*, whom you call Moors, came to be united under a great leader, Tariq ibn Ziyad. He was not a hereditary leader in your sense, but a man who had gained the respect of the our various mutinous tribes, which was a feat in itself. The great Tariq, may his soul wander paradise, amassed a great army at Tangier and from there set sail to Iberia, which was then a patchwork of petty Christian tyrants, each constantly at war with each other as we unfortunately are now.

"The voyage must have been dreadful for our men, for we Arabs are people of the desert and are not natural sailors, unlike you Portuguese that live upon the ocean. God was kind, and the crossing went without major mishap. Within two years, our armies had swept the petty tyrants aside, as if they were dead flies upon a table. From this patchwork arose the Moorish kingdoms of Toledo, Malaga, Badajoz, and Granada, the latter of which still stands, though I fear not for much longer.

"At that moment, Islam had reached its farthest boundaries as well as the height of its culture. You Christians have purposely neglected to document the history of our benevolent rule. There were no forced conversions. Your religion was not outlawed. Muslim, Christian, and even Jew lived side by side, perhaps not in complete harmony, but in peace nonetheless.

"We introduced irrigation into your arid peninsula and brought and planted orange trees that we imported from Cathay. Look to your words, Christian; everything from your word for lettuce, *alface*, to tax collector, *almoxarife* comes from Arabic. Listen to your music, Christian; I have heard it and find the same mournful lilts in your *fado* and the war cadences of the Tuareq in the flamenco. Finally, look at yourself; why did you think you could pass for an Arab among our shepherds if your blood was not intermixed with mine? I, Beni ibn Hamid, have read of our greatness and have often wept, for we as a people have fallen from a great precipice. I am speaking not of the mere loss of Toledo or Malaga, but of the loss of tolerance. Our scholars and leaders now take the Koran more literally than spiritually and have become more like your fervid Christian proselytizers who believe you can convert souls with a sword. People behave like nails: the harder you hit them on the head, the deeper ingrained their own beliefs become.

"Your prince strikes me as a pragmatic man who uses his religion when it suits him. He says he wants to convert the Negroes from paganism, but he really wants to enslave them. We Arabs enslave Negroes, but at least we are not hypocrites. We do not try to convert them; we sell them to enrich ourselves. Your prince even trades with his professed enemies if it suits him; I know he trades with us."

I remonstrated that I knew of no such case and that it was the Moors who had stopped trading with us after the fall of Ceuta.

"Please, João Fernandes, you are my guest, and by customs of hospitality, it would be an insult to contradict you, but it is well-known that your prince's squire, Leonel Gil, trades frequently with our northern tribes, even trading cannons for gold in Tangier and Fez. For this duplicity and silence, Gil has been appointed *almoxarife* of Lagos. Your prince has also established trading houses in our port of Massa, where he exchanges Negro slaves captured by some of your captains for wheat from our Sous plains. Yes, as you said, you are a poor kingdom. This poverty has made your prince a master of casuistry, quickly abandoning professed ideals when these ideals interfere with his goals. Do not look so alarmed, João Fernandes, I do admire him, for he is the future, as he is intrinsically Godless, no matter how saintly he behaves. It is the Godless that will inherit this earth, while the believers must wait for paradise."

At this point, my host became silent and pensive, but I felt it would be a discourtesy to interrupt his revelry. I sat and waited until the silence became deafening, so I took it upon myself to pour some tea into his cup.

"Thank you, my Christian friend."

I asked him if being a Christian and a friend were not a contradiction.

"No, João Fernandes. I see that you have taken the immense trouble to learn our very complicated language, thus you must be a friend of the Arabs in some way, though perhaps not Islam in particular."

I then asked why he thought his world was in decline, for the Ottomans were amassing to take Constantinople in the east while the Castilians were still unable to dislodge them from Granada.

"Ah, quite a question, but misguided. Military triumphs are ephemeral; they come and evaporate, like morning dew. Culture is more enduring. You see my precious books? Well, my collection is now a rarity in the Arab world, a world once replete with scholars. When we were lords of Iberia, every noble home either had books or aspired to own them and every man of note perforce had to be literate, while your

Christian princes were generally rude bullies with not a whit of intelligence. Now I see your libraries grow as ours wane, and each of our successive generations grows more ignorant while your posterity thrives. We invented the astrolabe, but is it you who actually use it. You Christians interpret your silly Bible as necessity demands, whereas our pedagogic imams take the Koran literally. We have lost our flexibility. The proof is that you sit here beside me, speaking Arabic, while I know no one of our young men who could speak your convoluted language.

"It is written that we Arabs are the sons of Ham, a son of Noah who himself was a descendent of the great prophet, Abraham, the father of all our peoples. We share so much, but man is a petty inventor of small differences, exploiting this narcissism to inspire hate. It is because, in truth, we are all little men, jealous of the few hectares God has judiciously put on earth to try our mettle and that we try to possess in our brief lifetime. It is a sin inherent within all men to overreach, lest our stomachs go empty. And so we fight for these hectares, we Arabs disunited despite kinship, while you Christians rally under your prince's banners. It is a battle we must lose since clans cannot withstand mercenaries. To grow old is inevitable, and to become disillusioned is a pity. Ah, I am tired, and so I wish you *Masal el full*, an evening of fragrance."

The next morning, with tears in our eyes, Hamid and I bid farewell to each other. I pressed upon him the remainder of my salt, which he could not refuse per the rules of hospitality. I wished that he may wander in paradise, eating lamb and lentils. He wrote me a letter of recommendation to a relative who was permanently camped at a place called *Waden*, again to the east. Several times during my journey to Waden, I was tempted to throw the letter away since I could not read Arabic and was afraid of its content. For all I knew, Hamid could well have instructed his relative to murder me. I willfully allayed my fear and retained the letter, trusting in Hamid's erudite tolerance.

Waden was the first permanent looking place that I had yet encountered, with mud buildings that were mixed with some sort of mineral that rendered them pinkish when the sun was at a low angle. As I approached the town, I raised my right hand in the sign of peace. My new host read the letter of introduction with some overt difficulty. His name was Imsalah ibn Karah. He was anther of Hamid's nephews. He had the same dancing eyes and the same amused, crinkly smile that made you like him from the start. Though not as learned, his eyes looked like they could pierce armor. His full black beard was contrasted by dazzling white teeth, while his cheeks were set high up on his face, giving him an aristocratic mien.

When we sat down upon his richly textured carpets inside his home, I noticed that he was much more wealthy than his uncle, but there were no books in evidence. When our tea was served, it was unsweetened, which may have accounted for Imsalah's pearl white teeth. We dutifully went through all the preliminaries, praising God and sipping tea, when he fixed me with a level stare that stabbed me like a shoemaker's awl.

"My scholar uncle gave me my living as a leader of caravans, so I owe my fortune to him, and any friend of his is a kinsman of mine. He tells me plainly that you are a *kafir* but a friend as well and that I must trust my judgment as to what I should tell you."

I sat erect, hoping that my friends revelation would save me from having my throat cut. But he smiled that disarming smile and slapped my knee playfully and ordered more unsweetened tea.

"What does your country offer us in trade?" he asked with an unbecoming drool.

Nervously, I mentally went through our meager inventory: salt, textiles, horses, cork, and fish.

"Pah, what about guns?"

I stammered, for I felt as though I was swimming among crocodiles and had no authority to trade our precious imported cannons. I felt my life was at stake, as Imsalah, though affable, was unlike his uncle; he was only a businessman. If I could not serve him, he might be likely to kill me or simply send my out into the desert without my aged camel. I prayed he would simply kill me; it would have been much more merciful.

So I congealed my quivering intestines into a simulacrum of a hero's heart and said that, yes, guns might be made available, for gold. I hope Your Majesty forgives my audacious independence, but I needed some bargaining leverage.

"Gold! That is a truly rare commodity. We ourselves are hampered in its supply. It comes from the land of the Negroes, where we refrain to go. Some of them are cannibals, and it is said that the marshes swallow men. Our horses cannot survive, and even our camels die of disease. Whenever our men try to penetrate the jungle in *razzias*, or slave hunts, shit-stained arrows rain upon them, making their wounds gangrenous within minutes in the dense miasma. The Negroes are fearless, and we hear they worship trees and vultures and frequently eat the heart of their enemies.

"We have ceased the *razzias* but prefer to trade with tribes that bring us enemy slaves. The Negroes understand slavery, as they practice it themselves. You must get friendly with a fierce and warlike tribe and let them do the raiding for you. They are finicky, but salt is something they always esteem.

"We do trade some textiles with the powerful Wolof for a trickle of gold. The real riches come in the form of black gold, Fullah Negroes, which we sell in Fez. They are vigorous, and almost half of them survive the journey. Trust the Wolof; they are fierce hunters and trustworthy."

I then elected to tell him a truth, that our kingdom was

a virtual fount of salt. A great deal of the coast is low lying, allowing the tides of the ocean to bring in the sea where we trap it in square pools. The unblinking Lusitanian sun then does its magic and evaporates the water, leaving the sea salt behind. Sea salt is delectable and coarse. Salt we have aplenty. It is gold that we lack.

Imsalah nodded in reflection and called for more tea while I internally ached just for a sip of that pale red wine, almost a rosé, native to my dear, beloved Evora, home of an old Roman temple to the huntress Diana.

"Gold is not possible. It is difficult to obtain, even with our connections into the land of the Negroes. You may invest in their pestilent jungles if you wish, but as a friend of my uncle, I would dissuade you, as you will not come out alive. Your head may very well wind up in a crocodile's stomach, and hyenas will feast on your liver.

"But bring me your salt and your Saxon cannons, and I will trade black gold, Fullah Negroes. They make excellent slaves. The men are muscular, though short-lived, while the women are voluptuous, with large breasts and none of our Muslim nor your Christian women's inhibitions. They delight in rape and look at you with a smile as you thrust into them, unlike your own insipid Christian virgins who never seem to enjoy it, even with their husbands, so I am told."

At this point, the prince interrupts Fernandes's narrative and asks him about the caravans. There was a decided note of discomfort in Henry's voice, and Fernandes apologized for the rude words, saying that he was only repeating what Imsalah had said.

It is appropriate that Your Majesty should inquire about the caravans, for the very next day, a line of waddling camels came into Waden. In all honesty, I was disappointed at its paltry size, as I only counted thirty-six animals. Most of the camels were burdened with packs, so I could not see what goods they were transporting. One of the beasts was laden with six elephant tusks, which I am told are very valuable.

Another three camels bore chained Negroes, two to a camel. They were a sorry-looking lot, keeping their eyes on the ground so as to not show they were weeping.

As the caravan entered the town, the women began to ululate strangely. At first, because of its shrillness, I thought it was a cry of alarm, but then I gathered from the expressions on the men's faces that it was a sound of welcome. I could not understand how they were able to make such a strange noise since their mouths were hidden behind their *yashmaks*.

That evening, a feast was prepared, and some of the sheep and goats were slaughtered and roasted. Two of the men from the caravan brought a hallowed-out tree trunk filled with a pasty, revolting-looking stew that they called *gosh-gosh* and set the makeshift trough before the Negroes who then kneeled and ate like pigs. I know they are pagans, but my heart ached at the ill-treatment.

A large fire was lit, and the men of the village and the men from the caravan danced around it while singing songs in praise of Allah. It was festive and happy, save for the misery of the poor Negro slaves who lay chained in the shadows, unnoticed and uncared for by the celebrants.

The leader of the caravan was called Abdul Al Taraq and was a good friend of Imsalah. Abdul was a short man with a hoary mane of whiskers. The skin of his cheeks resembled leather from the constant exposure to the elements. I tried to engage him in conversation as to what kind of goods he was bringing from the south, but he proved evasive, answering me in the most general of terms. I dared not press him, for I could see that he was becoming suspicious of me.

The next morning, I was up early to watch the caravan depart, hoping to espy what was in the packs, but to no avail. One thing did strike me as strange; I counted thirty-five camels, one less than had arrived, but I assumed that one of the beasts must have gone lame and had to be left behind.

The time was soon approaching for my rendezvous with

our ship, and I felt as though I had discovered little of worth
by way of useful information. That evening, I sat outside my
hut in abandonment of mind and body. I was depressed with
my efforts and so let myself wander into the realm of idleness
of the mind, which is truly easy to achieve, especially in the
magnificence of the starlit desert. Suddenly, the shadows I had
been vacantly staring at seemed to move, and I aroused myself
into a state of full alert. Peering intently into the darkness, I
noticed the furtive movements of someone who must be in
pursuit of an evil act. I watched as the shadow approached
Imsalah's hut, and then I saw the glint of the blade reflected
from the starlit sky. Unsheathing my own blade, I approached
the shadow while sounding an alarm. It was one of the men
from the caravan, and as we stood face-to-face, he sneered at
me with such contempt that his look nearly unmanned me.

"*Quss ummakh*," he spat at me as he thrust his blade
toward my abdomen. This was a mistake on his part, for he
had over-committed himself, and I sidestepped his attack
while using the advantage of my longer reach to slash at his
face. I felt the blade make contact and heard the dull rasp
of the steel scraping bone. He screamed in pain as a bloody
gash appeared on his forehead. Bleeding profusely, he was
blinded.

At this point, the men emerged from their huts, each
armed with a gleaming knife. My antagonist was easily
disarmed by two men who held his arms behind him at such
an angle that, I judged, would cause great pain.

Imsalah emerged from his hut, and I explained to him
what had taken place. He ordered his would-be assailant
searched, which initially resulted in mundane findings, such
as some coins and some dried meat, but then pellets were
found on him that looked to me like rabbit droppings. This
caused great excitement among the gathered men.

"Ah, an assassin," said Imsalah. "I don't even have to ask

who sent you. Assal, go fetch your sword and cut the dog's head off."

Assal obeyed with an alacrity that led me to believe that he looked forward to the grisly task. The assassin was tied with his hands behind his back and made to kneel. Assal then brought his blade down with all his might, and with that single, well-delivered stroke, the assassin's head fell to the ground like a hollow coconut. Blood began to pulsate from his neck as his heart continued to beat. Then his flesh quivered and was still, with the blood now flowing evenly from his neck.

"I owe you a great debt of gratitude. Come into my hut."

We sat upon Imsalah's luxurious carpet while he ordered his woman to bring tea. I then asked him how he knew this man was a paid assassin. He opened the palm of his hand as revealed the pellets.

"You see this? It is called hashish. My learned uncle would tell you that the word 'assassin' literally means 'hashish smoker,' as it is used as a means of payment for murder. I know who sent him: the whore's son, Bassal, who claims that I cheated him when I served as a *sheikh al-kara*."

I asked what use was this hashish.

"Ah, Christian, it's delectable. It comes from the faraway land of the Afghans who grow a plant you call Cannabis. The sun is strong there and land fertile, and so the Cannabis oozes a sticky resin. The Afghans, who are all lazy dogs, then drive their long-haired sheep through the fields of Cannabis. The resin adheres to the tips of the wool, and they simply cut the ends, mix it with camel dung, and roll it into these pellets. When you smoke it, you are transported outside of reality. Your trifling worries are left behind. Let us light a pipe."

I watched as Imsalah shoved a pellet into a pipe and applied a burning faggot to the bowl while inhaling deeply and then held his breath. He then offered me the pipe, but I was loath to partake of it. Which one of us has not accidentally breathed in the smoke from a fireplace? It burns your throat and lungs, causing uncontrolled coughing spasms. But again, the rules of hospitality mandated that I accept. I imitated Imsalah and was surprised to find the smoke to taste sweet and mild. My lungs felt no discomfort. We took turns until the pellet was consumed. Imsalah, smiling broadly, wished me a fragrant night and retired.

I went back to my hut and sat looking at the stars, feeling that I had never seen anything more beautiful. There they were. I had looked upon them all my life, so how could I have ignored their fascinating beauty for so long? I do not know how long I sat there in wonderment, for time had ceased to exist as a frame of reference.

The next morning, I awoke clearheaded but famished. Luckily, there was still some mutton left from yesterday's feast, which I devoured like a man who has not eaten for a week. I then went to say good-bye to my host, for the time for the rendezvous was fast approaching.

"Ah, my Christian friend. I again thank you for saving my life. I should not tell you this, but the gold your prince seeks lies south of here, in a land we call Senegal. It is difficult for our caravans to penetrate the jungle that surrounds it, but your sailors may be able to reach it with relative ease. You must sail south until you come to a great river. The river is navigable, so you can go up it. I am told that the currents are not strong. After some leagues, you will come to a large village, and you can trade with the Negroes to receive gold for salt, which they prize."

I thanked him profusely, for I knew the value of the information he had just related to me as well as the internal difficulty he must have experienced in telling a secret to someone who might use it to hurt his people.

Emerging from Imsalah's hut, I found a young camel with my saddle on it.

"It is for you," Imsalah said. "That old beast you were

riding would never make it to the coast. Camels do not make a big fuss over dying; they just sit down and expire with no prior warning. This beast is young and strong and will get you to your destination. May God go with you."

With that, we embraced and kissed each other on the cheek, as is their custom. As I left, I must admit feeling a bit low-spirited, for I had come to like Imsalah. In fact, I had come to like the *Imazighen* as a people, though they did possess their faults. They were generous to the extreme but indeed quarrelsome. Yet they did not discriminate, as they were just as quarrelsome with each other as with foreigners. I have come to the end of my narrative and hope Your Majesty is pleased with my humble efforts.

س

I fear I have set upon a dangerous path. If I allow my people to get too close to the Moor, learn his customs, speak his language, the Moor will no longer appear like the menace I need him to be. I know it is a maxim that we must know our enemy, but will he remain an enemy with understanding? I need the Moor to remain despised, for the common foe provides the cohesiveness I need of my men. Without the threat from outside, our unity would disappear like the sea froth upon the sand. I cannot dare let the tolerance learned from proximity with the Arab infect my army for God's will. This João Fernandes no longer sees indistinguishable Moors but individuals with names and personalities. This is a dangerous attitude. But what am I to do? I need more information.

The courage of this man astounds me. Would I venture thus into the desert? I fear not. Yes, my Lord, I admit fear. I am often afraid, afraid of delving too deep inside myself, afraid of staring too intently into a mirror, afraid of the significance of my tortured dreams. Yes, dear Lord, I have read in the Bible that dreams have meaning. Would that I had a Joseph to interpret my dreams. Then, yet again, do I dare learn? Perhaps they are best left undeciphered, lest the interpretation send my soul to perdition. As João Fernandes would probably wish, it is better to let sleeping hyenas lie.

CHAPTER TEN
TANGIER

Often, the mood of an assembly, a court, or a large household is determined by the mien of its master. Sagres was no different. Henry's demeanor was manifest in the perfervid activity, tolerance for opposing opinions, and seriousness of the scholarship. It was uncanny how such an overtly religious man could impress a secularity on his household. In the discussions of geography and other sciences, class distinctions were blurred by the issues at large, as native intelligence and acute minds superseded rank. As Henry himself was a somber individual, the wags at Sagres had to curb their wit while the gourmands and worshippers of Bacchus had to constrain their appetites and thirsts. These sacrifices were generally made willingly in return for the privilege of being among stimulating company in a constant search for the light of truth as a candle dispels the superstitious shadows.

Then suddenly, one day, without any explanation or warning, the openness of atmosphere changed as Henry did. He become more secretive, meeting strangers behind closed doors, sending an unaccustomed pallor over Sagres that muted the once lively discussions and put an end to the more rambunctious arguments. It was as if a huge vat of cold water had been poured on a raging fire.

Unknown and unannounced visitors would sidle along the corridors, hugging the jagged walls as if they wished to disappear within them. It was impossible to keep track of these comings and goings. The scholars and adventurers of Sagres quietly speculated among themselves as to the significance of these activities, mostly in fearful anxiety, for it is human nature to expect the worst when the status quo is upset. The most hopeful and optimistic opined that Henry was simply planning another expedition to Guinea. This conjecture was rejected by the majority who rightly claimed that, if that were true, Henry would have consulted with them. No, the thinking went that Henry was up to something quite different from the exploration of Guinea coast, which was a just enterprise motivated for the extension of God's glory and private profit, those two motivations never having been mutually exclusive in anyone's mind.

As I have repeatedly stated before, dear reader, Henry's mind was in constant motion, much like the Atlantic that abuts our small nation. His brain was forever active, in constant turmoil and work. I often wondered how he could possibly sleep, given the pervertedness of his mind. This was not just another expedition down the coast of Guinea, but something more furtive and assuredly darker. Then, just as suddenly as the secretiveness began, the *sub-rosa* meetings stopped and Henry emerged from behind closed doors. He had removed one mask to don another; now he was all smiles and uncharacteristically affable. I and others were enlisted to plan feasts across our kingdom, inviting the high born and low born, wealth was the common denominator. Henry traveled the length of the kingdom, hosting lavish pageants, garnering the support of the nobility and impressing the easily impressed merchants who were only too willing to lend their financial support to the as yet unnamed endeavor. All he would say was that it was for the greater glory of Christ. Many just wanted to support any enterprise he favored in order to gain his favor. The merchants were lavish with their contributions since they had been enriched by Henry's influence. The nobles were not as generous, as they were not as rich, but contributed beyond their constrained means, for it would have been dangerous to displease the powerful brother of the king.

Our king was now Dom Duarte, Henry's older brother, who had assumed the throne in 1433 upon the death of the great Dom João I. Dom Duarte was named after his Plantangenant uncle, Edward of Lancaster, but unfortunately, namesakes do not inherit personalities. In outward appearance, Dom Duarte was like his brother: inordinately tall and with the same well-proportioned face but lighter in complexion and thin limbed. His favorite activity was reading, and he needed spectacles to do so in comfort, though the court physicians warned him continually that excessive reading was bad for his health. Unlike Henry, Dom Duarte suffered from a variety of ailments, the most prominent of which was dyspepsia. Thankfully, his mild disposition counteracted the ill humor that usually accompanies this ailment.

Dom Duarte was basically a good man, eager to do the right thing; in fact, the common opinion was that he was too good a man to sit on the throne, if you, dear reader, will pardon my irreverence. Ruthlessness is a good trait for a king to have. The ruler who puts himself above his subjects is likely to meet success, as he will cower potential enemies and silence criticism by second-guessing pesky nobles. Dom Duarte's deference to the members of the court invited petty squabbles, so the palace was in a constant state of inertial flux. While a king may listen to advice, he must be resolute at the time of making a decision. No matter what qualms the king suffers internally, once the decision is made, he must act as if he is of one mind and show no ambivalence. Dom João

I possessed this seeming resoluteness of mind, and people follow the kind of man who appears to be absolutely sure of himself, though I suspect that even the great Dom João I must have suffered from internal doubts. If he did, to his credit, he never showed it.

In contrast to his father and younger brother, Dom Duarte possessed a febrile character, bookish and anxious to please. He dreaded offending anyone, a fatal flaw in a leader. Most detrimental to his reign was the general opinion that the king was too differential to his Aragon-born wife, Leonora, whose loyalties were too closely tied to Castile for the people's comfort. Indeed, it was well-known that the king was caught in a vise between two powerful *éminences grises*: his wife and his younger brother. Dona Leonora's influence was attenuated by her unpopularity with the nobles and the people of our kingdom. As such, she was constantly attended by a retinue of Castilian bodyguards, as she rightly feared for her life.

Henry reigned in a parallel realm. My prince did not seek permission from his brother, nor did he go to court to explain exactly what he was planning. Leonora was said to frequently complain to her suffering husband that his younger brother believed himself to be above the vassalage he owed the king. It was whispered that Dom Duarte bore Henry's freedom of action because he feared his resolute and courageous brother more than he feared his impressively willed wife. It is a pathetic kingdom when its subjects pity their king. Dom Duarte's vacillations put us at risk, and many, including your loyal servant, longed for the days of Dom João I's firm hand. There were even careless whispers of replacing Dom Duarte with Dom Pedro or Henry himself. To their credit, neither brother ever gave the slightest encouragement to fan these flames.

Dom Duarte frequently convened the *Cortes* to get the advice of his noble-born counselors. In so doing, the king ruled by consensus, which meant that precious little was ever accomplished. Dona Leonora was another matter. Her will was steeled and dedicated to the preservation and augmentation of the legacy of her two sons: Afonso, the heir to the throne, and his younger sibling, Fernando.

As a foreigner, Dona Leonora was distrusted by the *Cortes*, especially as it was commonly known that Aragon was making overtures to Castile for the unison of the two powerful kingdoms. The nobles of the *Cortes* were of the opinion that Leonora's ultimate aim was to include Portugal in this new union, perhaps maneuvering for Afonso to be crowned king of this new superpower. This was unacceptable to the old nobles who had fought and shed tears of blood by Dom João I's side at Aljubarrota; it would be too dangerous for the Portuguese lamb to try to manipulate the Castilian wolf. These veterans and their mangled bodies served as the kingdom's conscience. These men possessed the moral authority to speak their mind, and their unanimous opinion was that Dom Duarte might have made a good school master, though he was a poor king, especially when contrasted with his father. Nonetheless, he was the king, and their main effort lay in keeping Leonora from wielding too much influence. And so the affairs of our kingdom limped along as a drunkard teetering along a ledge.

ي

Henry's money-raising activities did not go unnoticed by the court. Now, dear reader, you will forgive me if I resort to the prevailing gossip, but it was said that Dona Leonora demanded that her husband summon his brother to Lisbon that he may explain these activities to the king. Leonora might have rightly feared that the audacious Henry was planning a coup. Despite his natural inclination toward avoiding all confrontation, Dom Duarte sent a messenger to Sintra, where my prince was then entertaining the local dignitaries and wooing their support for the still-unspecified enterprise. Henry calmly read his brother's command, nodded a dismissal to the messenger, and proceeded with the festivities, taking an uncharacteristic sip of wine.

When Henry refused to comply with his order, Dom Duarte was befuddled. Dona Leonora was livid, and the gentlemen of the *Cortes* were mildly amused. To use the ugly vernacular circulating at the time, Henry was pissing on Lisbon from the prominence of Sagres. Since Henry was seen to be thwarting Leonora rather than disrespecting the king, a silent cheer could be discerned among the nobles. The people were more direct: "fuck that Spanish bitch and the boat she came in on" was commonly heard in the taverns of the capital.

Ever wishing to avoid trouble and to placate everyone, it was the king who set out to Sagres to go meet with his younger brother. It was a serious lapse in protocol but indicative of the strength of the king's and Henry's respective wills.

Now, dear reader, I will happily dispense with hearsay and gossip to return to eyewitness reporting, for I was present when Dom Duarte and his modest entourage arrived at Sagres. The king was greeted in a perfunctory manner by his younger brother, as if his visit was some sort of ill-timed inconvenience. Henry's deportment toward his sovereign bordered on that fine line between rudeness and fraternal intimacy. To Duarte's credit, he bore his brother's demeanor with the magnanimity of a gracious man, although with uncharacteristic frailty for a king. There is a fine line between compromise and cowardice. An unspectacular meal was quickly prepared, and a privileged few sat in the rotunda, with a great fire blazing against the cold mist of the sea. The sea was winning the argument.

Dom Duarte possessed no inner stratagems that I was aware of; he was rather a simple and direct man, so he asked his brother what he was up to.

"What have you heard, my lord," asked Henry, the infinitely more complicated man relative to his brother.

"Nothing more than you are traveling the realm, raising money and men. We can only assume that you mean to raise an army. As king, I demand to know for what purpose you intend to use this army."

"For the glory of God and to aggrandize our kingdom."

"That is an evasion, dear brother. Remember that I am king and that you would not dare answer our dear departed father in such a flippant manner. It is a gross disrespect to me and my throne for you to act without first consulting me."

"You are correct, my lord. I must stop myself from loving you too much as a brother and begin respecting the king. What I will tell you must remain among us here. I intend to take Tangier."

There was almost a visible pall in the room; the only sounds were the crash of the waves against the massif below and the impotent crack of the logs in the fireplace. I could see that Dom Duarte was trying to digest, with some difficulty, the import and consequences of this information. It was quite evident that the king was taken aback by his brother's audacity and disrespect of protocol.

"Why have you not consulted me first?"

"My lord, remember our father's secrecy in the preparation for the attack on Ceuta? Remember how he kept Europe guessing, lulling the infidel into complacency?"

"But he was the king."

"I do realize that, but I felt I should test the purses of our country before bothering you with the weight of the enterprise, for it might not have proven feasible, and I would have put this added worry on Your Majesty's head to no purpose. Remember, your health is not what it should be, and I would rather spare you any stress."

"Did you consult with the Pope on whether it is proper

to take from the Moor what has always belonged to the Moor?"

"Dear brother, the Pope will go along with any displacement of the Moor. I should think His Holiness would only be too happy to see Christianity's realm increase. Would it comfort you if I were to obtain a papal bull authorizing the attack?"

"Infinitely, but you should have discussed this with me before. My health is not as fragile as you think."

"But, Your Majesty, I am not asking a single *real branco* from the crown. In this way, if I fail, the failure will be completely my own, but should I succeed, as I have every reason to think I will, the conquest of Tangier will contribute to your glory."

Dumbfounded and at a loss for argument, Dom Duarte was evidently out of his rather circumscribed depth. He looked to his right, where Dona Leonora would have sat had she been present. Seeing his brother's perturbation, Henry promised to come to the court and give a full explanation of the plan once it had been fully funded and finalized. With the perfunctory mollification, we all retired to the chill of the night.

س

At an appointed time, Henry arrived in Lisbon, accompanied by a magnificent entourage of mounted men-at-arms, and rode to St. George castle, overlooking the city. Resplendent with royal woven robes, my prince strode into the small throne room and presented himself to his brother and king. Dona Leonora sat at his right, bristling with rage as evidenced by her pursed lips. To his left stood their bother, Pedro, and their half brother, Count Barcelos, now showing his age with a gray beard that was only intermittently sprinkled with the dark hairs that once had covered his intense visage.

My prince's apparent insouciance further irritated the

queen, which in turn discomforted the king. Dear reader, I seriously thought that my prince's behavior was not suited to the occasion. After the greetings, it was Count Barcelos who broke the silence, inveigling his younger half brother as to the wisdom of taking Tangier when the Moor was still upon our own peninsula in Grenada. He was adamantly of the opinion that an attack on Tangier would lead to disaster, as its garrison was better fortified than Ceuta had been.

"Tangier lies leagues inland, so there can be no surprise from the sea. Furthermore, you would deplete our kingdom of men at a time when we are surrounded by enemies," he said with a sidelong glance at Leonora. "Moreover, the Moor still occupies our soil with his unholy hold on Grenada. It is there that we should attack."

Henry replied without a trace of sarcasm in his voice that the esteemed count and half brother had also stated the same opinion on the attack on Ceuta. He reminded the count of his arguments, but in the end, it was Dom João I's plan and audacity that had won the day.

As far as the count's fixation on Grenada, my prince deftly reminded his half brother that, were we to undertake such an expedition without the prior approval of and alliance with the Castilians who had always laid claim to Grenada, it would be a provocation and an invitation to war. The count countered by saying that an alliance with the Castilians would most likely lead to at least a partial grant.

"The Castilians have always thought they can rid our peninsula of the Moors unaided. But even if they were to accept our help, they are dogs and piss drinkers. We would gain nothing but their contempt," said Henry, his voice still even.

Dona Leonora could no longer contain herself and jumped up, tight fists at her side and extremely red in her complexion.

"Dom Henry, you insult my family, and I will not have it.

You forget your place in this court and by your words show disrespect to your king and queen."

"My lady, with your marriage to my brother, you came to a new family and pledged new allegiances. All ties to Castile should be severed in your mind and heart. I am sorry if I offended you. Not all Castilians are piss drinkers; some are dung eaters."

The court exploded with uncontrolled laughter, forcing the queen to sit in defeated rage.

Now Prince Pedro calmly steeped into the fray, pointing out that, unlike Ceuta, Tangier had never been part of the Christian Visgoth kingdom of Mauretana Tingitana, and therefore, we did not have the right to usurp their territory simply because they were infidels.

It was a rarity to see my prince smile; his countenance always bore the severity of an austere elder of the Church. So when he now smiled, it was a bit of a shock to the assembly who wondered, I am sure, whether he had lost his mind. Gesturing to one of his minions, he produced what turned out to be a papal bull from Pope Calixtus III, authorizing the attack on Tangier provided the Portuguese were willing to join a joint Christian force to drive the infidel out of Constantinople. The prince now backed up his trump card with words.

"There is no philosophy or precedent that protects the infidel. It is our Christian duty to drive the Moor not only from traditional Christian lands, but off the edges of the earth, until there is one true religion."

These words and the unexpected papal bull quieted the assembly of men but not Leonora who had by now regained a modicum of composure.

"I agree with the king, my husband, and your brothers that this endeavor is ill-advised. With *our* kingdom stripped of a good portion of its fighting men, it would be an invitation for Castile to attack."

The irony of Leonora's warning, a constant pro-Castilian

voice in the court, was not lost on my prince, nor on Pedro and the Count.

"Would true Christians take advantage of other Christians while there are on a crusade?" asked Henry, this time his voice rising. "I propose to take Tangier for the greater glory of God. I intend to do so with His succor, and I name my nephew, Afonso, as my second in command. For his loyalty to my crusade, I intend to make Fernando my sole heir."

"Afonso is only six," gasped the queen.

"It is a symbolic appointment so that his house may share in the booty."

Again, my prince had produced a trump card. I could see the wheels of the queen's mind turning upon their pragmatic cogs. Her oldest son, Afonso, was the heir to the throne, but her youngest, and none-too-secret favorite, Fernando, had no assured livelihood, for he owned no lands. My prince was the lay governor of the Order of Christ, the inheritor of the fabulous fortune of the Knights Templar, reputed to be interred somewhere in the Order's monastery at Tomar. She was plainly willing to jump at the chance to bestow these riches upon her child. With this one grandiloquent gesture, he had appeased the she-wolf. She would of course support my prince, but not in public, as she could not be seen to reverse herself. Her counsel would come in the seclusion of the bedroom. Henry was shrewd to manipulate a mother's concern for her son.

The next day, Henry and his entourage were treated to a feast; there was suckling pig roasted to salivating glory on a spit, its skin appetizingly crisp; delicious warm bread, fresh from the oven; and magenta wine from some of our best vineyards. It was indeed a sign that we had gained favor at court, for Leonora was not known for her generosity.

I, now at my advanced age, will not lie to you, dear reader. After his announcement making Fernando my prince's sole heir, I was a bit concerned for my own welfare. Henry had repeatedly hinted to me that the loyal members of his household would be provided for in the event of his death. Did that mean that we were all to be disenfranchised now that he had made the child Fernando his sole heir? How could I approach my prince with such a self-interested question?

During the feast, the king and queen joined us. Dom Duarte announced that, after careful consideration and prayer, he was prepared to endorse his brother's crusade. Both Dom Pedro and the count of Barcelos remained adamant in their opinion and argued with the king that the project remained ill-advised. But now, armed with his wife's steel will, Dom Duarte remained steadfast in his support, and his brothers fell silent, their arguments exhausted.

"I have confidence in my brother's great endeavor and believe it to be for the greater glory of Christ, our Savior. I am confident of a victory, but I now wish to add a simple request and modest advice. Everyone knows of my brother's righteous Christian valor during the conquest of Ceuta. Some retractors have even referred to it as savagery. So I caution you, once the city is taken, to be lenient. Spare lives and be most merciful with the women and children. Let it not be said that we are part heathen ourselves.

Be sure to send scouts to reconnoiter the garrison, as I have heard it to be well defended. Do not try to assault the walls directly, but let the Saracen come to you and attack. When they come in range of our cannons and culverins, unleash Christian fury in all its righteousness."

The king's advice was met with a general respectful silence as he resumed his throne, his self-consciousness apparent. The meal continued with minimal conversation, as each person mused his own grievance while secreting personal ambitions.

As we departed, I noticed that Henry's complexion had darkened into a crimson shade. I recognized this look well and knew that he was enmeshed in the tentacles of rage, yet he refrained from giving vent to that black ire in public. On the long coach trip back to Sagres, I did hear him murmur a few words, of which "pompous ass" was repeated more than a few times, and I also heard him referring to an "ignorant dandy fart" who was trying to tell him his business. These words were clearly enunciated, albeit *sotto voce*.

When our train of horses reached Sagres, my prince's mood eased, and he began busying himself with the preparations for the endeavor. He bid me to remain at his side, as he intended for me to write the *Chronicles on the Conquest of Tangier*. Stammering and hemming and hawing, I asked whether I remained as a consideration in his legacy.

"Do not confuse politics with duty. It serves my interests to promote my nephew; that does not mean I will abandon my household," he answered, and I took heart.

س

The next few weeks evaporated in a whirlwind of activity as Henry hosted feasts to gain additional financial support. He was expert at coaxing the wealthy merchants with the prestige they gained from sitting at the same table with him. As usual, Henry remained abstemious, partaking of little food and no wine.

We were at Sintra, hosting such a feast, when a lone noblewoman walked unescorted to our table and greeted Henry. It was Dona Eulalia, brazen as ever. Nervous, deferential merchants quickly slid over to make room for this noblewoman who sat at Henry's right side.

"Madam, you have grown stouter since we last met."

Tactfulness with women was never one of my princes strong points.

"Thank you for noticing, my lord. They say it is a sign of health and a clear conscience. I do enjoy my food. I am not a dainty woman. My lord, I have heard that you are raising an army, but there are various rumors as to the use this army will be put to. Your half brother, Count Barcelos, is campaigning to use your army to take Grenada. As I have often said before, I think it ill-advised to attack and take Grenada. My cousin, the king of Castile, would never allow it, and I am certain it would mean renewed war."

"My brother can bluster and fume all he wants. It is *my* army, paid from *my* pocket, and I will decide what use to put it to."

"I am sure you will employ it to aggrandize God's majesty. Tangier would be a suitable target, as, besides serving God, it is the terminus for many caravans bringing gold from the interior. Remember my offer regarding the Genoese trader that serves my household. He frequently goes to Morocco and would not cause any suspicion."

"I thank you, madam, but I possess all the intelligence I need."

Dear reader, I was nonplussed, for indeed, I was unaware that Henry had already sent scouts to reconnoiter the city. Henry remained a mystery to me.

س

I was at my appointed place and time in Lisbon, attending upon the vast business of spending a fortune on the provisioning of an armada, one of many minions set in motion by Henry. Enrapt in my duties, I did not notice the approach of the soft, deferential footsteps of the youngest of the princes, Fernando. I looked up to encounter a distraught face, not yet hardened by the heartlessness of a man's, and eyes red from weeping.

"Is my bother Prince Henry about?" he asked plaintively.

Before I could answer, Henry, in all his majesty, strode into the room, his words entering before his form as he dictated instructions to a shuffling scribe who was doing his utmost to keep up with his master's gist. When Henry noticed his younger brother, he abruptly ceased dictating, and I noticed his resolute visage change into some semblance of warmth as an ever-so-faint smile alit upon the corners of his mouth. This youngest of the brothers had always been a favorite of his.

In my own personal opinion, which I am happy and free to share with you, my dear reader, Dom Fernando was perhaps the best of the issue from the commingling of the Houses of Aviz with the *Plantangenant*s. At sixteen, he was almost as tall as his brother but still retained the softer face of the child, still trusting and pathetically vulnerable to the slightest perceived hurt. It was no secret that he both admired and adored his older brooding brother who reciprocated his love as much as his austerity of character allowed. My prince's stern demeanor always softened perceptibly in the presence of his young brother.

"My lord brother, I have heard that you have appointed my cousin and namesake, Fernando, as your sole heir. So be it, but I am distraught that you have named my other cousin, Afonso, as your second in command. What have I done to have fallen in your esteem?"

Henry's face clouded in confusion as he sought to reconcile ambition with emotion. The cogs in his usually fluid mind jammed, as he was visibly taken aback.

"I want to go with you to Tangier," said this man-child, "even as a groom, should you ordain."

"Fernando, you are but, but, fourteen—"

"I am sixteen, much older than my cousin whom you have chose as second in command. You were not much older than me when my grandfather allowed you to come along to take Ceuta."

"No, it is too dangerous. I will not have it."

"Would my brother deny me the privilege of serving God and my king? It is time for me to earn my spurs. I beg you, please."

The boy prince choked at these last words in order to stifle another onslaught of weeping. Henry remained ashen and silent. Fernando was teetering on that cusp between the child and the man, not yet one nor emerged from another. It was plain that Henry was at a loss whether to comfort the child or rebuke the inchoate man. Unable to decide, Henry chose the easiest and most cowardly of paths.

"Very well. You may come along as my personal attendant and man-at-arms but only on the condition that you obey every command I give you without question. I will breach no arguments nor tolerate any favoritism based on family ties."

Fernando's face changed as if an alchemist's magic turned lead into gold, from utter despair to complete rapture. I have never since witnessed such a metamorphosis of emotion. He kissed his brother's hand with unearned thanks. He was a magnificent child.

س

With the coffers replete with donations from both generous and disgruntled, the money was paid out to some of the merchants and shipwrights that had donated it in the first place. Contracts were signed, and the percentage of the booty and future lucre from the enterprise was apportioned to the various shareholders. The provisioning of the ships and boarding was expeditious, as we as a nation had become adept at launching fleets on short notice. It was late in the hot, merciless month of August in the year of our Lord 1437 that our ships sailed from various ports in our small kingdom. We were instructed to rendezvous at Ceuta, just a half day's sail from Tangier to the east. The weather actually turned tolerable aboard ship, thanks to the ocean breezes laden with the misty nectar that flew off the white caps, which served to cool the stagnant August air. Despite the pleasant weather and the calm ocean, Henry remained uncomfortable with the sea and remained quite pale for the entire short voyage. He chose to stay in his cabin for the voyage, which had been provided with a private privy. When we arrived at Ceuta after a short three-day crossing from Lagos, young Prince Fernando was already there and eager to secure his own name in history. Assembling ashore, we were greeted by the old soldier and stalwart governor of Ceuta, Dom Pedro de Meneses. He leveled an eye at my prince and said that he had heard that the king had given him sage advice on the upcoming attack and that he hoped Henry would heed it, just as he had heeded the advice proffered him after taking Ceuta. My prince said nothing, but his face spoke volumes as it turned that peculiar crimson color that silently bespoke of curbed rage.

These ironic preliminaries finished, Dom Pedro de Meneses said that he had bad news. There were not enough ships to transport the proposed force of fifteen thousand men, so barely sixty-eight hundred men-at-arms, foot soldiers, and bowmen had landed with but a few horses.

"If Your Majesty's goal is Tangier, as I suspect, I must advise against it, as this present force is insufficient," said the old soldier with all the confidence of his nature and station. His years of service to the crown endowed him with a certain amount of veneration and the right to speak his mind.

That evening, Henry consulted with his commanders, including Dom Pedro de Meneses. My prince looked intently at the map spread before him.

"What if, instead of attacking Tangier, as most everyone expects by now, we sail to the Grand Canary and wrest it from the Castilians?" Henry proposed.

"Your Majesty has maneuvered well, keeping Europe in doubt of your ultimate target. Therefore, Juan of Castile has already sent reinforcements to the Canaries in the event your thrust against Tangier was merely a feint," informed Dom Pedro de Meneses.

Crimson faced, bared teeth biting lips, then the conscious imposition of control.

"Then we will have to make do with what we have. Governor Meneses, how many men can you spare from your garrison?"

"None. But I imagine Your Majesty will insist. I have fifteen hundred men. Take the majority of one thousand of the best, but I must warn Your Majesty that you will leave Ceuta dangerously undermanned in case of attack."

"We must take that chance."

"Then I beg to come along," said the old soldier.

"Your presence would be invaluable Dom Pedro," answered Henry graciously.

 س

Unlike Ceuta, the fortress of Tangier was not directly located on the coast, but a few leagues inland. Thus our men were forced to disembark and set up camp, making sure to erect a temporary stockade in case of a surprise attack from the enemy. There was no hope of complete surprise. Henry ordered preparation for the attack that he planned for the next day before the Saracen governor had a chance to send for reinforcements from nearby Fez. That evening, Dom Pedro de Meneses strongly advised my prince to leave a protected corridor to the beach in case we were forced to retreat back to our ships.

"That would sap the moral of our men," countered Henry. "It would serve as a signal that we expect defeat. There will be no corridor. The only direction we will go is forward. Besides, I cannot spare the men."

I could see that Dom Pedro wished to press his argument, but that would be an insult to the prince, so he kept his silence, though it was with some overt pain that he restrained himself, like a man holding back a huge amount of intestinal gas.

ﺵ

The next morning, we set out toward the city. We made a sparse perimeter, for we had not the men to properly constrict the walls and set up the cannon where we thought the walls to be weakest. To our undying chagrin, we found that the scaling ladders we had brought along were too short, so there was nothing to do but retreat back to the stockade in order to construct longer ladders. Dear reader, I am sure that I was not alone in wishing that my prince had accepted Dona Eulalia's offer to send her Genoese scout to reconnoiter the city, yet no one in the camp dared point it out.

At the time, we were unaware that the governor of Tangier was none other than Salah ben Salah, the defeated governor of Ceuta. He had gained some hard-learned lessons since that defeat, and as soon as our ships were spotted, he had immediately sent out an urgent request from the vizier of Fez, Laraque, who was known for his fervent hate of Christians. The vizier readily complied, and unbeknown to us, reinforcements were already on their way while we frittered our time building scaling ladders.

The next morning, we again invested against the city. Again, the lack of intelligence plagued our efforts, as the cannon we had brought proved to be too light to breach the massive walls. Meanwhile, our men suffered heavily from the rain of arrows that fell on them from above. Time and time again, our ladders were set up against the walls, and our brave men would rush up, only to have the ladders pushed off the wall at the last moment, injuring men and damaging weapons. The heat was almost as bad as the arrows, weakening our men, so they had to return to the stockade to drink, lest they faint from exhaustion and thirst. The air was so thick with humidity that it proved to be a chore to inhale. The attack was a failure, and Henry ordered a cease-fire and general retreat to the stockade.

That evening, Henry sat in counsel with his commanders. He was plainly in a foul mood, as he had fully expected another easy victory as had occurred at Ceuta. Perhaps Dom Pedro de Meneses could have told him that such victories are rare and take much more planning and thought than my prince had invested in this campaign. If Dom Pedro thought these words, he did not express them. One of the commanders— sorry, dear reader, I forget his name—suggested that we remove the heavy cannon from our ships and bring it to the city walls. The proposal was discussed in earnest but finally rejected on the grounds that it would take too long and that reinforcements from Fez were sure to arrive soon before we could muscle the cannons into position. Moreover, it would leave the ships defenseless against attack by Moorish corsairs. Though usually shy of engaging our ships, the corsairs could be made bold if they saw us removing the heavy cannon.

It was the prince's younger brother, Fernando, who proposed to mass our attack on a small section of the wall. In this way, our bowmen and our culverins could keep the heads of the defenders down while we massed our ladders. After only a token discussion, Dom Fernando's plan was accepted, much to the elation of the young prince and novice soldier.

The next day, the heat was as oppressive as ever. We all intrinsically knew that, if we were to succeed, it had to be done quickly, for the men would not be able to stand prolonged strenuous activity. Our men massed at the section of the wall deemed weakest, where multiple scaling ladders were set. Our bowmen and culverins kept up a steady fire of arrows and shot, so the defenders dare not raise their heads to push the ladders away. The walls were beginning to be breached as more of our men went over and began fighting on the parapets. Before we could raise a cheer, the reinforcements from Fez arrived and began attacking our rear. Screams of pain mounted, and in the midst of my terror, I was taken how culture defines the sounds we make as we die. The Saracen cries of death were unlike our own; they were high-pitched screams, a prolonged *yih*. Our men died with grunts of resignation, cursing their fate then quickly mumbling words of prayer. There was again nothing to do but retreat to the confines of our stockade. It was our forces that were now under siege.

ﺱ

Blessed rain fell on our withered faces and lips the next morning. Welcome though it was, we were under siege, surrounded and outnumbered. Dear reader, I must tell you that I was petrified, for I am not a trained soldier who has come to terms with death, since death is a soldier's business, but a scholar who expects to die in his bed surrounded by doleful-looking loved ones. I could only imagine my prince's consternation and utter humiliation at not having heeded Dom Pedro's advice to leave a defended corridor to our ships. To his credit, Dom Pedro said nothing.

Days accumulated into weeks, yet the Moors did not attack our stockade. Luckily, there was a well within our wooden walls, but soon food would start to run short. The Moors were surely aware that they had only to keep us in their vise and that, sooner or later, we would starve or be forced to surrender unconditionally. Salah ben Salah was having his revenge for the loss of Ceuta.

Then the weeks amassed into a whole month. In early September, our situation worsened, as additional Saracen reinforcements arrived under the command of Laraque himself. Our men, now defeated and afraid, began to slip away at night to the safety of the anchored ships, while some even walked back to Ceuta. Mass desertion would soon be inevitable.

Our commanders began to press Henry to ask for terms of surrender. My prince was above all a pragmatist, so sullenly he agreed to meet with Salah ben Salah. As he rode out of the stockade on his white Arabian, I could see his abject depression as he kept his eyes on the ground, up to the moment he came up to his Moorish counterpart.

We could see Salah ben Salah openly gloat in Henry's wounded pride. They spoke for a few minutes, and then Henry slowly walked his horse back to the stockade, again with his eyes planted on the ground. Even before he could dismount, his commanders crowded around him asking what terms were offered.

"They will allow us to return to our ships, provided we lay down our weapons, that I give my word that I will return Ceuta to them, and that we leave behind an important hostage to assure my compliance."

With this sullen deliverance of news, Henry retreated into his tent; discussion of the terms would have to wait until evening. We all milled around in front of my prince's tent, though no one spoke, wishing to keep his counsel and fear to himself. None of us, save for Henry, wanted to be physically alone.

That evening, our commanders somberly went single file into Henry's tent. No one spoke for some time, each afraid to break the silence, afraid to point out the obvious. It was Dom Pedro who dared to break the gloom, and I believe we were all thankful for his courage.

"We must not lay down our weapons. I propose that Your Majesty agree to the terms, but when we leave, we leave armed, for the infidel is treacherous, and I will not tolerate to be put at his mercy, of which he has none."

No one had the manhood to counter, so Dom Pedro de Meneses's words were agreed to tacitly.

The next morning, it continued raining mercifully, for the droplets disguised the tears that freely flowed from our eyes. Henry again rode out to meet with Salah ben Salah. Their conversation this time was much shorter than the first. When Henry returned, he announced that we would leave in two hours to the general muted cheer of the gathered men. The commanders were hurriedly summoned to his tent and waited for Henry to break the silence.

"I have agreed to leave behind my brother, Prince Dom Fernando, as hostage and guarantor of the terms that I have personally stated, namely, the return of Ceuta to the Moor."

There was much false protesting among some of the commanders, but it was just for show, and there was little choice. For his part, Prince Fernando said nothing; however, his countenance had turned deadly pale. So in evidence was Fernando's discomfort that Henry addressed him directly.

"Dom Fernando, you are to be taken to Asilah, the private residence of Salah ben Salah. He has assured me that it is a luxurious palace and that you are to be treated as befits your station. You may even take along your household to ensure your comfort."

My heart went out to the poor child, for he was little more than a boy. Despite the terror he assuredly suffered, Dom Fernando stood erect, though we all could see that his legs were shaking as if he were in the grips of a deep fever.

"I will do as my brother commands," the man-child said bravely, barely holding back his tears.

With that, he summoned the men of his household and walked toward the city. He did not turn back to wave, but walked on his wobbly knees with the resoluteness of his father, Dom João I. As he disappeared into the arms of the enemy, I remembered thinking that he perhaps was the best man of us all.

We assembled quickly, as there was no need to decamp. The Moors were nowhere in evidence, so we made a defensive formation and began to march toward the beach. We were a diminished but still formidable fighting force, and we marched briskly forward. Even our wounded marched with the swagger of the undefeated.

We could now see the masts of our ships. A crowd of

Moors had amassed at the beach, most of them smirking while a few gawked at the first Christians they had ever seen. Then a cry arose from them; they had noticed we were armed.

"*Quss ummakh*," they spat out disparagingly and closed in on us with lips curled in hate and unsheathing their scimitars. They were outraged at our blatant violation of the terms of surrender; however, we were fighting for our lives. Their outrage was no match for our desperation.

As if we were one man, we unsheathed our swords and fell on the heathen, quickly widening the corridor for our escape. There was no need to kill, as maiming was easier and served our purpose better, for the wounded man was carried off by two comrades, reducing the number of adversaries. Our men, overwhelmed with the pent-up frustration of five weeks of siege, struck out at limbs, tearing ligaments and breaking bones. The Moors were loath to advance on our determination to live, and we soon reached the beach.

To our collective dismay, we discerned the dust of cavalry on our left flank. It was Laraque, trying to cut off our escape. Some of our men despaired and dove into the surf, only to drown, weighed down by their cuirasses.

Thanks to God and some human forethought, our ships were double anchored, with their broadsides facing the beach. As the Moors came out onto the beach, our heavy cannon opened fire, sending red-hot balls of destruction that raked through the oncoming cavalry, causing eruptions of blood and sinew of both man and horse. The cannon maintained its deadly barrage, allowing us to retreat to the safety of our ships.

As we departed, with sails bulging, men lay about the decks in gleeful exhaustion. Many of them had loosened their bowels during the frightful fray, so there was a pervasive, acrid smell of shit. Others just lay there crying, incredulous that they were still alive. I myself vomited in a mixture of terror and relief. The smell of our pathetic human cargo would have turned a camel's stomach.

My prince ordered to be put off at Ceuta and disappeared into the bowels of the city. I knew enough not to follow. There would be no need of me for the time being, as there would be no *Chronicles of the Conquest of Tangier*. No word reached me from Henry, save that I was to change his sole heir from Fernando to Afonso who stood in line for the throne. I did not even wonder why the *infante* did this; his brand of political alchemy was beyond my poor ken.

س

I saw him again in the nightmare that has become my dream. His face, once rounded and pink with childhood, is now drawn, his eyes sunken into abysmal pits. That cherub that had once toddled after my footsteps was now a ghost, a remnant of a human. I saw the welts on his back from the blow of the Moor's whip, and his wrists were chaffed raw from the weight of the shackles. The black holes that should have been his eyes bore into me in unavoidable accusation.

"Why did you abandon me to the Moor, my beloved brother? It was I who loved you when everyone else feared you. You were both father and mother to me since I had none. I trusted you above God."

His black holes pin me where I am like the butterflies we used to impale on felt. I want to run, but my legs are paralyzed. I am bursting to look away but cannot; every muscle in my body has mutinied. I am a total prisoner. My tongue lies mute with an outrageous impotency. I cannot even plead a release from that magnetic gaze, transfixing me with the guilt of ages. Another phantom approaches. This one is clouded in mist, or is it floating veils? A female. As I breathe relief at an expected mercy, I see she has been made hideous with death, her face crowded with festering buboes, with creatures undulating under her pallid skin, craving to infect me as well. She takes the boy's shoulders in the possessive manner of a mother and grins at me, exposing green, uneven teeth.

"Why did you forsake us?" she hisses. I can smell the foulness of her

breath project over to me. Then they both spread their arms as if to embrace me in death. Unwillingly, I feel myself drawn along toward their fetid bodies and somehow know that, if I allow them to embrace me, I will join them in their tragic hell. Or perhaps not. It is I who will be interred and they released. I am still struggling to move but cannot as I float with relentless destiny toward them. The harder I resist, the quicker I am drawn to these demons, and I feel warmth down the side of my leg. I gasp at reality. I have pissed my bed.

CHAPTER ELEVEN
INTRIGUE

We were a diminished force on the slow, shameful voyage back to Ceuta, certainly diminished in numbers but, more importantly, diminished in spirit. The loss of one's comrades from a successful endeavor is tragic and also glorious, but when failure is encountered, the loss turns wasteful. The majority had escaped with their lives but left a great deal of their dignity on that Moroccan beach, together with the battle banner the Moors had captured and waved at us as we sailed away in our misery.

Despite the cooler breezes, the men remained sullen. Conversation was totally absent, and the men communicated with grunts and the monosyllables needed to sail the ship. Henry was nowhere to be seen on the deck. I last saw him slither into the stern castle. I surmised that he must be brooding in his cabin.

Ceuta was sighted on the second day, but there was no general cheer from the crew and men as was their wont upon arriving safely at a friendly port. The ships were silently provisioned and made ready to sail for the longer voyage home. Just before we were to raise anchor, I saw Henry furtively emerge from the stern castle and quickly board a waiting aviso that rowed him to shore. No one dared to comment.

Henry immured himself somewhere in the bowels of Ceuta for the next three months after the fiasco at Tangier, an exile within a place of exile. For weeks on end, he did not communicate with anyone; however, we knew he existed and was in health through the laconic missives sent by Dom Pedro de Meneses who had resumed his post as governor at Ceuta. What was going through my prince's mind during those months remained a mystery, as he did not communicate his state of mind to anyone to my knowledge. I can only imagine his turgid mind reliving the events at Tangier and wishing to change his decisions, perhaps even ruing his hubris.

Of course, there were the inevitable gloaters at the court, in particular, the prince's half brother, Count Barcelos, who had repeatedly warned the king against the prudence of the endeavor. I must admit, dear reader, that the count's frequent reminding us of his ignored advice became loathsome to my ears. In contrast, my prince's full brother, Dom Pedro, who had also advised against the investiture, remained silent, appearing to empathize with his brother's anguish in the first failure of his life. There were also other gloaters among the lesser nobility, as small-minded men appear to take great pleasure in the contretemps of the great. Yes, dear reader, for all the cracks I began to see in his once sublime character, I did ultimately believe, as I still do, that Henry possessed a singular driving force within himself that most men do not have but that remains the object of envy from the less-gifted populous. While the great majority of us are condemned to mediocrity, Henry's intrinsic ambition and sense of mission impelled him toward both great accomplishments and great disasters.

In November, following the ill-fated expedition, Dom Pedro de Meneses sent Dom Duarte an uncustomary long and detailed report. In that month, the sands of the Sahara had cooled sufficiently to make traveling across the desert less odious. Dom Pedro de Meneses reported that none other than Salah ben Salah had arrived at the city's gates accompanied by a small entourage. Among the members of this well-appointed entourage was the hostage, Dom Fernando, mounted on a magnificent dappled Arabian stallion. The animal was nervous and full of energy, impatiently trotting back and forth so that Dom Fernando could barely control the pent-up life that wanted release. Dom Pedro de Meneses stated in his letter that the prince looked to be in good health, but his face bore a worried and pallid expression. Dom Pedro de Meneses was too tactful to say outright that Dom Fernando was afraid, as any normal man would be, but especially a lone boy. Salah ben Salah announced that he had come to lay claim to Ceuta in return for the release of Dom Fernando, as promised under the terms of the truce agreed upon at the Tangier siege. At the sound of Salah's voice, Henry suddenly materialized at the walls and ordered our cannon trained on the Arab chieftain. Henry plainly stated that he was not ready to surrender his city. The gray pallor on Dom Fernando's face whitened to a bloodless gleam while his eyes widened in disbelief. Dom Pedro de Meneses reported that the boy was visibly shaken by his brother's refusal to exchange the city for his freedom.

Dom Pedro de Menses said that he was as confused by my prince's deportment as Salah ben Salah but did not protest the order to train the cannon on the Moor. After all, Ceuta was Henry's personal property while Dom Meneses served under his prince as caretaker. There was nothing for Salah ben Salah to do but retreat back to Asilah, leaving behind many shouted curses and abusive descriptions of promises given by infidels. Dom Pedro de Menses did note in his report that Dom Fernando was forced to dismount his steed and made to walk. This indignity was in full view of Henry and no doubt meant for fomenting second thoughts. We were later to learn that, upon returning to Asilah, Salah ben Salah withdrew his lavish treatment of his guest turned abject prisoner so that Dom Fernando was forced to borrow funds from Genoese merchants to feed himself and his household.

The arrival of Salah ben Salah to claim his city revived Henry who immediately emerged from the stupor of self-indulgence. In that same November, just days after he had sent the Moor away, Henry sent his brother, the king, a proposal. In it, Henry suggested that the king call on Castile and Aragon to jointly raise twenty-four thousand men in tandem with our own kingdom. He offered himself as commander of this new, glorious expedition whose objective would be to take Tangier and then Fez itself, the capital of Morocco. Dom Duarte, usually demure in his private opinions, was plainly shocked at Henry's proposal to entreat the voracious Castilians and explicitly admit weakness. Moreover, it obviously pained our poor king that Henry apparently had no regard for the wellbeing of their young captive brother. It was painfully evident that Henry's ambition to conquer Morocco remained superior to the concern he owed his family. The whispers at court grew louder, excoriating Henry on his callousness. Dom Duarte ordered Masses said for his young captive brother so as to shame the obdurate Henry into doing the right thing. If that was the king's intent, his hints fell on a hardened heart as raindrops upon barren granite.

Dom Duarte paced to and fro, caught in that typical indecisive vise that was unfortunately part of his character. Unable to come up with any direction on his own, he decided to call a session of the *Cortes* in order to convince Henry by the force of the body's moral suasion to cede Ceuta and gain Fernando's release. As I have often said, dear reader, Dom Duarte was a good man, artless to the forces of vested interests. There were many members of the *Cortes*, both noble and merchant, who were profiting handsomely from provisioning the garrison at Ceuta. These men obfuscated the debate, resulting in long, drawn-out sessions that reached no conclusion. The king and the *Cortes* were like a ship caught in the doldrums, a stilled vessel upon a stilled ocean.

Amidst all the inertia of the court, Henry slipped back to Sagres and again cloistered himself, ostensibly mourning his captive brother, even though it remained in his power to free him. Although Henry's mortal body remained interred at Sagres, his influence was projected at court, as he continued to press the king to approach Castile as an ally for the conquest of Morocco. To add to his burden, the king's own wife, Dona Leonora, supported Henry, urging him to reach out to her cousin, the king of Castile, and offering herself as intermediary. Our poor king knew no peace, as he was assailed by contravening advice from all sides. Pressed to act, he remained motionless.

To escape the cacophony, Dom Duarte retired to his private chambers, receiving only his confessor and his two young sons, Afonso, the heir apparent, and Fernando. It was indeed a mistake for Dom Duarte to create such a power vacuum, as there were many who would gladly fill it, chief among them his own half brother, Count Barcelos, now recently made duke of Braganza. This freeze in activity went on into the next year. Then in mid-February, one of the deadliest of times of the year, Dom Duarte suddenly took ill, and in a matter of days after his first symptoms of nausea appeared, he died in violent agony. Many speculated that the king had embraced, even sought out, death to be free of the extreme unease of wearing the crown. The peace death brought must have been sweet to one who had desired it so much in his short life.

The king's death was a shock to me. As I have already mentioned, dear reader, Dom Duarte did not possess the robustness of health that his brothers, Henry and Pedro, enjoyed. It was for that reason that Dom João I did not take him along to conquer Ceuta, though he was of age to win his spurs. Having said this, he was not exactly a sickly man either. His sudden death immediately caused suspicion, and his brother, Dom Pedro, called for physicians to examine his dead brother's body in order to determine whether he had been poisoned in the Italian manner. Leonora, the queen and Dom Duarte's widow, refused to allow her husband's body to be mutilated, as it was against the sacred precepts of our Church. Her refusal was Catholic and proper but elicited even more suspicion, especially among the more viral Castilian haters in the *Cortes*. Their suspicion was aroused to a febrile state when Dona Leonora declared herself regent until the heir, the six-year-old Afonso, would come of age. To many members of the *Cortes*, Dona Leonora's behavior was tantamount to an admission of guilt for the murder of her husband.

Leonora's pro-Castilian inclinations were well-known. Her assumption of the regency was therefore anathema to the members of the *Cortes* and threatened civil war should she pursue her plans. Paranoia prevailed as many nobles and prominent merchants, including the duke of Braganza, began hiring food tasters. The duke was especially vociferous in accusing Leonora, with Dom Pedro as accomplice, of having murdered the king. Confusion reigned, as no one knew whom to trust.

Throughout this anomie, Henry remained ostensibly sequestered in Sagres but continually sent missives pulling strings, cajoling, coaxing, and, as last resort, threatening. It was largely as a result of Henry's *éminence grise* that the *Cortes* appointed Dom Pedro as regent, thoroughly rejecting Leonora's claim to the post. At the appointment, the duke of Braganza immediately left the capital and cocooned himself in his fortress at Braganza, rightly fearing his half brother's wrath. With Dom Pedro as regent, Dona Leonora's position also became perilous; however, Dom Pedro reassured her that she, as the mother of his nephews, had nothing to fear from him. Still fearful of her situation, Dona Leonora proposed cementing their relationship further by marrying her six-year-old heir to the throne, Afonso, to Pedro's equally young daughter, Isabel. I could see Dom Duarte mentally sharpening his quill as he pondered Leonora's proposal. To no one's surprise, he agreed. The ludicrous ceremony took place at the Jeronimos Monastery, where the children repeated their vows by rote, and a modicum of normalcy returned to the court.

At this point, Henry emerged from the incubating solace of Sagres and came to Lisbon to pay his respects to the new regent. Dom Pedro received his reclusive brother with grand ostentation, thankful for his support. As reward, Dom Pedro granted Henry a monopoly on all trade out of Guinea and reappointed him as governor of Madeira and the Azores, making my prince the virtual king of the Atlantic, though I am positive, knowing his iron appetite, that Henry still coveted the Canaries.

I was surprised by my prince's ability to rebound from abject defeat to ascendancy with one deft maneuver. I must admit to my own weakness of person as I gloated at the thought of the duke of Braganza now cowering behind his walls, fearing the appearance of an army headed by Henry to exact vengeance for all the times the duke had attempted to thwart him.

ي

The uneasy equilibrium attained at court did not last long, as, again, bare-toothed havoc was let loose. A nondescript member of Henry's household claimed to have intercepted a letter from Dona Leonora to her cousin, Juan of Castile, conspiring to raise an army to attack and incorporate our kingdom within Castile. This man was summoned to court to deliver his proof to the regent, and to my utter surprise, I recognized Nuno, the ham-fisted hostler I had met at Tomar and who I had hired to accompany me to the tavern. He was now under Henry's employ.

With the ludicrous emulation of what he had seen his betters do, Nuno bowed three times to the regent and handed in the letter with a flourish of his thick wrist.

"This is not the queen's hand," remarked Dom Pedro with what sounded like disappointment.

There were mummers in the court until individual voices gathered like small currents to amass a wave upon the shore and almost unanimously hit upon the sands of a conclusion to say, "a scribe, surely the bitch used a scribe."

Dear reader, I do wish that justice was indeed blind, but most often that goddess does tend to do what is expedient. The hearsay served too many purposes, so Leonora was immediately impugned and delivered to an unanimous verdict: guilty. No one thought to ask the thick-armed hostler where he obtained such an incriminating document. Dom Pedro broadcast the news, gentleman that he was, to give his sister-in-law time in which to flee. He was not as ingenuous as his dead brother, Dom Duarte, but he was almost as peace loving and had no wish to shed blood, especially that of a woman who was both his sister and mother to his nephews.

Leonora was quick to grasp the overt cues. Afonso was too young to help her and would remain safe with his uncle. She left our kingdom unimpeded and turned up, unsurprisingly, in the Castilian court at Toledo. Her flight was accepted as proof of guilt by everyone in the *Cortes*, while the people rejoiced in good riddance to Castilian rubbish, forgetting she was from Aragon; it was all the same to the populous.

ي

Peace at the court again threatened to prevail as the regent, Dom Pedro, consolidated his position while bearing genuine affection for his underage nephew, Afonso, who was destined to become Afonso V upon coming of age. My prince, Henry, was now a frequent visitor to the court of St. George, often bringing exotics from the voyages of his captains from Guinea. To the young *infante's* delight, Henry presented him with a striped horse our Roman uncles called a zebra. Many of our knights tried to mount the stallion, but to no avail. The animal not only summarily threw them off but, unlike any horse we knew, he would fasten his long, yellowed teeth upon the fallen rider, releasing his pernicious grip only when several men kicked him repeatedly in his grotesquely large scrotum. Even then, the victim had to scamper quickly, lest the animal vise his jaws again on any exposed flesh. There were few volunteers after just three attempts. After brief debate, it was unanimously decided to slaughter the animal; however, the meat proved to be to no one's liking, worse than a horse. Nevertheless, the zebra loomed as a sensation to the boy who would someday be king and who implored his mystical uncle for more exotics as a child implores a parent for toys.

Henry complied, presenting the child king with ostrich eggs (the actual parents were too fierce and quick to be captured), civet cats who promptly pissed on all the settees, marking their territory, and a baby elephant, which had, unbeknownst to anyone at court, cost the lives of three men to separate her from its mother.

The young king was especially delighted with his counterpart in the animal kingdom and called for mare's milk to feed the sweet giant. The baby sucked on a two-liter bottle, which quickly was exhausted. The child who would be king ordered more milk, and to everyone's astonishment, the beast consumed four more demijohns before rocking itself to sleep.

It was at this inappropriate time that our thick-armed, ham-fisted Nuno, his cheeks flushed from unaccustomed good wine, chose to wonder aloud what a baby elephant might taste like. There was an ominous silence, and it took all the joint efforts of the regent and my prince to dissuade the young heir to the throne from hanging the drunken hostler who had suddenly grown pale and sober. For his own safety, at least that is what my prince claimed, he dispatched Nuno on a mission out of the capital. The reality was that Henry was in need of the peasant's thick-armed amorality. Nuno was to serve as Henry's liaison to the exiled queen, Leonora, in Toledo, a totally inappropriate choice in my opinion, but my prince's mind worked in mysterious ways.

ي

Seven eventful years passed under Dom Pedro's regency, and Afonso came of age at fourteen. Afonso had inherited the robustness of both his grandfather and his uncle, Henry. He was long limbed and showed a distinct promise of growing taller than his uncle. Like his grandfather and uncle, Henry, Afonso was also fond of all virile activities, such as hunting, archery, and tilting, and at fourteen, he could hold his own against full-grown knights, though I am sure that many a knight fell off his horse purposely to aggrandize the self-esteem of the young king.

Afonso, still in his tender years, was mature enough to know he was untried. Upon coming of age, he asked his uncle, Pedro, to remain as Regent and help him ease into the throne, a remarkable astuteness for one so young. Of course, Afonso's request resulted in a rumble of complaints from hushed voices, as various agendas were thwarted should Pedro remain as regent. Chief among the frustrated agendas was Pedro's adamant refusal to countenance any further investitures into Morocco, much to my prince's consternation. The former Count Barcelos, now duke of Braganza, must also have fumed since he was forced to remain behind his own walls, a self-immured prisoner.

Events are uncanny in their unpredictability. We are all blind men stumbling along winding paths that lead to doom, death, and damnation, with chaos as the only certainty. I know, dear reader, I grow cynical in my old age. News reached the court that Dona Leonora had died. This time, her cousin, the king of Castile, allowed the body to be examined, religion be damned, and the physicians found poison in her stomach. The boy king was inconsolable, for the bond between a male child and his mother is the strongest of all invisible tethers.

The duke of Braganza came slithering out of his fortress and begged an audience with his nephew. Afonso still deferred to his elders and could not refuse a request from his oldest living relative. The duke lamented the news of his mother's murder and, with no proof in hand, blamed his half brother Pedro, claiming he could produce witnesses from Toledo to corroborate his accusation that the actual murderer was under Pedro's pay. The boy king was malleable and easy to persuade. Moreover, the child wanted immediate revenge for the murder of his mother. Most adolescents suffer from impulsive behavior, and an adolescent king is no different. The boy was in a painful quandary, for he loved his uncle, Pedro, almost to the same measure as he had his mother. He sent a command to his uncle, Pedro, to step down as regent, which was immediately obeyed. Now the situation became a tinderbox in need of a spark.

ي

It was at this point that my prince elected to go to Lisbon to plead for his brother. Henry never traveled without an entourage, to reinforce his own importance, and I was part of that retinue. Upon arriving at St George's Castle, Henry was escorted immediately to his nephew's private quarters. I was privileged to be present for this tête-à-tête, as I had become a mere shadow of my prince, visible but not tangible.

Dom Afonso was disconsolate at the murder of his mother. Henry embraced his nephew, lamenting his loss while saying that his brother, Pedro, was incapable of such an effeminate act of murder as poison. The child king listened with all the devoutness he owed his famous uncle.

"But who could have done this?" the boy tearfully asked.

"Your dear mother, through a guiltless act of birth, had many enemies. She might have pled our case in the Castilian court, garnering even more enemies there. Let me intercede with my brother, Pedro."

Afonso's face flushed with gratitude, and he again embraced his uncle, hoping that he would prove that the guilt lay elsewhere. Now, dear reader, I was not present at the meeting of the two brothers, as Henry had ordered me to return to Sagres. Apparently, he did not wish for any chronicles to be written about the upcoming encounter between Pedro and himself. But what I can tell you, dear reader, is the truth as I discovered it in the aftermath of the coiling intrigue.

Dom Pedro received Henry with all the artlessness that a man asserts to greet his brother. He denied having anything to do with Leonora's death, and Henry was quick to assure him that he at no time harbored any doubt that he was guiltless.

"But, my dearest brother, there are serpentine tongues that hiss calumniations into your poor nephew's innocent ears; our own brother, the duke of Braganza, is prominently among them. He remains a quizzical man to me, but I understand his natural resentment. He would be king if not for a small accident of birth. He hates us, the legitimate heirs of Dom João I, with an unfathomable loathing, and at this time, he possesses Afonso's gullibility. The boy is understandably desperate to avenge his mother's murder, and the duke has convinced him that you are culpable. The boy loves you too much to order your execution, but I am afraid he will banish you from our lands. You must plead your case personally to him. But beware; do not go to Lisbon unprotected. My squire, Alvaro Vaz, pays for personal retainers and is willing to accompany you. Afonso trusts him, as he was his tutor at arms. I would not want to see you banished, as I would miss you deeply."

These are the words my prince was reported to have said, more or less.

ي

Alvaro Vaz was a visual paradigm of an old soldier: long limbed, gaunt body, high cheekbones, scarred vertically and horizontally from old wounds. He had aged well; his gray hairs endowed with the look of the sagacity he did not possess. Like most men past the prime of their bodies and mind, he would recount past battles to anyone unfortunate enough to be caught in his company without a polite excuse to escape. He had served three *infantes* as master of arms and was rightfully proud of the trust the royal family had invested in him. Old men usually grow fat with the contentment of years and abandonment of vanity, but not Alvaro Vaz. When he told one of his stories, his eyes lit up as if he was not just reliving the experience, but actually there. Dom Alvaro was esthetic in lifestyle, eating and drinking sparingly and trying with futile desperation to hold onto the sinews that allowed him to wield a heavy broadsword. Though shrunken by the erosion of time, Dom Alvaro still held onto to the last vestiges of strength that he had once possessed. Though he frequently missed the gourd target with his broadsword, he was better in body than most men of his years, though slightly worse for wear as far as his mind was concerned. In all honesty, he was a senile nincompoop.

It is said that we progress from the infancy of the young to the infancy of the old. At sixty-three years of age, Dom Alvaro weighed as much as when he was sixteen. He had lost all his teeth, so he was forced to revert to eating the mash served a babe. There were times he was found wandering back roads, lost as a child, but there was always a Good Samaritan to bring him home. In summary, he would have been a wise choice for my prince to pick as his brother's protector some twenty-five years before, but poor advice now.

But Dom Alvaro's elation and energy proved to be infectious to the depressed Dom Pedro. It was difficult not to exalt in an old man who had found a use for his life after so many years of quiescence. His duty was clear: reconcile the king with his uncle.

Despondent, Dom Pedro took to overindulging in wine, a behavior that he had never displayed before. Dom Alvaro did not see his guest's behavior as overindulgence; he rather encouraged the *infante* to try all his vintages, of which he was justifiably proud. Dom Alvaro's estate bore a multitude of olive trees and good, fat sheep. The cheese and olives complemented the wine, so Dom Pedro was thankful for the gustatory diversion that palliated his misery to a small degree. Dom Alvaro was attentive to ensure that his guest's plate and wine goblet were always full. The wine, pungent and strong, alleviated the pain of contemplating banishment.

With innumerable olive pits strewn on the stone floor, dozens of warm loaves of bread consumed, and two demijohns of magenta wine addling their brains, Dom Alvaro conceived of a plan for reconciliation. They were to regally march on Lisbon, accompanied by all Dom Alvaro's retainers, totaling one thousand festooned cavalrymen, the horses' manes decorated with ribbons and furbelows, and five hundred pantalooned infantry. Dom Pedro, leading this entourage, would present his case to the king.

"Why the entourage? Could my nephew not mistake it for aggression?" hiccupped the *infante*.

"A king is not impressed by small entourages," slurred Dom Alvaro, uncharacteristically heavy with wine and food.

"Agreed."

And so everyone went to fall into Morpheus's embrace, with the certainty that a wise decision had been reached. I had known that enthusiasm was contagious but had never guessed that senility could be as well.

ي

For the next week, Dom Alvaro was all activity, while the more wine Dom Pedro drank, the more inspired the plan appeared. Dom Alvaro spared no expenses, sending agents into the *Alentejo* to purchase prize horses. If you looked carefully, you could almost see a youthful bloom return to his once sallow cheeks.

Then, with Dom Pedro at the head and Dom Alvaro at his right, the entourage left for Lisbon, the horses' manes pleated, their coats shiny with balm, and their tails up in the air, as their riders had stuffed red peppers into the animals' anuses so that their tails would flail out. To this day, dear reader, I still remain curious as to why Dom Pedro, usually a model of good sense, failed to recognize the insaneness of this grotesque parade. It was as if Dom Pedro was like a man blinded by the low winter sun, disoriented and divorced from his prudent character. In this, his time of trouble, he put his faith in the infectious optimism of a senile old man. And so they set out with innocent flamboyance and not even a thought to consequences. The march was not a march of an army, but a parade, and so it proceeded slowly. Dom Alvaro, rosy cheeked and in good spirits, feasted his fifteen hundred men at every stop, providing meat and wine in abundance, further allaying any doubts that more sober minds might have harbored.

Although the overtness of the preparations and the parade obviated any need for spies, spies were nonetheless employed by the duke of Braganza who dutifully, and with what I might add to be misplaced gusto, reported to the young king the progress of the "army" set out against him. The affection that the young king might have felt for his uncle was canceled by the anger he harbored over the murder of his mother and rage at his uncle's apparent treason. Afonso's child wife, Isabel, tried to plead on behalf of her father, arguing that Dom Pedro was too noble a man to be guilty of such an effeminate act as the poisoning of a woman, but the boy king would not hear her counsel and ordered her locked up in her quarters. Remember, dear reader, there is no greater bond between humans than that of a mother and son; it is stronger and more pliant than between a mother and daughter since it is devoid of same-sex jealousies.

Meanwhile, the duke of Braganza obligingly prepared the king's army for the impending battle. With no care toward pageantry, the duke quickly assembled thirty thousand men. With the speed that the army was amassed, it might have even been said that the duke had made prior plans for such an eventuality.

ي

It was April as Dom Pedro still leisurely proceeded to the capital. April is a joyous time of year in our small kingdom as the songbirds return from their sojourn from the dark lands to the south. The white and red oleanders are in full bloom, and the jasmine caresses the air with its sweet perfume. The land is festooned with all the glory of the perverse colors that nature can produce, leaving even the most accomplished artist in awe. The wonders of this gay flora must have further addled Dom Alvaro's judgment, and Dom Pedro remained unaware that their movements were being closely watched and misinterpreted in Lisbon. With the situation progressing ominously, my prince decided to hurry to Lisbon to intercede for his bother, Pedro. I was bid to accompany him in case

Henry performed feats worth recording. With the immediacy of desperation, Henry was received by his nephew, the child king, who was in the throes of anguish, caught between anger and the lingering love for his uncle.

Afonso's young face was bloated from private tears, and when he looked at Henry, it was with a plaintive "what shall I do" prayer that denoted a paralysis of decision. He already had listened to the duke of Braganza's self-assured advice, now here was another uncle, perhaps to speak to him words to the contrary. I could already tell, dear reader, that Afonso expected Henry to defend his brother, Pedro. I suppose he even looked forward to hearing good words said about the uncle he could not help but still love.

To his and my own surprise, my prince's defense of his brother could at best be described as tepid. Henry did not even try to deny that his brother's guilt in the murder of Leonora, but rather, he tried to justify the act. He pointed out to the grieving child that Leonora had indeed been harsh with Pedro and that Pedro himself was beset with a multitude of ills, including a sickly wife, the loss of the regency, and now the threat of banishment, which, to him, was tantamount to a death sentence, for where could a pauper prince find sanctuary? To my astonishment, Henry never once repeated Pedro's own claim that he was innocent of Leonora's murder.

The boy with the responsibility of a man praised Henry's devotion to his brother, but the words were flat, without conviction. A silence then ensued, and we were dismissed. In my humble opinion, there was nothing in my prince's actions that day that merited being recorded.

ي

It was early May by the time the column of rosy-cheeked warriors arrived at the outskirts of the capital, their helmets festooned with daisies. Upon reflection, it is ironic that Dom Pedro unwittingly courted death at a time of year when the earth is bursting with life. The now-verdant hills were opalescent with varying hues of buttercups, daffodils, and poppies as nature pranced upon the earth, scattering her wondrous colors. Outrageously hued butterflies flitted about as if they too were joining in the celebration of the return of pullulate life. The slanting, stinging sleet of March was not even a memory as the warm zephyrs that arose from the Atlas Mountains embraced the men mindless of the boundaries set by men they had crossed. Dom Alvaro's furbelowed retinue had grown stout with all the feasting and drinking they had partaken along the way. At the head of the "army" rode Dom Pedro, sure that his nephew would believe his innocence.

With colorful pennants waving in the gentle breeze, the small army paraded toward Lisbon. As they passed, villagers applauded the handsome army and occasionally slipped bottles of wine to the bedecked soldiers. It was homemade wine, light and sweet, and it flowed down one's gullet with deceptiveness, making men giddy and filling them with false courage. As they approached the city's outer villages, carnations were thrown at the men from balconies by pretty young girls while older women cried, remembering other such gay marches, perhaps lovers who never returned. Nostalgia makes a fool of us all. The men were full of the righteousness of their cause, though I suspect that none of them could name what the cause was. They were happy, well fed, well dressed, and well lubricated, nothing like the ragged but efficient army that Dom João I led into the field against the better-clad Castilians.

ي

Meanwhile, the child king was totally dependent on his uncle, the duke of Braganza, to lead out his force to meet the enemy, as Afonso was still too young to have earned his spurs. The duke was now past sixty but still rode a horse like a man in his prime. Moreover, he exuded all the confidence that comes with experience. He was a source of comfort to the young king, like a grandparent who comforts a frightened child after his first beesting. With sincere sagacity, the wizened duke bade his nephew remain inside St. George's Castle and went forth to meet the enemy.

In the early mist of the morning, the duke led his thirty-thousand-strong force out of Lisbon, with horses and men slipping on the mossy, dew-laden cobblestones. There were no cheers, no flower petals strewn at their feet, no wine to send them off. Their faces were grim. They fully knew what their mission was, and it was a righteous one: earn money to feed their families. The pay was good, and there was also a possible reward, a fortune to be gained. The duke ordered Dom Pedro's coat of arms, a large red cross with a hawk and castle on either side, displayed on the side of the road. Each man was to take note. As they passed the standard, a crier announced that anyone who decapitated the bearer of this standard and delivered the head to the duke was to be awarded fifty *dobras*.

This was a fortune to be earned, and each man knew what it meant: the purchase of a tavern, perhaps where he could live off the vices of other men, never again toiling in the fields, hands raw and bleeding, fingers frozen to the hilts of their hoes. Here was a mission worth going on.

The duke had predetermined where he would meet Dom Pedro's clown army. He had chosen a prominence near a small village called *Alfarrobeira*, where he entrenched his cannon overlooking a small vale that hosted the road to Lisbon. His mounted men were formed along the ridge from whence they could sweep into the enemy's flank, dispersing the festooned lines. After a single charge, the archers would let fly three volleys, and then the infantry would mow down the survivors.

As Dom Pedro's column approached, the waiting men whispered to each other, asking for reminders as what the standard they were seeking looked like. They were mostly given wrong information by their colleagues. Officers went up and down the lines, hitting those who spoke with the flat of their swords to silence them.

There was no need for quiet as it turned out, for Dom Alvaro's men marched to the deafening beat of drums and the wails of Galician bagpipes. As they marched in unsteady precision, they sang lusty songs at the top of their giddy lungs. It was, after all, May.

I do not suppose that any men who have breathed air had so brusquely been catapulted from utter bliss to complete terror in so short a time. Cannon fire rained into the core of their lines as bodies shattered into bloody mists and lumps of torn flesh. No one knew which way to turn to escape the onslaught, so they clashed into each other. Though their weapons were polished, they were not prepared for fighting. As they ran back and forth like rabbits who had forgotten the entrance to their warren, mounted men cut a swathe through their lines. Screams pierced the air, echoing off the ridge, as uncompromising steel encountered mere bone. They were all in hell and had not thought they could sink any deeper into perdition until the arrows began raining on them like fatal hail. More screams ensued as the haphazard projectiles found targets that no one would have conceived—a man's eye socket, through another man's cheek, impaled upon a knee cap, or piercing innumerable buttocks, these last the lucky ones.

They had not marched out as soldiers, but as actors treading upon a long stage, yet something inside these beleaguered men oozed into their blood, acting like a catalyst, and suddenly, they were soldiers again. They grouped into an orderly circle and locked shields against the vicious arrows. Quickly sobering, there former gaiety was now replaced with a fierce determination to fight back, the kind of anger that does not contemplate death.

With their diminished ranks but undiminished fortitude, it must have been a sight to behold. If it was so, as indeed I am sure it was, the duke's men were an unappreciative audience. As the intrepid survivors formed ranks, the duke's men, both mounted and on foot, charged with only one thing in mind: to find the man with the standard and chop his head off.

It took but ten minutes for the remaining survivors to be slaughtered. Poor Dom Alvaro was said to be brought down by a man not half his age. Since he bore a standard, and his killer had forgotten what he was looking for, Dom Alvaro was beheaded as he lay helpless on the ground.

It was a mounted man-at-arms that brought Dom Pedro's head to the duke, though there was a general remonstrance among the lines, accusing the current bearer of the prince's head of murdering the real winner of the ghastly trophy. The duke, however, was in no mood to determine justice and paid the bearer his blood money. The battle was over. The festooned soldiers of Dom Alvaro had died bravely, if perhaps not too wisely.

ي

The duke outfitted a decent-looking retinue from his rag-tag bunch to accompany him to Lisbon so he could report the victory to the king, if that is what slaughter was being called. Upon his return, there were still no cheers. This was a battle between their own people, to be mourned, not celebrated.

With great pomp, the duke went up to St. George's Castle and entered the master hall, bearing a burlap bag. The boy king sat diminutively on a throne that had been constructed for his oversized grandfather. It was noticed by all that the king sat at the edge of the seat, as if he wanted to escape the duties of the throne.

The child on the throne looked at the duke and the burlap bag with obvious conflicting emotions. His contorted peach-fuzzed face said that, yes, he wanted news, though he dreaded what he may hear and further dreaded what he may see.

The duke, as if trained in the theater, simply placed the burlap bag at his nephew's feet. There was utter silence in the great hall, a rare occurrence, where even the slightest whisper reverberated off the stone walls. It was more than a silence, more like a vacuum, as though even if someone would have uttered a sound, it would have been sucked up into the stillness of the moment.

The boy king was perplexed, but clearly his uncle wanted him to unwrap the burlap bag. He descended from his oversized throne tentatively, like a child who still feared the goblins that live under his bed.

With trembling fingers, he undid the twine and then let out a scream—it could have been either the scream of a woman or the scream of a boy not yet past puberty—as Dom Pedro's head fell onto the stone floor, barely recognizable with death's grimace overlaid with clotted blood and with one eye open and the other shut. The boy king looked upon his uncle, the duke, with all the revulsion of one as yet unschooled in the cunning of court politics.

"Get out," he shouted, his voice breaking.

"Get out," repeated the second command in the more even voice of a man.

The duke merely smiled and bowed, retrieving the offending head as he withdrew. As he left, I thought I could hear the entire assembly exhale in relief.

I remember thinking, dear reader, how perverse our world is. Poor, innocent Dom Pedro had been murdered for an act that I suspected my Prince Henry had ordered. Despite my revulsion, I could not help but admire Henry's adroitness. I must say that I did not exactly feel sorry for the ever-scheming Leonora, but Dom Pedro had not deserved such a fate. It was at that moment that I began to believe that there is no rational justice guiding our world and that there is no sense in what fate people got.

 س

The webs I have spun have trapped the un-cunning as the hapless flies they are, ensnarled and eliminated. It is the maestro indeed who uses his cat's paws to maximum advantage, never sullying his own hands for all to see. Let that contemptible bastard do my work and be blamed for it. Sheep were born to be shorn, and lions must kill to survive. All this I do believe to the marrow of my bones, yet I need Dominicus to bring me ever-stronger dreams to keep the ashen visages at bay and to stay that inky darkness from crawling under the door and suffocating me in my sleep. My brothers were all good men but weak in resolve and small in their ambitions. They believed in heaven, so I have dispatched them to it. My gentle nephew will never forgive the duke of Braganza for killing and then mutilating his beloved uncle. Even that idiot, Nuno, has done well; he is so obtuse in his self that no one would ever suspect him of a sophisticated murder. I am not free to act freely, no constraints, no gentle persuasions, just orders given and obeyed. My destiny awaits, and I am extending my hand so that it may lead me down that glorious path of immortality, in God's service.

CHAPTER TWELVE
RAZZIA

As you must have surmised by now, dear reader, Henry was a complex man, and like all other complex men, he mistrusted his fellow human beings, as he imagined their motivations to be cloaked in hidden agendas as his were. I always imagined him as prodded by a two-pronged pitchfork, one tine representing divine curiosity and the other base greed. I never knew which prong was impelling him at any given moment. Perhaps it is because we are all a mixture of good and evil intertwined, each angel or devil predominates as if they are on a child's teeter-totter, coming to the fore as the situation dictates. I do admire Henry's subterfuge in keeping it secret from me which prong was impaled on his arse. In the meantime, a third prong arose, like the delayed tooth of a child, namely, finances. The building and provisioning of a ship is a costly affair. Money must be paid up front, as no shipwright, smith, or merchant will agree to postponed payment since the lumber, iron, and victuals they must purchase must paid for up front as well. No assurances of promised booty to come will take the place of current gold *dobras*. The depths of the coffers of the Order of Christ were a secret known only to Henry and perhaps his wretched confessor, Frey Dominicus. I imagined these coffers as fathomless, but perhaps it was not the case. By temperament, merchants are cautious men who will not extend credit, even if they could. So it was either money up front or no ships. I began to suspect that those storied coffers may not have existed at all when I witnessed Henry imploring financing from those wary merchants who nervously smiled without committing. They were walking a tightrope by denying money to Henry. To be honest, I applauded Henry's cautiousness with the vestiges of the funds of the Templars, as that could have meant that there would be more left to me, or so I thought at the time. Funds needed to be procured to continue Henry's ambitions from somewhere other than the Order of Christ. But where?

"We must find a way to self-finance as we proceed," Henry declared. He put his obstinate hands behind his back and began his usual pacing to and fro, his frustration with the merchants evident, but there was a balance of dependence between him and those very same merchants. I am again reminded of a child's teeter-totter caught in a horizontal position with equal distribution of weight with the landing of a butterfly on either side to sway the issue of gravity.

The butterfly alit with its customary whisper. I do not know who of the accumulated sages at Sagres suggested it, perhaps one of the Arabs, for it was an Arab solution: razzia. In the absence of the precious yellow metal, we would avail ourselves of black flesh that could be traded for gold.

Of course, the subject was never actually discussed aloud nor was it approached head on. Instead, euphemisms were employed, and so we were ostensibly on a mission to save the Negro's soul and other conscious-saving platitudes. Henry neither spoke out for nor against slaving, so it was commonly agreed that his silence constituted tacit support. One can always argue that, at times, base means must be employed toward the accomplishment of noble ends. There were also the exotics that could be sold in order to help with the finances.

There was also the ticklish task of finding and selecting leaders to undertake these self-financed voyages of exploration. Mindless broad backs were in abundance, but actual leaders were rare. Henry needed someone with just enough intelligence so as not to be sly, a man in possession of heartless courage who would not flinch in the application of necessary cruelty and either keep compassion at bay or dismiss it altogether, a man who was not gratuitously brutal but could employ brutality as a tool. As hard circumstances make for hard men, Henry was fortunate in finding astute men willing to undertake what some may say is devil's work but done for the greater glory of God and Henry.

Having been frustrated with the conquest of Morocco, my prince now returned his attention to the conquest and discovery of *terra incognita*. It was not long after the Tangier disaster that he sent ships farther down to explore the unknown coast of Guinea. The ships and provisions were indeed expensive, and Henry had to burrow deep into his coffers to finance the expedition. The first to be recruited as captain was Diego Afonso, a crude man and all but illiterate, but an able sailor willing to risk his life for a share in the gold my prince sought, yellow or otherwise.

In the spring of the year of our Lord of 1438, Diego Afonso set sail with no particular fanfare from Lagos in command of three caravels. Early in 1439, he returned with two ships, having left one behind at a place he called Arguim Island, with the intention of setting up a *feitoria* there. He was wise to do so, for the trading post would draw natives from the interior to exchange their chattel for salt, which is abundant in our kingdom but rare in Guinea. Henry recognized the value of the web that Diego had spun, so although Diego had failed to find gold, my prince received him in the damp rotunda at Sagres, granting him a prolonged audience, as

Henry wished to learn of the particulars of the voyage and his reasons for establishing the trading post at Arguim Island. Diego's report was not a soliloquy, for he left large gaps in his narrative, necessitating that my prince interrupt him frequently to complete his report evenly. As I have already mentioned, Diego Afonso was an unschooled man with a thick tongue that slurred over the few words of vocabulary he commanded. Rather than repeat his tortured narrative verbatim, I think it would be best to paraphrase it for your convenience, my dear reader.

The small fleet proceeded down the coast and around Cape Bojador without incident, as now their rudders indicated the locations of all the dangerous submerged sand bars and reefs. The winds were favorable, and the water casks remained near full, thanks to the frequent rains that the crew caught in the folds of the canvas and barreled. Consequently, they boldly sailed on past Porto Galé. The shoreline continued unremarkable until they reached a deep-water bay, where the ships anchored. Diego named the bay Angra de Santa Maria and erected a wooden cross to claim the land in the name of my prince. Henry interrupted and asked what kind of wood the cross was made of, to which Diego answered, resinous pine. "That cross will not last a month before the insects and climate eat it. Pray continue." Henry determined that later voyages would take along inscribed stone pillars called *padrãos* so that his claims to the land would have more permanence.

As per the now-established custom, four mounted men set out to explore the interior. Only after a short while, they returned with an unwilling guest, a Moorish goatherd that they had encountered nearby. He was an old man, well past forty and shaking in fear, for we were clearly infidels. His eyes bulged in anticipation of his murder and, because he was toothless, his trembling chin beat against his beaked nose. There were a few of our men who could speak basic Arabic, and upon hearing his language, he calmed down, for we must be perforce somewhat civilized.

His fear was completely eliminated when our men set down a rug and offered him tea.

"Why have you taken me away from my goats? There are jackals around, and I cannot afford to lose a one," he said irritably. When Diego promised to return him, he visibly relaxed, as though he were in his own abode. He told our men that he had heard other, more educated men of his tribe refer to this land as Mauritania, in honor of its Moorish population. Yes, he said he knew there were caravans that came up from the south, but their routes were well into the interior, assiduously avoiding the coast so as to be safe from the infidels. He winked at the irony of his words and then smiled, and our men smiled back in a sort of backhanded collusion. He apparently had come to the conclusion that there were good and bad infidels. He was sincere in his pledge, saying he did not know the provenance of the gold the caravans sometimes carried, only opining that it must lay much farther to the south. He did know that, some sixty leagues to the south, the land turned lush, as there was much freshwater. Diego thanked the old man and kept his promise, ordering one of the horsemen to return him to his unguarded flock.

When the horseman returned, he had a most curious large dead bird draped across the mane of his steed. It had small wings, apparently flightless, and a hilariously curved bill, making it look like one of those silly marionettes. Our man reported that there were masses of these silly-looking birds just half a league away, and he said that they were easy to hunt, as they did not flee. With Diego's consent, four horsemen went in search of these birds and came back with two each. They said their movements were equally as absurd as their appearance, and so they had christened *doidos*, our word for crazy.

As there were three ships in the fleet, there was room for what had been previously superfluous personnel on prior voyages. A priest had accompanied our small armada, and before departing, he said Mass in front of the wooden cross on that sun-baked beach. The men were only too happy to be allowed to remove their cuirasses and casques that seemed to trap the sun's heat, keeping it near their skin while not allowing any breeze to wash over and evaporate their sweat. After Mass, wine, thick-crusted corn bread, olives, and cheese were distributed among our men, resulting in an increase in the good humor. The *doidos* were also cooked, and their meat was found to be surprisingly delicious. Subsequent captains never failed to stop to hunt the *doidos*, until there were no more to be found. Because of their stupidity, the creatures became extinct. When they did set sail, it was with light hearts and energetic hands, as full bellies often engender good humor.

It appeared to everyone aboard that God must have been pleased with their homage of the Mass, as the breezes stiffened, taking our ships quickly into uncharted waters. Being the good sailor that he was, Diego was careful to take depth soundings and recorded his findings on his rudder. With such a breeze at their stern, it was difficult for Diego to stop, as all true mariners are entranced by fair winds. He said he felt the hand of God pushing them along to their destiny. When our ships sailed into a vast school of fish, some of them jumped out of the water in surprise and right onto the decks. They were strange fish that the crew had never seen before. They had spiny backs that made them difficult to clean, but they proved delicious in the stew the cook made with rice, garlic, and onions. Surely, God was sending them another sign, and the already high spirits continued on their ascent.

After five says of sublime sailing, the lookout spotted land off the starboard side. This was indeed puzzling, as the coast of Guinea lay to port. As they approached, land appeared on the port side as well, so it was determined that the sighting to starboard must be an island. The island looked lush, the shoreline choked with vegetation, indicating the presence of abundant freshwater. Their water casks were adequate, but freshwater was always welcomed.

As they approached the fertile island, Diego again cautiously took depth soundings and ordered sharp eyes to the prow to look for submerged rocks or reefs. Much to everyone's surprise, the water remained deep almost to the shore, providing a natural anchorage. Dropping anchor some twenty strokes from the shore, every available glass was trained on the island; however, the vegetation was thick, so the interior remained a mystery. Thus occupied, it fell to the lookout to warn them of an approaching strange sight.

All glasses immediately trained on what looked like a giant bird trying to lift off the water as gulls do with their feet running on the surface while desperately flapping their wings. Some of the more superstitious men began praying, for if such giant birds existed, assuredly the tales of huge sea serpents must be true. But as the giant bird approached, fear turned to wonder as a large canoe came forth. Muscular Negroes stood on the canoe, using one leg to propel the vessel, while balancing themselves with their remaining leg. As the canoe came alongside our flagship, a single robed man sat among the tall, bare-chested Negroes.

"*As-salaam aleikum*," he shouted, to which someone immediately responded with the ritualistic response, "*Allah ma'ama.*" Peace and understanding were immediately established between the parties, as the language of Allah had been spoken and hospitality mandatory.

The robed Moor called himself Khalid ibn Fanouk, and he said he was the emir of the Sanhadja. The Negro leg-rowers were his personal slaves. The rules we had learned called for tea, which was brewed, and the emir was politely bid to sit as our men eyed the brawn of the Negroes with curiosity.

For many of our men, if not all, this was the first time they had gazed upon these creatures who looked so much like brown gods, their muscles clearly delineated and their teeth in extreme whiteness in contrast to their ebony skin. It was reported that our men wondered how they could keep their balance on the canoe as they rowed, for there was nothing to hold on to. As the Negroes' chests heaved from the effort of rowing, our men marveled at the size of their nostrils that allowed for the intake of twice as much air as our own thin noses. One common puzzlement the crew shared was why such strong, virile men would subject themselves to slavery, taking orders and abuse from the pudgy Khalid whom they could so easily overpower. Of course, none of us knew of the severity of the slave hunters Khalid employed and the unmentionable retribution an escaped slave suffered.

Khalid told us that his village was on the mainland and that his people lived off the sea. He called the island before us Arguim and informed us that, while it was uninhabited, it nonetheless belonged to him. Khalid confirmed that there was plenty of freshwater on the island as well as many fruit and nut trees.

Wishing to avoid any unpleasantness, Diego asked the emir if he would be willing to sell us Arguim Island.

"Do you have horses?"

"Yes, but only four, and we will need them," answered Diego with an honesty that the emir accepted. We had brought some trading goods, principally, linen cloth and, of course, salt, but the emir was disdainful of the uncut material and, for some reason never explained, had no need of salt. He said that he bought ready-made garments from the caravans, having neither the patience nor the industry to convert cloth into apparel. Our interest piqued at the mention of caravans, and Diego, perhaps unwisely, showed his curiosity too blatantly. The emir grew suspicious and refused to tell us whether the routes of the caravans came near the coast.

Other goods were shown to the emir, as well as some of our native provisions. Although he confessed that his religion forbade it, he sheepishly offered to trade the island for five tons of wine. After some ritualistic haggling, the price was reduced to four tons, and the deal was completed.

Diego left one ship and its crew behind, transferring most of the tools to them so they could build a *feitoria*. For his part, Khalid agreed to spread the word of our presence on the island and our willingness to trade. With the establishment of the *feitoria* on Arguim, our ships could sail less laden with water, which could free space in the holds for trading goods, such as salt, wheat, ready-made garments, or whatever could be traded for gold.

The audience was over, and my prince was pleased with what Diego Afonso had accomplished and discovered, rewarding him commensurately. We had established an important foothold on the continent.

ي

The ensuing years attracted very little gold to the *feitoria* on Arguim Island. Henry was disappointed at the lack of progress, as were many of the adventurers at Sagres. Wheat proved to be the most sought-after commodity, but it did not produce gold. The natives traded odds and ends—captured animals, some malagueta peppers, a tusk of ivory now and then, and an occasional captured slave—but not a single ounce of gold. This disappointment led my prince to lease the Arguim *feitoria* to a group of Genoese merchants for ten years. The Genoese had ready access to Moroccan wheat, which we did not, as well as ready-made garments and so were willing to pay a stiff price for use of the *feitoria*. The income would thus provide Henry with funds to continue farther south in the hope of finding gold.

And so our voyages continued, captained by desperate

men and crewed by voracious ones. There is a great deal to fear in someone else's desperation, as they are usually unafraid of death, which will only release them from their misery. One captain, whose name I cannot remember, returned with salted elephant meat for the prince's approval. He had not found any gold and was grasping at hope like a poor man who finds a copper ring and thinks it must be precious. The meat was cooked and served in the rotunda at Sagres but proved sadly lacking in edibility; even the mastiffs refused to eat it. Ivory, not the meat, remained the elephant's true value. My prince was still convinced that Guinea held vast riches, though these riches were proving elusive.

ي

Carlos Tristão was a brash man, not yet twenty-five. When he spoke, he would put his hand on the hilt of his sword, as if daring anyone to disagree. To God's credit, but nothing to do with him, Carlos was a fine-looking man, with a sharp aquiline nose, forehead, and jaw. Unlike the previous young men who flocked to Sagres to wage their lives against fate, Carlos belonged to the nobility, but although he was not poor, he remained a desperate man. His desperation was not in lack of sufficient food, but an insatiable hunger for fame, the food the dead eat. In this, and the fact that he was able to finance the expedition out of his own pocket, he served my prince's purposes well enough.

Carlos provisioned two caravels, wisely choosing an old Guinea hand, Antão Gonçalves, to captain the second ship. Antão had already captained a ship far down the Guinea coast and knew all the hazards lurking just below the surface of the sea. On a previous voyage, he had discovered a small island where a colony of seals lay basking and ordered them slaughtered for their pelts and oil. These goods alone had paid for the entire expedition; however, Antão had also distinguished himself by penetrating the interior and returning to Portugal with three Moorish captives who were donated to the Jeronimos Monastery, where they were put to work on the vast gardens. There had been slaves in our land since time immemorial, as attested by the dim Latin books, almost deliquesced with age, that listed the Iberian slaves of Roman households.

The two caravels set sail, and again, the voyage proved tranquil, as our mariners had gained experience and confidence in their abilities while remaining respectful of the more powerful ocean. Arguim Island was easily reached, and off the port horizon, the lookout spotted what indeed looked like a giant bird attempting to lift off the water. This time, there were no imprecations from our men, as they knew it must be the emir, Khalid, coming out to greet his civilized infidels and, perhaps, to barter for more wine. It proved to be a grievous mistake on the part of the Moor to judge all infidels by the ones he previously encountered, for the schooled Carlos was nothing like the nearly illiterate Diego. The latter, it turned out, was the much more humane man. In Carlos's case, his education exacerbated the cruel streak he harbored in his breast.

Carlos ordered his best bowmen into the riggings to take careful aim. He admonished the archers not to hurt a single slave. As the unsuspecting emir approached the lead ship and shouted his ritualistic greeting, the only reply he received were short-shafted arrows from crossbows, shot at such close range that the hapless man was impaled onto the bottom of his canoe. Our mariners, by unmistakable signs and signals, ordered the Negro slaves aboard, where they were shackled and stowed into the airless cargo hold. A culverin was then aimed at the canoe and fired, sending it and the impaled, slain occupant to the bottom. As Carlos reported, there were no tears or jubilation from the Negroes who instinctively knew that they had just exchanged masters.

The two ships continued down the coast in search of suitable anchorage but found none, as sandbars guarded the shores. The farther south they went, the more lush the shoreline. The ships then came upon a small, deep-water inlet with a proper beach. It was always preferable to land on beaches, thus avoiding ambushes from hidden foes. Spy glasses were trained on the sands, and human footprints were clearly discerned. Dropping anchors, Antão shouted across to Carlos that he wanted to volunteer to go ashore. Perhaps he was motivated by courage, but I suspect, dear reader, that Antão did not trust Carlos to share his booty with him and so wanted to ensure his own slave cargo.

Antão put out his longboat, with twenty heavily armed men to accompany him. Once ashore, two men were assigned to guard the longboat while the rest slithered in a single line into the interior. There were clearly delineated paths, so it was not long before our men came upon a thatch-roofed village.

The jungle is a strange place for someone not born into it. You would think the dense vegetation would isolate people who lived relatively near to each other. A man can walk or crawl amidst the thickness of it and not notice that a battle royal is taking place between two ant civilizations. I think of the foliage as walls that separate people from each other, but in reality, the jungle sends messages through its mist; the heart-shaped leaves tell each other's secrets. In reality, it is much like our grapevines that almost immediately deliver rain water to nurture their thirsty roots. Whether by drum or runners, the villagers apparently knew that our intentions were not peaceful. Women and children fled while sturdy male Negroes ran out to defend their village, armed with colorful, long, wooden shields and wooden javelins. Alas, for these brave defenders, it was wood against steel. Carlos had not skimped on the weaponry, and each man was sheathed in cuirasses and wielded a sword made out of the best Toledo steel. Although thrown with remarkable accuracy, the javelins harmlessly shattered against breastplates and greaves. Shouting Portugal and St. James, our men charged at the bewildered phalanx, killing three of the now-unarmed defenders with viscous swipes of their brutally sharpened swords. Upon witnessing the easy slaughter, the remaining defenders fled into the jungle while our men gave chase. Not all the populace had fled; some women, children, and old men had remained behind. Our men now culled their captives with leisure and method, taking only young, healthy-looking males. These were rounded up and laden into Antão's ship.

That evening, Antão was invited over for a meal on Carlos's flagship. After describing his encounter at the village, Carlos bade Antão kneel and knighted him for prevailing in what I believe was a decidedly uneven contest. Dear reader, if I appear cynical, you are correct in assuming it. I do not know whether Carlos, though noble, had the right to knight Antão, but my prince did not question the privilege that Carlos had appropriated. It has been my experience that the meek do not inherit the earth. My prince gave no indication of whether he disapproved of the emphasis Carlos gave on slave hunting over exploration. Carlos had, after all, funded his own expedition, and Henry was perhaps only too glad to receive his royal fifth.

Carlos and Antão unloaded twenty-four healthy Negroes at Lagos. Almost as if by magic, an impromptu market appeared, and the slaves were quickly sold, for labor was in short supply in the sugar mills and rice fields. The value of a young male Negro was established as being worth thirty-five gold *dobras* or four thousand *real brancos*, a veritable fortune to the poor men of the crew, now no longer poor, that had accompanied Carlos on his razzia.

Closely watching the proceedings on the beach was the treasurer of Lagos, Lançarote da Ilha, who was amazed at the prices this black gold fetched. As he watched, Lançarote made plans.

ي

Lançarote was a wealthy man who, like a great many other wealthy men, wanted to amass even more wealth. Dear reader, I do not claim to understand this perverse motivation, for a person, no matter how rich, can only reside in one palace at a time and can only drink from one golden goblet at a time as the erudite Hamid had said. Everything else is superfluous. When is that thin line crossed between greed and intrepid ambition? This same opprobrium that I apparently harbor against Lançarote could equally be leveled against my prince. Both men were driven by secret hungers that I still cannot understand, even with retrospective old age.

In the year 1444, just after Carlos Tristão's voyage, Lançarote da Ilha financed the building of six caravels, vessels much larger than their predecessors by some five tons. He enlisted well-tried captains, including Estevão Afonso, Rodrigo Alves, João Dias, João Bernades, and Gil Eanes; the latter was the first captain to round Cape Bojador. Henry must have anticipated his royal fifth with a serene pleasure.

Boldly, the ships set out from Lagos, sails all concave with friendly breezes and a stalwart crew. We could now risk sailing deeper draft ships since the Guinea coast was no longer a complete mystery. Each ship carried a stone *padrão* for claiming new lands and providing ballast, along with wheat and rice for possible trading.

Apart from the provisions, Lançarote made sure that his armada was the most imposing force ever thrust down the coast of Guinea. The ships were so well ballasted that even the neophytes did not get seasick, much. Adding to the ballast were dozens of shackles, ugly things exhuming misery in their iron blackness. They were like that proverbial elephant in the room, very visible yet unmentionable. Experience was ingested, and we were confident of the breezes and knew where hazards lurked. We were home on a familiar sea and had become at least partial rulers of the Atlantic along with Poseidon and his Roman bother, Neptune.

And so with the assurance of past experience, Lançarote sailed past Porto Galé, past Porto Branco, and deep into the land of the Negroes. Lançarote had made no pretenses with my prince; his was purely a slaving expedition, with discovery as only secondary to his purposes. Henry remained a passive but expectant partner.

Once Porto Branco was rounded, they sailed on past the West Nile river, which the natives insisted on calling the Senegal. They tried to put to shore several times, only to find that proper anchorage was not available, and when the water may have been deep enough, there was no unobstructed beach on which to disembark safely. One time, there was both anchorage and beach, but hordes of mosquitoes drove our men off before they could row ashore. Later captains venturing into the interior would describe how black clouds of these insidious insects drove off mighty herds of elephants. God has never showed His reasoning behind His creation of such malevolent tiny insects that only wreak misery on man and beast. But I suppose God is ultimately wise, and our rapacious and arrogant race needs these diminutive adversaries to remind us of humility.

These cogitations are my own humble musings. Lançarote was a braver man than I, but I suspect he must have cursed the black clouds that had no respect nor fear of cannon and steel. These creatures are merciless, and all our casques did was trap them near the men's pale-skinned, thin faces, where they could feast at their leisure. With the coast more familiar, Lançarote had not bothered to bring horses, as they would be useless in the jungle and, moreover, easily succumb to the miasma of the jungle. Horses are fragile creatures, unused to the noxious ardors that humans endure for the sake of survival. They are easily susceptible to the flux and die without the protest of humans who persist on living beyond their use. We live so much longer and do not part with life without argument and pain.

In addition to the grains, the hold was also filled with the salted fish we call *bacalhau*, olives, olive oil, and some ready-made garments obtained from Genoese merchants, should an occasion for trading arise. The Moors remained adamant, refusing to trade with us until we relinquished Ceuta. Only God knew how poor Dom Fernando was faring given my prince's steadfast refusal to honor his word.

History later relieved me of my curiosity. I was to learn that the sweet young prince was transported to Fez with but one attendant. His household had been beheaded by the Christian-hating Cadiz of Fez, Laraque, who was now Dom Fernando's jailor. The poor boy was put to work in the Cadiz's gardens and given only half rations so that he was slowly starving to death. But I digress.

Returning to Lançarote, his ships rolled on like snails upon a dew-filled leaf: at their leisure and enjoying the voyage. It was Lançarote's intention to trade his grains and other goods for black gold, the human ballast he would need for a safe and profitable return. After briefly stopping at Arguim Island to top off his water casks, the armada ventured forth, with each poor man aboard imagining the sweeter life they would lead upon returning home, that is, if they were not hacked to death or impaled on a javelin.

Some of the older men dreamed of the land they would finally buy or the house they would build. The younger men may have thought of the beautiful girls they might marry. These pent-up aspirations may have been vented in sighs that further billowed the sails.

Having not found proper anchorage nor anyone with whom to trade, it was Lançarote's plan to sail past the cove where Carlos Tristão had landed until he came upon coastal villages that could be raided, thus saving time looking for Negroes while also avoiding the dangers of investing into the jungle. Indeed, he was fortuitous, for just ten leagues south of Carlos's cove, the armada came upon a large coastal town with a multitude of thatched roofs. On the sun-blinding beach, natives could be seen in all their peaceful tranquility. Men about the sands absent-mindedly mended their fishing nets while naked children ran into and away from the foamy surf in a universal game that children share. Women sauntered from hut to hut, young babies at their breasts, in search of chatter to break up the monotony of the day. It was evident that peace prevailed among these people, and they had not had yet heard about the metal-wearing cannibals. There were no lookouts posted, so our ships were able to sail right into their aqua bay without being noticed. Such was their preoccupation with the sweet luxury of their quotidian lives.

There was no time to be lost as each caravel launched a longboat in the water with thirty strong backs to man the oars. The inhabitants had been caught unawares, sitting in their huts, sipping fermented goat milk, crouching on the beach, mending their fishing nets, and even napping in the warmth of the low, late afternoon sun. Their delicate bliss was about to be shattered like a thin, fine wine glass thrown upon jagged rocks.

The first longboat to put ashore was led by one Martin Afonso. His men quickly fanned out and herded 165 captives of all ages into the convenient kraal, located in the middle of the town. They emptied the kraal of the few scrawny cattle within and crammed their living booty inside. The captives were so dazed that there were no attempts to resist.

As João Bernades's longboat approached the shore, he spotted a canoe loaded with young, muscular men pulling on the paddles for their dear flesh, for they had heard of the cannibals who wore metal coats and ate men raw. He set out to intercept the canoe. Our men were strong and avaricious, but the Negroes were terrified, so try as he could, Bernades was unable to close the gap between his longboat and the canoe. Frustrated with his lack of progress, Bernades ordered two bowmen to shoot at the paddlers in order to reduce their number and speed. The arrows found their targets, embedding their barbed shafts deep into the well-muscled backs of the Negroes. At each hit, Bernades told us he winced in dismay at the loss of another thirty-five *dobras*. After five of the paddlers had either been killed or wounded, their longboat finally began to close the distance, taking fifteen Negroes: ten remaining male adults and five children they were trying to save. In a rage, Bernades unsheathed his sword and murdered the wounded.

In all, the raid on the town yielded 235 Moors, as Lançarote insisted on calling them. Aware of possible mutiny over the spoils, he wisely approached the lucky Martin Afonso and loudly suggested that the plunder was to be divided equally among all. Martin was said to be enraged, but when the other captains put their hands on the hilts of their swords, there was little to do but agree since, if he had insisted on hogging the loot, he surely would have been murdered. They distributed the cargo evenly among the six ships, lest anyone dare to run off and return home while their human ballast cries below deck, beseeching deaf gods.

ي

The masts of the returning ships were spotted by a fisherman, mere dots on the horizon. The fisherman rowed ashore and shouted the news to everyone he encountered, and soon there was an expectant crowd gathered on the fog-shrouded beach at Lagos. Word was sent to nearby Sagres, and by the early afternoon, my prince had arrived to welcome Lançarote and his men home. The unloading of Negro slaves was not a novelty in Lagos, never on this expected scale and from tribes so deep in the continent. People actually wondered whether they were human like the ones brought thus far or perhaps whether they have an eye for a belly button, as they had heard that such creatures existed deep in Guinea. Lançarote and his captains first came ashore to present themselves to Henry who greeted them warmly. It was determined that the human cargo was to be divided into five equal lots, with one-fifth of the best going to my prince.

Then came the longboats, laden with their weeping, shackled prisoners, not of war, but of economics. Families huddled together, shivering from fear and the unaccustomed cold mist of the upper Atlantic. Mothers held their children tightly against the spray, intrusively cold upon their unaccustomed skins. Despondent and despairing, the women wailed without restraint, causing their children to scream at the unfathomable terror that grips a child when he sees adults cry. The men wept quietly at their impotence to affect the situation. For the sake of decorousness and to shield priests' eyes, the women had been draped in loose-fitting burlap sacks. The men were not given the same courtesy; their shivering nakedness added to the abasement of slavery. Some only wore rags, while others wore nothing at all. The ships' crew was given its instructions to separate the slaves into five equal groups of men, women, and children. This could not be accomplished without separating families. Our mariners had apparently grown callous from their participation in the razzia and ruthlessly pulled babies out of their mothers' arms while attempting to whip the hysterical woman back into submission. As mothers, the whip did not seem to restrain them, necessitating two strong men to drag them back to their group by their ankles as they screamed, while their men were barely restrained at sword points. In order to protect themselves from their own consciences, our mariners had ceased thinking of these poor wretches as humans, only as so many *dobras*. The wailing and weeping rose to a crescendo, so it was not possible to discern a single voice; they all combined to sound like a howl from a single gravely wounded animal.

It was heart rendering to watch children being separated forcibly from families, their arms outstretched, fingers curling and finding no purchase, no sympathy, no humanity. Many of the onlookers also began to weep silently while urging the mariners to stop renting families but were paid no heed. One fisherman tried to stop a child from being dragged off only to receive a meaty fist on his face.

Dear reader, I will confess to you that my own eyes began to sting as my tears swelled. When I could no longer repress them, the accumulated globules of tears ran freely down my cheeks, disappearing into my beard. I looked up at where my prince stood atop his dappled Arabian and saw no emotion, no pity, just a blank stare, as if he were watching a stew come to a boil. His face could have been chiseled in stone for all that it betrayed. Henry calmly accepted forty-six of the best men, women, and children, even as parents were whipped to make them release the children from their desperate embrace. I did not remonstrate, and it is to my shame to this day. At the time, I justified my cowardice by assuming the weeping had unmanned me. There was the image of Henry also, stoic as a statue immune to weather and human suffering that raged on that beach, and there I was, indeed most of the populous, reduced to a spineless jellyfish. In the gist of our collective souls, we knew that what was taking place was wrong; God could never condone such atrocity. But we, the weepers, were weak. I wondered if that is what differentiates the strong, to be able to rise above mortal men and not act like a man by expelling any compassion from your soul. I looked at the assembled fishermen and their wives who wept at the scene of agony as I did. I then looked upon Henry's calm visage, which betrayed no emotion, and I judged myself and the assembled humans lacking in the cold reptilian ichors that make some men great. We were weaklings unable to adapt to the realities of objective economies, holding on to our pathos. We were told that the Negroes were heathens, yet they reacted much as we would at the loss of their children, at the loss of their freedom. We saw them gnash their teeth in despair, just as we would have done in their situation. We empathized like the weaklings we were. The strong remained stonily unaffected.

Lançarote's voyage was deemed a huge success, making the men who accompanied him, if not exactly rich, at least comfortable for the remainder of their lives. Henry donated two of his slaves to local Churches and sold the rest. If he could have at the time, he would have sent fifty ships down the coast of Guinea, manned with poor men, lead by intelligent brutality, if not for the chronic shortage of ships. It was the rare caravel that survived more than two voyages. The corrosive seawater rotted every timber that came in contact with it, and the only salvageable parts were the masts, and then, even the masts sometimes failed to escape the corrosive salt-laden sea air. Wood and men are all inevitably consumed by the sea.

Despite the shortage, the nobleman Carlos Tristão was able to purchase a single serviceable caravel, albeit at an exorbitant price. He related to my prince that, this time around, he would be more interested in discovery as opposed to slaving. I could tell by my prince's bearing and tight smile that he did not believe him. As for myself, I did espy a tiny glitter of sincerity. Carlos did not, after all, have to explain his motives to Henry, as he was again bearing the entire cost out of his own purse. Henry's concern was that he receive one-fifth of the booty Carlos could prize from the continent. Yet I am sure it was not his only concern. Henry was transfixed in his curiosity, much like one of those beautiful butterflies impaled on a collector's velvet cloth. I was never sure which motive was in prominence, avarice or curiosity.

Circumnavigating the Moorish prominence of Guinea that juts out into the ocean, Carlos confidently sailed on. In late April of 1446, Carlos's ship had reached a river that he had heard about from natives from the north that they had called the Gambia. The current emanating from the river was too strong to attempt any riverine exploration; moreover, sailing up a river had already proved too dangerous. Even weak currents carried along the detritus of the forest, including whole trees that could easily punch a hole through a ship's hull. Also, as our ships of exploration had increased in size, their draft had deepened, making them susceptible to sand bars. Narrows made it impossible to map these ever-moving sand bars while also making maneuvering extremely difficult.

The only solution was to send two longboats up the Gambia, each manned by ten rowers. Carlos himself captained the first longboat, leaving but five men aboard the double-anchored ship to ensure its position against the current shooting out from the shore. The men strained against the river's strong current, but their sinew eventually prevailed against nature. The shore along the river looked ominous, as a thick wall of vegetation prevented anyone's eyes from penetrating past the shoreline. Imaginations were allowed to work their sinister alchemy, so many of our men thought they saw yellowed, famished eyes of creatures staring at them as their salivating maws prepared for a feast of human flesh. A stiff breeze also impeded their progress, adding a burning pain to strained muscles, but it also kept the dreaded black swarms of mosquitoes from tormenting our men's exposed, sweat-sodden bodies.

As they rounded a bend, the river narrowed while the current strengthened, requiring our men to double their efforts to maintain their momentum against nature, which inevitably always wins. Again, it was a mixed blessing, for the strong current also drove the deadly river horses away. These beasts were known for toppling boats when we inadvertently got too close to their young and for ripping the helpless humans to shreds with their large teeth. They were worthless, as their ivory was not prized and their flesh tasted worse than that of the elephants. In the years to come, many more of our men were lost to these fierce vegetarian beasts than to all the accumulated carnivores of the black continent. It is a rare sea captain that does not train cannon on a river horse to avenge the death of some relative or friend. The men who descend into the innards of hell need little incentive to kill since their own lives are constantly at risk. Why die alone? Besides, the river horses, when on shore, made such excellent targets, and it was amusing to watch the crocodiles come to tear the still-living animal apart. Ignorance does not engender much compassion for the fauna of our world. Sorry, dear reader, again, I digress.

As the river deepened, the current suddenly eased as our men leaned over their oars, mouths agape with exhaustion. Just as their gasps for air slowed, the sky grew thick with arrows shot at them from both sides of the shore. The arrows were small and came at them with little thrust, indicating primitive blowguns. At first, our men were not overly frightened, as these small projectiles were more of an annoyance than a fatal threat, like the black flies that plagued but did not kill.

Each longboat was armed with a culverin placed in the bow, and our men fired blindly into the green wall. Each time they fired, they found targets, indicated by screams of agony as limbs were torn off torsos. It was both heartening to kill the hidden enemy and worrisome, for the forest must be thick with attackers if they could hit so many with blind shots.

It was then that men who had received scratches from the darts started becoming paralyzed, then gasped for air for a few moments, and then died. The arrows were poisoned, and the slightest cut meant almost instant death. Our men were now afraid.

Carlos ordered our boats to turn around to escape the swarm of deadly arrows, but the river was so narrow that the extremities of our boats came close to shore. As prows and sterns approached the shoreline, attackers emerged from the screen of the dense forest. These were not the timid fishermen we had encountered on previous voyages, with their useless wooden javelins; these were Mandinka warriors armed with double-tipped iron spears, unafraid of our culverins and steel and determined not to be taken and eaten by these rapacious pale men with their black beards.

Carlos's longboat was boarded, and viscous hand-to-hand combat commenced. Carlos was seen wielding his Toledo sword with effect, cutting a fatal gash across a Mandinka warrior's throat. Blood spurted from the severed artery of the dying man, as his heart must have been beating at its full capacity, and covered Carlos's face, temporarily blinding him. Just as he was trying to wipe the viscous fluid from his eyes, another warrior boarded his boat and thrust his spear with all his muscular might, piercing Carlos's cuirass and instantly killing him. More warriors swarmed aboard and soon every one of our men were dead.

As the Mandinka's celebrated their victory over what they believed to be cannibals, the other longboat escaped with just two of our men left alive, Andrea Dias and Alvaro da Costa. It is their eyes and my subsequent interview with them that makes my narrative of what happened to the ill-fated expedition possible.

Now riding with the current, the two survivors made their way back to the caravel. They joined their five comrades and, in a remarkable feat of seamanship, made their way back home to tell their story of murder and mayhem. Upon hearing of the carnage, Henry ordered that the river be renamed Rio do Tristão, but to my knowledge, the natives still refer to it as the Gambia.

ي

Despite the massacre, or perhaps because of it, many desperate men remained willing to go on the slave hunts, as the possible reward still outweighed the risk in their estimation. My prince continued to countenance slaving as reward for audacity and a means to fund his curiosity and greed. Of course, it was also helpful that he received his royal fifth for every successful razzia.

Such an intrepid soul was Gonçalo de Cintra who purchased Carlos's still-serviceable caravel and refitted it. There was no shortage of men eager to join him, and he was able to select the strongest brutes. Despite his uncompromised intention to go slave hunting, Gonçalo gladly took along a Jewish cartographer from my prince's household along with a scribe who was assigned to protect Henry's interests. My prince had grown wary of his unscrupulous captains. It was true that he depended on their brutal courage, but it was also true that he mistrusted their motives, which mainly enriched themselves at the expensive of the world. My prince strongly advised against just concentrating on slaving, reminding Gonçalo that there were other riches, perhaps more valuable than slaves, such as gold and ivory. Moreover, these riches could be obtained without the attendant hazards that accompanied the razzias. There was also information to be obtained, such as the routes of the caravans and where they were most vulnerable, namely, closest to the coast. If the *sheikh-alkara* led his camels close to the coast, these caravans could be raided; let the heathen do the work while we simply reap the treasures. In addition to gold and ivory, Henry gave Gonçalo a list of other items he would be interested in that included civet musk, malagueta peppers, and a substance he said was called hashish by the Arabs, said to enlighten the mind and get us closer to God. Gonçalo listened dutifully, taking copious notes, but his actual actions betrayed his pen's feverishly moving nib as it scraped across the rough parchment.

Using Carlos Tristão's rudder, Gonçalo sailed beyond

Rio do Tristão, though even his crew stubbornly referred to it as the Gambia. He was determined to avoid the vicious Mandinka and hoped to find more docile tribes farther south. Sailing twenty leagues past the Gambia, they came upon a natural harbor that they named Heron Bay, owing to the large population of these birds sunning themselves on the beach. Again, a longboat was lowered with twenty-two heavily armed men manning it and Gonçalo at the tiller. Reaching the beach with its unobstructed views, the men carefully explored the interior. Before they even walked fifty steps, they were met by two-hundred Sine and their ferocious iron spears. Of course, our men did not know the name of the tribe at the time, but we were beginning to differentiate. It is indeed an ignorant man who claims that all Negroes are alike; are all Europeans alike? All attempts to speak to them proved fruitless, as they spoke no Arabic. They had heard of the cannibalistic metal men and set upon our mariners without flinching from our well-aimed crossbows that penetrated their wooden shields, driving us back to the beach with their heft of numbers and willingness to die on a battlefield as opposed to a kitchen. As they retreated, they found the men guarding the longboat had been slain, their throats cut as evidenced by the black pool of blood their heads lay atop of. Worse, the longboat had been hacked to pieces.

Of the original party, only six men remained alive on the beach, including Gonçalo himself. Gonçalo's companions quickly stripped off their heavy cuirasses and greaves and plunged into the barrier of the surf with determined strokes. Unfortunately, Gonçalo could not swim, a common shortcoming among our mariners. The men in the water did not look back to watch his fate, and the sound of the surf drowned out any screams he may have emitted. We can only hope that Gonçalo was granted a swift death. Again, an undermanned caravel was courageously sailed back home, the survivors able to tell the tale I have just narrated to you, dear reader.

ي

Still, there were hungry men willing to risk a possible spear in their abdomen or a poison arrow impaled in one's cheek. These quick deaths still seemed preferable to slow starvation at home. I will name some survivors of some voyages. There was Diniz Eannes da Grã, Alfredo Gil, the privateer known as Malfado, and Lançarote da Ilha who returned to Guinea with the largest fleet ever, twenty-six ships that returned with nearly five-hundred Negroes. During these slaving expeditions, new lands were incidentally discovered, such as the Cape Verde Islands. These voyages were made by hard men who were unafraid of the Mandinka or the Sine. Dear reader, I must admit a certain admiration for them, for now, the contests were more on an equal footing, as our cannon was of limited use within the canopy of the forests of Guinea. Yes, these men dispensed death, but they accepted that they were likely to be killed as well. No longer were we preying upon the defenseless. We gathered slaves, even as sometimes half our men failed to return from the razzia. This mutual slaughter continued for three more years until 1448 when Henry completely changed his mind on active slaving. From then on, trading relationships were the priority.

I do not believe my prince was driven by any innate sense of morality by coming to this conclusion, nor did he claim to. His impetus, as always, was practical. We were losing men at a distressing pace, as fathers died faster than they could be replaced by their sons. Our kingdom had never been a very populous one, as our soil was niggardly and could not produce the abundant grain harvests available in France or England. Destitute widows and orphans added to the kingdom's burden, hallow-eyed reminders of our national guilt. There was a surfeit of groom-less would-be brides, destined to barren lives. At this pace, there would be no kingdom left, and we would fall as easy prey to Castile.

Ever the pragmatist, my prince recognized that the Negro population grew denser and more fearsome the farther south we ventured. Our reputation was at a nadir with the natives who were sure to extract life for life. My prince was equally aware that the Negro tribes were at continual war with each other. His new stratagem was to find the strongest among the Negro tribes and make them allies in the plunder of other tribes. In this way, the slave trade could resume without further disastrous loss of our men. The profit he received from selling slaves could be put to use on further exploration of the continent, which remained his passion. Henry may have had a hard heart, but he possessed an agile brain that was quick to adapt to changing realities. *I saw them strewn upon that mist-clouded beach, screaming and weeping, and, may God forgive me, my loins hardened. The delineations of muscle and sinew on their ebony skin, those white, flashing teeth gnashing in impotence, they were more magnificent than the most prized Arabian.*

I also saw my own people sobbing at the spectacle and was tempted to be moved as they were. Compassion is a weakness to be weaned away from, much like from a mother's breast. I cannot think of them as humans or else I would lose my mind. Their screams were but some caws of distant seagulls or the last and final grunt of a pig upon the slaughter, ambient sounds that one must grow indifferent to. Their wailings have no significance.

They worship spirits, numerous ones, hidden in trees and mindless, soulless animals and believe that good and evil are in balance with amoral consequence. The victor can be either, depending on pure happenstance. This is a damnable amorality. They believe in omens and say that the trees were once humans and that the animals of the jungle harbor ancestors who either transgressed or pleased the gods, depending on the animal avatar. Lions were noble ancestors while jackals and hyenas base ones. They have never heard of our Lord Jesus, which perforce gives me complete license over them. They are my clay as innocents, without the Moor's perniciousness over the truth of their religion over ours. They will make for easy conversion and guarantee my entry into heaven, despite my sins. Yes, I will earn a place in Catholic empyrean by converting this naïf and keeping him away from the talons of Islam. I will not let Frey Dominicus flagellate me tonight, as the razzia is an innate good. I am leading them to God while at the same time financing my sacred mission of exploration. It remains the ends, not the means. Still, I am well aware that there, but for the grace of guns and steel, go I.

Chapter Thirteen
Modus Vivendi

*H*is name was Alvise Cá da Mosta, a Venetian mouthful that my prince, in one of his rare moments of caprice, shortened to his endearment for him, Cadamosto. The nickname quickly took hold, and everyone called him by it. He was only twenty-two years old when he appeared at Sagres to offer his seamanship services to my prince.

"Your experience has only been in the tame Mediterranean, Cadamosto. The Atlantic is vaster and largely unknown," chided my prince.

"My lord, you can just as well drown in one fathom of seawater as ten," retorted the Venetian with that wry smile of his that quickly thawed the ice in people's hearts.

If there had been any young women at Sagres, they most likely would have fallen in love with the youth. As it was, his beauty was wasted on the wind-swept walls of the rotunda, where he spent most of his time, looking over the shoulders of his elders while they perused maps and speculated what might lie beyond the edges of the parchments. He asked many questions, not fearing to show his ignorance but avid and open in curiosity. The gathered sages indulged him with patient explanations, which he ingested like a hungry puppy. It was impossible to become annoyed with his persistence. He was treated like a favorite nephew by everyone, including Henry.

Cadamosto was easily as tall as my prince and also like him, clean-shaven, with thick black hair that cascaded down his forehead like a bunch of grapes. His smile was infectious, exposing even, white teeth and causing two dimples to implode on each of his rosy cheeks. His constant good humor did much to increase his already formidable attraction, his green eyes forever twinkling. Cadamosto also possessed the unrestrained optimism of youth; this attitude and his natural beauty were irresistible, making everyone want to be near him in the hopes of infection.

My prince was no exception; it was plain for us to see that he had succumbed to the handsome young man's charm. When in the company of the irrepressible Cadamosto, Henry's usually dour face erupted into smiles, and at times, he even joked with the members of his household. Cadamosto's beneficial effect on Henry was appreciated by and endeared him to the members of his household, such as myself, who had to come in daily contact with Henry's dark moods. Happily infected by Cadamosto's good humor, Henry's own dark moods lightened. It became more pleasant to be in his presence. He could cajole any favor from anyone, and so it was not long before the irrepressible youth began at first trying to persuade and then begging Henry to be allowed to captain one of his expeditions. We were all aghast at his request, as we were reluctant for him to leave and rightly feared for his safety in our avuncular affections for him. But with the demon myths of Cape Bojador dispelled and our rudders gathering information on the sailing routes, the danger, while still considerable, had diminished. Moreover, we all knew Cadamosto would not be denied and would go somewhere else to find his adventure and slake his curiosity.

In the end, Henry's pragmatism held sway over his affection, as it invariably did.

Henry decided that Cadamosto was the most likely ambassador to send to establish relationships with tribes that could be persuaded to become trading partners, and perhaps even allies. It was a judicious choice, in my opinion, for if there was anyone who could charm the venom out of a snake, it was Cadamosto. In the year of our Lord 1447, Cadamosto set sail on a caravel provided by my prince. He had already received instructions from some of the old hands at Sagres on which tribe to approach, namely, the Wolof.

Though Muslim, the Wolof wore their religion lightly, not letting dogma interfere with trade or some of the pleasures forbidden to more iconoclastic believers. The Wolof enjoyed wine and smiled easily when in good company, dining on good food and in good cheer. In our past brief encounters, our mariners had found them to be pleasant people. When Cadamosto returned from his voyage seven months later in late 1447, he had successfully established a *resgate*, a small trading post usually composed of three to four men, in the Wolof-controlled coastal village of Mboro. Despite his charming Portuguese, accented in Italian that sweetened the vowels, removing the bones from our tongue, his command of our language was not fluent. So with your indulgence, dear reader, I will take the liberty of paraphrasing his report to Henry.

The Wolof are ruled by an absolute monarch called the damel of Kayor. His subjects are forced to approach him naked, groveling on the ground while throwing dirt on their heads. Although severe with his own people, the damel was a hospitable host, graciously accepting the four tons of excellent wine we had brought as a gift in Your Majesty's name. We also presented him with seven arrobas of salt, a brass-plated cuirass and several bushels of malagueta peppers, which the damel found very flavorful when added to their rather drab cuisine, which consists of rice, lentils, and goat meat. Lamb is especially prized but saved for feast days or high occasions, and when times get hard, camel is added to the menu. The malagueta peppers did much to add spice to their simple fare and worked miracles in disguising the rancid taste of camel meat. The damel especially highlighted the peppers as items of interest for future trading.

The Wolof raided to the south, capturing Sine and Ibo slaves, but assiduously avoided the savage Mandinka. Cadamosto asked the damel through the combined effort of various interpreters if there was some way he could intercede with the Mandinka on our behalf, adding that it was also our wish to trade to them.

"The Mandinka are silly, superstitious people who believe that gods inhabit their trees and wild animals. They hate you Portuguese because they think you are cannibals," commented the damel while absentmindedly chewing on a sun-ripened golden date.

"I am not Portuguese," responded Cadamosto in his usual disarming way.

"Then I will try to send an emissary on your behalf. He might be killed, so I will choose someone from my wife's family. In return, you must promise to bring me more of these magnificent peppers on your next voyage."

A rate of exchange was established; a horse would be worth nine to fourteen Negro slaves, depending on the condition of the horse and the slaves. Before departing, the damel gave Cadamosto a gift of a twelve-year-old girl of extraordinary beauty.

"For your prince, to thank him for his gifts," said the damel. Cadamosto thanked his host with the expected profusion of ritualistic homage to Allah and set sail, leaving five unmarried men behind to man the *resgate*. Cadamosto set a course back to Lagos to report his success to my prince.

"You have done exceptionally well, my dear Cadamosto," said Henry.

I had never heard use such a term of affection to anyone, but we all pretended not to notice, lest we embarrass Henry or Cadamosto.

At this point, Cadamosto ordered the twelve-year-old girl to be brought forth and presented her to my prince. She was a vision, dressed in a white linen dress so stiff that I doubt she could have sat down in it. A wreath of fresh daises coroneted her oval head, and she possessed a pretty face set atop an elegantly long neck. She patted into the austere round room on bare cat's paws feet, immediately brightening it. She did not walk, but rather glided, as if she were glissading on a sheet of ice. Her mien gave every indication of entitlement, most likely having been pampered all her wonderful life because of her rare beauty. There was an audible hush in the rotunda as she floated in; the only sound that could be heard was the susurration of her linen dress. Females were a rarity at Sagres, save for old, crone-like servants.

"I have named her Zucchera, my lord, as she has a sweet disposition. Her name means 'sugar' in Venetian," announced Cadamosto with some pride.

While all eyes were greedily trained on the girl, I stole a peek at my prince who turned crimson and was visibly upset. After a period of twenty heartbeats, he seemed to compose himself.

"When next you meet the damel, you may thank him on our behalf. As for the girl, I will make her a gift to the Carmelite nunnery at Evora, to be trained as a novice. Such beauty belongs to God."

Each man present, including myself, repressed a gasp of horror at the thought of condemning this gossamer creature to the dark, narrow rigors of the convent. The mapmaker that called himself Jonah whispered angrily between his clenched teeth, "Why does God give all the walnuts to people with no teeth? Virtue can be carried too far."

I could not answer his quandary, for it is indeed perverse that some seemingly privileged men disparage what others would give their lives for. Every man was thinking of the waste of depositing this flower onto such barren ground, yet no one appeared to give a thought of how this pampered flower might wilt without the sunlight of adoration. As for myself, I envisioned a sad ending for this poor, ethereal child.

That evening, the usual austere round room at Sagres was lit with an abundance of candles and played host to a hastily improvised feast of fish and fowl, including some delectable *doido* bird meat. Our honored guest, Cadamosto, partook of much white wine and was giddy, his voice rising in merriment. I corner-eyed my prince who usually scowled in disapproval at the slightest sign of intoxication, but I saw nothing but content equanimity on his face. I found my own mood elated by the conviviality and drank more wine than I usually dared in my prince's company. It was good to see Henry smiling widely, shorn of his hair shirt and donning a human skin. Adventurers toasted to each other's success, cartographers complimented their rivals' skill, and everyone was in a jolly mood. I saw Henry take a sip of wine without his usual reversion and laugh at a poor joke that Cadamosto made. We all live in fear that the happiness of a singular moment will burst like a soap bubble. It is this fear that tempers our ability to loosen and give into hilarity when fortuitous opportunities come our way. But that night, no one worried about the threat tomorrow brings but feasted upon the giddy present.

Just as I sat there, wishing that this evening be prolonged into eternity, a messenger came in and delivered two notes to my prince, with a sense of extreme urgency. Upon reading both notes, my prince gallantly bade everyone to continue eating; as for him, he had to set off for Lisbon immediately on some important business. The rest of the company tried to follow his dictum, but the spell of the evening had been broken. I simply followed my prince, according to my perpetual duty.

ي

The first note related to the Castilians. There was a new king on the Castilian throne, an earnest young boy, too young, and perhaps too weak-minded, to possess his own opinions. Juan II was primarily guided by his overly devout Dominican tutors who, unlike our friends the Wolof, wore their religion as if it were chainmail. Under their order's aegis, Castile was being cleansed of heretics. Their ominous influence had already spread to neighboring Aragon and even usually recalcitrant Catalonia. Their intolerant eyes now cast their narrow gaze at our poor kingdom that, according to them, was replete with heretics, atheists, Jews, and Moors, while our own clergy did nothing to contain their poison. It is true that our own clergy was lax in many ways, including living in open marriage to women and fathering children by them. It suited us to have men, not saints, intercede with God on our behalf.

The boy king of Castile had sent emissaries to our own equally young monarch, Afonso V, Henry's coddled nephew. He was proposing to allow us to welcome the foreign inquisitors into our nation to rid us of the scourges of heresy and Jews, as our own clergy seemed to have no interest in orthodoxy. Our young king saw no reason why he should not allow inquisitors to cleanse our lands, and it was this leaning that induced certain members of the *Cortes* to send a message to my prince, warning him of the probable outcome. These members of the *Cortes* were, of course, motivated by the preservation of their own interests rather than any devotion to tolerance. Many of the members of the *Cortes* traded profitably with so-called heretics and Jews; their businesses would suffer at the expulsion, if not outright murder, of their business partners. While the confessors' duties were only to God, theirs was to the shareholders.

Afonso received his famous uncle with a mixture of relief and trepidation of a child who still must raise a hand to seek the comfort of an adult's warm palm.

"You have heard of our cousin's petition?" the boy asked anxiously.

"Yes, precisely, and I hurried here to lend what little wisdom I have been able to amass during a long, arduous lifetime."

My prince listened solemnly and patiently at all the logic the Castilian court gave for being allowed permission to rid our kingdom of the vermin, as they put it. After the boy finished his tentative speech, my prince paused, as if to consider what advice to give.

"My lord, the Castilians suffer from extreme passions. It has been my experience that any decisions that arise from passion are invariably poor ones. The best minds work with the iciness of indifference. The Castilians will tell us that the Jews and the Moors that live in our kingdom are intrinsically evil, and I agree with that assessment, but there is such a thing as a necessary evil. Take war for instance, even the pestilence that wrecks havoc on us makes the survivors stronger. We are better Christians from being able to live next to the heathen and maintain the integrity of our faith.

"The inquisitors will also tell you that these infidels trespass upon our Christian shores and make use of our tolerance for their own convenience. My lord, I maintain that if they use us, we also are using them. We are richer for their presence. It is a rare game when both sides can win. Yes, they will say that I have vested interests in that my cartographers are mostly Jews and Moors, but what of their interests? The Castilians are avaricious, and what better way to prepare for an ultimate invasion than by doing it gradually? If you allow these Castilian priests into our realm, their armies will not be far behind."

Our young king was persuaded and chose to accept his uncle's advice and told the Castilians that their inquisitors were not welcomed. Dear reader, I must confess that I was again impressed with the persuasive power of my prince. Was he protecting self-interests? Most assuredly so. Did he care whether he was acting in a righteous manner? Absolutely not. Henry acted out of what was purely convenient; he pursued the shortest route that allowed him to reach his goals with the least amount of expense or resistance.

Yes, I did mention that there were two messages delivered to the rotunda. The other was a simple announcement: Prince Fernando, held captive for eleven years, had finally died of starvation.

ي

In the spring of 1449, Cadamosto headed back to his *resgate* at Mboro commanding two caravels and one clumsy flat-bottomed *bau*. Our mariners were by now confident enough with the voyages to risk taking along less seaworthy vessels. The advantage of the *bau* was her larger hold, which was crammed with horses for trading. The Wolof, much like their Arab cousins, prized horses among all animals, preferring their majesty to that of graceless humans.

The five men he had left at Mboro were still alive and well, greeting their companions with the enthusiasm of men who had not expected to survive their ordeal. They proudly showed the amazed Cadamosto the gold they had accumulated from trading trinkets with the surrounding tribes, as well as with the dreaded Mandinka, through the intercession of the Wolof. It was not an immense fortune, perhaps one hundred *dobras*, but it was more gold than anyone had yet procured from the past expeditions.

Cadamosto led a string of the best horses to the main village and presented them to the damel along with five tons of our kingdoms best and stoutest wine. He also presented him with three bushelfuls of malagueta peppers, for which the damel was truly thankful. The men left behind had mastered the Wolof language and served as interpreters.

"You are most welcome, my friend. I like men who keep their promises. I have also kept my promise to you. My silly brother-in-law was not slaughtered by the Mandinka after all, and that is bad news for me. But the good news for you is that he has convinced the Mandinka that you are not cannibals, and their king, Batimansa, is willing to receive you."

Cadamosto thanked the damel graciously, invoking Allah's generosity many times, as per custom.

"What of the girl I gave your prince? Did he like her? Has she borne him many sons?"

Unable to look the damel in the eye, Cadamosto mumbled something to the effect that our prince was so pleased with his gift that he donated her to the service of our God, which is a great honor.

"You have strange customs, but if your prince was pleased with her, then I am happy."

ي

After two weeks as guests of the damel, Cadamosto set sail for the Gambia to the south and his appointment with Batimansa. The damel's brother-in-law had gladly volunteered to come along as guide and interpreter, which somewhat mollified the worried Cadamosto.

I say Cadamosto was somewhat mollified, dear reader, because deep in his bosom, Cadamosto remained afraid of the fierce Mandinka, the assurances of the damel and his brother-in-law notwithstanding. The slaughter of Carlos Tristão and his men was still fresh on everyone's mind and, worse, on their imaginations as well. He ordered his men to keep a close eye on the brother-in-law, lest there be some treachery afoot. Cadamosto dared not share his secret trepidations with his men since they were even more doubtful of the reception they were to receive and were on the verge of mutiny, not wishing to go up the Gambia River. Everyone had heard of the slaughter of Carlos Tristão and his party, which by now had taken on exaggerated proportions, with the men not only killed, but eaten as well. Cadamosto was only able to keep order by the prospect of the gold that he dangled before each man's wild imagination each day.

Not daring to have idle hands about him, for idle hands can turn lethal, Cadamosto set the men to make-work tasks: scrubbing the deck, refitting the masts with new sheets, and fishing. Though there was no shortage of food, fresh fish was always welcome. The men were grateful, for the not-so-subtle subterfuge and set about their labors with a gusto that served to somewhat belay their fear. A haggard old hand, perhaps the oldest man in the fleet, quipped, "Those savages won't be happy with me, for they'll find nothing but bone and gristle." It was a stab at levity and was received with tight, nervous smiles.

The lookout sighted the Gambia River, and the men's stomachs tightened in anticipation of being pierced by a spear. Three longboats were launched from each ship and were rowed up the Gambia, which remained the Gambia. No one referred to it as the Rio do Tristão, as if it were bad luck to do so.

With the damel's brother-in-law at the prow of the lead longboat, the party rowed up the river, now aware of its currents and quirks. The damel's brother-in-law stood up and began shouting a greeting. As no one understood exactly what he was saying, one crewman unsheathed a dagger, ready to kill him in case of betrayal.

The longboats uneasily floated past the site of Tristão's

ambush as each man tightened his sphincter muscles to restrain the evidence of his fear. Off the left bank, a large village appeared, and four canoes came out toward them. As men prayed and tried to repress sobs and shit, or tried to swallow but found their mouths too dry, shouts were heard from the canoes, and a man stood up with his right hand open in the universal sign of, if not at least friendship, then that no hostilities were imminent.

The canoes surrounded our longboats, resulting in many anxious, furtive glances from our men. Rather than as an attack, the flotilla of canoes was intended as an escort and led the longboats to a dock, where our men disembarked.

Their chief, Batimansa, was an immensely fat man, his flabby arms easily the width of most men's thighs and with a protruding stomach that rested on his knees. He sat on his makeshift throne, reinforced by many slats of hard wood. Around his enormity sat almost equally fat young women who looked upon our bearded men with obvious aversion, as if they had never seen such ugly creatures. For all the king's obesity, his warriors were fit and muscular. Batimansa's heft obviously was a mark of rank and distinction. Unlike the Wolof, his subjects did not grovel before him, but only lowered their heads slightly when addressing him.

At the approach of our timid men, he smiled, showing his even, white teeth. His incisors were studded with diamonds. Of course, our men did not fail to take notice, inspiring awe and avarice as counterweight to fear. Again, their own expectations of wealth were piqued by the sight of Batimansa's diamond-studded teeth as greed trumped fear.

The damel's brother-in-law, for that is what everyone called him, not bothering to learn his name, translated that Batimansa bid us welcome. Gifts of salt, olives, wine, and a brass-plated cuirass were presented to the king. He magnanimously accepted these gifts without much in the way of thanks. It was his due; after all, we were the visitors to his realm.

As the king spoke, our men noticed damaged cuirasses displayed atop poles surrounding the village. These were obviously the trophies from our last encounter with the Mandinkas. To their common horror, our men realized that it was Batimansa who had ordered the slaughter of Trisão's party. Sphincter muscles were again tightened as hands were squeezed upon weapons, each man secretly determining their distance from the fat savage. It fell to the outwardly calm Cadamosto to impose order in his frightened men.

Too fat to move himself with any ease, Batimansa gestured for Cadamosto, the obvious leader, to sit on a stool placed before him. To allay our men's evident fears and perhaps to avoid spontaneous battle, women brought wooden cups of fermented goat's milk to them as they looked upon their bare breasts with lecherous and hungry eyes. Batimansa spoke through the damel's brother-in-law.

"My friend, the damel, has told me that you are not cannibals, but warriors like us. That is good, for we despise cannibals; better to die of starvation than commit taboo. You have given him horses; why have you not brought horses to me?"

The efficiency and speed of communication in the interior of Guinea was astounding, thought Cadamosto. He also thought that the best way to respond was with the absolute truth.

"King Batimansa, the climate where the Wolof live is amenable to horses. They will die here in the jungle, as they are not used to the heat and have no defense against the insects. They are delicate animals."

"Then they will die, and you will bring me more."

"As you wish. I have some horses in one of our ships and would be glad to present them to you as our gift before we leave."

As this, the king smiled and nodded, saying something intelligible to his retinue. Then with great difficulty and aided by two strong warriors who served this purpose, the king rose and disappeared into his hut, leaving Cadamosto pondering. The damel's brother-in-law explained that tonight there would be a feast in their honor. For now, the audience was over, as the king had retired for his afternoon nap.

Cadamosto took advantage of the respite to gather his men and give them instructions regarding their comportment while in the Mandinka village. Despite his youth, he was already a man of the world and had not failed to notice his sex-starved men leering at the bare-breasted Mandinka women.

"Remember, we are their guests and unfamiliar with their customs. In our country, if someone is caught ogling at your sister or wife, it is a severe insult. Let us assume that it is the same here. If anyone causes any trouble, it may mean death to all of us. Remember Tristão and his party who offered no offense other than showing up?

"I can see by your faces that you believe my counsel is wise; your faces are sober. Let us keep it that way, for the inner demons of every man is released by drink. The goat's milk is fermented and stronger than our wine. Let everyone be modest in its consumption, as we are unfamiliar with the drink's effect. If I catch anyone drunk, I'll put him in shackles and stow him into the hold in the company of any slaves we might gather. Moreover, he will not get any share in the booty we bring back.

"If you feel insulted by any man, swallow it. Everyone is to keep their weapons sheathed. I will personally kill anyone drawing a blade. Be modest in all appetites, speak among yourselves in moderate tones of voice, and refrain from raucous laughter, lest the Mandinka think you are making jest of them."

Our men listened to Cadamosto's orders of the day with

heedful ears. Even the most rebellious of them understood the need for absolute decorum.

That evening, fires were lit, and what looked like several large deer and a wild boar were roasted. Cadamosto had four of his men row back to the lead caravel to bring back some of the fish they had caught on the voyage, ordering the cook to make the stew that had been so popular with the mariners. The Mandinka tasted it and, with nods of approval, devoured the fish stew with evident gusto.

The feast went well. Batimansa, unused to the furtive kick of our stout wine, became drunk early on. Luckily for our men, he proved to be an expansive drunk; the wine did not release any demons, but rather it elicited a hitherto hidden generous nature. By late evening, Batimansa was extolling his new friends, lauding their polite manners. How could he have thought that they were cannibals?

"You have not brought any of your wives?" he slurred, to which Cadamosto replied that most of his men, including himself, were not married.

"Do you prefer boys then? Some of our warriors are that way, and it is accepted as long as they are fierce in battle."

Through the damel's increasingly drunk brother-in-law, Cadamosto explained that it was our custom not to marry until we had procured our fortune in order to support our wives and issue. Batimansa's eyes went agog, and he laughed at such stupidity.

"A man's loins must have release, or he will go insane. I will give you and your men wives while you remain our guests."

Before Cadamosto could remonstrate that it was not our custom, Batimansa was shouting orders. Some forty young girls were dragged before him; all were sobbing loudly and beseeching the king. When Cadamosto asked the damel's brother-in-law what they were saying, he smiled wickedly and told him that they were begging the king not to give them away to such ugly, smelly beasts. He further freely translated that the women complained that we all stunk of rotting flesh and that they were repulsed by us, not wanting to bed with us, even for one night. The damel's brother-in-law obviously took pleasure in making the gratuitous translation of the insults, and Cadamosto understood the damel's dislike of this petty man.

Perceiving his authority questioned by mere women, Bantimansa's expansive mood turned venomous as he threatened to kill any girl who disobeyed. Meekly, they went to sit by the side of our men who could not believe their luck yet remained attentive to decorum, lest this be some sort of test. Batimansa then presented Cadamosto with one of his fat consorts who immediately sat next to the handsome young Venetian without complaint, though she did hold her nose at his smell.

"You, as their chief, may have a handsome, fat woman. Let the others bed with stringy, ugly girls."

Batimansa belched and fell into a deep sleep, the wine vapors bathing over him like a warm blanket in an early April chill. Noting the interrogatory looks that his men were throwing at him, Cadamosto went to them to give them further instructions.

"Do not be rapacious nor rough. The king presented us with temporary wives while he was drunk and may come to regret his generosity in the morning. Treat these girls with the same courtesy you would treat a wife back home."

"I beat my wife every day," said the old, grizzled wag who had previously boasted of being composed of just gristle and bone. Cadamosto shot him a murderous look, his tacit point taken.

"I also suggest we all bathe since our smell must not be pleasant after so many weeks at sea. We have grown accustomed to our own stink, but apparently it is loathsome to the women. I am ordering you all to bathe before lying with them. And for Christ's sake, wash your blouses and pantaloons as well."

Throughout that night, quiet sobbing emanated through the thatched walls as girls submitted to the muted carnal passions of our men. Cadamosto himself was circumspect and did not describe in detail his own experience with the handsome fat woman, much to the overt relief of my prince.

Despite Cadamosto's fears, Batimansa remained benevolent, not seeming to regret his generosity of the prior evening. He granted permission for Cadamosto to build a *feitoria* at the mouth of the Gambia River. Again, Cadamosto picked unmarried men to man the *feitoria*, only this time, there were no sad faces, as the men so chosen were only too happy to remain behind.

Returning to Lagos, Cadamosto reported the particulars of his voyage to my prince who was again pleased. Cadamosto was eager to refit his two caravels and obtain another two *baus*, as the returning *bau's* timbers were rotted. His intention was to return to his *feitoria* with more trading goods, including horses, that could be bartered for slaves. Uncharacteristically, Henry tried to assuage Cadamosto's eagerness and bade him rest at Sagres for a time instead of immediately putting back to sea, but the young Venetian's blood was aboil with zeal, and he was in a hurry to make his fortune. My prince could not convince him otherwise and finally gave in to his eagerness to get underway.

ي

When Cadamosto returned to his *feitoria* at the mouth of the Gambia, it was already late autumn of 1450. He found all his men alive and well and even content with their lot. In the ensuing months after he had left them, the men had traded salt and wine for civet cat musk, malagueta peppers, apes, and parrots. The Mandinka also brought captured slaves but wanted horses in return, which were in short supply after Cadamosto's gift to Batimansa. All had gone well, save there was no gold. Cadamosto noticed the presence of their "wives," each rotund with child. There already had been a birth in the village of a cocoa-colored girl, neither Negro nor European. The men at the *feitoria* jokingly referred to her as a *mula*, our word for mule, which is the issue of a horse and a donkey. During Cadamosto's stay, more women gave birth to these so-called *mulas* who became so plentiful that an elongated, more human term was coined: mulattoes. These children scampered about with their darker playmates, oblivious to man-dictated racial divides. Their mothers seemed to have lost their initial abhorrence of our men, given the relative good treatment they received at their hands, as Cadamosto's prior admonitions had been heeded to the letter because of their fear in being surrounded by the relatives of their wives. The men had behaved with the same strict decorum first mandated and only occasionally beat their wives when called for, such as in the burning of a meal. Besides, it is well-known that a husband must occasionally beat a wife, albeit with a light hand, or else she may grow jealous. Our men doted on their children as our people tend to do, which further endeared them to the women, for it is also well-known that a kindness to one's child is doubled in the mother's estimation.

The horses were unloaded from the *baus*, and other trade goods replenished. Cadamosto set sail with his four ships steering farther south, now venturing into unexplored territory. They sailed on by the featureless coast until they spotted a huge promontory that resembled a sitting lioness. Cadamosto noted the promontory on his rudder so it would be recognized by future mariners and called it *Serra Lyoa*, or Lioness Mountain.

Beaches abounded with unobstructed views, though the approaches to them remained shallow, necessitating the ships be anchored too far from shore. Our rowers would have been exhausted by the time they reached the beach and too weak to fend off a possible attack. Cadamosto therefore continued on until he could get closer to shore.

Eventually, a natural harbor was discovered, barely a league offshore. Longboats were launched and landed with a soft scrape as the wood of the hulls touched upon the coarse sand, almost pebbles, with Cadamosto steering the lead longboat, as was his wont. The climate was pleasant, with cool onshore breezes, and there were numerous signs of inhabitants, such as footprints, rotting canoes, and ragged fishing nets strewn about the beach. Cadamosto and his men explored the interior, finding suitable freshwater. Building a rudimentary perimeter, they made camp uneasily, each man feeling the prickle of malevolent eyes staring at him from deep in the forest. The vegetation was thick, allowing imaginations to conjure hidden monsters.

The next morning, Cadamosto led a column of men into the interior in search of the natives but found no villages. Evidence of habitation continued to appear, but the natives themselves proved elusive. Trying to lure them out, Cadamosto ordered that bags of salt be left in the clearings of the forest as gifts. The next morning, the bags of salt had disappeared, and in their place were satchels containing tiny gold nuggets. Encouraged by the outcome, Cadamosto set out more numerous yet smaller bags of salt, but found them untouched the next morning. Doubling the salt, small satchels containing gold nuggets appeared in place of the vanished salt. This silent trade continued for months, our men never getting a glimpse of their counterparts. Cadamosto sent back one of his ships with his rudder and instructions for a rendezvous at *Serra Lyoa*. Cadamosto remained with his three ships, fortifying the basic perimeter until it resembled a small fort. The climate remained relatively benign, so no one was stricken with the flux or succumbed to the vapors emanating from a small swamp nearby, those evil vapors that the Italians refer to as malaria. With food and freshwater bountiful, only two deaths occurred during the months of waiting for the relief ships to arrive.

In the late winter of 1452, three caravels and a single monstrous carrack appeared offshore. At first, the presence of the carrack frightened our men, thinking the intruders were Castilians or even French. To everyone's relief, the lookout decried the blue and white pennants indicating that they were indeed Portuguese, and our men rejoiced. The fleet was captained by one Pedro da Sintra, sent by my prince to relieve and resupply Cadamosto. Unfortunately for all concerned, the two captains took an immediate dislike to one another, even before each man could discover the other man's deeper, often hidden, character and motives for being present at this particular time and place. Each man assumed their worst estimations of the other, not bothering to confirm their suspicions. It is a strange phenomenon that I have often noticed, how two people, upon encountering each other, can either immediately like or dislike the other without bothering to get acquainted with their respective characters. It is as they are foes, avatars from a previous life, reigniting in their previous passions.

Physically, the two men could not have been more different. While Cadamosto was lithe and ethereal, da Sintra exuded an inelegant raw strength from his squat body like some men exude odors. His hands were that of a brute, with short, thick fingers that appeared capable of uprooting a tree. You could never imaging these hands caressing anyone or anything. His forehead was salient, jutting out like that of an ape. However, these brutish simian features belied a native intelligence that made many men underestimate him.

To Cadamosto, Pedro da Sintra was an interloper, intent on usurping the valuable *feitoria* he had established at considerable risk to his life. He did not believe what Pedro da Sintra told him regarding his instructions from Henry. As far as Pedro da Sintra was concerned, this effeminate-looking man was arrogant in the extreme and, moreover, avaricious. While Pedro da Sinta had paid for the outfitting of his own ships, Cadamosto had been regaled with his ships by Henry. This privileged treatment infuriated Pedro da Sintra. Here was this man, a foreigner to boot, refusing orders from an overly indulgent patron, in essence calling him a liar without overtly saying so. The stage was set for armed confrontation, as each captain led a loyal and quarrelsome retinue of men.

Driven to the brink of action, Pedro de Sintra's head cooled, and he backed off. As I had said, he was as astute as he was excitable. In the current situation, his sense of self-preservation came to the fore. Cadamosto was a favorite of Henry's, and if he were to do him harm, he surely could not safely return home. Pedro da Sintra therefore proposed to take his entire party of men and go into the interior to make direct contact with the elusive natives.

"Why?" asked Cadamosto. "The system of silent trade is working fine. Why tamper with an instrument in no need of repair?"

"First, because those are my orders from Prince Henry, to befriend the natives. Second, we must find out whether salt is the only medium of exchange they will accept. Perhaps we could get even more gold for other goods, even trinkets," responded Pedro da Sintra with evident impatience.

"If anyone is to make contact with and befriend these natives, it will be me," said Cadamosto with a certain pride of ownership and defiance that da Sintra was forced to concede to for the reasons already explained.

In the mild non-winter of *Serra Lyoa*, Cadamosto set off at the head of a small column of men so as not to frighten the obviously timid natives. He had no reason to believe them to be hostile, as he had established a sort of relationship with them through the silent trade. As they proceeded, the evidence of habitation increased, as they found foot-hardened paths that led to a large village. In front of the village, a phalanx of tall warriors stood, wielding the much-dreaded doubled-pointed iron spears, similar to those of the Mandinkas.

Cadamosto raised an open right hand and approached the phalanx like an experienced matador who, although cognizant of the danger, outwardly shows no fear. The warriors remained impassive to his gesture of peace. Clearly, they resented his intrusion into their privacy, as evidenced by scowls and hisses. To illustrate to them who we were, Cadamosto slowly produced a bag of salt from under his tunic; again, there was no response. A tall, lanky warrior emerged from the phalanx and seemingly berated Cadamosto, waving a long, flexible tree branch at him as if he were a tutor dissatisfied with his charge's poor work. There could be no mistaking his meaning as his unintelligible words were hurled at Cadamosto like the volley of batteries of artillery. Despite all his efforts to palliate, the screed continued unabated, perhaps encouraging conflict.

At this impasse, Cadamosto thought there was nothing left to do but intimidate with a show of strength. He had prudently brought a culverin along, which he ordered aimed at a nearby baobab tree. The natives watched in fascination as our men limbered the cannon and ignited the fuse. The resulting explosion unmanned the natives as they exhaled in awe. Upon impact, the tree trunk shattered into splinters, and the mighty tree fell with a swoosh of leaves and branches. With this demonstration, the lecture ceased abruptly, and the lanky warrior returned to the phalanx, which wordlessly withdrew into the village, leaving our men bewildered as to how to proceed.

Seeing no obvious alternative, Cadamosto ordered his men to follow the retreating warriors into the village. It was the usual tranquil scene, with chickens scratching in the dirt for insects, men crouching in front of primitive furnaces or working clay wheels, and curious women espying them from the darkness of their huts. The children had no such reticence; they crowded around the strangers, touching the gleam and unrelenting hardness of their cuirasses and casques.

There was the usual kraal in the middle of the village, with those strange humped backed cattle that were no longer strange to the men. Off to the west was a large hut that must house their leader or at least someone of importance. There was a raised porch where an old man sat on a stool; his white whickers contrasted the ebony shine of his face. He bore no expression; his face was a blank. Cadamosto placed a bag of salt at the old man's feet, at which the old man nodded, bidding him to sit. There was no stool provided, so Cadamosto had to sit on his haunches in discomfort.

The old man spoke no Arabic but did understand a few words of Mandinka, of which Cadamosto had a very cursory understanding. Their tribe was called the Mende, and they were primarily herders of cattle, though they also cultivated sorghum and legumes, which were introduced to them by Arabic traders. Communication proved to be painfully slow as the sun rose higher. The chief, whose name was Pdende, pointed to the culverin, indicating that he would be willing to trade gold for it. Cadamosto astutely agreed since the Mende would not have the gunpowder nor iron cannonballs to make the weapon lethal.

Pleased by this progress, Pdende ordered sorghum beer to be served to our thirsty mariners. Though sour and unpleasantly warm, our men imbibed deeply, unaware of the beverage's furtive potency. As in the past with the Mandinka, our men were served by bare-breasted, nubile, young women who did not seem to find them overtly repulsive as the Mandinka girls had, perhaps because our men had become accustomed to frequent bathing.

Bereft of admonishments, the men gulped rather than sipped the strong beer and quickly lost any inhibitions they might have harbored upon entering the village. These were the same men that had confronted and befriended the ferocious Mandinka. Surely, the customs of the Mende would be similar. As Cadamosto talked haltingly to the chief, he had not noticed the excesses of his mariners.

Uncertainty about the responsible party lingers today, but one of our men kissed a naked breast as he was being served more beer. In the scheme of outrages, it was not a very grievous one, but it proved to be an anathema against the unknown code of the Mende. Perhaps she was someone's cherished daughter or overly protected sister or even a beloved mother. Before anyone could react, the offender's cuirass was pierced with a spear wielded by a short, squat warrior. The thrust was so powerful that the point of the spear pierced through the body of the dying or dead man who, mercifully, quickly succumbed to the latter.

Instinctively, Cadamosto began to unsheathe his sword. It was a disastrous offense since he did so in proximity to the tribal chief. Before the point of the sword could clear the sheathe, two spears were mightily thrust into him from his left and right, transfixing him so he seemed unsure of which way to fall, until he collapsed dead face down, blood flowing out from the edges of his cuirass.

Quickly sobering, our men fell upon their attackers with all the outrage they owed to the murder of their beloved leader. Two of our men salvaged Cadamosto's inert body, leaving the original offender to rot. The Mende, mindful of the culverin and sharp steel edges of our swords, kept their distance and let our column retreat without pursuit.

ي

Pedro da Sintra was now in a quandary. He could take revenge on the Mende, killing and taking slaves, or he could try to repair the damage caused by the breach of etiquette. After all, not many lives had been lost, and we bore the worst of it with our two dead against none of the Mende. His calculation was heavily influenced by the probable opinion that my prince would have of his conduct. Knowing that Henry was, above all, a pragmatist, he decided on mending the tattered bridge. Besides, the Mende had gold to trade and were more valuable as counterparts than slaves.

His overtures to the Mende were well received, and apologies were given and accepted. Pedro da Sintra remained some months at the *feitoria*, amassing both gold and the courage with which to face my prince with the news of the death of his favorite, who some of our men unwisely referred to as Henry's lover. When Pedro da Sintra overheard one such careless jest, he had the offender stripped naked and bent over a barrel and ordered someone who had no love for the man whip his buttocks raw with a bamboo cane. I doubt whether the unnamed offender ever sat down comfortably. What I do not doubt is that all such jests immediately ceased.

In the fall of 1454, Pedro da Sintra set back to Portugal, as the prevailing southerly winds were at their weakest at this time of year. He sailed to Cape Verde, where a slave-gathering *feitoria* had been established, and dropped off his small human cargo of slaves and proceeded, without incident, to Lagos, fortified with the three hundred gold *dobras* he was to present to my prince. He was, he told himself, blameless for Cadamosto's death, and the gold would surely do much to mollify Henry's possible wrath.

ي

Henry was disconsolate upon hearing the news of Cadamosto. Even the gold that Pedro da Sintra presented him with did little to assuage his grief. He accepted Pedro da Sintra's story and did not fault him in any way. Henry also acknowledged that Pedro da Sintra was correct in establishing trading relations as opposed to taking revenge. Henry also approved that Pedro da Sintra had buried Cadamosto under a stone *padrão* inscribed with his name. Despite the gold that been found, which otherwise would have given rise to much talk, the audience with Pedro de Sintra was short.

It was at this point in the year 1454 that Henry disappeared from Sagres, indeed, the face of the earth. Of course, I knew where he was but dared not let anyone else in on his secret hideaway. It was not even a village, but a small cluster of three pastel-colored houses not three leagues from Sagres. It was there that my prince cloistered himself, feeding immodestly on self-pity. There were, of course, bizarre rumors since my prince had enemies who wished him evil repute. There was talk of all-night debaucheries with captured Arab catamites and overindulgence of wine and something called hashish. In all honesty, dear reader, I can neither confirm nor deny these vicious calumnies.

Meantime, the chain of *feitorias* seemed to work by itself, un-captained and unled, like a pendulum set to motion. Our Mandinka and Mende allies captured slaves, which they sold to us. These slaves were then transported to Cape Verde, where ships from all over Europe would come to buy them for coin. The slaving industry, once centered in the Mediterranean, was now an Atlantic enterprise, and we were the kings of the Atlantic. In later years, our mulattoes, now grown men and irresistible cinnamon women, were entrusted with the management of the Cape Verde *feitoria*.

There were also more voyages to Guinea, though none of them ever got beyond *Serra Lyoa* in my prince's lifetime. The riches of Guinea continued to be harvested without Henry's oversight, though he passively received his royal share.

ﺱ

That cursed Frey Dominicus says nothing, not a word; he just scowls at me in his imperiousness but continues to slavishly do my sinful bidding while he ascends higher on his moral ladder. I have lost count of the pipes I have consumed. My head feels like a sodden sponge, unable to think beyond my next craving. I have wolfed down food with unaccustomed appetite and poured sweet new wine into my throat in long-abandoned drafts. The food and drink satisfy as never before, the vivid flavors of the meat enhanced by the cool tartness of the wine. I do not recognize myself in these telluric appetites.

How ever much I inhale the sweet, camel-dung-laced smoke, eat the flesh of a calf, or imbibe in the September new wine, my grief cannot be assuaged. That ever-imposing sadness lies in wait like a thief in the night, ready to plunge the dagger, the reminder that he is dead and that my eyes will never look upon his beauty again nor my ears be favored with the soft wilting music of his dulcet voice. He is dead, and I will never again drink in his sweet aura, warm myself in his lithe presence, or even imagine what that soft cheek must feel like. That cheek is no more, long rotted away, devoured by little, ugly fiends that crawl upon this ugly earth, feasting on transient beauty and rejoicing on the final and lasting triumph of pernicious vileness over ephemeral adornments of the flesh. When I think of his face eaten by hordes of unfeeling larvae, I find myself weeping.

It is then that I call out to that beast, Frey Dominicus, and I watch him approach me in all his majesty of righteousness, his cavernous face drawn tight in a grotesque grotesque smile. I know why he smiles, the brute. He is looking forward to his reward. Frey Dominicus has never sinned, and he was born poor. He feels superior to me. As second my servant and first my confessor, he is cognizant of my profligate sins and my deep, deep humanity, despite my noble birth. Here I am, a prince of the House of Aviz who must prostrate himself for a sinless son of a peasant. I am doubly abased, for Frey Dominicus has no human appetites; he is a stone. His only pleasure seems to be lording over the humanity. Does he sleep? Does he even eat? I have never seen him do either, and in some of my most abnormal states, I often wonder if he can bleed. What does God think of me? I wonder. I know what Frey Dominicus thinks of me, but it is not the same judgment as God's. I cannot rise above my flesh. This weakness is an eternal torture. Oh, my beloved!

I am sorely tempted, very sorely, to take the gold he brought me and outfit an armada of vengeance, to mandate these brutes that I command to seek out these savage Mende and kill every single one of them, drink their blood, rape their women, and hack off the genitalia of the men and stuff them in their dead, gaping mouths. I can do this; I am a prince of Portugal, and I have the resources, but it would accomplish nothing but to dissipate my goal. It would not bring Cadamosto back to me. Yet when the wine tempts my anger . . .

Here he comes, that squalid piece of excuse for human flesh. He is ambling down to me in full superiority in doing my latest, most base bidding. His ugly smile is drawn tight in anticipation of the punishment he must wreck on me for the greater glory of God and his own hapless soul. I see that he is salivating with aforethought. His whip awaits and is still thirsty, still clotted with blood coagulated from frequent past offenses. Tonight, Frey Dominicus will delight in stripping my flesh of its pride and punishing the hedonisms that lurk in my soul and will not be removed. Yet before I will endure his lusty whip, I will have this boy.

CHAPTER FOURTEEN
TERRA INCOGNITA

After months dispersed with long absences, Prince Henry began to appear regularly at Sagres. The trading structure he had imposed had continued to function without his direct control, so his fifth flowed in with a regularity that mitigated the less-than-spectacular amounts of gold. For the first time in cognizant history, our hitherto poor kingdom possessed sufficient gold to mint our own coins, the Cruzado, upon whose face was cast the image of a crusader from whence the coin took its name. The other European coins were soon disparaged in favor of the nearly pure gold of the Cruzado. The Dutch gilders, the Genoese florins, and the German thalers had been adulterated over the decades, as they were constantly recast to remove their silver so they were gradually made almost worthless. But men are ever inventive, especially when there is profit to be made from fools, and soon, fake Cruzados were circulating, iron painted with a thin veneer of yellow paint. Merchants of all levels took to biting a coin to see if the soft gold yielded an indentation to their teeth. The Cruzado was king, and we, once on the periphery of Europe, were quickly becoming its center, especially as the Atlantic was yielding more riches than the tired, old Mediterranean.

Prince Henry's appearance had changed markedly. Once ascetically gaunt, his face now appeared puffed and darkish like an overly ripe grape. I could plainly see his veins outlined on the side of his nose and the unmistaken beginning of jowls. As he always had worn loose robes, it was difficult for most people to tell whether he had gained weight, but since I had spent so much time in his proximity and had a more practiced sense of his heft, I could discern that he had put on as much as a stone. He also appeared less energetic; his movements, once vigorous to the extreme, looked slothful and determined, as if moving his limbs took concentrated effort. After all, it was the year of our Lord 1553, and Henry had advanced to the ancient age of 59, a rare feat in our time when flux, unbalanced humors, dyspepsia, or an impacted tooth can claim a life, as man's existence is but a vulnerable flame on a candle set atop a mountain so that the slightest breeze can extinguish it.

Apart from his demeanor, others changes manifested themselves. Although still publicly abstemious in his diet, I did notice that he ate with more appetite than before. After noonday meals, he now retired to his quarters for an uncustomary nap, a luxury he had never allowed himself in his previous avatar. Were the weight of the years finally crushing my indomitable prince? I believed so, and I dreaded the inevitable fate that time would wreck on me, eventually slowing my gait and curving my spine from the heft of time. We only notice how old we are getting in relation to those around us. The shock we get from seeing someone from our youth now an old man is sobering, especially when our surprise is met with its equal, for if the acquaintance looks old to us, then we must look old to him as well.

It was generally assumed that Henry had absented himself from Sagres because he was grieving for the death of his younger brother, Dom Fernando who had died in poverty in captivity. Henry did nothing to dispel this general belief; he even encouraged it, sighing when his brother's name was mentioned. Henry ordered many Masses said on behalf of his brother's soul and even contemplated aloud requesting that Dom Fernando be made a saint by the Vatican in recognition for his martyrdom at the hands of the infidel. Such was his outward pathos, so many forgot that it was Henry who was responsible for the agonizingly slow death of that poor child in a devilish Moor dungeon. Those of us who did remember kept their own counsel.

They were, of course, all curious to know where Henry had disappeared to, but he did not volunteer the information, and no one dared ask. Henry still religiously attended the gatherings in the rotunda, where the best minds opined on the mosaics of the rudders in order to piece the world together. He mostly listened passively, only occasionally asking a question or making some remark on what had been said. One subject that always got his interest and participation was the best method to explore *terra incognita*.

With the steady trickle of gold coming from the slave trade and other endeavors, there was now no shortage of wealthy adventurers willing to finance their own expeditions under Henry's aegis. My prince now had the luxury of choosing whom to allow to pillage in his name. To this end, his judgment served him well, for he had always been a good determiner of character, or lack thereof. Henry had the gift of seeing through the most skilled artifice and right into the meat of a man. So while many offered their money and services, few were chosen.

س

Over use and experience, the caravels were improved. No, not by great leaps but by small incremental steps, the way a child learns how to walk. A shortened sheet here, the trimming of a sail there, and our ships became increasingly more maneuverable and more seaworthy as different calking mixtures were tried with each succeeding in sealing the hulls tighter against the ever-attacking sea. Each small improvement correlated to a larger increase in audacity. Our mariners lost their awe of the sea but wisely retained their fear of its immense power.

As could be expected, our dry docks were overrun with Aragonese and Venetian spies acting the parts of merchants interested in purchasing a vessel. Henry forbade our shipwrights to sell any but the older models, some of the hulks that miraculously had survived as much as two voyages to the coast of Guinea. Shipwrights were admonished not to talk to strangers, even if they spoke perfect Portuguese. To put shark teeth into the admonition, he sent agents into the dockyards to test the obedience of the shipwrights, carpenters, and sail makers. The agents asked questions with vague promises of recompense. Anyone found leaking information was brought uncomfortably to Sagres and given a very stern lecture. These were valuable craftsmen, not to be wasted with revenge. Usually, the warning was sufficient to seal their mouths, even from their wives. Henry could be very intimidating. Still, he knew that ships were in plain view and that, eventually, their secrets would be unlocked. But the rudders were another matter.

The rudders were amassed and kept in a secret vault at Sagres. I do not know of anyone he trusted with the key but himself. Of course, there were many learned men who had memorized pieces, but the entirety of the painfully gained knowledge belonged to Henry alone. Woe to the spy who tried to steal these secrets, for there would be no stern warning before he was beheaded, that is, if he was lucky enough to be merely beheaded. All secrets are transitory, but Henry

hoped to retain his dominion over the Atlantic for as long as
he could.

The hubris of our mariners grew in proportion to the
possible rewards but in disproportion to the remaining
dangers. Each day, my prince was besieged with ever more
outlandish proposals. One wanted to sail up the West Nile,
which everyone already knew was the Senegal, into Egypt.
Henry, never one to suffer fools, even wealthy ones, ordered
the master of arms to place a healthy foot on his arse.
Another would-be explorer claimed he could round the cape
of Guinea in one fell swoop, never stopping until reaching
the Indies. Henry dismissed this crackpot in anger, though
he did not order arms laid on him. Before the continent could
be rounded, *feitorias* had to be established to resupply ships;
there was no caravel that could sail onto the enormity of
the Atlantic and the daunting Indian Ocean on the faith of
foolishness alone. Rounding the continent was an incremental
exercise, much like the gradual improvement of our ships.
Henry communicated to me that he feared that rounding the
cape would not be accomplished in his lifetime. As it turned
out, his fear proved correct. The coast of Guinea stretched
southward to perdition and eternity, or so it seemed.

With trade doing well in the known world we had
discovered, there was little financial impetus to continue
the discoveries. Most petitioners merely wanted to go over
known routes to enrich themselves further, but Henry was
never one to share in assured or low-risk enterprises. There
were sufficient means at his disposal, and now his better
nature took hold, his curiosity of what lay beyond.

س

He was not a very imposing man, at a height that barely
reached Henry's shoulders, nor was he particularly young, an
asset Henry valued in his explorers, for age breeds caution.

His girth and habiliment betrayed him as a rich man. His hair had receded past the middle of his head, and his forehead glowed like a harvest moon. Worst of all was his propensity to giggle like a young woman when he was nervous. His name was Joaquim Andrade, one of the many merchants who had become wealthy on the Guinea trade. Although he dabbled in many articles, his main commerce was slaves, and it was slavery that had made his fortune.

Like many men who come upon wealth, Joaquim believed that he was exceptionally talented. It would never have occurred to him that he was simply a lucky man, made so by the misery of the Negroes and the need for labor in our disease-decimated Europe. We had still not recuperated from the last plague, which took Henry's mother, Phillipa. Therefore, despite his less than impressive credentials, Joaquim felt entitled to opine with the assurance of a man accustomed to being listened to. In short, he was a pompous idiot, but as he had been instrumental to my prince's finances a number of times in the past, Henry tolerated him with an even temper and even attended to some of his ideas. In return, Joaquim bore my prince a slavish devotion, something Henry prized.

On the Saturday following Good Friday, Joaquim showed up at Sagres at the head of a caravan of five drays, all heavily loaded.

"Lent is over, my lord, and I bring fresh meat and stout wine to celebrate the rebirth of Christ and our earth," he exclaimed, frequently giggling between words.

Joaquim Andrade may well have been unfeeling to the plight he doomed his slaves to; he could be a bore, but no one ever accused him of not being generous. The wagons were arrayed with horizontal poles from which hung fat, recently slaughtered capons and thick sausages; there were suckling pigs in cages squealing in protest for their mothers and pine boxes brimming with fish, each with the telltale bloodied eye, which meant they had been caught that very morning. One dray was pulled by a team of four oxen as it groaned under the weight of a tremendous cask of wine. Even the ascetic Henry could not help but smile at the cornucopia that Joaquim had brought.

Not trusting the curmudgeonly hags of Sagres's rather austere kitchen, Joaquim had hired his own cooks who quickly began preparing the feast for that coming evening while ignoring the curses the hags heaped on them. That evening, the good food and wine put everyone in a festive mood, and I was reminded of that other time when Cadamostro was last with us. Apparently, so was Henry, for his smiles were admixed with sadness, and he returned to his abstemious manner in regard to food and drink. While quiet himself, his presence was not heavy enough to intrude on the prevalent bonhomie, and I was grateful for the *beau geste* on his part.

It is rare that we lose ourselves in the present moment and not think of the past or anticipate some future event. We are usually in despair for this particular moment to lapse so we may have a chance at happiness in the next. It remains a mystery to me why we all insist on the postponement of happiness. I have come to the stark conclusion that if you are not happy in the current moment, then you never will be. But that night, with a hearty fire keeping the Atlantic at bay and the raucous laughter of men ringing in my ears, I did not feel the passage of time, for I was in the moment. I was happy.

Indeed, I had so abandoned myself to the camaraderie of the present that I had not looked at my prince for some time. As a rule, I scrupulously observe him for any sign of displeasure, and I am constantly on the alert for his beckon. But that night, I had lost myself, laughing, eating the delicate meat of suckling pig, and trying to outdo the stories I heard from the companions at my table. It was only when one of the servants tapped me desperately on the shoulder that I noticed Henry, irritated by my lack of attention, was waving me over to his presence. As I approached, I noticed that Joaquim Andrade was sitting at his right side, his face flush with a foolish smile.

"Go bid the servants set a fire and light lamps in the rotunda," he ordered.

I knew that there was no fire in God's world that could expel the dampness from the rotunda, but the servants made a good show of it.

س

With the flicker of flames from the giant hearth dancing eerily on the walls, Joaquim Andrade carefully unfolded an ancient map, the parchment yellowed with age. The map must have been three decades old and dated from the discoveries of the Atlantic isles. We all bent over to examine the map as Joaquim began to explain.

"You will see the Açores plainly where they should be, my lord, the correct latitude and longitude. But as you can also see, there is a land mass farther to the west. It must have been sighted by one of our mariners from afar since the rudder lacks detail. It is my contention that this land mass is the eastern coast of Guinea and that our mariners have inadvertently almost circumnavigated the globe."

"But what of the Indies?"

"I believe India lies to the north, for as you can see, this land mass indents."

"Are you saying we can get to India easier by sailing west?"

"This is what I believe my lord, and I am willing to invest in an expedition, of course with your permission."

I could tell Henry was intrigued with the prospect. Seeing his opportunity, Joaquim continued.

"As you see, my lord, the prevailing winds run southwest, which means we can arrive on one tack. This would save considerable time and money. Fewer slaves would die during the voyage, and we would need less provision."

Joaquim had run out of arguments, but he had no need to proceed, as I could see that my prince was intrigued enough to gamble Joaquim's money and life on this venture.

 س

In the intervening months, we all forgot about Joaquim. The duke of Braganza, Henry's half brother and, in my opinion, the murderer of Leonora and Dom Pedro, had died and was buried with great fanfare. His sons had come of age and one especially had caught my attention. His name was plain enough, João, but he was a most astute politician. Rather than shunning his father's enemy, Dom João II assiduously courted Henry's favor and flattered his intelligence with many questions on the science of navigation. He asked to visit Sagres and was, of course, admitted. Whether his interest was feigned or actual, I could not tell.

Henry was cordial toward Dom João II but never actually friendly. Come to think of it, he was never really open with any man that I know. Dom João II's affiliation with the man who had too frequently tried to thwart him was too close. Moreover, the resemblance between father and son was unfortunate: the same intensity, the same thick eyebrows that bespoke of excessive masculinity, and the thick, raw hands of a common laborer or a murderer.

Dom João II possessed his father's quick mind and was soon as much a master of navigation as any sage at Sagres. It was then that I realized that his interest in the science was genuine and admixed with my prince's motivators, namely, curiosity and avarice. Their shared interest and goals did much to assuage Henry's suspicions but not eliminate them altogether.

Dom João II believed rounding Guinea to be the best

route to India. When Henry told him of Joaquim's theory, he laughed dismissively.

"The man's a fool. Surely, there is a land mass to the west of the Açores, but it is decidedly not Guinea nor does India lie to the north in those colder latitudes. God did not make this world so small as that. It is vast, like its creator. But, my lord, I do agree on your reasoning to let the man try. After all, it is his money and his hide he risks. But you will see that the true route is around the horn of Guinea. I have even thought of an appropriate name for the cape, Good Hope. What say you, my lord?"

"It is indeed apt."

As I have said, Henry was always cordial to Dom João II but never expansive.

س

The sun, the earth, and the sea were all in synchrony that year, and the harvests were bountiful. The markets brimmed with vegetables, fish, and meat, and prices fell so much that even the poor could afford a joint of mutton or a dozen mackerel. Although it was an uneasy one, peace did prevail nonetheless.

We are not generally a cheerful people, perhaps because we have suffered so much without cause or explanation from God. Our music reflects our character; it is morose and replete with star-crossed lovers. We are natural pessimists. Yet in that late summer, the mirth in the air was palatable, like a warm mist that soothes. I would dare say that some of us became giddy, laughing aloud at the slightest hint of a joke. Even the sparrows appeared fatter than usual.

Ships arrived with their holds laden with cargo and even some gold from the slave trade. The breezes were stiff, and everyone reported good sailing with no time spent in the doldrums. Henry's fifth arrived unmolested at Sagres since, with the disappearance of desperation, there was no need to rob and risk one's neck. In the cobblestone streets of cities and towns, children played merrily and cooperatively, with none of the usual bickering that arises when stomachs are empty. The children frolicked, rosy-cheeked and squealing in their joy, barely able to contain the life in their youth. All the confluences of fortune were favorable, fishing nets replete with silvery wagging tails, trees groaning with fruit, their branches nearly touching the ground, and peace, sweet peace.

The clerics never tire of saying that we mere mortals can never fathom the infinite ways of God. When fortune smiles, we must be thankful for His generosity, but when fortune frowns, we are not to imprecate but, like Job, remain patient and accepting in His mysterious ways. Now, dear reader, as one of those dense mortals, I am not in a position to question God's infinite wisdom, but then again, He did allow us a brain, and that resulting faculty must perforce be put to use.

In my personal vision of God, He is merciful and infinitely generous. My God would not stoop to silly tests of faith like those He put Job or Abraham through. We are His children, and parents do not torture their offspring, but rather carefully nurture them and be willing to suffer in their stead. So I will admit to confusion when, in the midst of this idyll, for what is happiness but the lack of misery, an intruder slithered among us: plague.

س

It had been many years since the last pestilence struck, taking Henry's mother, Dona Phillipa, as well as half the populace of our kingdom into its black bosom. We had forgotten the ferocity of the plague and how the invisible evil can wrack woe upon our frail bodies. Many had not been born since the last plague and were caught unaware and unprepared for the misery of seeing mothers, brothers, friends, and neighbors shrivel in fever then tremble in pools of foul-smelling sweat and ultimately die in agony, unreleased by unconsciousness. People locked their doors against the invisible intruder, furtively looking out their windows to see if they could somehow forestall death. The wealthy had their food delivered to them, using pulleys to hoist baskets of larder through windows. No one dared venture far from home for fear of contracting the pestilence from some bestial spirit. Experience had taught the elders that the best chance of survival was to isolate oneself away from their fellow human beings. Many believed that the sickness was spread through evil stares and more deaths ensued with witches burned and warlocks stoned, their lifeless bodies then burned. Death was about like a startled stallion, spreading misery and grief. It became a common sight to see drays laden with corpses to be burned as children or parents followed their kin, shedding impotent tears. Wails of despair echoed off uncaring stone walls.

At Sagres, life went on, but carefully. Voices were hushed, as though we were all afraid to call attention to ourselves, and we all treaded lightly, as if we were walking upon eggs. Red warning flags were hoisted so that out mariners kept to sea. At Sagres, we looked suspiciously into each other's faces, silently interrogating each other for the first symptoms of the plague. We constantly peered in mirrors at our own terrified visages, frequently thinking we saw signs to our immediate horror. With time, the symptoms did not become manifest but left us heaving in fright nonetheless.

Like all innate scientists, Henry kept a meticulous log of where the plagued ravaged, which was almost everywhere, and where, for some inexplicable reason, the sickness spared the population. As could be expected, the more remote regions suffered much less, as if the pestilence had a poor sense of direction and got lost. Henry also kept a detailed list of friends and acquaintances who succumbed to the disease, noting their age, gender, weight, right down to the number of teeth that remained in their mouth at death. My prince was naturally searching for some common trait that made one person susceptible but not another, but alas, the plague appeared to strike at random, killing the young, the infirm, and the hale indiscriminately. I had the sad occasion to see this latter list and was distraught to find so many names I recognized. There was Vasco Martins, the veteran of Ceuta I had interviewed at his tavern, as well as his beloved son and inchoate scholar, Felipe. I was surprised to find Nuno, the thick-wristed hostler, among the dead and truly saddened when I discerned Darfum's name. For some reason, Henry had underlined it, whether he was saddened too or whether Darfum was the first Negro to be brought down by the plague, I could not say.

As the pestilence continued to rage, Henry asked a number of physicians residing at Sagres whether they would be interested in performing autopsies on the dead to see which organs were affected by the disease. They all begged off, as they were certain that such a procedure meant sure death and that certainty instilled enough resolve in their spine to deny my prince's curiosity. Besides, one said, it was a sacrilege and against Catholic doctrine to desecrate the human body that once housed the immortal soul. The point was made to assuage Henry's displeasure and avert any possible punishment. Henry appeared mollified, but I knew that he never let mere dogma get in the way of his curiosity.

The plague began to fade, much like the fever of a cold as the body begins to regain control of itself. Henry's entries into his log of doom became sparser until, at last, they too had run their course. Church bells pealed over our kingdom in thanks for deliverance. In truth, the living had much to be thankful for, but what of the dead? There were no dirges, no solemn knells for them, as we live dogs always will have the advantage over dead lions. But I still persist in wanting to know exactly what we had to be thankful for; was it that God did not completely annihilate the human race?

س

The spring the air smelled fresher, and everyone appeared to take greater delight in the return of the early blooms as an assurance that life would go on. The early spring cabbage had never tasted so good, and the cold mountain water slaked our thirst as it had never done before. Death's proximity can make for the full enjoyment of life's more simple pleasures, which we often take for granted.

At Sagres, we returned to our duties with a renewed fervor. Much had been neglected during the reign of the plague, for no one wanted to begin a task that might not be finished. As such, the backlog of tasks was formidable. In the middle of our diligence, a runner arrived from Lagos with news that masts had been sighted to the southwest. As we lived in constant fear of attack, the announcement was received with foreboding, especially since our ranks had been decimated, and we were weak to defend ourselves. Another runner arrived some hours later to announce that the pennants were indeed Portuguese. In our troubles, we had forgotten about Joaquim Andrade.

س

I barely recognized Joaquim when he limped into the rotunda. He had gone completely bald and had lost all his teeth to scurvy. His once plump body was now gaunt, and his once fat, rosy cheeks had inverted into pale, concave hollows. He limped in slowly and with the small steps of an old man wracked by rheumatism and afraid to fall. We were all agog to hear his tale, especially since he looked like he might not survive to tell it. In the story, he told he did not giggle once; gone was the jocular soul, replaced by a ruined hulk of a man. My prince is indeed wise to avoid sailing the seas at all cost. I shall try to paraphrase his tale as closely as I can, for he was not a glib speaker.

 س

My lord, we left the Açores well provisioned and with a stiff wind at our stern. We were sailing southwest and all the time getting closer to the equator, so the days grew warmer and, after a month, intolerably hot. I was soon forced to start rationing water, but luckily, there were intermittent cloudbursts that partially refilled our casks. The sea was too deep to catch fish, so we made do with biscuits and hard tack until we could barely stand the sight or the smell of that wretched excuse for food. Still, the breezes remained stiff, inflating both the sails and the crew's morale, for there is nothing a true sailor likes best than a fair wind, the feel of the prow cutting the sea, and a boiling wake to show our progress. A sailor delights in the sway of the ship.

As we traveled farther south, the rainstorms became more frequent and torrid, as if God had unloosened the heavens and released Noah's flood upon us. With the relief from the water ration, the crew's spirits revived. Their spirits were further elated when we started to catch fish. This manna from the sea was much welcomed, but it also meant that the sea floor was reaching up to us as we traveled. Land, we reasoned, must not be far.

Some two weeks went by, and our weak flesh had been replenished by the plentiful water and fresh fish, which we called St. Christopher's fish, as it had carried us across a vast ocean, and none of us recognized it by any other name. It was then that the lookout spotted birds, a sure sign of impending land, and I had the lads limber the longboats and sharpen weapons in preparation for landing. Most of our gunpowder was damp and useless, as the rains had partly flooded the holds, owing to the warping of the hatches with the severe changes in temperature. We sailed on confidently and with the prevailing wind pushing our ships to our destiny. At first, the lookout could only make out a vague haze, perhaps land, perhaps an expansive cloud cover. After months at sea, the crew's as well as my excitement was palpable; it glowed around our bodies like an aura. We would have blown into the canvas had that helped to determine whether it was land or just a ruse of nature. But the wind remained stiff, and we cut a thin swathe through the trackless sea.

Three days after spotting the hoped-for land, we could definitely see its shape and contours and not just the false promise of it. I ordered depth sounding taken, lest we run aground, and positioned sharp-eyed men on the bow to look for submerged reefs or rocks. As I have been told by my father, there only two kinds of ships: ones that have struck rocks and ones that have not struck them, yet. Shortening sail, I approached this inviting new world cautiously as a man who enters a strange house uninvited. I trained my glass on the shore and was blinded by the sun-bleached sand that glowed as a luminous ribbon. There were no signs of life such as ragged nets strewn upon the beach or rotted canoes. There was only the roar of the surf as the waves appeared to touch and retreat from the scorching heat of the white sand. Beyond the wide beach, the forest was dense. The trees were all bright red like the remaining embers of a once raging fire. The lookout trained his glass but could see nothing beyond the density of the ember trees that he called *brazas*, after our word for vivid red embers. The trees were so-called from then on.

The water proved deep and allowed us to approach the shore at a close distance. I ordered both caravels double anchored and launched longboats. After months at sea, we wobbled on the beach in expectation of sea rolls. The steadiness of the land felt strange to us at first, until we grew accustomed to the lack of movement. My lord, I had never seen such multicolored birds as I did upon that shore. There was one that could hardly fly because of its enormous, wonderfully colored beak. We spent weeks investing into the interior, but found no sign of human life; there were no paths beaten into the jungle floor. Flora and fauna abounded, and one of our men reported spotting a huge, beautiful cat. There were also packs of huge, rat-looking creatures that proved to be very tasty, more like rabbits. The trees teemed with strange, succulent fruit, so even the most scurvied among us was soon cured.

We built a fortification out of the hardwood trees in prudence, though against whom, I knew not. Each day, we cleared more path and invested farther into the forest. I sent parties in sixes, two to clear the path, two to watch their backs, and two to guard the rear. So there were six swords in all and two culverins that I am sure grew heavier as the sun rose to its apogee. I forbade the men to remove their cuirasses, for which I believe they both cursed and blessed me at the same time. I was despairing of finding anything but pesky mosquitoes and dense jungle when one of the parties brought back six captives: four men and two women.

They were small creatures and timid as deer. They looked almost identical to us with the same straight black hair, broad noses, and waif-like bodies. They were all almost totally naked but for a loin cloth made of some lizard's skin. The men sported some sort of bone that pierced their septum, which caused much wonder among us. But soon, their curiosity over the pierced men gave way to lust, as the women were bare breasted, I do beg Your Majesty's pardon. Some of the men grabbed the women or girls, for in truth, I could not tell which by their lustrous black hair, and dragged them away. We had been at sea for months, and my heart did go out to the screaming women, but I felt powerless to stop the men, as I feared a mutiny had I tried.

As we all knew a smattering of languages, we tried to communicate with our captives, but they remained passive, as if they were incomprehensive of what had happened to them. Finally, we grew tired of trying to communicate with them and loosened their shackles and gave them food and water, though they did not touch or even acknowledge the presence of the victuals. Shrugging, we retired for the night. In the morning, we found all four men dead with the food untouched. They had all shoved dirt into their mouths until they suffocated, so had the women when our men finally had left them tied to tree trunks.

The news of our intentions must have traveled through the vines of the jungle quickly, for every time we briefly encountered these naked natives, they vanished into the dense flora. Often, one or two of these dwarfs would stop for a moment and shoot darts at us from blowguns that fell harmlessly to the ground, as they did not dare get near us. We often came upon their depopulated camps but found nothing worthwhile. God had indeed neglected these creatures, for there was not a single metal implement to be found. Their huts were made out of twisted vines with not a hint of masonry anywhere. We could not even find a single piss pot; again, I apologize for my coarse language, my lord. These creatures, who looked like men but were not, lived in prehistory. Our most base citizen is much richer in knowledge.

I would not accept that I had happened upon a primitive world and sent out parties in search of a civilization. I ordered some of the men to remain behind and guard our boats and pan the nearby streams for gold. I encountered many empty camps, their inhabitants warned of our approach and recently scattered, as I could tell by the still-smoldering fires. It occurred to me that the only true value in this wretched jungle were the natives themselves, even as slight as they were in contrast to the robustness of the Negroes. But how to capture them in their own environment, given their evasive nimbleness?

One of our men was an experienced hunter and had served Your Majesty on your trips to the royal lodge. He suggested that we build an enclosure from the extra prow nets we had on board then funnel the natives into it like the cattle they evidently were. We then set the men out into the jungle to form a huge arc, and at the appointed time of the sun, they began beating pots against each other, banging casques together, anything to make hellish noise. On silent command, the arc of men began to converge, driving frightened monkeys, birds, and natives before them. The monkeys swung over us in the canopy, the birds flew over us, but the natives conveniently ran into the maw of our trap. After counting about one hundred head, for that is what I believed would fit into the holds of our ships, we shut the trap. Upon finding themselves enclosed, some of the younger men began scaling the netting with the dexterity of the monkeys that had already passed over and had to be knocked down with pikes and culverins, yet they got up again and started to scale the netting anew, only to be knocked down again. After a number of iterations, one of our men grew angry and fired his culverin into a climbing would-be escapee. I was about to discipline him when I noticed that the natives had stopped trying to escape and were gazing in awe at the severed corpse in wonder, for he had been shot at close range. The women all huddled in the middle of the compound, each with an infant in their arms or at their breast. They howled as though the world was coming to an end, for indeed, their particular world had.

The women's wailing continued into the night, driving some of our men to desperation, as no one could sleep through the cacophony of misery. As men picked up swords, they had to be restrained as they would have killed the slaves. I must admit to some consternation of my own, as these creatures did not possess the stoic acceptance of the Negroes who understand what has happened to them and consent to their fate with morose silence. The wailing of the women must have stopped sometime before dawn. I am myself not sure, as I must have dozed off. When I awoke, I went to the compound to find the guards I posted asleep and had to boot them awake. They did not apologize nor did I remonstrate. There was a mist in the compound as the heat of the sun admixed with the cooler air that had hugged the ground. As the mist lifted, I could discern the naked bodies and assumed they finally were asleep. But then I saw that there was no movement in their ribcages to indicate breathing, and I immediately knew they were all dead.

Mothers had suffocated their infants and then stuffed dirt into their mouths until they suffocated, so had the men. These people were so backward that they had no concept of slavery and, as such, are worthless.

س

Joaquim's voice echoed off the uncaring walls of the rotunda until it faded as no one wanted to break the spell of his tale. Joaquim himself slumped in his chair from the effort it had taken to recount his peregrination to nowhere. I deduced that the poor man, for now he was indeed a poor man, having squandered his fortune on the vainglorious pursuit of fame and fortune, would not live for much longer. The plague had taught me both the overt and subtle signs of impending death. Joaquim would not survive to the winter.

"You have done well, Joaquim Andrade," said my prince without a trace of facetiousness. "I will ask you to help update the rudders. It is well to know where we should not bother to explore. This new *terra incognita* shall remain so."

س

I had to lock and bolt my door to that lunatic Frey Dominicus. He would not stop ranting that Andrade had stumbled upon the original Garden of Eden and that the naked savages he found there were God's original children and direct descendents of Adam and Eve. He kept haranguing me that it was our duty to send ships to preach the word of God to these creatures and defend them from any interlopers who would enslave them. Who in this predominantly sane world would go through the expense and effort to enslave these sub-savages; they cannot even understand the concept of slavery! They simply eat dirt and die. They are useless as slaves and even more useless as converts. Dominicus still thinks that I financed expeditions to Guinea to bring God's light to the dark Negro; he is an utter fool. Yet he has no problem with Negro slavery. He is a contradiction, and contradictions in men usually pique my interest, but not that stick of a sorry excuse for a soul! Strange though, I would have never thought him capable of pity.

There he is again, banging at my door with his rat's claws. I tell him that, if he does not go away, I will set the dogs on him. He is frightened of the mastiffs, and I often set them on him to amuse myself, especially after a flagellation delivered by his pitiless hands. Despite the pain from my new welts, I cannot keep from laughing as that stick hikes up his skirts and runs on those spindly legs. The mastiffs usually overtake him and shred his cassock but are trained not to touch flesh. No, Dominicus, I am not in the business of saving souls, perhaps not even my own.

They tell me I have done much in my lifetime, as if all my accomplishments are behind me. The smarmy fools say it only to flatter for minutes after the sinister compliments a request ensues. The pagan Greeks, whom I admire secretly, say that no man truly dies as long as his name is remembered. If this is so, then my name will be but a whisper while the likes of Alexander, Caesar, and Richard of England will be shouted. Perhaps I will be merely of paragraph in the tomes of history; I may not be truly dead, but neither will I be truly immortal.

I do not trust this dogma that states that the soul is immortal. I see that it is useful dogma, for it makes our peasants docile, and they would never put up with their earthly existence otherwise. Yet I still doubt this afterlife. I have sent men beyond Cape Bojador to find the river of Senegal. I know the river exists, because men have returned to tell me, so but no one has ever returned from the afterlife to tell me it exists. If I confessed my doubts to the inflexible, unthinking Dominicus, he would try to have me burned at the stake, my title and position notwithstanding. I sometimes toy with the idea of telling just so that I may have an excuse to have him killed. Fanatics bore me; they cannot see beyond the blinders of their own convictions and are consequently stunted men, if indeed men at all.

What if there is no afterlife? What if, after death, you simply returned to the nothingness of before you were born? I am a prince, I am sentient, and I therefore possess the license to question this dogma inside my head. Did God create man, or did Man create god? Are we so in awe of temporary mysteries that we need the solace of a being all powerful, all protective, all wise? But He is not all powerful, or else, why do we have the intelligence to create better ships. He is not all protective; ask the dead from the plague. And if He was all wise, I would think He would have created better images of Himself. Explanations of mysteries keep coming to the fore almost every day as our world becomes less intimidating, and as such, we have less need of God.

I have witnessed the most venal of men rewarded in their mortal lifetime with wealth, health, and happiness while the good and humble man suffers in penury and dies in abject misery, convinced his reward will come after death while his uncaring overseer will perish in eternal flames of hell. I know something about hell; it may exist, but if it does, it is here on earth. Everyone, especially the clerics, thought the seas beyond Cape Bojador were filled with monsters, but it was not so. What if the Church is wrong about hell too?

Perhaps these mental metaphysics are just ways for me to justify my sins, which are plentiful, and mortality? I fear airing my doubts. Without the assurance of punishment in an afterlife, we would all be free to indulge in the basest of appetites without consequence, without the need to have Dominicus flagellate me. I wish it were so, but I cannot break free of my conscience. If there were no heaven nor hell, anarchy would reign, and we, the nobility, would be crucified by the long-suffering populace. So I will keep these thoughts to myself, but it is lonely to ponder alone without the resistance of a bright mind. My sins cannot allow for the cultivation of love, of a companion that I can tell all to. I am alone in a world of people. Alas, I have never cultivated a confidante and would never dare to.

I am through for the evening, exhausted from the painful introspection.

Dominicus is not present to give me my dram that guarantees dreamless slumber, and I do not dare to call him, for he will inopportune me with his mania. I have in me a playfulness that would invest the funds to let him go on his mission to convert these savages, but I fear that even they would find him too stringy to eat. I have never liked religious men; they have no motives; they have no brains. He is banging at my door again, and the mastiffs are in a playful mood. I will let him in.

Chapter Fifteen
A Modest Conquest

*I*n the year of our Lord 1456, the seemingly eternal war between Christianity and Islam continued to teeter-totter, much to the utter frustration and perplexity of either side who both claimed that God was with them. God's infinite and mysterious wisdom must have tested the patience of many believers. In the West, Christian armies had liberated the Iberian Peninsula from Muslim rule in the prior century, leaving only the pesky enclave of Granada. Our great king, João I, had crossed the Pillars of Hercules and taken Ceuta, establishing a foothold on Moroccan soil. Our mariners had succeeded in circumnavigating the Muslim kingdoms of North Africa and wresting the slave trade from them, obviating the importance of their slow and inefficient caravans. However, in the East, the Turks had taken Constantinople, committing numerous sacrileges, such as converting our sacred churches into mosques. The Pope, Calixtus III, called on Christianity to rise up and gather a huge army to attack the interior of Turkey and, from there, go westward, driving the infidels from our holy city of Constantinople and into the Dardeneles to be crushed by the vise of Christianity. Even I recognized that it was a ludicrous plan; the Pope was no military strategist. Despite the obvious impracticality of the Pope's plan, several European monarchs gave it serious thought. One such monarch was our own king, now a man of twenty-five, Afonso V.

Afonso was an impressionable young man, given to short bouts of feverish activity and then long spells of lethargy. He was, moreover, morose, and I believe that he secretly felt he did not deserve to sit upon a throne made powerful by the exploits of his grandfather and uncle. Afonso both wanted to achieve great feats while despairing of being able to do so at the same time. The call to arms by the idiotic Pope must have appealed to his search for his destiny, for he lacked inner vision and perforce relied on the spirituality of the clergy to guide him to his proper place in history.

The king must assuredly have felt his mortality leaking out of his body. He was much like his father, Dom Duarte, and given to fits of dyspepsia and plagued by insomnia. He lamented that he lacked the strength of his mother, Dona Leonora, who would have lived to a wizened old age had she not been poisoned by his uncle Pedro, or so he believed. He naturally feared that he was destined to die young, like his father. The court physicians were on constant call to examine a suspicious lump or some unexplained rash.

This torment of an early death drove the young king mad with the desire to leave his imprimatur on history while he still lived. He remained well aware of his relative inexperience and knew that he needed the advice of a warrior he could trust. His uncle, the duke of Braganza and the avenger of his mother's murder, was by now long dead, but hardly forgotten. His troublesome legacy persisted, represented by three quarrelsome sons who all tightly gripped their father's torch of ambition and who eyed the throne with the same cupidity that the duke had displayed throughout his long life. They disagreed with each other about everything, save that the House of Braganza should supplant the effete House of Aviz on the throne of Portugal.

The most astute was the middle son, whom, dear reader, you have already met, Dom João II. Perhaps the duke had named this son João purposely so as to remind everyone of his lineage from Dom João I, the great liberator and the true conqueror of Ceuta. Of the three would-be heirs of the House of Braganza, João was the most tactful, never actually mentioning his direct lineage to the king but alluding to it constantly without seeming to do so. João's boon and problem was that he was his father's son, and the duke retained many enemies, even after death.

The duke was also not forgotten by the widows and children of the men who had lost their lives at Alfarrobeira. Such was their resentment that his sons were forced to station a twenty-four-hour guard at his tomb to prevent these aggrieved relatives of his victims from relieving themselves or otherwise desecrating the duke's elaborate stone marker. João was therefore challenged to rehabilitate the name of the House of Braganza without denigrating what he believed to be the spent House of Aviz, personified by a weak, vacillating king who was presently at a loss of where to direct the very limited resources of the kingdom.

There was no one Afonso could comfortably turn to for advice but Henry who had mysteriously disappeared over the past few months. The king sent word that he wished to consult with his now-famous but reclusive uncle. The word reached Sagres and was heard by ears, namely, those of Frey Dominicus who knew the whereabouts of his congregation of one. Ultimately, word did reach my prince that his nephew, the king, was anxious to speak with him. Ever heedful of protocol, Henry presented himself before his nephew and sovereign at St. George Castle in Lisbon. Afonso was glad to see his famous uncle and quickly outlined his plan to raise an army for the invasion of Turkey with the intent of eventually retaking Constantinople. He added that the Pope was granting indulgences to anyone who participated in the conquest. Henry lost no time in dissuading his militarily naïve nephew from undertaking such an unwise endeavor.

"My lord, the Turks number in the hosts of millions and will be defending their homeland. As attackers, we must field three men for every one of theirs, an impossibility for our poor kingdom. Moreover, our armada must perforce be such a size that it would be easily spotted on the crowded Mediterranean, eliminating the necessary element of surprise. We are primarily a naval power, while the Turks rule the land. They will not fight on our terms, and it would be ruinous for us to fight on theirs. It would be a disastrous expedition; our army would be completely wiped off the face of the earth and sent to heaven, where it could not defend us from the avaricious Castilians."

I have described before that my prince's physiognomy had changed much for the worse. Comparing his current appearance with that of his previous one, I could not believe how much he had deteriorated. The debilitations of old age usually creep up slowly like thieves in a thousand nights, stealing the resiliency of our youth and replacing it with gradual infirmity. It had not been so with Henry, as he had appeared to have aged geometrically within these past few months.

His once ruddy face had turned pale and puffy like one of those delicate pastries that rise in the oven. Fatty pads appeared under his now-sunken eyes, and on each side of his bulbous nose were red star bursts of capillaries. His hands and fingers were gnarled in arthritic deformity, shaking as I had never seen them do before. There was a new presence with him, a boy servant who kept himself facing my prince's back and who did not take his eyes off Henry's breeches. I suspected that Henry had succumbed to incontinence and that it was this boy's exclusive duty to watch for signs of an accident and be ready with a change of breeches and linen. Even his once resonant voice now vacillated much like that of a boy's upon reaching puberty. His old friends at court were shocked at his appearance, for an old friend is the truest mirror.

Perhaps his body had become infirm, but Henry's mind certainly remained intact, for he argued well against the Turkish expedition, presenting his logic in natural sequence, convincing the king quickly and efficiently. Afonso was not likely to change his mind under the sway of other less competent counselors once Henry finished with his arguments. As long as Henry remained near his nephew's ear, the king was not likely to proceed along foolish paths. Given the precariousness of our kingdom's fortunes left in the hands of inexperience and glory seeking, Henry's duty was obvious. Henry acceded reluctantly to his duty, although he was equally reluctant to display his infirmity.

"What about Tangier?" asked the king. "You know the defenses well, and we would not make the same mistakes."

"Again, we fall short in manpower, as the Moors have strengthened the city's defenses since our last attempt. We must use what advantages we have, namely, our navy. The Arab is a poor sailor, their dhows are clumsy, fit only for transporting wheat down the tranquil Nile. They are frightened of the ocean, as their dhows are unseaworthy and ride too low in the water to mount cannon. We must attack a coastal target where we will be unchallenged on the water."

"Very well," conceded the king, none too pleased with lowering his expectations. "But it must be a target of importance. One more thing, uncle, I will need a loan from you to equip ourselves."

"But I have no fortune. The money that comes in from the Atlantic Isles and booty from Guinea is barely sufficient for the upkeep of Ceuta and to finance my expeditions."

"What of the treasure of the Templars?"

"My Lord, that belongs to God."

"I see; you have already promised it to all the members of your household that have served you loyally for all these years. Uncle, I will not argue as to the provenance of the money, but I will need at least ten thousand gold *dobras* to build and buy one hundred ships and enough arms for seven thousand men."

"Let me see what I can do, as I possess various markers that I can call. However, I will put a stipulation on my effort. If I succeed in raising the funds, then I will choose the target to be attacked."

"Agreed, provided it is impressive enough for my name to live on after my corporal body is dead."

ي

In that year, 1456, Henry did call on all the people who owed him money to pay, but the funds he raised proved to be woefully short of the amount needed. Henry sat in the rotunda at Sagres, brooding over the wane of his influence, when a visitor arrived. Into the male sanctuary of Sagres, Dona Eulalia thrust herself onto his solitary musings like an errant cannonball, beginning to speak to Henry even as she burst through the doorway.

The years had been kinder to her than the intervening months that weathered my prince. She was even stouter than the last time I had seen her, but her step remained energetic. Her face, though plump, was unfurrowed by wrinkles and still displayed that wild resolve of someone who knows her mind and will not be dissuaded by trivial arguments. Though often suited, even into her old age, she had never married, having once chosen a mate and been rejected by him. She got right to the reason of her visit.

"I have heard that you are in need of money for the

invasion of Morocco. You are fulfilling your destiny, albeit at old age. I have come to help."

Henry was stunned and visibly at a loss as to what to say.

"But, madam, it is a vast sum. I need some six thousand gold *dobras*."

"I will lend you that amount without interest, provided I receive half the plunder you take, of course, in addition to the full repayment of the principal."

"Madam, I will not marry you in return for this loan if that is what you still seek."

"Posh. The repayment of principal and half the booty are the only conditions I place on the loan. At one time, I did entertain a union between us, but at our ages, the issue of marriage is quite ludicrous. You've turned into a decrepit old man, and a pervert too from what I've heard, while I'm a fat old maid. I have survived the pestilence while all my male relatives succumbed, leaving me the sole heir of our house. I have been made richer in *dobras* but miserably poor in the years of life that remain to me. My lands are well-cultivated, and the serfs who work upon them are well fed. I must put my money to some greater use, and I have always believed that somehow you were my instrument. The financing is not a favor I bestow upon you or leverage for me to gain what you are unwilling to give, but merely a way for us to fulfill our common destinies, for I fear I will not see you again after we part, judging by your sickly appearance and that boy who keeps staring at your breeches."

Age had made Dona Eulalia even blunter than she had been in her youth and more resolute of character. She was fearless in the face of life's random occurrences.

Henry agreed, and the documents were quickly drawn and signed, and Dona Eulalia departed as suddenly as she had appeared.

ي

Henry was always at his best when he was absorbed in simultaneously attending to multiple tasks. In his twilight years, his energy was like one of those stars that burst brightly before extinguishing, exhausting their remaining fuel in a lavish swan song. While attending to the armada, he also retook his interest in exploration of the coast of Guinea, though I must confess, not with the same intense passion he had once displayed. Our old, squat friend Pedro da Sintra again volunteered to lead an expedition. He certainly did not fit the usual mold of Henry's explorers, since he was not in financial distress any longer, nor was he particularly young. If I were to be pressed to venture his reasons for going, I would venture that he had grown weary of the sedentary peaceful existence he had led after returning from Guinea. Some men become vitiated to adventure as others do to wine.

With his greed tempered, Pedro da Sintra set sail in the voyage-friendly spring of 1456 and wandered aimlessly along previously explored coastline until he passed the Gambia River. Anchoring some twenty leagues south of the mouth of the river, he chanced upon a tribe who called themselves the Bulums who came out to meet them in a large, forty-man canoe that they rowed with their feet. Our mariners were now accustomed to such sights and were sanguine, as they had learned to read the various signs of malevolent intent. The Bulums did not seem warlike in any outward manner, yet weapons were cautiously kept at the ready, though inconspicuously so.

Upon visiting their village, our men learned that, despite their outwardly peaceful nature, they did make use of poison-tipped arrows and wielded fierce-looking assegais, though these weapons served mostly for defense and hunting. The males also pierced their genitals, a custom our men found strange and which highly disturbed the young *pagens* who were more susceptible to the bizarre than our older, world-weary mariners. The Bulums were willing to trade for the small amount of ivory they had, but they had no gold and were largely ignored and bypassed on subsequent voyages.

Diego Gomes was one of the last captains to sail under Henry's auspices. Gomes was particularly interested in going up the Gambia River farther than previous expeditions had. He outfitted two special longboats for this purpose, reinforced with perpendicular struts so as to hopefully survive being rammed by a floating tree trunk. He then lashed the longboats upon davits on the port and starboard sides of his carrack and, in 1457, set out. Rowing up the river, he and his party passed by known and now friendly villages. They rowed on until they reached a land the natives called Kuntar. Canoes came out to greet our men, and Gomes was taken to meet their chief who called himself Nuimi-Mansa and who spoke fluent Arabic but treated our sailors cordially, despite his knowledge that we were the Moor's enemy.

As I have already noted, dear reader, I believe in a strange alchemy that either makes men immediate friends or life-long enemies upon first sight of each other. In this particular case, Nuimi-Mansa took an immediate liking to Gomes and his party of men, even though he innocently stated that he thought their flesh resembled that of a dead man buried for three days and then unearthed. Gomes was quick to take advantage of this initial goodwill and indulged the chief who was enchanted with the taste and effects of our robust wine. I suppose the strict word of the Koran had not reached Nuimi-Mansa, so he wore his religion like a woman's veil in Church, that is, lightly. Our explorers were always more comfortable under these circumstances when religion did not preclude camaraderie, perhaps because they too bore their own religious convictions with a dollop of practicality, despite overtly manifesting firm belief. In our times, it was merely a manner of surviving and eliminating obstacles. These men resembled water that, aided with gravity, always finds the path of least resistance. With two men of such like minds, they were sure to become fast friends. It was more practical to do so.

Gomes and his men were aware that they were by watched from the shadows by Arab *marabouts* who naturally did not wish them well. The *marabouts* had been trading with the chief and were rightfully afraid of being replaced by us. The Arabs looked upon the unfolding events with the consternation but could do nothing, as they were outnumbered by our men. All they could do was quietly curse us from the darkness of their huts from which they dared not venture, for our swords were well sharpened and oiled. But come nightfall, Gomes knew that the *marabouts* would slither out from their lairs and blather dark afflatus into Nuimi-Mansa's ear. Gomes deduced this likely event and wisely chose to remain close to his newfound friend.

The Arab merchants had taught Nuimi-Mansa the value of gold, so Gomes was aware that he could not dare offer trinkets in trade, so he dealt with him honestly. The chief was so pleased with the deportment and honesty of our mariners that Gomes convinced him to expel the *marabouts*. A Franciscan friar had accompanied them on the expedition who managed to convert Nuimi-Mansa and many of his people to Christianity. The king was baptized and chose the name Henry in honor of my prince. Upon Gomes's return and report, Henry, for the first time, appeared to be more delighted with the conversions than the actual procurement of gold. Henry sent three more Franciscan missionaries to Kuntar in the following year, cautioning them to respect their flock and adding that he would not countenance the priest lying with or marrying native women, as missionaries are apt to do when far away from the authority and moral suasion of the Church. It is a phenomenon I have often witnessed, where, as men approach death, they try harder to mollify God.

ي

In September of 1458, ninety ships carrying sixty-five hundred heavily armed men sailed from Setubal for an attack on an undisclosed Moroccan city. Henry had not forgotten the lesson his father had taught him regarding the element of surprise. The armada was ostensibly commanded by the king, Afonso V, though Henry retained the real leadership since the king deferred every decision for his uncle's approval. Henry had appropriated one of the larger carracks, customizing it with private quarters, including a privy, in the stern. Only he and his servant were allowed aft.

As the armada approached the Moroccan coast, the mercurial king pressed Henry to attack Tangier instead of his secret target. It took all my prince's suasion and patient argument to keep the king from overriding his counsel. Henry was now 64 years of age, an old man grown cautious with the accumulation of experience. He revealed to the king that the target was Alcácer Ceguer, a fort midway between Ceuta and Tangier. When he learned of his uncle's plan, the king was not pleased. Moreover, it did not make him happy when the king also learned that Alcácer Ceguer meant "small castle" in Arabic.

The armada gathered in the deep bay in front of the fort, disgorging forty-five hundred men on the shore, out of range of the guns mounted on the crenulated walls of the Moorish fort. Our fleet now went to work, bombarding the walls with impunity as our ground forces made it suicide for any defender to risk sticking his head above the walls. After two days of successive broadsides, the walls were breached, and our ground troops poured into the fort. The six hundred or so defenders immediately laid down their arms and surrendered.

Obeying previous instructions given by my prince, there was no carnage, and we spared all lives. The wealthier captives were kept for ransom, while the others were simply released to walk to Fez. The victory was utter and complete, yet the king complained openly that we had used a sledgehammer to drive in a simple and small nail.

"How can this small victory compare to what my grandfather achieved?" lamented the king. Henry paid him no heed, convinced that the victory was attained honorably. Our men rebuilt the walls of the fort, taking special care in reinforcing and elevating the walls facing landward since there was little to fear from any Arab navy. Leaving the fort in the capable hands of my friend, the governor-general, whom the reader will recognize from the start of my narrative, our fleet departed with victory pennants waving majestically in the stiff wind.

Within months of our departure, the Moors attacked Alcácer Ceguer twice, but without proper ships to bombard the seaward walls, their attacks were repulsed with little loss of life on our side but serious losses from the invaders who were limited to the landward attacks. As with Ceuta, many members of the *Cortes* complained that Alcácer Ceguer was a useless prize, draining money from the treasury for its upkeep and defense and contributing nothing in return. However, there were also members in the *Cortes* that profited handsomely from selling the provisions to the garrison, the very same ones who profited from Ceuta. These men of power could naturally be counted on to defend the prudence of the conquest. Henry had given his nephew an easy victory and perhaps a line or two in the thick annuls of history.

ي

Henry became ill in late October of 1460 of an undiagnosed malady. For the convenience of the reader, I will call it old age, a sickness we must all succumb to eventually, that is, if violence or an accident does not visit us first. He was not in a position to complain, as he had enjoyed a long and vigorous life, enjoying robust good health until almost the end. Save for the lack of progeny, which he did not lament, he had led a full life.

For weeks, priests and well-wishers gathered at his bedside, praying for his soul, while Masses were said in his honor all over our nation. His soul would go well recommended, and Henry encouraged this community of prayer, as if hoping to sway St. Peter. I was one of the last people to be ushered into his presence.

"My dear friend, Zurara, after I die, I am commissioning you to write a vast chronicle of my life. I am aware that some wrongs may have been committed but always with the proper ends in mind. I authorize you to convey that I am sorry for the misery I may have caused to the bodies of men to save their souls, for it is well-known that the health of the immortal soul is more important than that of the transient body. But you must also point out that, in these last years of my life, I have attempted to expunge any unintentional evil by good works. You must state that clearly in your chronicle.

"Remind my people that I have given them a world to explore. Someday soon, I believe our explorers will reach the tip of Guinea, rounding it to reach India. Let the explorer who finally rounds it call it the Cape of Good Hope as Dom João I suggested. I die fearing no man but fearing only God. Pray for me."

س

Was it only a few scant years ago that I was young and robust? How could this misfortune happen to me so quickly? I can still vividly remember the vigor I possessed in my limbs and feel I can still remember wielding a sword with that same strength, but when I try, I can barely lift it, let alone wield it. So it must be true; I am dying.

I pray the unintentional evil I have committed is interred with my bones and devoured by the limestone while all the good I have intentionally done remains public. In my defense, I can say that no man is all good or all evil, but an admixture of the two. Those who claim complete goodness are most likely hypocrites, while those who claim to be completely evil are insane or somehow demented. As such, there are no extremes, and there can be no absolute brightness of heaven nor inky blackness of hell, just the gray existence that can only be defined in retrospect. We ourselves cannot define the moment we live in; history must determine its virtue or lack of it.

Death is inefficient, as it retards the intellectual evolution of mankind. Here, we the sentient are accumulating knowledge throughout our lifetimes then reaching the epitome of our learning only to die and have another generation start all over. Yes, our progeny may read the written material we leave behind, but not having experienced our lifetime, they will not fully understand and are most likely to commit the same blunders we did in our own youth, the warnings notwithstanding. The written word can only convey so much information; it is hard experience that teaches indelible lessons. As it is, each generation must start over; we advance by crawling on our bellies like the worms we are rather than soaring effortlessly like the falcons we are not.

I have heard of a religion beyond the Indies where the worshipers believe a man is reborn infinite times. Depending on how he has conducted his life, the man is reborn elevated or debased from his previous station. A noble existence will engender an even nobler rebirth, a prince or a king, while a base existence will result in coming back as an animal or even an insect. It is a religion I can relate to, for it allows the progression of the human spirit and preserves the precious acumen we accumulate with great difficulty, immense pain, and wounded pride. This religion, like our own, offers immortality but with a catch, much like ours. We may be reborn in heaven or hell, while these faraway practitioners believe we may be reborn kings or cockroaches. Judging by the number of kings as opposed to cockroaches, I would suspect most of us fail and descend the latter of spirituality. It is all the same.

No man is ever really ready to die, not really, even those who would be released from pain; they would much rather endure the pain than die and be released from it as well as everything else grown dear. My own learning is not complete, and my curiosity is far from slated. I dare say I will always thirst, even after rounding the horn of Guinea, for I would want to know what lies beyond and then beyond that until my own Tower of Babel is erected and I can look God squarely in the eye. No, I am not complacently going into that bitter darkness but begrudgingly and full of complaint. Let some less worthy man die in my stead. There are so many small men while I deserve some consideration, but then again, there is no deserving. The evil both prosper and die as do the good; there is no differentiation, merely happenstance. Do I blaspheme? Do I dare, now at the precipice of life and end of all hope, still cling to hubris and at the same time pray for salvation, or at least redemption? My name and legacy are dear to me. I must preserve them.

I have called my lackey confessor into my presence and hope that his cavernous face is not the last I see. He is an ignorant man but faithful to his ignorance. Frey Dominicus grins at me, revealing a hideous lack of proportion, for he truly believes that I go to a better place. He is a fanatic, and because he is, he is the only one I can trust to do my bidding after my corporal authority can no longer exert itself. I confess the same sins I have been confessing for decades and make the same act of contrition and receive the same absolution, which he gives without pause. I have promised so many times before that I will endeavor not to commit the same sins, only to falter and do so again. It does not matter to Dominicus as long as my acts of contrition are heartfelt. It is a way out religion allows for the continuance of sin, for if we had no sin, we would have no need of priests to forgive us.

After confession, I give him my instructions; my refuge is to be razed to the ground and all its residents put to the sword mercifully then buried in unmarked graves. I explain that they are inherently evil, as they abetted me in my sinful ways. He nods energetically, looking forward to the task. I then give him a list of confidantes that I suspect may have deduced my parallel life with the same instructions. I will lament the death of none of them, save Zurara who has served me well, but he has been close to me for too long and is too intelligent to survive my demise and perhaps sully my name with innuendo. Alas, he must die.

There is a modicum of comfort in knowing that, as I die, I take my household along for company into the hereafter, much like the ancient pharaohs of Egypt. I send Dominicus away to his errands and dismiss the physicians who withdraw without protest, for none of them want to be present at my death and possibly blamed for not being able to save my life.

I am alone as I have been throughout my life. It is a warm, reassuring company, as I can be as weak and sobbing as I please. I reflect that, in my lifetime, I have stolen the mystery of the earth much like Prometheus who stole fire from the gods and gave it to mankind. Deprived of its monsters, the sea is now ours to explore and exploit. I stole that mystery from the gods and bestowed it to men.

A massive pain presses upon my chest, and I find it impossible to draw a breath, yet I remain stoic and do not call for the physicians, as I know all they can do is send me into oblivion with their Oriental potions, and I want to live to the very last second. I review a lifetime barely conscious. I have killed my precious brother, Fernando. I allowed him to slowly starve in captivity rather than render the fortress Ceuta to the Moor. The wrong I did to Fernando is counterbalanced by the good of defeating the Moor. This sin is equiponderant to the virtue of thwarting God's enemies. I do not fear this sin, but the omission of action I do fear. I have stolen the slave trade from the Arab, but what of it? The slave is destined for slavery and better at our hands than those of the heathen. I have made the vast Atlantic a mare nostrum and forced the European principalities to pay tribute in order to be allowed to sail on it. I have conquered much of the coast of Guinea but am now powerless to overcome my own frail mortality.

Another wrenching spasm of pain, and I now almost look forward to release. There is another Cape Bojador awaiting me, and I will dismiss its myth as well. I peer anxiously into the gloaming of my chambers as the candles flicker helplessly to hold back the night. I am vainly searching for an omen, perhaps a fiery cross or a golden chariot that will differentiate my death from countless others. There is not even a glimmer, as God has not seen fit to honor my demise or send a sign that I will be welcome in His universe.

Yet another spasm of pain, this the most terrible one so far. I am spent and unable to inhale, though I try to draw in breath in futile desperation. Life is pernicious, and we hold on to it as long as we can. For someone who has lived as long as I have, death will not come easily, as I will fight it tooth and nail and spit to the end. I am still trying to inhale but cannot and decide to call the physicians, but no remnant of voice is left in my collapsed lungs. Death strangles me like a merciless python. I try to fight, but death only presses itself upon me with more determination. Death tells me to let go and die, but I fight and continue to try to breathe. I will not oblige, but death will not yield either; it is indomitable. Countless others have struggled in vain against it and have lost. Death wins, and I reluctantly release myself from the pain that assured me that I was still alive. I die with my eyes wide open and my jaw agape as if in wonder but confident that the sarcophagus awaits and the limestone will devour my flesh and crumble my bones to dust. Speak of me often and render me immortal.

EPILOGUE

*J*have been told that my prince died peaceably in his
sleep on November 13 in the year of our Lord 1460 at
the perhaps overly ripe age of 67. His peaceful death
was in contrast with the way he had lived his life. Henry's
mortal remains were entombed in a limestone sarcophagus
within the great cathedral at *Batalha*, the burial place of the
House of Aviz. I often wondered at this word "sarcophagus,"
and so I studied it to find it comes from the Greek and it
means "flesh eater" for the limestone quickly disposes of the
soft tissue and ultimately grinds the bones into white powder.
And so Henry's flesh was soon consumed, but not his legacy,
for that was not buried along with his mortal remains. It is
interesting to note that the king, Afonso, ordered that no
date of death be inscribed on his tomb, as if implying that
his uncle's memory was eternal.

Henry's sole heir, his nephew, Dom Fernando, inherited
nothing but debts; Henry died penniless. As far as the
Templar treasure, it proved nonexistent. Henry merely used
this chimera of a fortune to convince merchants and nobles
to lend him money, which he never paid back, including Dona
Eulalia's huge loan. I suspect Dona Eulalia never expected
repayment, and her claim on half the booty was smoke to

obscure her true intent of giving him his chance to conquer Morocco. In a sense, it proved to be her dowry to Henry. We, the members of his household, who all had been promised pensions from the treasure, received nothing. Upon learning of the empty promise, I grew extremely bitter at having to work into my old age, but thankfully, time has attenuated any ill will, as I have come to accept what I cannot change. Naturally, I wrote no chronicle of Henry's life, and I do not fear his retribution in my next life.

But in this corporal life, I do fear Henry. Soon after his death, many members of his household began experiencing accidents out of proportion to the odds. One inexplicably fell from a window and crushed his skull upon the cobblestones below. Another apparently was trampled to death by his own horse, and still another drowned in a bathtub. I lay no claim to extraordinary intelligence, but I am also not a fool. It was clear that Henry's lanky hand was thrusting through his limestone grave to murder the members of his household who had been closest to him. My itinerant lifestyle had perhaps spared me, but I knew that it would not be long before the murders caught up with me. I am not naturally a brave man, as I believe I have confessed before. I kept on the move, not revealing my next destination to anyone. I survived, if but for a time.

The worst of it was in the lonely black hours of the night, where every creak of an old house, every breeze that sent a shutter swaying would cause me to jump out of bed, ready to flee in a moment. I would go into a terrified frenzy at the wail of a cat in heat. If the murderers did not kill me, then my perpetual anxiety and lack of sleep surely would.

In that moment of terror, I could not fathom why Henry wished me dead, why he would want to murder his most trusted servants. I was reminded of those old kings in Egypt who, in their unbounded hubris, would have their whole household of slaves, concubines, and wives interred along with their remains so that they could serve them in their afterlife. Surely, Henry would not have such grandiose delusions. But who can tell what dementia comes to a man on his deathbed?

I thought of a dozen different possible escapes only to almost immediately discard them as ludicrous. I then thought of escaping abroad only to remind myself of Leanor whose murder was committed from afar with ease. Besides, I only know our language and would surely starve for lack of employment.

Then one horrible night while I bore the excessive heat of our summer at Faro, it came to me. I should go to the end of the earth where no one would want to follow since I would not present a danger to whatever it was that must be kept secret. To my mind, that terminus was Alcácer Ceguer. I arrived on a supply ship in secrecy and bribed the captain well while also promising him a stipend from future income so that he would have cause to wish that I continue to live. The man also bore Henry no love, as he had been passed over many times for a captaincy on one of the expeditions that made the returnees rich. The governor-general received me with courtesy and asked but one question: "Do you play chess or *shesh-besh*?"

When I answered in the affirmative, he was delighted, and we have become fast, if not odd, friends ever since. At Alcácer Ceguer, I finally felt safe, and peaceful sleep returned to me. The howling wind of the riff and the rush of the surf upon our walls act as sedatives. No one can approach me in stealth; they would have to arrive by ship, and the governor-general deals severely with assassins.

Within the walls, I have found the tranquility of a newfound asylum, which has allowed me to regain my composure, for a panicked man does not think properly. Why did Henry wish me dead? Was it pure vainglory? Did he really think himself a pharaoh? I have treaded this particular path and various tributaries countless times, and I must confess that I do not know. My guesses are absurd, so I have stopped trying to understand Henry's intent. I could barely understand his actions when he lived, let alone his motives from the grave.

How can a man of Henry's magnitude be measured? Does he defy the normal yardsticks we apply to ordinary people, or does he merit some special gauge we set aside for great men? These questions are beyond my ken, dear reader, so perhaps you can provide a more adequate answer than I. With the advantage of retrospection, I can say that Henry did both great good as well as great harm, as he himself seemed to be aware of from the complexity of emotions he sometimes let escape.

Certainly, his sponsorship of the voyages of discovery must go down in history as a great achievement, though I must confess that, since his death, the Lisbon merchant, Fernão Gomes, has sent his ships farther down the coast of Guinea than Henry did during his entire lifetime. Fernão's merchant ships have reached the land of the Mbundu and the Ovimbundu in a land they call Nha Gola. However impressive these investitures are, they would not have been possible without Henry's innovative spirit of discovery. It is easier to follow footsteps than to blaze trials. Some of our cartographers now speculate that it will not be long before the tip of Guinea is reached and rounded to reach the emporium of India, bypassing the Arab block. If this feat can be accomplished, it is largely due to the efforts of my prince. Fernão's achievements are merely mercantilist; they lack the fanfare of Henry's pure curiosity.

Henry also slew dragons, sea serpents, and all the other monsters of superstition with his insistence on sailing beyond Cape Bojador. In doing so, he made the world safe and somehow smaller. He settled desperate, landless people on fertile Atlantic islands, creating land like God in Genesis, reducing the misery of our population. Our tiny kingdom, but a shoreline with a small country attached to it, is now a naval power thanks to Henry, and English, French, and Castilian ships must pay us tribute to sail on our Atlantic, though I do not know how long we can preserve this supremacy against these more populated nations who must also have their intrepid men among their vast desperate numbers. Henry must also have the gratitude of a legion of desperate men that made their fortunes sailing under his pennants.

Henry belongs not only to our small kingdom, but to the greater world since he never hesitated to invite men of all nations to work with him at Sagres. Many of his detractors who now have the advantage of live curs over a dead eagle now gnaw away at his legacy, accusing Henry of casuistry. Perhaps he did not have any intrinsic ideals, only goals to be attained, but in the pursuit of these goals, he practiced tolerance and patience, virtues most of his detractors lack.

There are also those who claim that my prince was avaricious in his mania for gold. If he was indeed such a greedy man, why did he die penurious? Curiosity is an expensive habit. It is my belief that Henry pursued wealth not for its sake alone, but to feed his mind. In his single-minded pursuits, he did bring much misery to many people. I am thinking most notably of those poor wretches who were sold as slaves on the beach at Lagos and all those who came after them. His indifference to their suffering does not speak much about the charity of his soul. In this, Henry's casuistry weakens, as I do not believe that saving a soul is worth enslaving a body. This may sound like heresy, but here in Alcácer Ceguer, I am beyond the reach of the inquisitors and, hopefully, Henry's henchmen. Henry did not invent slavery; this scourge has been with us since time immemorial. He merely wrested it away from the Arabs who plied it strictly in the Mediterranean while he made it an Atlantic enterprise. What I cannot fathom is why Europe continues so avid for more Negro slaves. At the rate the Europeans are bringing slaves from Guinea, they will need to discover another continent to make proper use of their manpower.

There was a devious side to my prince's character. I remain convinced that he had a direct hand in Dona Leonora's murder as well as an indirect responsibility for the death of his brother, Dom Pedro. Then there is his reprehensible behavior regarding the slow death of his younger brother, Dom Fernando. Only time will be the judge if the retention of Ceuta was worth the agonizing death of that trusting young boy. If there is a place in hell reserved for Henry, it will assuredly be due to his indifference to the suffering of his young brother.

As to his personal morality, I cannot judge with any semblance of surety. Outwardly, he was a paradigm of probity, but with so much talk of unspeakable things, who can know the truth? We are all petty rumor mongerers, as our own lives are small and we feel the necessity to steal majesty from the great. If he indeed led a double life, he was a hypocrite, but he was not alone in this. Men can often be both devils and angels at different times and under varying circumstances. The rumors aside, Henry performed enough public acts to be properly relegated a place in history, neither a complete saint nor utter villain.

ي

And so, dear reader, I have come full circle and returned to my present existence here at Alcácer Ceguer. I am fully aware that I am a mere interloper upon a noteworthy story. If I am to be remembered at all, it will be as Henry's panegyrist. With these pages, I hope that history will be kinder to me and not judge me solely on the sugary chronicles I wrote to make an easy living. I know I exaggerated the good done and ignored the evil, but I am merely mortal, with an innate desire to seek pleasure and avoid pain. Soon, I will die, and I hope, dear reader, that you are not too harsh in your opinion of my life and that you will say a prayer for my soul as well as for Henry's. I fear we both may need them.

About the Author

Francisco V. Martins was born and raised in New York City. He earned a Ph.D. in Comparative Literature from City University of New York and an M.B.A. from Columbia University. He lives in Bermuda where he works for a bank. The Prince of Ambition showcases his parents' native country, Portugal.